DARK CORNERS OF THE NIGHT

THE DARK CORNERS OF THE NIGHT

ALSO BY MEG GARDINER

Ransom River
The Shadow Tracer
Phantom Instinct

UNSUB NOVELS

UNSUB
Into the Black Nowhere

JO BECKETT NOVELS

The Dirty Secrets Club
The Memory Collector
The Liar's Lullaby
The Nightmare Thief

EVAN DELANEY NOVELS

China Lake
Mission Canyon
Jericho Point
Crosscut
Kill Chain

THE DARK CORNERS OF THE NIGHT

AN UNSUB NOVEL

MEG GARDINER

BLACK STONE
PUBLISHING

Copyright © 2020 by Meg Gardiner
Published in 2020 by Blackstone Publishing
Jacket design by Stephanie Stanton

Printed in the United States of America

33614081621764   First edition: 2020
978-1-982627-51-5
Fiction / Thrillers / Suspense

1 3 5 7 9 10 8 6 4 2

CIP data for this book is available
from the Library of Congress

Blackstone Publishing
31 Mistletoe Rd.
Ashland, OR 97520

www.BlackstonePublishing.com

For the librarians,
who open the world of knowledge to all of us

Stars, hide your fires;
Let not night see my black and deep desires.
—William Shakespeare, *Macbeth*

THE DARK CORNERS OF THE NIGHT

1

March

Caitlin Hendrix thundered down the off-ramp hard past the speed limit, into the smoke. The haze obscured the skyline and hung a red pall in the morning sky above the Berkeley Hills. Nine hours after the blast, Temescal Hospital was still burning.

On the radio, reports were grim. *"Oakland authorities confirm multiple fatalities …"*

Caitlin punched the steering wheel. "Goddammit."

She slewed to a stop in the hospital parking lot and her skin turned cold. Ladder trucks ringed the building, spraying stubborn hives of flame. Search-and-rescue teams combed the smoldering ruins of the ER with dogs, hunting for trapped survivors.

"Latest in a string of bombings that spans the country …"

Caitlin jumped from the car and was blinded by acrid smoke. At the yellow perimeter tape a police officer raised a hand to keep her back.

She flashed her FBI credentials. "ATF?"

The patrolman pointed toward the hospital's crumbled façade. "They went in."

She ducked under the tape and ran. The ER entrance was a gaping hole half-choked by debris. She climbed over unstable slabs of concrete and rebar, picking her way through. The wind gusted. Ash flicked her face, hot.

It seemed impossible that anybody could have escaped this place alive.

From the eddying smoke, a specter emerged. A red bandanna was tied around his face. A badge hung from his neck. ATF—the Bureau of Alcohol, Tobacco, Firearms and Explosives.

Caitlin scrambled through the rubble toward him. Sean Rawlins saw her and his shoulders dropped. Her throat went dry with dread.

Her best friend had been on duty as a nurse in the Temescal ER when the bomb exploded. Michele Ferreira—whom Caitlin had been trying to reach for hours. Michele was the reason she'd flown all night from DC to get here.

"*She's not answering her cell*," Sean had said on the phone, his voice like broken glass. "*Nobody knows.*"

The attack on Temescal was a massive escalation in the bomber's campaign. It was a devastating turn in a case Sean had been working for months. And it had done more than bring disaster to the East Bay. Because Michele was more than Caitlin's friend. She was Sean's ex-wife. The mother of his little girl.

Caitlin grabbed Sean's arms. He was dirty and hollow-eyed. A tremor ran through her.

He pulled down the bandanna. "They found her."

His voice was raw. Caitlin's heart fisted.

Behind him shadows solidified from the smoke. A search-and-rescue team emerged from the ER, their hard hats and yellow vests filthy. They were lugging a basket stretcher.

In it, unmoving, lay a small woman in raspberry scrubs. Her shirt, her face, her crow-black hair, were caked with concrete dust and matted with blood. The rescue team hadn't bothered to cover her broken form with a sheet.

Grief raked Caitlin's throat. Her friend was shattered, her skin the gray of a stone angel.

Then Michele's chest rose.

"Oh, my God," Caitlin said.

Sean nodded. "Come on."

Her heart gunning, Caitlin clambered through the rubble ahead of the rescue team, checking step by step for stability.

"Follow my path," she said.

Sean grabbed the stretcher's side rail to help steady it. A mass-casualty triage unit was set up across the parking lot. They rushed toward it, tears burning Caitlin's eyes.

"Michele," she whispered. *Forgive me for ignoring you. Forgive me for doubting you. Forgive me for waiting to reach out until you were already in the maelstrom of blood and fire.*

When the rescue team set the stretcher down, paramedics swarmed. A nurse and trauma doc swooped in. They waved Sean and Caitlin back. From the bottom of an ocean, Caitlin heard *Red tag*—the triage term for patients who were in danger of death without immediate treatment.

She grabbed Sean's hand. She rarely prayed, and never aloud, but heard herself saying, "God—help her. Do it now."

Michele coughed. The doctor said, "You're safe, you're out." He gave Sean a look, concerned but calm and competent. *Got this.*

Sean seemed to unspool, and he relinquished responsibility to the medical crew.

"Michele," Caitlin said. "Breathe, girl. Stay with us."

Briefly, Michele opened her eyes. Her gaze reeled, but she found Caitlin and Sean. As the trauma team beetled around her, she lifted a hand and spread her fingers. Reaching. Letting them know she was there.

Caitlin raised a fist. "Fight, Michele. *Fight.*"

Michele squeezed her eyes shut.

Sean slipped his fingers between Caitlin's. She clutched his hand. Then grabbed him and held him tightly.

"She's going to make it. Understand? She is," she said.

"No question." He clasped her to his chest. "No chance in hell she won't."

Throat scored with dust and ash, for a moment Sean sounded overwhelmed. Then he took a long breath, and Caitlin felt his fury distill. He peered at the smoldering hospital.

"It's in there. Somewhere. The key." His voice once again had glass in it. But not shattered. Sharp. "I'm going to find it. And I'm going to get this bastard."

Ragged joy, relief, and savage purpose filled her. "You are."

He took her face in his hands and pressed his forehead to hers. "Thank you for coming. Thank you for getting here."

He smelled of smoke and sweat. She kissed him roughly and tightened her arms around him.

The sun hung red in the air. The question hung between them.

Did the Ghost do this?

2

December

Winter, two A.M., and a Santa Ana wind was scouring Los Angeles. Hot and gritty, it keened over skyscrapers, through canyons and barrios, past the Hollywood sign, over flickering holiday lights, along the freeways, across the rippling surf. And through him. It sharpened his vision and clear-cut his path.

The neighborhood spread across the hillside like a fungus. Below him the lights of the San Fernando Valley prickled in the black air. The moon slicked the sky, whitewashing the street. He paused the music and pulled out the earbuds. The rivet-gun beat of Ministry's "Stigmata" evaporated. The hiss of the 101 freeway replaced it.

The road noise obscured his footsteps. The moonlight cast his shadow on the grass as he crossed the lawn. Thin, silent, smooth. His shadow—the only companion he could trust. As black as his baseball cap. His hoodie. Jeans. Gloves.

Light on his feet, he strolled around the side of the house, dragging his fingers along the stucco.

He found the open window at the back.

He stood for a minute. The night and the wind filled him with command. He licked his lips. His knife sliced the window screen. His shadow invaded the house before the rest of him.

The Christmas tree was a dark pyramid in the living room corner. Presents hid beneath it, wrapping paper quicksilver in the moonlight. He absorbed the stillness. An electric hiss seemed to saturate the air.

He sheathed his knife. His shadow slid past framed photos hanging in the hallway. Family fun shots. Fathermother. Grannygramps. At the end of the hall he paused and nudged wide a door.

In the master bedroom a man and woman lay asleep, shadows and headlights skittering over them as cars passed on the freeway. The couple's heads were barely visible on their pillows. Hiding. (*Not any more. I found you. I know what you are.*) He raised the gun.

It felt weightless in his grip. Felt like truth.

It meant revelation. Here, inexorable, undeniable. The sweeping headlights gave him enough light to line up the front and rear sights.

He held for a second. Extending the moment, feeling the bubble expand toward the bursting point. In the bed, the sleeping man breathed.

Oh, no you don't. I saw that.

He fired.

The blare of the gunshot jerked the woman awake. "*Jesus*, what ..."

She lurched like a shot dog. Sleep-drunk. Confused. She felt the hot blood that striped her cheeks. Touched her face. Looked at her husband.

"Andy—oh, God, what is ..."

She turned, saw him, and stopped. He could be no more than a shadow at the foot of the bed. The Undoing.

He tracked the pistol and lined up the sights again.

She stumbled from the bed, hand out to ward him off. "No—"

He squeezed the trigger.

As the echo of gunfire faded, he exhaled. Silence swelled. *Told you.* They had seen. *Showed you.* He soaked in the sight for one final second.

Down the hall, a voice called out. It was small and tentative.

"Mom? Dad?"

The intruder turned. In the darkened hall stood a young boy. First grade, maybe. Flannel pajama bottoms and what looked, in the thin moonlight, like a Star Wars T-shirt.

The intruder sauntered out of the parents' room toward him. The boy dashed into a bedroom and slammed the door.

The intruder slid along the hallway, gun barrel dragging on the wall, shadow wiping the photos. Fathermother. Babybrother. *Here, kiddie kiddie.*

The bedroom door was flimsy particle board. The house was flimsy suburbia. He jammed the gun in the waistband of his jeans, raised his boot, and kicked the door open. It broke like Styrofoam.

The lightless room looked empty. He walked in, took a slow look around, strolled to the far side of the bed and back. The silence was distorted now—by breathing. He crossed the room and threw open the closet door.

Inside, the boy crouched in a ball. He was hugging his sister.

Their eyes, staring at him in the moonlight, were enormous.

3

When Caitlin climbed from the FBI Suburban, a bloodshot sun hung between the palm trees. The street sloped toward to the 101 freeway and the checkerboard sprawl of the San Fernando Valley. The mountains at the valley's far edge were brown, furrowed, and under the blowing Santa Anas, shockingly clear. Mid-December, and it was in the high seventies. Caitlin's black suit absorbed the heat. Her auburn hair wraithed around her shoulders.

Her colleagues from the FBI's Behavioral Analysis Unit got out and shut the Suburban's doors with a hard clack. They'd driven here straight from LAX. Unit Chief CJ Emmerich and Special Agent Brianne Rainey regarded the house.

Police tape batted on the porch. Emmerich, spare and angular, panned the property, the street, the neighborhood. His suit jacket flared like a wing in the wind.

"No trees in front. House is completely exposed," he said.

Rainey set her hands on her hips. "How'd the killer see it? As a juicy target? Asking for what he wanted to dish out?"

Rainey's gaze, smooth and cool, took in the house with seeming dispassion. Her voice was calm, her bearing even, her clothes chic, braids pulled into a high chignon. But Caitlin sensed Rainey steeling herself for what lay inside.

"He slunk in the back," Caitlin said. "He saw but wanted to remain unseen."

The front door opened, and two LAPD detectives stepped onto

the porch. They were from the Homicide Special Section of the Robbery-Homicide Division and were the ones who had requested the BAU's assistance. The BAU usually consulted on cases from Quantico. But Robbery-Homicide had gotten Emmerich, a legendary profiler, to jump on a cross-country flight with two of his agents. Receiving a call from such heavy hitters—detectives who handled mass murders, serial slayings, and LA's highest-profile killings—meant the case was a five-alarm fire.

Caitlin shot her cuffs. "Into the breach."

They walked toward the crime scene and the LAPD detectives came into the afternoon sun. The older of the two extended his hand.

"Dave Solis. Appreciate you coming so quickly."

Solis was in his early forties, solid, his white dress shirt bleach-bright in the harsh daylight. His partner seemed to squint against its glare as she shook their hands.

"Talia Weisbach."

Weisbach was as slight as a yellow jacket. Her curls were shoveled atop her head. Her face was grim.

"This way."

The house was chillingly quiet. The patrol cars, the ambulance, the medical examiner, and the crime scene unit had been and gone. Door jambs, walls, and the windowsill in the living room were sooty with fingerprint powder. The window, the killer's entry point, faced the patio and back fence. Emmerich paused to evaluate it. The small yard was enclosed by white oleander.

Caitlin stopped beside him. "Hedge, fence, single-story homes on all three sides. Coming in that window, the intruder wouldn't have been visible from any neighboring houses."

Emmerich checked out the Christmas tree. Presents were arrayed beneath it. "Looks undisturbed."

Solis grunted. "Theft doesn't seem to have been the primary objective."

They turned toward the hallway. Though the lights were on, it resembled a forbidding tunnel. Solis led the way.

The bodies had been removed from the master bedroom. Their blood remained. It covered the bed. It soaked one of the pillows, red drying to brown, with a watery ring along the stain's outer edges. It splattered the headboard. Caitlin tried to absorb the scene impassively. The iron tang in the air made that viscerally impossible.

Emmerich stood in the doorway to get a broad vantage on the room. "Same MO as the first two attacks?"

Weisbach nodded and pointed at the coagulated blood on the pillow. "Husband was shot first. Andrew McKinley. Then the wife."

"Did the killer take anything besides their wedding rings?"

"Don't know yet," Solis said. "House wasn't ransacked. Killer left jewelry, cash, phones, laptops. Car keys. But relatives haven't been able to bring themselves to look at photos of the scene, much less to walk through the house and tell us if anything's missing."

Solis' voice was deep and surprisingly gentle. He rounded the bed to indicate a smear on the hardwood floor. "We think he stepped in Daphne McKinley's blood when he approached her body to take the ring. Then wiped the shoeprint off the floor. And off his shoe."

"With?" Emmerich said.

"A corner of Mrs. McKinley's nightgown."

Solis peered around the gloomy room. Yellow light filtered through opaque shades. The windows faced the street, and the police didn't want anyone to get a look inside.

Solis' shoulders looked laden. He had ashy circles beneath his eyes. "If he took anything else, we haven't found evidence of it. No fingerprints, no blood smears on dresser drawers, jewelry boxes, cabinets."

"Gloves?"

"Presumably."

Same MO. The McKinley murders were the killer's third attack in Los Angeles County in two months. All late-night home invasions. Robberies that opened with double murder. Male-female couples: two married, one long-term partners.

Rainey stepped out of the room into the hall. A dozen framed photos glinted dully on the wall. Halfway down, a smashed bedroom door dangled from a broken hinge.

Drawing a slow breath, she walked toward the doorway. When Caitlin caught up, they pushed the broken door fully open.

The bedroom belonged to a little girl. Pink accents, American Girl dolls. A globe on a bookshelf.

Rainey's voice was tight. "The children?"

Detective Weisbach drew near. "With their grandparents."

Caitlin stepped inside. The air felt cold. The closet door gaped open. Above the bed, long scratches striped the wall. They looked like the claw marks of an unearthly wolf, ripping into the house from another dimension. The iron tang again reached her nose. The claw marks had been drawn in blood.

She turned to Rainey. "We need to talk to those kids."

4

A towering Christmas tree dominated the grandparents' San Fernando Valley home. Its gleaming cheer was smothered by the airless grief in the living room. The grandmother sat on the edge of a wingback chair, a soggy tissue clenched in her fist. She hunched as if she'd been punched in the chest. But she watched Caitlin and Rainey with a black-powder stare, ready to fire on them if they asked questions she objected to. Caitlin couldn't blame her.

The children sat side by side on a sofa. Noah and Natalie McKinley were six-year-old twins. Brown hair, sturdy limbs, gleaming eyes. Silent.

Caitlin assessed the kids' emotional temperature, caught Rainey's eye, and signaled: *You lead.* Rainey pulled a dining room chair next to the sofa and sat down, close but not crowding the children. Her tone was tender.

"Tell me what you saw. What you heard."

Noah's shoulders bunched inside his Batman T-shirt. He stared at the floor. A jet passed overhead on approach to Burbank Airport.

"I know it's scary to remember," Rainey said. "But you were very brave. You helped your sister."

She glanced at the little girl. Natalie was holding a stuffed bear, squeezing it repeatedly, almost rhythmically. Trying to soothe herself, Caitlin thought.

Softly she said, "You can tell Agent Rainey whatever you're thinking about. Anything at all."

Noah eyed Rainey with something like suspicion, maybe disbelief.

But Rainey's gaze was direct and genuine. Caitlin knew her as forthright and incisive. Ex–Air Force, she was one of a rare number of female African American FBI special agents. Whether in the field or an interrogation room, she was commanding.

And she was the mother of twin boys herself. Her way with kids was completely natural. Even at such a wrenching moment, she was calm, warm, and respectful. Caitlin hung back. She had a good rapport with children—she was close to Sean's daughter—but she wasn't a mother herself. She let Rainey attempt to work her empathetic magic.

Rainey leaned her elbows on her knees, getting to eye level with the boy. "You got out of bed and went into the hall."

Noah looked at her. After a moment he dipped his chin. *Yes.*

"Did you turn on any lights?"

He shook his head. "I heard a noise." His halting voice was little more than a whisper. "I got up and went into the hall and called to my mom and dad and ..." He breathed. "Saw a shadow."

Rainey waited. After a few seconds, Noah went on.

"A man," he said.

Progress. She held onto his gaze. "Can you tell me what the man looked like?"

"Gigantic."

"Did you see his face?"

Noah shook his head.

"Did you see what he was wearing?"

"No. It was dark." He kneaded his fingers together. "He had a gun."

Across the room, the grandmother stifled a cry. She turned her head to the wall and squeezed the sodden tissue.

"Did the man speak?" Rainey said.

The boy's chin trembled. He shook his head.

"What happened then?" Rainey said.

"I ran into Nat's room." Noah's eyes shifted to his sister. She sat stone still beside him. "Nat was standing there. She was shaking." He looked at Rainey. "I hugged her and thought we should climb out the window, but Mom and Dad were in their room and what if they needed help and …"

The grandmother stood up, fist pressed to her lips. Caitlin understood her distress but didn't want her to interrupt the boy's story.

Noah, however, seemed unaware of her. "Then Nat pulled me into the closet. I pushed the door shut and we got … we got small and tried to hide behind the toys because … because …"

The tremor in his voice set a nerve ringing behind Caitlin's eyes. He looked so fragile. Caitlin knew he had indeed been brave—he'd demonstrated a level of courage no kid should have to summon. And retelling it so freshly, to strangers, was a burden unfairly placed on his small shoulders.

Christ in hell.

Hunting serial predators was what Caitlin did. The more challenging and urgent the case, the more dangerous the UNSUB, the hotter her blood sang. The clearer her vision became. The wider awake she grew. The work was important. It kept people alive. It put killers in prison.

And interviewing orphaned first graders sent an arrow through her. She inhaled and blinked and tried to lower the shields.

Rainey's tone was kind. "Noah, you're safe. You can tell me, and it won't make it happen again."

He turned to her, his eyes burning. "Then he kicked the bedroom door down. And we tried to not make any noise, tried to be like bats and blend into the dark but I heard him breathing and walking and he pulled open the closet door, pulled it open *hard*, and …" He stopped. "I heard his voice."

"He spoke to you?" Rainey said. "What did he say?"

He shrugged.

"What did his voice sound like?" Rainey said.

"Man's voice."

"Do you remember what he said?" Rainey asked.

The boy nodded. In the hall, a clock ticked.

The little girl, Natalie, was wringing her hands. She had dropped her stuffed bear.

Caitlin knelt by the girl's side and handed her the toy. It felt damp, perhaps from being held to Natalie's face while the little girl sobbed.

"Did you see him?" Caitlin said.

The girl nodded tightly. She whispered, "Eyes."

"What about his eyes?"

The child raised her hands, palms out. "Eyes were on his hands."

An electric shock seemed to run down Caitlin's arms. She exchanged a sharp glance with Rainey.

"What do you mean?" Caitlin said quietly.

"He opened the closet door and saw us. He had gloves on but he pulled them off. And he had eyes on his hands."

"What did the eyes look like?"

Natalie spread her fingers. "Big black eyes. Wide and scary."

Noah nodded. "He drew eyes on his palms. And he said …"

The look in his own eyes lengthened to a thousand-yard stare. He seemed lost, back in the closet, trapped by the gunman who had killed his mom and dad.

Caitlin leaned forward. "What did he say?"

The boy's lips seemed to move without volition, as if speaking in another voice. "'I am the legion of the night.'"

Jesus. His monotone sounded like an incantation. And beyond a six-year-old's vocabulary.

"You seem really sure that's what he said."

"He made us say it back to him."

Caitlin fought a shudder.

Rainey's face went stark. "Did he say anything else?"

Natalie's voice was tiny. "'I am beyond good and evil.'" She inhaled. "He made us say that back too."

Noah stared through Rainey now, to a moment somewhere beyond the room. "The darkness ate him. He wasn't there anymore."

The grandmother stood frozen, her face as pale as the paint on the walls.

"But his voice stayed," Noah whispered. "It told us who he is. He's the Midnight Man."

5

The wind buffeted the Suburban as Rainey drove downtown, her expression tense and pensive. Unnerved by the McKinley twins, thoughts roiling, Caitlin silently flipped through local radio stations. "Jingle Bell Rock." "Little Drummer Boy." *"Two more people shot to death in their bedroom …"* "Run, Run, Rudolph." *"Nobody's safe. This guy crawls through your window? You'd better have a gun."*

I am the legion of the night.

She turned the radio off. "I know we only landed three hours ago. We're still gathering information. But this UNSUB's like nothing I've ever dealt with."

They swept through a curve past Dodger Stadium. She realized how she came off. Overmatched. Spooked.

"That sounded dramatic," she said.

Rainey's tone was grave. "That's not drama, that's your finely honed intuition telling you to freak. This guy's off the chart."

Downtown Los Angeles came into view, an Emerald City cluster of skyscrapers, ruddy in the lowering light. Caitlin put down the sun visor. She'd been with the FBI for eighteen months, was officially still under Emmerich's mentorship in the BAU, but had worked a slew of difficult, violent serial crimes. She was no longer a rookie. And this case chilled her.

The UNSUB seemed less a man than an evil energy given human form. A shadow roaming loose under the glittering lights of LA, anonymous among thirteen million people, swooping in to kill at random.

"This case is some WFS," she said.

"What's that?"

"Weird Fucking Shit."

Rainey gave a low laugh.

"Need to find a key to opening his head," Caitlin said.

"Just be ready for what pours out."

LAPD headquarters was a sleek stone and blue-glass complex across from LA's iconic City Hall. Outside, flags buffeted and palm trees bent under the wind. The side of the building that faced Spring Street featured irregularly spaced windows, designed to thwart snipers. To Caitlin the place felt shiny and too new—cool lighting, flat-screens, sleek phones, and computers. She thought it still needed some breaking in. She had been born into Cop World, the daughter of a homicide detective, and even now felt most comfortable in the clamorous, grungy world of street policing. She was glad to see smudges on the doors of interview rooms.

The LAPD and Los Angeles Sheriff's Department had formed a joint task force to investigate these killings. Caitlin and Rainey found Emmerich upstairs in the Homicide Special Section, where a war room had been set up.

Caitlin dropped her computer case on a conference table. Emmerich, standing across from her, lifted his head from a file.

"The children?" he said.

"Told us stuff to make your hair stand on end," Rainey said.

"More bizarre symbols," Caitlin said. "And occult-style proclamations."

As Emmerich raised an eyebrow, Detective Dave Solis approached with another man.

Gil Alvarez was the LA Sheriff's lead investigator on the task force. He was sucking avidly on a toothpick. *Smoker trying to quit*, Caitlin thought. His jeans had a sharp crease ironed down the front. He looked like a kettle working to a boil.

Alvarez shook hands. "Welcome to the arena."

He openly sized up the FBI team. He seemed to approve of Rainey's straight back and direct gaze and the ease with which she wore her

Glock 19M on her right hip. He gave Emmerich a longer once-over—maybe measuring the breadth of his shoulders and the force of his gaze. Alvarez's glance at Caitlin was brief. It seemed to say, *Baby agent.*

She hoped she was way off. She hoped her own radar needed calibrating, and that Alvarez's intensity didn't equal hotheadedness.

She knew that three prides of lions had gathered in a single den.

"Let's go through the attacks chronologically," Alvarez said. "Solis, you want to start?"

Emmerich gave Caitlin and Rainey a cool glance. *Bide your time. We'll get to your report.* Detective Solis rolled up the sleeves of his ice-white shirt, turned on a flat-screen TV that hung on the wall near the conference table, and put up crime scene photos.

"Benedict Canyon," he said.

Caitlin had examined some of these photos already. But seeing them on the large screen gave the images extra weight and solemnity.

The first photo showed a mansion. Ultramodern, plate glass windows, a steep driveway, laurels and eucalyptuses screening the precipitous hillside. Inside, the walls were supernova white. Or rather, they had been. Until the killer infiltrated the house like carbon monoxide, silent and invisible, and started shooting.

In the cavernous master bedroom, Joel and Jessica Peretti had been killed as they lay spooning. Standing at the foot of the bed, the killer had put bullets in their heads from four feet away. A halo of blood spread across Jessica's pillow like a saint's starburst crown.

"After shooting Mr. and Mrs. Peretti, the killer proceeded down a hall to their seven-year-old son's room. He pushed the boy's door open. The gunshots had already woken the kid up, and he saw a shadow in the doorway," Solis said. "Standing there. Motionless, holding a handgun. The kid started crying. The killer disappeared."

"The killer knew the boy had seen him," Caitlin said.

"Kid was six feet away, howling in his face."

She didn't think the UNSUB was surprised to find a child in the house. Did he *want* the boy to see him? Did he stand in the doorway to make sure the kid felt his presence, and knew he'd been ... what? Spared? Taught a lesson? Destroyed?

Detective Alvarez, sucking on his toothpick, put up photos from the second crime scene, in Monterey Park, a bedroom community east of downtown. A Spanish-style house on a suburban street. The kitchen window, its flimsy lock jimmied. James Chu, face down on his bed, dead.

Alvarez approached the screen. "The first shot hit Mr. Chu below the ribcage." He gestured at a dark entry wound on Chu's bare back. "He made it to his elbows before the second shot hit him in the head."

Chu had been young and fit. On his nightstand a James S. A. Corey novel sat open. *Nemesis Games*. Caitlin had read it. Read the whole Expanse series. Chu never would.

What a goddamned waste. Always.

Next photo. Beth Lin sprawled on the floor, slumped against a dresser. Her hair waterfalled across her face. She was twenty-nine. She'd been shot in the heart.

"Lin wore an engagement ring, half carat diamond. It's missing. And Chu wore a simple silver ring on his right hand. The killer took that as well. Abrasions on his finger, postmortem."

Rainey leaned a hip on the conference table. "Did the killer think the couple was married? Or was he just stealing the jewelry he found within plain sight?"

Alvarez clicked to a new photo. An SUV on the driveway. Its back window had a sticker—cartoon figures of a family. Dad, mom, little girl in a ballet tutu.

"We presume he thought they were man and wife. Or that he doesn't care."

Rainey said, "The child?"

"Three years old. Unable to tell us anything useful," Alvarez said. "After he shot her parents, the killer walked into her room. Climbed on the bed. Marched right past her. Stood on her pillow and wrote this on the wall above the headboard."

He clicked. A new picture came up. Written in black marker, two words.

NIGHT MINE

Sharp letters, cramped, two feet tall. Caitlin knew it was her imagination, but the air in the war room seemed to taste coppery.

"Where's the little girl now?" she said.

"With an aunt and uncle. They're planning to adopt." Alvarez turned his face to floor. "Brutal, yeah. At least she has family."

He sat down at the conference table. His knee jittered. "What kind of killer threatens kids he's just orphaned?"

Emmerich straightened a folder on the table in front of him. His Tag Heuer dive watch shone in the afternoon sunlight. Subtly, everyone's attention was drawn to him.

CJ Emmerich had twenty years with the Bureau. Atlanta, Las Vegas, New York. Major crimes. Bank robberies. Militias. He'd seen every grimy stain on the bottom of society's shoes. He had a master's in psychology and a JD from Duke Law School. And he'd spent the last eight years in the Behavioral Analysis Unit, pursuing child abductors, terrorists, and serial predators. He held his counsel close to the vest. His jokes were rare, and dry. When he joined the team for a beer after a hard day, he was companionable but reserved. His hair was too short to ever let down. He captured serial killers.

He scrutinized the crime scene photos on the television screen.

"This killer is cutthroat but careful," he said. "He enters homes surreptitiously. He kills the men first because he considers them the prime physical threat to him. And because killing the men petrifies the women. It stokes his ego."

Alvarez watched him closely. Detective Weisbach walked over from her desk.

"He's virtually undetectable, until he appears as if out of a nightmare." Emmerich snapped his fingers. "Like that. He chooses houses that are completely dark, doesn't he?"

"Yes," Alvarez said. "The deputies who responded to the 911 call at the Chu-Lin house reported that there were no lights on. One thirty A.M."

"Christmas lights?"

"No. Chu and Lin were Buddhist. Had a tabletop Christmas tree, couple feet tall, maybe for their daughter, but otherwise no decorations." Alvarez removed the toothpick from his mouth. "Word gets around this guy picks out dark houses, we'll have an area-wide contest to out-dazzle each other for the gaudiest Christmas display."

Weisbach said, "What does he get out of terrorizing the kids?"

Emmerich studied the image on the television screen. The little girl's bedroom, the words NIGHT MINE scrawled above her bed.

"I don't know yet. But he's escalating." He gestured at the photos of the Benedict Canyon house. "In the first attack, the UNSUB shot the parents, then walked to the child's room. He opened the door but didn't go in."

"Afraid to?" Solis said. "Anxious to get away before the cops arrived?"

"Hardly. He had no physical fear—he'd just gunned down the adults in the house. He'd eliminated the immediate threat to himself. He lingered. He felt confident."

Caitlin said, "It was the opposite of anxiety. It was release. A display of triumph."

"He stood in the child's doorway. A figure of terror. Faceless, all-powerful." Emmerich walked to the flat-screen. "Then, in Monterey Park, he crossed the threshold into the child's room. He invaded her space, in a way that was both thoughtless and menacing. He climbed on her bed, trampling her most private—ideally *safe*—square of personal real estate. And he walked away acting as if he never noticed her presence. Of course, to the contrary, it was an almost ritualistic intrusion. A display. Meant to terrify a youngster barely old enough to talk."

He turned to the group. "Then the McKinley home."

Solis clicked up a picture of Natalie McKinley's bedroom.

"This time he didn't even pause to turn the doorknob," Emmerich said. "He kicked the door open, though it wasn't locked. He was violently asserting control. And he went much further in defacing the room and traumatizing the children."

Emmerich pointed at the photo. "Drawing on the walls in their parents' blood is a primal gesture. It invokes power. Pain. He arrived enraged. But he also came prepared to put on this show. This was transgressive—but controlled."

"Scaring the children into silence?" Solis said. "Intimidating witnesses?"

They all focused on the photo of Natalie's bedroom. Outside the war room on the street below, traffic growled. The low sun cast a cherry glow on the walls.

Caitlin spoke. "He not only left witnesses alive at every scene but made sure the children saw him. He's deliberately *created* surviving witnesses."

Emmerich eyed her, hawklike. Solis ran the back of a hand across the stubble on his chin.

"There's more," she said. "He wants the children to know who he is."

She walked to a whiteboard, picked up a marker, and wrote THE MIDNIGHT MAN.

Alvarez stood up.

I am beyond good and evil, Caitlin wrote. *I am the legion of the night.*

"And he drew eyes on his palms," she said.

"The actual fuck?" Alvarez said.

She and Rainey recounted their interview with Noah and Natalie McKinley.

"Iconography," Caitlin said. "Mythology, a worldview, something. He's got a narrative about himself." She reread what she'd written on the whiteboard. "He's creating his own legend."

"He drew the eyes on his palms before he entered the house," Emmerich said.

"Yes," Rainey said.

"He came with a script. From the word go, he planned to put on this terrifying spectacle for the children. It was a controlled display of aggression. Ritualistic terror."

"Nasty show to star in," Alvarez said.

Caitlin tossed the marker onto the table. "A killer's always the star of his own fantasy. The problem is, he can never perfect it. And the moment fades."

"So he tees up the next one," Alvarez said. "Infinite loop."

"Circle of death."

Rainey nodded at the whiteboard. "Where's he going with this? Grander shows?"

Caitlin clenched her hands. The memory of the children's bedroom, the claw marks on the wall, little Natalie's quiet horror, all hit her. Her skin crept.

"Let's just say it. He's not targeting couples. He's striking families with children. And he's becoming bolder." She looked at all of them. "What happens when he loses control?"

6

The concept behind behavioral analysis arose from a surprisingly straightforward insight: The criminal and victim must inevitably cross paths. When they do, at the crime scene, the offender's conduct leaves behind clues that reveal his psychology, his personality, and, inevitably, his identity. He might leave evidence or take evidence with him. Might pose victims' bodies, comb their hair, masturbate, cover their faces with a blanket. Bite them. Help himself to a beer.

To profile the Midnight Man, to turn the shadow into flesh, Caitlin and her colleagues needed to make sense of his crime scene behavior. In the war room, as the setting sun fired the windows, the FBI team spread files on the conference table. The mood on the floor had turned jangled. There was a sense of a heavy engine revving, a dynamo spinning up and throwing off sparks. The task force leaders conferred and handed out assignments to detectives: Hunt down videos from cameras within a two-mile radius of every crime scene. Canvas the McKinleys' neighborhood. Interview victims' family, friends, and neighbors.

Caitlin fanned crime scene photos across the shining tabletop.

Rainey inspected them. "The killer's getting into a rhythm. Definitely establishing a pattern of behavior."

Emmerich said, "Once could be happenstance. Twice is planning. Three times is ritual."

Caitlin said, "What he did at the McKinley house seems more than personal ritual. It seems almost ceremonial."

Emmerich turned his head.

24

"Rituals can be private," Caitlin said. "Crossing yourself. Obsessive handwashing. Ceremonies involve performance. A shared experience."

Emmerich became thoughtful. "Yes. Ceremonies are a formal observance to mark special occasions. Marriages. Graduations. Coronations."

"And ceremonies typically have assigned roles. Shaman, priest. Penitent, acolyte." She paused. "Victim."

Emmerich lifted a photo of Natalie McKinley's bedroom. "The Midnight Man prepared the ceremonial space. The claw marks he drew on the bedroom wall."

"What do they signify?" Caitlin said. "Wolf? Tiger? Eagle?"

"Dominance," Rainey said. "*He's* the wolf. The alpha. Apex predator."

"Marking his territory," Caitlin said.

She turned back to the files on the table. Among them was a fresh drawing, pencil on construction paper. It had been made by little Natalie, at Rainey's request, to describe the eyes on the palms of the Midnight Man. It was simple: the shape of a football, with a circle in the center and a black pupil within that, staring directly ahead.

"His ceremonial finale," Caitlin said.

Emmerich picked the drawing up. "Eyes. Windows to the soul."

"Omniscience," Rainey said. "Judgment."

"Watchfulness," Caitlin said.

"There's a counterpoint," Rainey said. "Covering the eyes creates mystery. It veils. Obscures the truth. This killer has never let his surviving victims see his face. I think he's doing more than merely hiding his identity. Covering the eyes is designed to intimidate."

Rainey had a background in military psyops. Caitlin took her at her word.

"What's he trying to *do* when he presents these eyes to the children?" Caitlin said. "Tell them they're being judged? *Owned?*"

Emmerich leafed through a printout. "Let's rewind to an earlier moment in this ceremony. Cleanup. Note what's missing from the crime scenes. Fingerprints. DNA. Cartridge casings—the killer polices his brass."

Rainey said, "I don't see ballistics. Didn't Crime Scene recover the rounds that killed the victims?"

Emmerich shook his head. "From the wound tracks, the killer was firing hollow-points. But he was close enough that the rounds exited the victims' bodies."

Rainey frowned. "What kind of a huge piece is he firing? How close to the victims was he? Good lord."

Hollow-point bullets expanded when they hit their target. Their pitted tips peeled back into a mushroom cap or starburst. The results were ugly. Instead of arrowing through a target in a fairly straight trajectory, a hollow-point formed a shock wave, cavitated, and essentially blew apart what it hit.

Most law enforcement agencies used them. A hollow-point could disable a bad guy with a single shot. In cop speak, it maximized stopping power.

And hollow-point rounds spent almost all their kinetic energy within a few inches of impact. They rarely exited a target's body and continued across a room. They inflicted maximum damage and remained inside the target.

Caitlin had been shot as a young deputy on patrol duty in Alameda County. The bank robber's bullet had punched through her deltoid without hitting major nerves or the brachial artery. If she'd been hit with a hollow-point round, she wouldn't have kept running toward the bank. She'd be missing an arm, or dead.

"Policing the through-and-through rounds is stratospherically careful," she said. "Or compulsive."

She picked up another file. "Know what else is missing from the scenes? Home security systems. He targets houses where no alarm system is activated." She turned a page, searching. "And, apparently— where there's no dog."

"He has burglary skills," Rainey said. "And he knows exactly what makes a home an easy target. No lights. No alarms. No barking."

Talia Weisbach walked over. The Robbery-Homicide detective's demeanor was reserved. Despite her volcanic curls and dentist's-drill energy, Weisbach could flatten her manner to a thin layer, smooth and opaque.

"You talked about what the killer's going to do next," she said. "We have no idea, and we don't know where he's going to do it. But you can dissect where he's been. You can give us a deep dive into the meaning behind some data."

"Is there a particular data set you want us to analyze?" Emmerich said.

Weisbach put up a map on the flat-screen television. The Los Angeles metropolitan area, from Zuma Beach to Canyon Country to the border with Orange County. She clicked, and three red dots appeared. The crime scenes.

"You're not all special agents and profilers in the BAU, right?" she said. "Your unit have a quant?"

"We have a technical analyst, if that's what you mean."

"Can this technical analyst crunch map data and develop a geographic profile of the killer's hunting zone?"

Emmerich eyed the projected map. The red dots were separated by miles, by mountain ranges, by city boundaries. He adjusted the band of his dive watch. It was a tell. He was uncomfortable. Maybe wary.

"Absolutely," he said.

"Good. If your guy can zoom in on the killer's home ground, we can tighten a noose on the bastard."

Emmerich scanned the map. "Three crime scenes give us little go on. But we have somebody who can draw an entire world from a few bytes of data." He turned. "Let's get Nicholas Keyes out here."

Rainey punched a phone number and walked across the floor as she called Keyes at Quantico. At the conference table, Caitlin examined a photo of the Monterey Park crime scene. The child's bedroom. The words scrawled above the little girl's headboard. NIGHT MINE.

"Thoughts?"

Emmerich's voice caused her to raise her head.

She lifted the photo. "The phrase is declarative. Possessive. So was the way he stomped across the girl's bed. Treating her as trash beneath his feet. Demonstrating his power."

Caitlin thought of the little girl—suddenly alone, grasping with both hands for a father and mother who had been annihilated. A coil of piano wire seemed to cinch around her heart.

"What's the girl's name?" she said. "Is there a photo of her?"

She sorted through printouts on the table. Found a family snapshot. The child had shining eyes, wide with curiosity and wonder.

"Hendrix."

"This UNSUB. He's black smoke. I can't see him."

"Caitlin."

He was across the table, his gaze pinning her.

"Yes, sir?"

"Everybody's shook," Emmerich said. "The public, the detectives, the brass. That's why we're here."

Her shoulders dropped. "No kidding."

"But we can't let it tip us off balance." His gaze drifted to the photo in Caitlin's hand. "Compartmentalize. These killings are distressing. The fact that children are traumatized is especially distressing. But I need you to bring your A-game to this case."

"Of course."

She barely got the words out before he raised a hand to forestall her saying more.

"I know Detrick took a toll on you."

Kyle Detrick and the Saturday Night Killer case had taken the BAU team to Texas and across the western US. Going one-on-one against a devious, manipulative killer had dredged up Caitlin's darkest fears and carried her to the edge. But she'd put it to bed. The case was considered a huge win.

"It took a toll on all of us," she said. "Main thing is—"

"Case closed, yes," Emmerich said. "You don't have to pretend it was a walk in the park."

Since the day she joined the BAU, he'd been trying to get her to open up. Emmerich had personally recruited her to the Bureau, and she sometimes thought he regarded her as more than a bright spark, an agent with investigative potential. That he had seen a street cop he could shape into a weapon. A Sidewinder missile, a heat-seeker who could sense the dank motivations of serial predators and lock on target.

She drank this work like spring water. She loved it. She felt addicted to it.

She knew that could turn into a problem.

When she first pinned on a badge, she'd written out hard rules for herself. *Dedication. Persistence. Job stays at the station.* Those rules were meant to erect an electric fence between relentless pursuit and dangerous obsession—a barrier her father had crossed, to his ruin.

Emmerich knew about her code. He understood and accepted it. But he wanted her to reset the boundary line. To slice into deeper psychological territory. He knew that meant exposing herself to emotional risks.

He didn't know what she feared might happen if she truly threw wide the gates.

"Detrick is done. For good," she said. "Don't worry about him."

"Noted. I also understand the strain the Temescal bomber has put you under."

Her face heated. At the mention of Temescal, Caitlin once again smelled acrid smoke and saw the search-and-rescue team hauling Michele Ferreira from the rubble.

Michele lived, she told herself. That was what counted. But nine months after the explosion, Michele was still battling to recover from critical injuries. Her fight was heartrending, not least because the case remained unsolved. Sean was working overtime on the investigation. Every day the bomber remained at large hit him like a rebuke and felt like a timer running out. And he had no evidence to either confirm or disprove that the Ghost, a killer he and Caitlin had faced before, was behind the bombings.

Caitlin kept her face neutral. "I know, boss. I'm just wrapping my head around these killings."

"This is a particularly tough case to work. Attacks on families. That it's happening during the holidays only makes it more emotionally fraught." He glanced around the room. "These detectives are feeling the weight. And you're picking that up by osmosis, because you're empathetic. Yes, I want you to put yourself in the UNSUB's head and decipher how he thinks. But step back from the turmoil the detectives here are dealing with. Fine-tune the edge."

Poker face, she thought. This killer was making her feel like nothing *but* edge.

"I'll work on it."

Emmerich leaned on the table with his fingertips, like a sprinter in the blocks. "I need you focused. And analytical. And that means keeping yourself from becoming too emotionally involved with the case."

He pointedly eyed the photo in Caitlin's hand. She wanted to clutch it to her chest.

"Otherwise you might as well have stayed at Quantico."

A sharp needle seemed to poke her in the forehead. She met his gaze. "Don't doubt my commitment."

He held poised, assessing her. She knew: she couldn't hold back, couldn't swerve, couldn't let her emotions or the messy world around her distract from this. *Job stays at the station.*

"Message received and understood. I'm here," she said.

"Good." Emmerich straightened. His expression softened. "The little girl's name is Maisie Lin-Chu. The situation's tragic but could have been even worse. Her aunt and uncle will take care of her. She'll be safe."

"We can hope," she said.

But she thought of the Midnight Man—a rip in the night—and drew a deep breath. Then straightened her shoulders.

"I'll start analyzing the evidence he takes and the messages he leaves," she said.

"Especially the eyes." Emmerich's gaze tightened. "Because there's something he wants us to see, and he's picking up steam."

Weird fucking shit.

Caitlin was packing her notes and laptop, preparing to head to the team's hotel to check in, when Detective Alvarez came through the war room. He had a sheet of paper in his hand.

The early night was closing in, a cool twilight falling on the city. Outside, skyscrapers lit the view. Headlights turned the streets into a moving grid of light. Across the street in Grand Park, the palm trees sparkled with white pinpoint lights.

Alvarez handed her the sheet. "Press release."

He had lost the toothpick but was gnawing on a piece of chewing gum. A pack of Nicorette peeked from his shirt pocket. *Good on ya, Alvarez.* Working a serial murder case wasn't conducive to kicking addictions.

The press release was brief and stark. It stated that the recent Southern California killings were believed to be the work of a single offender. Adult male who referred to himself as the Midnight Man. The killer targeted homes with no lights, no active security systems, no dogs.

And it warned the public that the killer had so far targeted homes with children.

Caitlin's attention lingered on that. "Including the warning is a gamble."

Alvarez bristled. "You think we should leave people in the dark?"

It would set Southern California off. The level of alarm would rocket into orbit. "Not at all. I agree with it. Warning parents that homes with children attract the killer—anything we can do to mitigate that risk is worth it."

"So what's the downside?"

"The Midnight Man will take it badly." An image of a black hole, a gaping heart ringed with teeth, came over her. "He doesn't want children warned or protected from him."

7

Maya Cathcart heard the sound from the depths of sleep. *Bang.* It jerked her straight up in bed, confused, heart racing. It had come from the front of the house, the living room.

Eyes gluey, she reached for her husband. Her hand found air. Terrence wasn't in bed.

She squinted, blinking, to read the clock on the nightstand. 3:12 A.M. She listened. Heard nothing now. The house was dead quiet. Street was dead quiet. As it should be, this hour, this little neighborhood in Arcadia. Terrence must have gotten up, gone to the kitchen, bumped something. But that noise.

It sounded like a gunshot.

For the tiniest fraction of a second, she held still, thinking: Couldn't be. I imagined it. Had to.

Then she thought: *Amelia.*

And Maya was out of bed, in her cami and panties, barefoot on the cold floor, rushing to the bedroom door, trying to hear past the thunder of blood in her ears. The baby's room was down the hall. Her own closed bedroom door told her that Terrence had gotten up some time ago. Because the baby was crying? No. She wouldn't have slept through Amelia's cries. Terrence must have gone to get a snack or watch TV and shut the door to let her get some rest. New mothers didn't get much rest. And she'd been dog tired.

Maya eased open the bedroom door. Her nerves felt covered in millipedes. The house was dark. Unusually dark, and she couldn't parse it, until she realized that the streetlight on the corner was out. A thin milk of moonlight spread across the living room.

In that moonlight stood a shadow.

Man-shaped. Tall, hooded, hands hanging at its sides. Its back to her.

The shadow turned its head. In profile, Maya could see that it wore a hoodie with a ball cap beneath. It stared across the living room.

Maya saw, by the corner of the sofa, Terrence's bare feet. Her husband was laid out on the floor. He wasn't moving.

In the shadow's hand, reflecting the moonlight, Maya saw the barrel of a gun.

Couldn't be turned real. Gunshot. Here. Now. She choked on a moan. *Terrence.*

Amelia's room was halfway down the hall, midway between her and the shadow. Maya could run, but the shadow could fire, and she wasn't as fast as a bullet.

She eased her bedroom door shut. Backed up, eyes wide now, knowing she couldn't make a sound, but she couldn't tiptoe because tiptoeing would take too long.

She hurried to the closet and inched the squeaky door open. She reached and pawed. The Winchester 30.06 shotgun was on the top shelf.

She pulled it down, hands shaking. She didn't turn on a light. Turn it on and for goddamned sure the shadow would know she was in here. She broke the breech of the gun and stared down the barrel. Turned it toward the window, the chalky moonlight. Inhaled. Empty.

The moan circled, deep in her throat. She reached into the closet again, fumbled on the high shelf, and found the box of shells. The cardboard was soft. How old were the shells? Five years? Ten? The Winchester had belonged to her grandfather, he brought it with him when he moved west from Texas after the war, he told her it had put food on his family's table and kept drunken peckerwoods from harassing him on his own property and he hoped she'd never need it but *damn, girl,* don't rely on anybody else for your life in the dark of the night. She'd fired it once, back when, and had kept it on the top shelf since Pap passed, and now, now, now …

Her hands shook as she grabbed shells from the box. A couple fell to the floor but she left them, kept loading, until she couldn't wait any longer. She crossed the room and threw open the door even as she slammed the breech shut, barrel aimed straight down the hall, and it seemed darker, seemed endless dark. She stepped into the hallway and couldn't see anything now, maybe tunnel vision. She put the stock of the Winchester to her shoulder and aimed down the hall but she couldn't fire until she knew where he was and she had to block the intruder's path to the nursery but couldn't pull the trigger blindly. She hit a light switch.

The Midnight Man stood outside Amelia's door. Motionless, silent, facing straight at her. He raised his head and the light hit his eyes. Maya gasped.

Not real, she thought. *Not possible. This?* Him? *All those people?*

He stared at her. The Winchester was heavy in her arms. She held it steady and pulled the trigger.

The old shotgun misfired.

The killer hissed.

No. Maya gaped at the Winchester in horror. In her peripheral vision, the shadow-made-flesh raised his handgun and charged down the hall at her. She flipped the shotgun around, grabbed the barrel and ran at him, raising it to club him, thinking, *My baby.*

He fired.

The blow, the blare, inflated into pain, solid, wall to wall. Maya keeled, knew she was going down, but the world seemed inside out, and her arms couldn't control the shotgun anymore. The floor hit her hard in the back, the light on the hallway ceiling directly overhead, and all was agony. She saw the Midnight Man swim into sight above her, his face, his expression. She heard the baby crying. She gritted her teeth and reached up, to claw him, his face, bring him down to her, because he had a gun in his hand and if she could bring him down she could take him with her, wherever she was going. Take him with her and leave Amelia here. She reached for the Midnight Man as he stood over her. Gun in his right hand.

Knife in his left.

He dropped to his knees at her side, breathing hard. He extended the knife. Maya swiped her fingernails at his face. He jerked back, but not quick enough. Then he raised the gun one more time.

8

Under the rising sun, the medical examiner greeted the FBI team outside the Arcadia ranch house. The San Gabriel Mountains were etched in shadow behind it. Hundred-year-old palms towered over the roof. A jogging stroller was parked on the front porch.

The ME was a solid woman in her fifties, Doris Park, and if Caitlin had been asked to describe her from a checklist, she would have picked "Seen it all."

Park warned, "It's bad."

The home of Maya and Terrence Cathcart was painted a happy yellow. The gardenias were sweet-smelling, rush hour traffic a distant whisper. Around the neighborhood, sprinklers misted neat lawns. Neighbors stood in knots, hands pressed to their mouths. The street was lined with police cars, an ambulance, and the medical examiner's van. None of it affected the Cathcarts. Nothing would again.

Caitlin, Emmerich, and Rainey signed into the scene and ducked under the police tape. An Arcadia PD detective stepped out the front door. He handed them latex gloves and paper booties.

What a way to get dressed for work.

"This way."

The house was sunlit and homey. Family photos covered the walls. A baby swing sat in the living room. Terrence Cathcart lay in front of the sofa, face up.

He was in his early thirties, athletic, African American, wearing Gap boxers and a gray Cal State Dominguez Hills T-shirt with a bullet hole in it. From the copious dark blood that soaked the shirt and floor, he'd been shot in the liver.

Caitlin peered around. Through the kitchen door, she saw a baby bottle standing in a pan of water on the stove. A half-prepared sandwich remained on a cutting board. Chicken, mustard, hunk of cheddar cheese.

The carving knife was in Terrence Cathcart's hand.

Beyond his body, a living room window was broken. The screen had been removed from the outside. Shattered glass littered the floor inside below the windowsill.

Whatever had happened, Cathcart had enough time to recognize a threat and confront the intruder. He'd gone down trying to protect his family.

Emmerich was somber. "Mr. Cathcart was the first victim?"

"Evidently," the Arcadia detective said.

He stepped aside to give them a view of the hallway. The FBI team silently took it in.

The young mother lay outside a door with a child's name on it in colorful block letters. AMELIA. Caitlin forced herself not to react.

Maya Cathcart was in her late twenties, petite but strong. She had a runner's legs. They were splayed awkwardly, the soles of her bare feet pale against her brown calves. A vintage shotgun—very old, maybe a family heirloom—lay beside her. Cathcart's hand loosely gripped the barrel, as if she'd tried to use it to bludgeon her attacker.

Close quarters. Deadly, no room for error, no escape. And the young woman had fought to the end. She'd made a stand, outside her baby's room, to her last breath.

The ME's assistant was kneeling beside Maya's body, bagging her hands in paper sacks.

Dr. Park approached. "There's biological matter and blood under her fingernails. She may have scratched her assailant. We'll send scrapings for DNA analysis."

"Good." Caitlin stared at the body. She couldn't bear to look. Couldn't look away.

Maya Cathcart had been shot once in the gut and twice in the face.

Caitlin forced herself to scan the hallway. She saw no ejected shotgun shells. No evidence markers. Maya apparently hadn't been able to get off a shot. The killer had fired multiple times, but Caitlin saw no cartridge casings on the floor.

"He policed his brass again?" she said.

The Arcadia detective spoke in hushed tones, as though not to disturb Maya. "Four shots fired, no spent cartridges. Of course, he may have been firing a revolver."

Caitlin pointed at a spot on the wall outside the baby's door. "He was careful."

A bloody palm print had been hastily wiped from the wall so it was unidentifiable. And a few feet from Maya's body, near the living room, a square of hallway carpet had been cut out and removed. Roughly eighteen-by-eighteen inches.

The ME gestured at Maya. "Careful is one word for it." She shook her head. "He pried the bullets out of her body with a tactical knife. And took them."

And Caitlin lost the battle to turn away from Maya Cathcart's face. Her breath snagged.

"He shot her through the eyes," she said.

"Then gouged them out with the knife to retrieve the bullets."

The ME's voice sounded distant. Caitlin stared.

She heard Rainey ask, "The baby?"

The Arcadia detective said, "With Social Services. Grandparents are flying in from Seattle." His voice was thin. "There's something you should see."

He called the police photographer over. The man approached, camera hanging from a strap around his neck. He clicked through shots he'd taken earlier and turned the viewscreen.

The photos showed the baby, Amelia, in the arms of a paramedic. She seemed about nine months old, eyes rimed with tears, soft curls stuck to her head. She appeared uninjured.

Rainey went incredibly still. "He drew an eye on her forehead in blood."

Under the glare of the camera's flash, the eye was clearly visible, covering the little girl's entire forehead.

Caitlin stepped into the nursery. She halted.

Eyes were drawn all over the walls. Some in blood, some in ink.

Caitlin's throat seemed to seize. Some eyes were the size of a fist. Some the size of a serving platter. Some, dozens, the size of a kiss. She stopped counting when she hit sixty.

Above the crib was written the word LEGION.

She needed air. She walked outside to the front yard. Emmerich joined her in the sunshine.

"You don't need to say anything," she said. "I'm fine."

"You're not. None of us are."

She threw a glare at him. "In that case? It's goddamn brutal."

Rainey emerged from the house, moving slowly. She never moved fast unless the situation called for it, and then she hurtled. But she was walking as if through syrup. Her hands hung at her sides.

Emmerich normally would have asked for impressions, comments, analysis, but he seemed to regard this as a moment of intermission. Fresh out of the gate on a sun-drenched California morning, and their world was peppered with emotional shrapnel.

Rainey gazed back at the house. Her jaw was tight. "The Cathcarts did everything they were supposed to do. They committed. Married, stepped up, took responsibility, created a home. Cherished their child. Then this. No reason, no purpose, just destruction."

Her gaze extended to the horizon.

Emmerich stared across the street at the clusters of neighbors rainbowed by lawn sprinklers. A news van turned the corner. An Arcadia police officer stepped into the road, hand out to stop them. The street, the crime scene, and the morning were simultaneously busy and empty, bright and broken.

Caitlin spoke quietly. "We're missing too much. We're not seeing his vision of the world."

Slowly, Emmerich nodded. "If we're going to profile this UNSUB, we have to travel LA as he does."

Rainey said, "What do you propose?"

Caitlin took in the cloudless blue sky, fresh and cool with the winter morning sun. But the killer attacked a sleeping city and infested its dreams.

"He told us," she said. "He's the Midnight Man. We have to follow him into that world."

A van from the County Coroner's Office arrived. Two attendants pulled a gurney from the back. A black body bag was tightly rolled and strapped down on it. They walked past the agents to the front door of the house.

Emmerich watched them pass. "We'll go tonight."

9

They rode out at midnight. Bundled in her peacoat, Caitlin slid behind the wheel of the Suburban. Rainey and Emmerich climbed in, Caitlin cued a playlist, and they pulled out. Nine Inch Nails filled the SUV and they flowed through the city like a black-lacquered bullet.

Olympic Boulevard. Koreatown. Hancock Park. Traffic, streetlights, empty sidewalks. Highland Boulevard. West Hollywood. Neon, bars. La Cienega. Caitlin drove and absorbed the vibe. When the playlist hit "Ruiner," Rainey cut a glance at her.

"Really? You think he's pumping himself up with this?"

"He's not listening to NPR," Caitlin said.

West LA. Cramped apartment blocks, twenty-four-hour gyms, KFC. Westwood. Dazzling and busy, with UCLA students, holiday shoppers, and moviegoers lingering for late-night entertainment.

But as soon as they crossed Wilshire, the night deepened and traffic ebbed. The sleek high-rise condos disappeared behind them and they were virtually alone on Beverly Glen. They rolled uphill, crossed the peak of the Santa Monica Mountains via Coldwater Canyon, and cruised through the Valley.

By three A.M., winding their way through tract-house neighborhoods, the streets had emptied. Trees loomed. Streetlights were far between. The view tunneled to the beam of the headlights.

The sleeping city felt eerily lonely.

Droning along Mulholland, the dashboard lights turned Rainey's face skeletal, and Caitlin got an unnerving sensation of dislocation.

The roads were deserted. From the top of the hills, Los Angeles was brilliantly illuminated. But it felt distant.

Even when they dropped back downhill to Sunset, the well-lit blacktop felt abandoned. Caitlin cut down an alley behind expensive homes. Garbage cans flashed past, construction fencing, guardhouses to gated compounds. Lights were scarce. Flickers, fireflies.

"Approach the gate and the floods come on," Rainey said. "CCTV. Doubt he goes through any entrance where he has to smile for the cameras."

They emerged in Benedict Canyon and headed uphill past mansions with topiary gardens. "The Downward Spiral" throbbed from the stereo. Fifty-foot palm trees picket-fenced past, there, gone, there, gone. Nobody else was on the road.

"He drives to the scenes," Caitlin said.

"Agreed," Emmerich said. "Getting up these hills would take hours without wheels. And his range—it's twenty-five miles east to Monterey Park. Thirty, thirty-five northeast to Arcadia. He's not walking."

"He has a vehicle. Or access to a vehicle. Or he steals cars and dumps them."

The houses thinned out. Eucalyptus trees thickened, and coyote brush grew wild along the shoulder of the road.

Privacy. Seclusion. That was what people paid for when they lived up here. Neighbors wouldn't be close enough to hear a scream or a cry for help. Or perhaps even gunshots.

After ten minutes of climbing steep switchbacks, they rounded a final bend. Caitlin pulled over, killed the engine, and they got out.

The Peretti family's house was dark. The wind scored through the trees with a heavy rush. Seed pods and dry leaves crunched beneath Caitlin's boots. At the bottom of the driveway she paused.

The eucalyptuses chattered in the wind. Ivy covered the hillside behind the house. Across the street was a construction site, a tear-down that had been cleared to the slab.

Emmerich surveyed the hillside. "He drove and parked on this road.

Not on an adjacent street. He didn't come over that hilltop behind the house. The terrain and vegetation's impossible."

The night was clear. LA was mostly overwhelmed by light pollution, but here, near the crest of the hills, surrounded by chaparral and canyons and sleep-locked homes—with no streetlights or even Christmas lights visible at this time of night—stars broke through overhead, spangled, vibrating. Cold light.

On the ground, all was shadow. They walked up the curving driveway three abreast. The house came clearly into view.

Caitlin slowed. "He saw it from this vantage, I'm sure. He got this view of it before he broke in."

"Agreed," Emmerich said.

The house was a showplace. Meant to draw in light, provide expansive views, give a feeling of air and height. Above it all. Soaring.

The air felt close and black. The wind scoured her.

The house, designed to glow with light, was a shell.

It was an abattoir. The slaughterhouse where a family was destroyed. It loomed silent and dark.

A shiver racked her. Though Rainey and Emmerich stood close on either side of her, she felt almost existentially alone.

This was the view the killer saw. A moonless night. The glass of the house dim, flat, black. The darkness mysterious, almost inherently frightening.

And this view had *excited* him. It had *unleashed* him.

It had sent him up the walk to the house, coursing with the urge to kill. It had propelled him inside, where the family woke to the realization that they weren't protected, weren't safe within their own walls, but were isolated, overcome, torn apart.

"The dread, the darkness—they *are* the Midnight Man," she said.

It was a terrifying thought.

On the cracked pavement of a vacant lot, the Midnight Man jogged past ragged weeds and broken bottles. The lights of downtown, the skyscrapers, the pillars of money, the glow of commerce, sports, shallow entertainment, the pond scum that constituted humanity, it all throbbed, mindless of him. The tangle of nearby freeways was a murmur rather than a gushing roar—an ultrasound heartbeat. He kicked an empty bottle of Thunderbird. It clattered, glinting, across the crumbling asphalt.

Nobody heard it. Even the homeless didn't hang out here at three thirty A.M., not on open ground.

He crossed the vacant lot and jogged along a railroad spur. It took him toward the decrepit, bristling heart of Los Angeles. The perfect place to blend in, camouflaged among the human rodents that swarmed LA. Among the trash and germs that constituted the life-form called *Homo sapiens.*

Old warehouses rose on either side of the railroad tracks. Parked cars, some abandoned, some stripped. If anybody slept in the cracks and doorways, they didn't stir when he loped past. Street lights buzzed on the corners, but the corners were far apart. The hum of electricity was to the west, in the gold-lit spires that towered overhead. Here, amid trash and graffiti and razor wire, he was cloaked. Especially when he stuck to the tracks.

At a split in the rails he ducked into the decaying zone that wasn't even Skid Row, but the ass crack of Skid Row. Checking his surroundings, he sneaked past a construction fence. Then slowed to a walk. He sauntered toward a dilapidated building marked for demolition.

Out of the open air, screened by the construction fencing, he pulled down his hood. He took the bullets from the pocket of his jeans. He held them in his palm. The metal was warm. It was irregular.

Personalized.

He rolled the rounds in his hand. The words coming from his mouth were mere mutters.

More to come. Next. Next.

He squeezed the bullets tightly and pressed his fist to his lips, then slid the rounds back into his pocket. He checked for hostiles one more time, eyes sliding across the view, ears tuned to rats' feet and drunks' stumbles.

It was just him. He slipped into the building and into darkness.

10

It was close to dawn when they circled back via the 405 and headed downtown. Rainey drove and Caitlin rode shotgun. Headlights pierced the deep blue of morning twilight. The city was stirring itself like the rough beast it was. In the wing mirror, Caitlin could see Emmerich's head bent to his phone. On the East Coast it was already office hours, and he was answering email.

Palm trees flashed past. Caitlin felt, as always, the push-pull of this city. Home of dreams, paradise, fragmented. The freeways were its arteries but didn't pump blood to its heart. They served as barriers, as corridors, passageways, pulling millions along in isolation. They were meant to be experienced in motion. Stop along the shoulder and the sense of displacement was inevitable, of being in a world that had suddenly become *wrong*.

Rainey's phone pinged. It was resting in a cup holder, and she glanced at the display but didn't pick it up. Both hands on the wheel, going sixty-five.

Caitlin said, "Want me to see who it is?"

"It'll be Bo. Or the boys." Her husband and twins. "Please—check that there's no school-day crisis brewing."

Caitlin snagged the phone. "Text and a photo. Breakfast."

The snapshot showed the twins, ten-year-old TJ and Dre, digging into scrambled eggs. When Caitlin showed it to her, Rainey's expression warmed.

Caitlin read the text. "'TJ wants to know how Santa can get to Wakanda if it's camouflaged from radar and satellites.'"

Rainey laughed. "TJ knows Mom and Dad are Santa and that Wakanda exists only in the Marvel Universe, but still." The warmth in her eyes lingered. "Tell him Santa magic doesn't need radar. And add kisses. Bunches of them."

Caitlin thumbed the message. She envied Rainey her family. Brianne Rainey was one of the few members of the unit who not only had young kids at home but was on her first marriage. Bo—Charles Bohannan—was a criminal defense attorney, former Air Force JAG.

Rainey sighed. "Christmas isn't coming for any of the families who lived in the houses we saw tonight."

"No," Caitlin said.

Rainey rested a hand on top of the steering wheel. "All these kids getting their parents ripped away … is he pretending he's *helping* them?"

Her voice was tight. Rainey was a vastly experienced agent, a cool, confident operator. She'd been with the FBI more than a decade. Worked counterintelligence, counterterror, and violent crimes before joining the BAU.

Usually she maintained a thirty-thousand-foot view of a situation, like a Predator drone circling the carnage miles overhead. Caitlin knew that she cared, deeply, about every case they investigated. That she loved the work, found it important. Caitlin had witnessed her put her own life on the line to protect others—to protect *her.*

Seeing a crack in Rainey's armor was jarring. Maybe it was fatigue, the gritty tiredness of pulling an all-nighter. Maybe it was being three thousand miles from home. Rainey's mouth was set. A vein was pulsing in her neck.

"The Cathcarts—those two went down fighting to save their family. That young mother, right outside the baby's room. Swinging, battering, clawing. And what he did to her …"

In the mirror, Caitlin saw Emmerich's head come up. He watched Rainey attentively.

"Maybe the killer was enraged that Maya Cathcart fought back," Rainey said. "Maybe he was excited. Maybe he wanted to punish the baby symbolically by drawing that monstrous eye on her forehead—and we *have* to figure out what the hell is going on with that."

"We will," Emmerich said. "It will provide insight into the UNSUB's fantasy. But I don't know if it's critical to stopping him. He may not fully understand its implications himself."

"Don't give a good goddamn about his insights into himself," Rainey said.

Emmerich let the remark hang. The Suburban raced along. The sun crested the horizon, golden, burning in the cold clear air.

"Brianne?" Caitlin said.

She changed lanes and passed slower traffic. "The Cathcarts. Hurts to see a young brother gone like that. A young sister."

She held her breath for a few more seconds, shook her head, and blew it out. "A *baby*," she said. "The killer getting closer now, touching her. *Defiling* the bond between a mother and her child by painting that little girl with her own mother's blood."

Caitlin's stomach clenched. She'd been trying to avoid feeling the pain, but Rainey's words punched through.

"While we were in spitting distance." Rainey rubbed her eyes. "Good Christ, I am exhausted."

Emmerich let her talk. They'd all felt this way at some point. They needed to get it out.

A Corvette blasted past them. Rainey watched it go.

She pointed at her phone. "My turn to pick the music, Hendrix. First playlist, first track."

Caitlin scrolled and hit PLAY. The Suburban filled with the voice of Maria Callas. *Tosca*. "Vissi d'arte."

"Betrayal and revenge?" Caitlin said.

"Turn it up."

The sun was fully above the horizon, needling the morning sky, when they pulled off the freeway downtown. They drove up South Main toward LAPD headquarters, the road wide open.

Caitlin saw him from the corner of her eye, across the street from the LAPD complex. A man leaning against the hood of a car. Rainey drove past him.

Caitlin spun in her seat to look out the back window. "Wait."

Rainey braked, eyes on the rearview. "Him?"

Caitlin's fatigue evaporated. "Yeah."

He was reading on a phone, head down. Jean jacket, Carhartt boots, eyes set. Caitlin jumped out and strode toward him.

"You."

He looked up. She kept walking. It was Sean.

His smile erupted. For a few calculated seconds he continued leaning against the car. He glanced at the idling Suburban and nodded a chin-up greeting to the people inside. Then he straightened.

She came up to him, her heart pumping.

"You didn't even mention that you were coming to town?" She set her hands on her hips. "Bastard."

"That's me." The grin spread. "Because you hate surprises. Absolutely hate them. Just look at you."

He pulled her to him and kissed her. She held her smile in check for a second longer, then threw her head back. She laughed. Her worries and tension dissolved.

"What's going on?" she said.

"Lead on the bombings. Have a meeting at the ATF Field Division in Glendale." He indicated with his thumb. "And you didn't tell me you were going on an overnight field trip. I've been waiting. Way past time for coffee."

"Let me finish up a few things here."

Behind her came Emmerich's voice.

"Hendrix. Grab breakfast and a nap." He raised a hand in greeting to Sean. "See you back here for the team meeting this afternoon."

"Thanks."

She nabbed her backpack from the Suburban. In the driver's seat, Rainey was craning her neck to get a good view of Sean. She had never met him. She put the SUV in gear and pulled away with sly grin on her face—maybe approving.

Caitlin hoisted the backpack and turned to Sean. "Breakfast?"

"That really what you want to grab?"

"Hell no."

11

The trail of coats and shoes and jeans led from the door of the hotel room across the floor to the bed. Pillows and covers lay askew. Caitlin and Sean lay side by side, face up, breathing hard. The morning light flickered on the ceiling, reflecting from the parade of traffic on the street below. Caitlin let out a whistle.

"I won that round," she said.

"It's not a contest."

"Twice."

Sean laughed. She stretched and rolled on her side. She was astonished at how wide awake she felt.

Sean ran a finger down her bare thigh. She was too energized, for once, to feel exposed. He was naturally unselfconscious. She instinctively felt the urge to turtle and protect herself from whatever he would discover by looking at her. All her life she'd believed that her heart needed to be hidden, encased in Teflon, or she would end up emotionally flayed. That letting anybody in was destructive.

It had taken her months to understand that Sean felt replenished when she came into his view. That she enlivened him. That she—Caitlin Rose Hendrix—could provide warmth and succor to another human being, merely by being herself. That he wasn't searching for flaws. Didn't watch to catch her stumbling. That when he looked and really *saw* her, he felt nourished.

That shook her. She was a child of divorce. Unhappy endings were her template. For a long time, she had felt like a tightrope walker who expected at any second to be shoved off the high wire with a pole.

But today she let him gaze on her. She gazed back.

She still felt invaded. But she stroked his cheek and let his breath and his fingertips pore over her body.

They'd sworn, *We'll work it out*. This, right now, was what *work it out* meant. They lived three thousand miles apart and found time for ephemeral moments of happiness.

He was a prize, and she'd be a fool to do anything except hold onto him. But if they wanted to make a life together, something had to change. Something that hadn't changed in the fifteen months since she moved to Virginia.

Her voice was soft. "Babe, I missed you."

He laced his fingers with hers and kissed the back of her hand, and she knew he understood the deeper meaning in her words.

She settled herself into the crook of his shoulder under the brilliant winter sun. "What's the lead?"

"Forensic analysis of the bomb debris." His expression was cool but curious. "We're off the clock."

Rule number one in the Caitlin Hendrix handbook: When you're off duty, you take off the badge. But with Sean on edge about the bombing case, she was suspending it.

It wasn't a sacrifice on her part. It was an indulgence.

She smiled to herself, recognizing the irony. "Just talk."

"We found a fragment of the wiring."

"When?"

"An ATF team has been sieving the rubble since the explosion. Hundreds of tons of it," he said. "Four weeks ago they found a fragment of the blasting cap. Amid debris that had originated near the seat of the explosion. Three days ago, at the facility where the county transported the rubble, they found another. With a sliver of wiring still attached."

"After nine months. God bless 'em."

He propped himself on his elbows. "A centimeter-long section of alloy. Enough to trace a manufacturer."

She sat up. "Sales records?" There was excitement in her voice.

"A wholesaler. First link in the chain. Inland Empire—I'm heading out there this afternoon."

She nodded. "Sometimes it ain't the big things. And you're a digger." She leaned over and kissed him.

After so many months of nothing, no headway, the investigation spinning its wheels, this was the first fresh evidence Sean had been able to tell her about. And she knew that this lead was incredibly tenuous.

"I don't want to jinx it," she said. "But damn."

"You can't jinx anything. I trust your insights and advice. I know you've felt frustrated too."

The case had become personal for Sean. And like him, Caitlin suspected that the Ghost could be orchestrating the bombing campaign.

The Ghost—the UNSUB who had helped the Prophet kill seven people in the Bay Area, including her father. The man who crucified her hand to a board with a nail gun. The killer who slipped away from the abandoned BART platform where she watched Mack die. The man who helped the Prophet set up explosives in the BART tunnel, then sabotaged them.

The shadow who sent her black lilies at Quantico.

He had warned her he'd be back. That he'd bring her down. He had *phoned her* at her desk at Quantico to make that promise. Telling her, without telling her, that he knew where she was, and how to touch her. Anytime he wanted.

She kept a forensic artist's sketch of his face tacked to a corkboard above her desk at the BAU. She had never for an instant taken his threats for idle boasting or mere taunts.

Was the bombing campaign that ensnared her friend and her lover part of his plan?

"It's one step forward," Sean said. "This guy is getting more sophisticated. And he wasn't a novice when he started placing his devices."

The bomber had coated one device with black paint. It indicated he knew that fingerprints and DNA could survive an explosion.

"He's wary and meticulous. But he may not know the advantage investigators have."

"Which is?"

"Bombs don't eliminate evidence. They create it," he said. "We have that sliver of wire. I'm going to trace it all the way back to this bastard's kitchen table."

"Hell to the amen," she said.

He smiled. His handsome face, his dark eyes, were a balm to her.

Throwing the covers off, she sprang to her knees and straddled him. "Round two."

He laughed. "You are the most competitive person I've ever met."

"You need a break?"

"If I did, at this point I wouldn't dare tell you."

He pulled her against him. His hands, his mouth, his heat poured over her. Caitlin pressed her lips to his ear.

"Don't want a break. Don't want to waste a second," she whispered.

When Caitlin woke, the light had sidled several feet across the floor. Noise from a construction site clanged through the window. She stretched with luxurious torpor. The bathroom door opened, and Sean stepped out, hair wet, a towel wrapped around his waist. He found his jeans and shirt.

Too soon, she thought. "You have time for breakfast before you go?"

He pulled on the jeans. "I'm not going. *We* are."

"Where?"

He nabbed his wallet from the credenza, stuck it in his back pocket, and picked up his phone. He read a message on the screen and smiled.

"Michele says hi." He typed a reply.

She pulled the covers over her shoulders. "Hi back."

"She's asking about the trip." Still reading the screen, he laughed. "I sent her a photo."

Caitlin's eyes popped. She bolted upright. "Of me? Us? Here?"

He swiveled, taken aback. "Of course not. Caitlin."

She felt her face redden. Saw *Sean's* face redden. He occasionally felt apprehensive that his girlfriend was buddies with his ex, wary that they would compare notes. Caitlin had always found his male insecurities—and ego—amusing. Exposing her own insecurities felt less funny.

"Sorry," she said.

He crossed to the bed and held out the phone. "This photo."

It had been taken on his flight to LA. It showed a little girl, her hand pressed to the window of the jet, absorbing the sky-high panorama with awe. Caitlin's anxieties sloughed away. She grinned.

"You brought Sadie?"

"Surprise."

"Sean Rawlins. You waited three hours to tell me this? Where is she? If you say you left her in your rental car, I'll place you under arrest."

"She's with my sister in Los Feliz. Getting to hang with her cousins for a couple of days."

"Days."

"I forgot to tell you. I'm staying in Southern California through the weekend."

"Double bastard. You let me think I had only one morning with you."

"You said you wanted a workout." He gave her a preposterously shiny smile. "Now get going, because I'm caffeine-deficient. And Sadie's waiting for us to pick her up."

Caitlin threw off the covers. "Then I must primp myself for Miss Rawlins. Out of the way, cowboy."

In-N-Out wasn't gourmet. But it was the best meal Caitlin had eaten in months.

The fast-food stop on Sunset overlooked the sludgy river of late morning LA traffic. Cheeseburgers and fries, coffee cups, and toys were spread across the booth's tabletop. At the counter, the crowd moved quickly. Some to-go customers took their lunches and began eating even before they reached the exit, unwrapping burgers and lunging for them with their mouths as they pushed the door open with their rear ends. Outside, cars and trucks inched toward the drive-through in a constant stream, like communicants at mass.

Sadie knelt on the bench seat, elbows on the table. Her soft hair had developed a curl. Her brown eyes, guileless and inquisitive, took in everything around her. Four years old, she was effervescent and unguarded.

She picked up a toy. "This one is Triceratops."

A year earlier Sadie had been into My Little Pony. As a kid herself, Caitlin had been into Power Rangers and Police Officer Barbie. For Sadie's sake she had trained in the fine art of styling Little Pony manes—and now the kid was into dinosaurs. The tabletop featured a prehistoric panorama.

Sadie pointed to one with wings. "This is Lolly. She's a Pteranodon. P-T-E-R-A-N-O-D-O-N."

"Wow," Caitlin said.

Sean leaned back, coffee in hand, and stretched an arm across the back of the booth. "She learned that from the Dino Songs album. Play it ten thousand times, you'll learn it too."

Sadie picked up a fearsome critter with tiny arms. "Tyrannosaurus rex. That means *tyrant lizard*. Her name is Cheeto and she's very gentle. You can pet her."

Caitlin ran an index finger down the T-rex's back. Sadie growled and made Cheeto leap at Caitlin.

Caitlin pretended to yell. A whisper-howl. "She's wild."

"Of course. She's the queen of the predators."

Sadie set Cheeto down. Her brow furrowed.

"She won't hurt you. None of them can really hurt you," she said.

"That's reassuring."

"They're little and pretend. Not like bears or a bomb."

Caitlin's breath caught. She flashed Sean a glance. He kept his face absolutely flat, but emotion shifted behind his eyes.

Sadie stuck a french fry into a splotch of ketchup. "A bomb hurt my mom."

"I know, sweetie," Caitlin said.

"That's why she was in the hospital. Her face was all scabby." Sadie ran her small fingers over the side of her own face. "She had operations. And her legs got broken. They were hung up on strings from the ceiling. She was in the hospital until summer and that's why my grandma came to stay with me and Daddy."

Caitlin had seen Sadie numerous times since the bombing, but until now, the little girl had avoided speaking about her mother's injuries. Michele had skated on the edge between life and death, and while Sadie hadn't been told how close it was, she knew that her mommy was very sick, and that every adult in her life was desperate with worry. Sadie was too young to understand what death meant. But she felt it when fear saturated her world.

With Michele home, her survival assured, Sadie seemed secure enough to talk. Caitlin thought it was a positive step.

"Lots of times my grandma stays with us now," Sadie said. "Mommy needs help. But I'm a big girl."

"And strong, like Cheeto," Caitlin said.

Sean briefly shut his eyes, then reached across the table and squeezed Caitlin's hand. He stroked Sadie's hair and kissed the top of her head.

At moments like this, Caitlin felt ashamed at her lingering anxieties over Sean's feelings for Michele. They'd been divorced for years. They both used the word *amicable*. Caitlin had never sensed any nostalgia for the marriage, had never seen any rekindled desire for Michele in Sean's eyes. Just stinging self-reproach that he and his college sweetheart couldn't make it work. Disappointment in himself for failing.

Of course, he and Michele had worked out a new relationship. By necessity. Distant at first, things had thawed in the last year, becoming friendlier—fond, even. That was a *good* thing, Caitlin reminded herself. Warmth was better than war.

Caitlin didn't think Sean was cheating on her. Not for a second. Still, she could never forget that Michele and Sean had something that she and Sean didn't. They had a family. And how Sean related to his family was out of her hands.

She dug her nails into her palm. *Let it go.*

Sadie stabbed more fries into the ketchup. She ate them heartily. Her gaze was earnest. "You can hold Cheeto, Cat. She likes you."

Caitlin wrapped the T-rex tight in her palm. *And so my Grinch heart grows three sizes this day.* "Thanks."

Sadie leaned across the table and lowered her voice to a conspiratorial whisper. "Think how big a T-rex poop was. *Enormous.*"

She popped back to her seat, both hands pressed over her mouth, stifling laughter.

With that, Sean's shoulders relaxed. He squeezed Caitlin's hand and smiled, rolling his eyes.

As they left the restaurant, Caitlin's phone pinged. An email from Emmerich. *Subject: Cathcart autopsy reports.*

She replied, *On my way in. Will read ASAP.*

Sadie said, "Are you having dinner with us, Cat?"

"Hope so."

Sadie didn't hold her arms out, but simply jumped into Caitlin's embrace. "You better."

Her hug was artless and loving. Caitlin kissed the girl's cheek. *Be happy,* she thought. *Be carefree. Let all evil stay away from you forevermore.*

12

On the playground at Bay Rise Elementary School, kids huddled at recess. The sun was white, the December sky crayon blue from horizon to horizon. Noise rolled across the playground. Kickball, foursquare, the third graders on the swings, soaring higher with every pump.

The sixth graders stood in a knot near the tetherball poles. Talking about the Midnight Man.

"He's a demon," Sam Hernandez said. "I heard my mom talking with Father Ortiz after church."

"Like a devil, for real?" Caleb Barnes said. "I don't believe it."

Sam bounced a ball. "Totally real. The demon possesses a person and takes over. The person becomes like an evil puppet. Haven't you heard of exorcists?"

Caleb grabbed the ball on the upward bounce. "That's in movies. Not the real world."

"Ask Father Ortiz. They have exorcists in the *real world*. Exorcists are priests and they throw holy water on the person and they vomit like a swimming pool of puke and the holy water burns their skin. The priests pray and show crucifixes and they drive the demon out."

"Where does the demon go?" Caleb said.

Sam grabbed the ball back. "Into another dimension. Or into somebody else."

Madison Little bit her thumbnail. "That's not what I heard. He takes kids with him after he kills their parents."

Sam and Caleb frowned. "Really?"

"Then he eats their hearts," she said.

"No way."

"Gross."

"Then I need one of those cop vests," Caleb said. "So he can't stab through it. Keep him from cutting mine out."

Olivia Chang kicked at a pebble. "I heard my mom and dad talking about how to protect our house."

Nervous eyes turned to her. Overhead, seagulls wheeled and screeched. The school was in the South Bay, a few miles from the Port of Los Angeles.

"They were talking about how to keep the Midnight Man out," Olivia said. "They won't even let me open the front door. They have to do it, then lock it again right away."

Madison continued biting at her thumbnail. "Our house is getting a burglar alarm. Dad said he never wanted one because they're superexpensive, but now nothing is too expensive. The killer knows how to break into houses, but no place has had a burglar alarm go off. The alarm would scare him away. Or at least wake us all up."

Sam shook his head. "Your house is safe."

"Why?" Madison said.

"Because it's just your dad and you and your sisters. The Midnight Man only kills people where it's a dad *and* a mom."

Madison's face flushed. "Really? Because who knows for sure?" She peeped at the kickball game. "So Jonah's safe, because he has two moms?"

"If he is," Sam said, "maybe we should all move in with him."

Logan Hanson said, "Security systems cost more than my mom earns in a month. My dad put burglar bars on the windows." There were nods among the group. Logan said, "I think we should add heat-sensing cameras."

"Like in *Predator*?" Madison said.

"Your dad let you watch *Predator*?" Olivia said.

The entire group gawked at her. Sam said, "We've *all* watched *Predator*."

Olivia seemed baffled, maybe a little embarrassed.

Hannah Guillory stayed quiet, listening to it all. The group was clustered in a circle. In the distance, a boy scrambled on top of the monkey bars and stood up. Quickly a teacher called out, telling him to climb off. The teacher strode across the playground, waving at the kid. No standing on top. That was the rule. That was to keep them safe. Too risky. Get down.

Hannah blinked at the sun. Her breath blew out in cold fog.

Keep them safe.

Bay Rise Elementary regularly held active-shooter drills. The teachers locked the classroom door and had them practice staying *perfectly silent* while they walked from their desks to the closets at the back of the room, ducking low when they passed the door because the top half of it was glass. They all climbed in the closets, squished, and Ms. Manabe shut the doors tight, and they stood there in the dark, not being *perfectly silent*, because Caleb and Sam could never stop snickering, and Olivia hated the dark, and Hannah got itchy standing so close to everybody for even only two minutes, and she knew they'd never keep perfectly silent or any kind of silent if it was real. If they had to stay inside for hours. Climbing out classroom windows would be smarter, she thought—should be every school's evacuation plan. But at Bay Rise they couldn't do that, they had to hide in the closets because the windows in the classroom were up by the ceiling, and to climb out they'd have to stack the desks and chairs and scramble over each other's backs and shoulders. But if an active shooter passed the classroom door and saw empty desks inside and high windows, he would know there was only one place everybody was hiding. And the glass in the door wasn't bulletproof.

The seagulls screeched and swooped onto the playground and battled over a dropped granola bar. They hopped and flapped and tore at it, each trying to get the whole thing.

Hannah turned away.

Active-shooter drills were terrifying. But a shooter was somebody you could see coming. When it happened, at least you had time to do *something*.

The Midnight Man just appeared, out of the dark.

Caleb held out his hands and Sam tossed him the ball. He said, "I'd put Legos on the floor inside all our windows so he'll hurt himself stepping on them if he's barefoot."

Hannah thought of her mom and dad and her little brother, Charlie, and felt blank.

If the Midnight Man materialized in your bedroom, what could a kid *really* do? Her hands felt cold.

13

In the war room, Caitlin sat at the conference table typing up her notes on the overnight ride-out. The building's unevenly spaced western windows provided a view across Spring Street, and she could glimpse the sturdy Art Deco façade of the old Los Angeles Times building. Around the room's open-plan floor, TVs played on mute, showing news feeds. She tried to ignore them. Otherwise it became an addiction. *Feed.* The word didn't just mean what was pouring out. It was what the people watching it felt an overwhelming need to do.

But she couldn't help noting that at least twice an hour, every channel cycled through the story, in bold red letters: MIDNIGHT MAN KILLS AGAIN. News coverage was ramping up. And fear in Los Angeles was intensifying. The city was itchy. And when a city itched with nerves because a killer was loose, the city bled.

She reread her notes. Across the room, a slender figure appeared in the doorway. He paused and peered around.

Caitlin's smile was spontaneous. She waved.

Nicholas Keyes raised his chin in greeting and headed toward her. He had a duffel over one shoulder and computer case over the other. Hands in the front pockets of his skinny jeans. His stride was a near lope. The young analyst was stop-sign tall, with Warby Parker frames, brown curls that flopped into his eyes, and an eager energy.

She stood to greet him. "Keyes. In person, on the West Coast."

"Hey. This our base camp?" He dropped the duffel beside the

conference table and surveyed the windows. "Sniper baffling. Clever. Sunny spot for such dark work."

"Glad you're here. Welcome back to California."

He half-smiled. "I love the smell of hydrocarbons in the morning. Smells like childhood."

At his desk, Detective Solis ended a phone call, smoothed his perfectly ironed white shirt, and came toward them with his hand extended.

Keyes shook. "Homicide Special Section. I'll try to live up to the standards your reputation demands."

Solis smiled in Caitlin's direction. "I like this guy."

It was a toss-off comment, but he was assessing Keyes to see if he was being obsequious.

"Keyes doesn't shine people on," she said. "He snarks, but he doesn't schmooze."

Keyes looked as if he could get knocked over by a floor fan running at low speed. He was the youngest member of their BAU unit, and with his checked button-down shirt and cheap Gap blazer, appeared like a youngster playing adult.

But Caitlin knew he had an analytical mind that only came with a rare confluence of inborn brilliance and years of intense study.

Detective Weisbach came over, her small frame almost vibrating with intensity. "Mr. Keyes."

"Nick."

Keyes was happy to leave it at that. Caitlin would have liked to proclaim, *It's Doctor Keyes.* But Keyes had told her what he thought of PhDs who demanded to be addressed as *Doctor*: they were hopeless narcissists.

He was hardly the only person at the FBI with a doctorate, especially within the BAU. His was in mathematics. Before joining the Bureau as a technical analyst, he had worked at NASA's Jet Propulsion Lab in Pasadena.

He unpacked his computer and notebooks and a camera. Weisbach propped her hands on her hips.

"What do you need to get started on the geographic profile?" she said.

He booted up the laptop. "Link to that big-screen TV."

Emmerich came through the door of the war room, talking to Rainey. At the sight of Keyes—on scene and already in action—his face brightened. Action was what they needed. Insight. Progress. A profile. An ID and an arrest.

Rainey approached the table. "*Privyet.*"

"*Tovarishch.*" He gave her a mock salute.

Russian. They must have binge-watched *The Americans*. Emmerich clapped Keyes on the back.

"I'm ready to roll," Keyes said, focused on his laptop.

He hit a key. On the flat-screen TV, a map of the Los Angeles Basin appeared.

He walked to the screen. "Quick refresh on geographic profiling. It analyzes spatial patterns produced by the UNSUB's hunting behavior and the sites he's targeted. From that we can build a map of a serial killer's hunting ground and predict where he lives."

The Sheriff's detective, Alvarez, strolled over. His toothpick was back today. With him came a detective from the Arcadia Police Department, newly detailed to the task force. His jaw was screwed tight with apparent stress.

"By target sites I mean locations where the UNSUB encounters the victim. Where he attacks. Where he kills. Where he dumps bodies. When you analyze all of those together, patterns emerge. Add the killer's hunting method and we can model how he chooses crime sites, which places he avoids, and where he goes to ground."

Keyes typed on his computer. Four red dots appeared on the flat-screen.

"The Midnight Man's kill sites." He gestured at the screen. "In this case, the victim encounter site, attack site, murder site, and dump sites are all apparently the same place—the victims' homes." His shoulders rose. "Data-wise, it's unfortunate. If this UNSUB spread out his work, we'd have better information to analyze."

"His work," Alvarez said. "That's a sick way to put it."

Keyes' expression was frank. "It's most likely how the killer thinks of what he's doing."

Caitlin felt a flutter, momentary queasiness. Plenty of cops talked about what serial killers did in exactly those terms. They simply didn't admit it, except late at night in the back of a dim cop bar. Her father had talked that way, he belatedly confessed—with shame.

Keyes showed no such compunction, because he wasn't speaking in terms of needing the killer to *keep working*.

"Because the Midnight Man attacks, kills, and leaves his victims in place, the primary crime scene is—as far as we know—the *only* crime scene. It means I have to get out to each location and collect as much data for interpretation and analysis as I possibly can."

He turned back to the screen. "It's going to be tough. But not impossible."

Emmerich had heard Keyes' talk before. More than once. Keyes was brilliant at what he did, but less than accomplished at public presentations. Emmerich pointed at the big screen—the four red dots spread out across the map of the Los Angeles metro.

"Explain what those four points tell you," Emmerich said.

"Yeah. The way humans move, search, and hunt are universal patterns," Keyes said. "Because the way *all* animals move, search, and hunt are universal patterns. We rely on routine. We use the least effort possible. We're comfortable in familiar geography." He shrugged. "We're fundamentally predictable."

He pointed at the red dots. "We know that serial killers hunt for prey in a concentrated area. And they do it in specific ways—far enough from their homes to conceal where they live, but not so far that the landscape is unknown to them."

"The farther away from their crib, the less likely they are to attack," Alvarez said.

"Just as the farther we travel from our homes, the less likely we are to shop for groceries. It's more work for us, it takes more time, and we feel less comfortable in a neighborhood we don't know well. We get lost. We don't know where to park. We aren't sure how to get back on the freeway to get home. It's a combination of time management, psychological comfort, and risk assessment."

He took off his glasses and cleaned them on the hem of his shirt. "Geographic profiling uses an algorithm that analyzes this distance decay and identifies the buffer zone around the UNSUB's home. If I can capture enough information, that'll let me zoom in on where the killer lives."

"So what does it take?" Alvarez said.

"Shoe leather, to begin with," Keyes said, and held up a hand. "Mine. You have enough to worry about."

"Roger that."

"I have to hit the street. I could sit at my desk at Quantico and pick apart five hundred crime scene photos, or zoom in on satellite images from multiple angles, but I wouldn't understand how a location *feels* in the flesh. Where the shadows fall at two A.M. under a full moon. How the traffic lights are sequenced late at night. Whether illegally parked cars get clamped on a particular street or a storm drain floods an intersection every time it rains. I need to get out there."

Weisbach nodded. "What do you need from us?"

"Maps, weather reports, a charger for my video camera. A car," he said, glancing at Emmerich. "And a bus map for the region. A pass for public transit, if you can arrange it. I'm going to find out how this prick is getting to and from the kill sites."

14

At eleven thirty P.M. the next night, the streets of Monterey Park were tranquil. The city, ten miles from downtown Los Angeles, was small relative to the megalopolis that engulfed it, and a home to thriving Chinese American and Vietnamese American communities. On its palm-lined boulevards a few restaurants and bars were open. Above the power lines and yellow streetlights, the winter sky burned brilliantly. The neighborhood where Beth Lin and James Chu had been shot to death was quiet and upwardly mobile.

Across the street from their home, shielded by the night, Caitlin stared at the empty house. The crime scene tape had come down, but a tatter remained, like leftover bunting from some gruesome party.

She crossed the street without leaving the shadows. The gate to the backyard swung open soundlessly. A Big Wheel sat forlornly on the patio, aimed at the sliding glass doors, as if waiting for the little girl who had lived here to come out and play.

The kitchen window over the sink had provided entry. The Midnight Man had jimmied it and slid inside. The spotless counters let him whisper into the room.

This night was still and cold. The Santa Anas were no longer blowing. Against the chill Caitlin wore a black watch cap and Under Armor running gear beneath her combats and FBI windbreaker. She raised the rifle nightscope and swept the yard. The view turned green, throbbing, pixelated. Nothing moved.

She walked along the back wall of the house, scope to her eye, and rounded the far corner. A specter boomed into shape directly ahead.

"Keyes," she hissed. "Damn you."

When she lowered the scope he disappeared, almost invisible in a black hoodie and jeans.

"How long have you been here?" she said.

"Three minutes."

She had dropped him off twenty minutes earlier, a quarter of a mile away. "Effing phantom. Did you come over the hill and climb the back fence?"

"No. Too many barriers to entry. The landscaping on the other side of the fence is cactus—a solid wall of needles. And the house on the right has a Rhodesian ridgeback."

He ambled toward her, jerking a thumb at the hillside behind the neighborhood. "Plus, the nearest road on the far side is half a mile away. It's a main thoroughfare, completely exposed, brightly lit. He wouldn't park a vehicle there. I came in the same way you did, through the side gate."

"Without being seen. Which convinces me the killer did the same." She frowned at him. "There's a Rhodesian ridgeback on the other side of the fence? You didn't even set it barking."

"Paintball taught me stealth."

She half laughed. "Ever think of applying to Hostage Rescue? You have the skills to be a sniper. Blending with the absolute dark like a ninja."

"The dark, that's the thing here, yeah," he said. "The streetlight's out. At every attack site, a streetlight's been out. And this road has more than one exit. He always chooses homes on streets with more than one escape route."

It had been two days since Keyes arrived in Los Angeles, and as far as Caitlin knew, during that time he hadn't done more than nap.

To prepare the geographic profile, Keyes had spent hours at each crime scene, learning the landscape and trying to understand it from the killer's perspective. He had walked. He had run. He had driven hundreds of miles. He traveled between scenes, backwards and forwards. He worked in daylight—and tonight, again, in midnight darkness.

Keyes turned toward the front of the house. "I think he parked on the street, under the broken light."

He towered over her in the dark, always an uncommon phenomenon because Caitlin was five ten and even taller in her Doc Martens.

"I do too," she said. "He gains a sense of power by standing outside a home's front door—the face it presents to the world—while the family inside is oblivious to the danger they're in. He wants to savor the sight, and the sensation that he's destruction itself, about to descend. And to bask in the thought that once he breaks in, all that will be left is death and fear."

He said nothing for a cold moment. "Deep," he finally murmured. He pointed at the corner of the house. "The gate."

"There's no lock on it. No mention of one in the police report. The toddler's too little to have reached the latch. This is a safe neighborhood. They didn't lock it."

"Safe neighborhood," he said.

She couldn't read his face. But his voice had an undertow.

She walked back across the patio. "He came in from the street. No lights on. No barking when he opened the gate. He prowled around back and saw a little kid's toys. No dog bowls. No curtains on the kitchen window. This was where he staged."

Keyes gazed at the sky. The half-moon going down. "He attacked at this time of night, but six weeks ago. The moon was a waxing crescent. It had already set."

"He calls himself the Midnight Man for a reason," she said. "The geographic profile includes the sky as well as the ground?"

"Yeah. It's weighed on by the whole solar system."

"And this guy waits to kill until the earth turns her back on the sun."

The cold felt bracing. If she suppressed her awareness that terror and murder had been unleashed within the house, the night seemed peaceful. The quiet was soothing.

"Safe neighborhood," she said.

"It didn't protect them."

She listened. The only distinct sound in the air was distant traffic. "Notice what we haven't heard tonight?" she said. "Sirens."

"It's a low-crime area."

"Exactly. But notice what we haven't *seen* in this neighborhood tonight? Cops."

He turned. "You're right."

"Not one Sheriff's car," she said. "Because low crime doesn't equate to a cop around every corner."

"Even though a double murder occurred on this street."

"The Sheriff's Department has upped patrols since the murders. Eventually a deputy will drive by," she said. "But low-crime areas don't generally have a heavy police presence. Residential street like this? You can expect *not* to see a cruiser most nights. I think he knows that."

She led Keyes out through the gate to the driveway. Peered up and down the road.

"That's what he's seeking out. Safe neighborhoods," she said.

"Why?"

"Maybe he hunts in low-crime areas because he figures people who live there take their safety for granted and set their defenses too low. And maybe ..."

She felt the emptiness, the black cover that the calm night provided.

"Neighborhoods like this one—the streets aren't dicey. The only threatening thing out here is *him*." A chill slithered down her spine. "What's the only unsafe thing in all these neighborhoods? Families."

Keyes' voice dropped to a whisper. "Damn. Yes."

"It's dangerous to belong to a family. That's the message." She turned to him. "And he doesn't just mean that families are in danger—he's saying families are *treacherous*."

Five minutes after leaving the darkened Monterey Park crime scene, Caitlin accelerated up an on-ramp onto the 10 freeway. Stands of eucalyptus swept past the headlights as the Suburban looped around a cloverleaf. She joined late-night traffic and rolled toward downtown LA, instantly anonymous on the ten-lane highway—an interstate that ran 2,400 miles across the continent and, she felt sure, had brought the Midnight Man to Beth Lin and James Chu's peaceful street.

Serial killers often used freeways to commit their crimes. So many, in fact, that the FBI had created the Highway Serial Killings Initiative.

She spoke quietly to Keyes. "It's impossible to believe that the Midnight Man doesn't use the freeways. Is there any way the HSK database will help you with the geographic profile?"

The initiative kept track of the number of bodies dumped along the side of the road. The FBI's ViCAP analysts had compiled a list of more than 750 murder victims found along or near US highways. And more than 450 suspects.

Many of those suspects were long-haul truckers. And most victims were truck-stop prostitutes. A driver could pick up a prostitute at a New Mexico truck stop, rape and murder her, and dump her body on a Colorado roadside hours later, before rolling on toward Wyoming. Neither the killer nor the victim would have any ties to the location. Without the HSK Initiative, local law enforcement agencies might have no way to link a murder in their jurisdiction to similar killings elsewhere.

"The HSK data won't be pertinent," Keyes said, "because he doesn't dump bodies at the side of the highway. But some of its paradigms will."

"Hunting style."

"Yes."

In the dark interior of the Suburban, he pulled down the hood of his sweatshirt. His hair was disheveled. His glasses reflected passing headlights.

"He roams," Keyes said. "I have a vague picture of him in my head, cruising the freeways late at night. Like this." He nodded at the road ahead. "But not with a pinpoint destination in his mind. More like listening to music, loud, and driving until his emotions reach a peak and he pulls off someplace that strikes him as promising."

"Mr. Data Analysis, going with a gut feeling?" Caitlin said.

"I have to consider all possibilities. It's fractal."

The big Chevy engine hummed as they rolled west. The cityscape filled the view alongside the freeway, hills and streetlights and railroad tracks, chain-link fences and night-dark businesses, hypnotic, repetitive.

"He's highly mobile," Keyes said. "I want to label that hunting style nomadic."

"Want to but you can't."

"No."

Nomadic killers traveled far more widely in search of victims. They killed and kept traveling. They were the long-haul drivers. Desert hitchhikers. Rich boys on round-the-world tours who strangled backpackers.

"The Midnight Man sticks to a single urban area," Caitlin said. "A vast urban area, but still. He roams—but always heads home. He has a single game preserve."

Keyes crossed his arms. A consternated vibe rolled off of him.

"What's bugging you?" Caitlin said.

"He's an outlier in so many categories," he said. "Something like sixty percent of serial killers murder at one location, then transport victims' bodies to a secondary dump site. And most of them attempt to conceal the bodies. The Midnight Man doesn't display his victims in public, but he does leave the dead in the presence of living witnesses." He seemed to fight off a shudder. "And he kills within the victims' homes, but he's not a stationary killer."

"No. He's a step over." Stationary killers committed their crimes at home or work. Black widows. Angels of death. "The Midnight Man commits his crimes at *homes*—but not his own."

The hillside campus of Cal State University Los Angeles went past, visible between oaks and scrub and firs.

Keyes watched the Suburban's headlights devour the concrete. "The house where the first attack took place. Benedict Canyon. Something keeps itching at the back of my mind."

"You wondering how far that house is from Ten Thousand Fifty Cielo Drive? Two point two miles as the crow flies."

"Two point seven by road." He eyed her, possibly surprised that she'd had the same thought as he had. He shook his head. "But the Cielo Drive address isn't visible from the Peretti house. If there's some resonance, I haven't found it."

"And at Cielo Drive, the killers didn't sneak in a back window. Tex and the girls went up the driveway to the front door with their knives out."

Ten Thousand Fifty Cielo Drive was the idyllic home in the hills where, on August 8, 1969, Sharon Tate and four others were slaughtered on the orders of Charles Manson.

Keyes nodded. "Unlikely it's connected, but I couldn't dismiss the idea. Los Angeles has quite the history of murder."

"Hillside Strangler, Night Stalker, Grim Sleeper."

"Skid Row Slasher, Black Dahlia, Sirhan Sirhan. The killer OJ's been trying to find since 1994."

"But even in this city, the Manson Family stands out," she said.

"Tinseltown. Look, Ma, my name's in lights."

His mordant tone surprised her. Late nights affected everyone, it seemed.

"If we presume the Midnight Man has staked out a defined target zone—Los Angeles County, roughly—what does that give us?" Keyes said. "He's a territorial killer?"

"Yes," Caitlin said, "but not a marauder."

The FBI divided territorial killers between marauders, who traveled less than five kilometers to kill, and commuters, who ranged farther—and who often stayed close to the major thoroughfares they took on their journeys.

"Yeah—he's got a big range both geographically and intellectually," Keyes said. "He attacks mansions and starter homes. He kills victims across the economic spectrum. Multiple ethnicities. He's comfortable in a wide range of environments—he has a large mental map. It makes the picture harder to bring into focus."

"He wasn't intimidated by driving into a multimillionaires' neighborhood," Caitlin said.

"Or entering a house where the victims might have spoken a different language than he does." He held up a hand. "Don't want to stereotype. But it's likely the killer is Caucasian, and Monterey Park is majority East Asian heritage. I know Chu and Lin were total Californians, fourth and fifth generation American. But I'm not sure the killer did."

"He may have lain in wait, close enough to hear them talking as they went to bed."

"Possible. And chilling," he said.

"But you're right—some killers would hesitate to enter a dwelling where the homeowners might speak a language they don't. It gives the targets an advantage against a lone assailant."

"The central issue remains," he said. "Four crime scenes don't provide enough data points to create a reliable profile. Right now, anything I produce will be uselessly vague. Blobs dropped on the map."

"Don't tell me we're sunk."

He pursed his lips. His usual energy had dimmed. Then he shook his head. "No. No matter how unpredictable the killer seems, his behavior won't be entirely arbitrary. Nobody's is."

"Even paranoid schizophrenics can be remarkably consistent in their delusional behavior."

"Right." Reviving, he turned to face her. "For instance, did you know? Research has found that right-handed criminals tend to turn left when fleeing but throw away evidence to the right."

She shot him a look. "Seriously?"

"And when hiding in buildings, most criminals stay near the outside walls."

The Suburban arced through a curve. "Wish I'd known that when I was with the Alameda Sheriff. Would have helped when I went through the door on a couple of meth lab raids."

He grinned. It made him seem not just fresh-faced, but impish. "File that tidbit away for tactical training. And pub quiz night."

She smiled. "You're confident that data analysis can help unmask this UNSUB."

"Absolutely. I can extrapolate from the target backcloth and environmental information. He's never attacked under a full moon. Every kill site except the Benedict Canyon murders is within a ten-minute drive of a freeway. All the nights of the attacks have been dry," he said. "Though LA's mostly dry, so weather might prove irrelevant."

"Don't count on it. Come on, Keyes—you lived here. In Southern California, people having heart attacks won't go to the emergency room if it's drizzling." She thought for a moment, then spoke more seriously. "It might even be more than that. Santa Anas were blowing on the nights of two attacks."

"Good point. Remember what Raymond Chandler wrote: 'On nights like that every booze party ends in a fight. Meek little wives feel the edge of the carving knife and study their husbands' necks.'"

She eyed him. "Chandler had it right."

Downtown LA came into view, skyscrapers sparkling in the cold December air.

"I'm still cross-referencing the murder sites with bus routes and Metrolink stations." Keyes ran a hand over his head. "And I need to factor in how close the crime scenes are to grocery stores, banks, and bars."

"You think he stops off for Oreos and twenties before grabbing a cocktail?" she said. "Or rather, cigs and a handful of singles before driving to the strip club?"

"A buffer zone will contain all those places," he said. "Where the killer shops, does his daily business, and relaxes. 'Normal life.' His off-hours, non-killing activities."

He stuck his hands in his sweatshirt pockets. "Five thousand murders go unsolved in the United States every year. The country probably has two thousand unidentified serial killers at large. Merely recognizing that a victim was murdered by a serial killer can be difficult."

The glitter of the downtown lights reflected from the hood of the SUV. "I have software that searches for statistical anomalies among 'everyday' murders, robberies, and assaults. It may separate the Midnight Man from the background noise so the BAU can home in on him. There *is* a pattern. And I'll find it."

Caitlin pulled off the freeway. At the bottom of the off-ramp she stopped at a red light. The drop in exterior noise created a disquieting sense of aural vertigo. Waiting at an empty intersection in the paved heart of a massive city left her feeling as if she'd entered a distortion field. A zone between worlds, where she was out of place and unreachable.

"Something about the absence of a law enforcement presence tonight is itching at *my* mind now," she said. "I presume you're checking how far each of the Midnight Man's attacks have been from the nearest police or sheriff's station. We also need to find out how far away the responding units were when the 911 calls came in. How long it took them to reach the scene."

"I can do that."

"I agree with you that his behavior's not completely random. He's not targeting neighborhoods haphazardly." She drummed her fingers on the wheel. "At a minimum he's situationally aware. He may plan in advance, study station locations. And ..."

A thought teased her, half-formed.

"What?" Keyes said.

"Shift schedules," she said. "Find out if any attacks have happened during shift changes. You'll have to check division by division because big outfits like the LAPD and LA Sheriff stagger shifts so the entire department is never in the middle of a changeover."

The itch, the teasing thought, grew stronger. "Cops are trained—I was trained—to consciously stay focused during the last half hour of your shift. To keep yourself from checking out mentally. But it's psychologically impossible to do that every single time you ride out. You get tired or antsy. In the last quarter hour of a shift, you're thinking about how to vector back to the station. You may take a direct route, instead of winding through back alleys or quiet residential streets."

"Which can leave safe neighborhoods even less likely to be patrolled than at other times." Keyes sat up straighter. "I'll have that information for you tomorrow."

"If anybody can pull this guy out of the data ether, you can, Keyes."

His eyes were nothing behind the red light reflecting off his glasses. "I appreciate that."

She meant it. Still, this killer's freakishness set him apart. He seemed to exist in an eerie crack where algorithms strained to reach.

The light turned green. She turned onto a vacant boulevard and headed for their hotel.

15

When Caitlin walked into the war room the next morning, sunlight reflected off silver tinsel somebody had draped on the flat-screen TV. It wriggled, centipede-like, under the heating vents. Caitlin set her computer case on the conference table and took a swallow of her Starbucks. It was eight thirty, and from the atmosphere, the LAPD detectives had been at work for hours.

Weisbach, phone to her ear, was avidly writing notes. In her V-neck sweater and gray chinos, she resembled a dagger dressed in casual corporate wear. The menorah on her desk caught the sunlight. Spotting the FBI team, she finished her call, stood, and walked briskly toward them.

Emmerich's face turned inquisitive. "Got something?"

Her holstered duty weapon rocked on her right hip. "Video."

Emmerich set down his coffee. Rainey exchanged a glance with Caitlin. Weisbach cued up a video on the flat-screen.

"We obtained this from the construction company that's building the house across the street from the Peretti crime scene in Benedict Canyon. Camera was a hundred twenty-five yards from the Perettis' driveway. The time stamp's been verified."

On screen, a still image showed the job site. The construction fencing. Trees along the street. The camera was mounted atop a construction shed on the driveway at the property. The black-and-white video captured about forty yards of the road. At a corner of the screen, the Peretti driveway was visible. The time stamp read 01:09 A.M.

Static electricity seemed to thicken in the air. Caitlin shrugged off a shiver.

Weisbach hit PLAY. The clock in the corner of the video began running.

"We had to manipulate the gain on the imagery to increase contrast." Weisbach's voice was low and urgent. "It's skewed, but clear."

The clock ran. Five seconds, six. A squirrel popped up and hopped across the construction site's driveway. With the gain turned up, the animal appeared blindingly, spookily white against the dark background. Eucalyptus leaves vibrated in the wind.

In the corner of the screen, a figure appeared. Walking up the street toward the Peretti home.

Almost as one, the FBI team drew a breath.

It was him.

Caitlin's impression that the UNSUB, the elusive Midnight Man, didn't fit within conventional boundaries, became abruptly, irrevocably amplified.

His back was to the camera. When he reached the foot of the Peretti driveway, he stopped. Stood. Stared. The clock ran. For thirty-two seconds.

He climbed the driveway and disappeared around the bend.

"He's inside for four minutes and thirty-nine seconds," Weisbach said.

They watched. At 01:15:22 a.m. he reappeared, coming down the driveway. Sauntering.

There was no other word for it. The figure walked loose-limbed and relaxed down the Peretti family's driveway into the empty road in the Santa Monica Mountains.

He wore a brimmed cap and hoodie, and in the low-light exposure appeared like a photo negative. Blazing white against the low-resolution nighttime background. Head down. Strolling along the middle of the street. Playing with something in his hand.

"Is that a phone?" Rainey said.

Weisbach stared at the screen. "Maybe."

The figure continued to amble down the center of the road toward the camera.

Rainey exhaled audibly. "I would call that a spring in his step. Good God."

Caitlin was enthralled and repulsed. The figure on screen had an unmistakable weightlessness in his stride. As if he was unburdened.

"He acts like he just won the Powerball," she said.

Emmerich's voice was low. "Postattack euphoria."

Rainey stepped closer to the screen. On the video, the figure twirled the device in his hand a couple more times, like an Old West gunfighter spinning his six-shooter. He stared at it. Then stuck it in the back pocket of his jeans.

"Phone. Hundred percent," Rainey said. "Unsurprising. But if he hangs onto it, and we can tie it to cell tower pings …"

That was far down the line. That was putting together evidence for trial. Caitlin couldn't tear her gaze from the screen.

"What was he checking? The time? His step count for the day? Social media?" she said.

For a few more seconds the figure on the video kept walking along the road toward the camera. Everybody gathered around the screen watched with quiet concentration.

The LAPD was undoubtedly already working to estimate the UNSUB's height, weight, identify his shoes—anything. From the distorted, low-resolution video, it was impossible to discern hair color or ethnicity.

"The stride," Emmerich said.

Weisbach nodded. "No sway. Narrow hips. Male. Probably young."

Keyes came in. "I have software that can break it down further and provide a statistical probability as to the subject's age."

Weisbach's eyes didn't deviate from the screen. "Do that."

The figure approached the nearest point on his pass-by. He was a heat map, and they couldn't see his face.

He passed from view and disappeared down the street, beyond the construction site. The leaves of the eucalyptus trees shivered as if in applause at his performance.

"Can you play it again?" Caitlin said.

Weisbach faced the TV. "Keep watching."

Caitlin straightened with curiosity. The video showed nothing except the empty construction site and vacant street. Twenty seconds passed.

At the right corner of the screen, twin beams abruptly illuminated the road.

"Headlights," she said. "Goddamn. He did drive. That's his vehicle."

For several seconds the beams stayed stationary. Then the light moved, rising, growing brighter. He was driving up the road toward the Peretti house. The street had an outlet at the top of the hill. But as the headlights crawled along the roadway, Caitlin became convinced that he wanted to pass by the Perettis' so that he could enjoy a parting glimpse of the crime scene—to savor his destructive power over the people up the darkened driveway. To grab a last delicious rush of death.

Caitlin pictured a map of the neighborhood. The car was heading north, uphill. From there it was a few curves to Benedict Canyon Drive, then a direct shot to Mulholland. Which could lead him anywhere. Hollywood. Santa Monica. The Valley.

The headlights crept, the car not yet visible. Definitely taking his time. *Come on, bastard.* A few more yards, and the car would pull into camera range. Her heartbeat had picked up. *Come on.*

The headlights halted. The unseen vehicle had stopped.

"What?" Rainey said.

The trees shivered in the wind. A second later, the construction fencing shook.

"Oh, no," Caitlin said.

The video camera swerved, abruptly pointing at the ground. It jiggled wildly. And went black.

"He scaled the fence, climbed on top of the shed, and ripped the camera out," Caitlin said, half distraught, half in wonder.

"He most certainly did." Weisbach crossed her arms.

"Were there signs posted outside the construction site, warning that it was under surveillance?"

"Small one."

"And he was smart enough to stop before driving his vehicle into view of the camera. Damn."

Emmerich rubbed a thumb across his chin. "The camera was uploading to a server off site?"

"Yes," Weisbach said. "Which is why it took us this long to obtain it."

"It's possible he thought he'd destroyed the recording itself," Emmerich said. "But more likely he knew that the camera was linked to a recording system elsewhere. Was the construction shed broken into?"

Weisbach shook her head. "No damage, no sign of attempted intrusion. No reports of theft. The camera was left on the roof of the shed, like it had merely fallen over."

Caitlin's wonder turned to cold awe. "This is one thorough son of a bitch."

"You got that right." Weisbach rewound the video. "But not thorough enough. We've got this image."

She stopped it with a clear view of the UNSUB walking down the middle of the road like he owned it. Owned the entire night. Caitlin stared at the image, trying to pull something, anything, out of the distorted pixels on the screen.

Who are you?

The figure didn't answer. Told them nothing. All she could see was a flash from his raging eyes.

16

Just after noon, analysis of the Benedict Canyon video came back. By comparing the known width of the road, the degree of grade on the hill, the height of the camera atop the construction shed, and the distance from the lens to the centerline of the roadway, Keyes and the LAPD's technical unit had extracted information about the UNSUB.

Five foot eleven, maximum. Perhaps five ten, discounting the shoes—a so-far unidentified brand of athletic shoe—and the hoodie, which covered a baseball cap. Stride length 29.2 inches. Longish for someone of that height, walking at a seemingly unrushed pace.

From the figure's speed and medial-lateral gait control, the UNSUB was under forty. And, from the length of leg compared to the figure's height, and the best estimate of the angle of the UNSUB's femur relative to the hips and lower leg, a man.

"Eliminated half the possible suspect pool, at least," Weisbach said.

Keyes opened his mouth to remark but caught the sardonic edge in her voice. Finding out that this serial murderer was *not* a man would have been a shock.

Keyes said, "I'll take another run at the video, see if I can draw out any information on what he's wearing. It's not like spraying luminol on a surface and seeing blood glow ultraviolet, but I may be able to manipulate the saturation and sharpen the contrast."

A still image from the video, blown up, was now tacked to a corkboard on a wall near the conference table.

A second still image, of headlights shining on the road, sat on the

83

table. Keyes picked it up. "I don't want to give *too* much weight to this, but I think his behavior with the camera is significant. A data point for the geographic profile."

At the table, Caitlin was examining a map. She looked up. "How so?"

"He didn't want the vehicle captured on video. That's why he ripped the camera down." Keyes handed the still to her. "He left the camera on the roof. And he didn't break into the shed to try to find the recording equipment. He knew the camera was uploading the video off-site."

She thought about it. "Experienced burglar."

"And I'm guessing he knows how poor most security cameras are. But that's not my point. He thinks he's anonymous. A shadow. There were no streetlights within two hundred yards of him. No security lights at the construction site. No motion-sensing lights. He wasn't worried about himself being identified. Just the vehicle. Why?"

Caitlin mulled it. "Because the rear license plate holder has lights to illuminate the plate number."

Keyes nodded, slowly.

"He knew the camera would catch a clear view of the license plate." She mentally cycled through the possibilities. "He could have disconnected the lights to darken the plate. But he didn't. Why not?"

"Because that would have put the vehicle in violation of the California Vehicle Code. And drawn the eye of an observant cop."

"He didn't want to get pulled over. He's not just careful. He's *incredibly* cautious."

"He's no McVeigh, that's for sure," Keyes said.

Timothy McVeigh, famously, had removed the license plates from the car he drove out of Oklahoma City after blowing up the Murrah Building. He had tried to anonymize the car. Instead, because driving without plates was illegal, the cops pulled him over. McVeigh never left custody again.

"The UNSUB takes care to stay within the law on his way to and from the crime scenes," Caitlin said.

"And he wanted to drive out of the neighborhood by heading north to Mulholland." Keyes began to pace. "*That's* why he killed the camera. He could have kept the car off the video by pulling a U-turn and heading south down the canyon to Sunset. But he didn't. That suggests his final destination was north. It suggests that in his mind, going south would have been an intolerable detour."

"And why would that be?" She pointedly raised an eyebrow.

Keyes nearly jumped. "The police station and shift data. Hang on."

He ducked to his laptop, hit a key, and sent her a file. As soon as she opened it, she felt a queasy excitement.

"Going south would have taken him toward the nearest police station. He was determined to avoid that. Damn." She speed-read the rest of the file. Raised her head sharply. "*Every* attack?"

He nodded. "All the murders took place within half an hour of shift changes at the nearest police or sheriff's station. You were right."

She straightened. "He's hyperconscious of law enforcement. He studies the cops. Us."

Keyes should have been gratified. Instead he seemed off balance.

"What's bothering you?" she said.

"Everything," he said. "Who the hell *is* this guy?"

By the time the white sun advanced to slant directly through the windows, Caitlin stood before dozens of crime scene photos she had spread across the conference table. Shots of the homes attacked by the Midnight Man. The claw marks. The words. The eyes. Alongside those photos was a fresh map she'd printed, highlighting the location of every LAPD and Sheriff's Department substation in the greater Los Angeles area.

In the center of the table sat a still image from the Benedict Canyon surveillance video. The high-gain ghost.

Emmerich came in, phone to his ear. He ended the call.

"You look glazed," he said. "Talk."

"It's too much, and not enough. It's literally all over the map and doesn't fit together. She gestured at the photos. "The crime scene drawings and messages are so obviously symbolic, and I'm not versed enough."

He lifted a photo. LEGION. Took a breath as if ready to comment, then set it down. "You aren't alone in that. Get a consult."

The BAU regularly reached outside the unit for expertise. In particular, it consulted with forensic psychiatrists, most often those at Walter Reed.

Emmerich scrolled through his phone contacts. "Dr. Penn is on vacation, but one of his colleagues should be available."

"I have a contact," Caitlin said. "A forensic psychiatrist who works with the San Francisco Police Department. She's on faculty at UC San Francisco Medical School."

UCSF was the top medical school in the country. Emmerich nodded approvingly.

"She profiled the Temescal bomber for ATF. Sean knows her," Caitlin said.

"Make sure this won't bust my budget and call her." Emmerich rapped the table with his knuckles and headed toward Detective Solis' desk.

An hour later, Caitlin connected a video call. On her screen, a woman appeared.

"Dr. Beckett," Caitlin said.

"Call me Jo. How can I assist the Bureau, Special Agent Hendrix?"

17

"I need to interpret the iconography at the Midnight Man crime scenes," Caitlin said. "The drawings and messages. And the UNSUB's behavior during the most recent attack."

"It's brutal," Jo Beckett said.

Beckett was in her midthirties, with alert brown eyes and a wide mouth beneath a cataract of brown curls. She wore a gold Coptic cross on a chain around her neck. Her gaze was direct, if carefully neutral. Caitlin felt, briefly, like she was being x-rayed. She guessed most people felt that way when they were face-to-face with a psychiatrist.

And she guessed that the psychiatrist knew it. But Jo Beckett, MD, was used to working with a wide spectrum of people. Prisoners. Violent psychotics. Cops. She conducted psychological autopsies for the SFPD and was a member of San Francisco County's Mobile Crisis Response Team.

"Special Agent Rawlins said to give everything to you, and straight," Beckett said.

Caitlin smiled. Jo's eyes widened just enough that Caitlin realized the doctor had spotted something personal in her response.

She shrugged. *Yeah.* Jo's expression remained guarded but turned lively at the edges.

The video link gave Caitlin a good view of Jo's San Francisco office. A bookshelf of medical texts. A photo of a man in a flight suit. Maybe Latino, definitely hot, standing beside a Pave Hawk helicopter. Caitlin recognized Moffett Field. He was with the 129th Rescue Wing of the California Air National Guard. Pilot or pararescueman.

Caitlin adjusted her screen and grew serious. "The Arcadia murders."

Jo's gaze flicked to her computer. Caitlin had sent her a long email, police reports, and crime scene photos.

"You want an explanation for why the killer dug the bullets out of his victims' bodies?" Jo said.

"To start. Beyond the obvious possibility that he was taking forensic countermeasures."

"You're asking why he shot Maya Cathcart in the face."

"To put it bluntly."

"How deep do you want me to go?"

"Tunnel to the core."

Jo paused, pensive. "Then let's talk about eyes."

Caitlin had a pen in her hand. She meant to write notes. Something in Beckett's tone left her hand hanging.

"Let's start with the eyes he's drawn on his palms and on the wall of the baby's room. It doesn't indicate a psychotic break," Jo said.

"If he was in the grip of a psychosis, we probably would have apprehended him by now."

"Precisely."

Killers suffering from delusions or hallucinations often didn't try to evade detection. Sometimes they didn't even understand that they were committing homicide. A need to escape didn't factor into their thinking. Those were in the killers the FBI formerly termed "disorganized."

"Does he mean it as a message?" Caitlin said.

"Possibly. The Evil Eye is a world-spanning motif. My Egyptian grandfather hung a *nazar* in his front window to ward it off." Jo raised a hand. "I'm not saying the UNSUB is from a Mediterranean background. Cultural cross-pollination has embedded the concept in our brains."

"Right."

"Archetypally, the eye represents consciousness and knowledge," Jo said. "But it also symbolizes the vagina."

Caitlin set down the pen. She didn't need to write that down. She'd remember.

She said, "I sense that the killer is attempting to create his own mythology—to present himself as an otherworldly nightmare."

"I suspect the killer *thinks* he's drawing eyes as a power move, to terrify people. He may be telling himself it's theater. A horror movie," Jo said. "But nothing is ever free from context and meaning. The unconscious, the shadow, are relentlessly present."

"You think this all goes back to his mother?" Caitlin said. "Something that classic?"

"Of course. But that's an insufficient explanation. And not helpful for your needs. Which I presume are to profile the killer, narrow the suspect pool, and create a plan for apprehending and interrogating him."

"That's the hat trick."

Jo held up an eight-by-ten color photo: the baby's room at the Cathcart home in Arcadia. Eyes, eyes, eyes in profusion on the wall behind her crib.

"Drawing eyes," Jo said, "suggests that the person feels they're being watched."

"In this case, aren't the eyes a message? To the victims and the world? *You're* being watched."

"Yes. But the reason the UNSUB sends that message is because that's his subjective experience." She examined the photo. "People who draw eyes are often observant and vigilant. The blood ..." She inhaled. "It's of course significant. Life's blood. Death. Menstrual blood. But the color itself. Red represents power."

Caitlin felt a frisson. "Power and control may be what drives him."

"I think you're right." Jo continued studying the photo. "Red can also indicate anger or a need to impose authority. Blood, war, and rage."

Some things were so obvious that they didn't need to be spelled out. Caitlin thought of Maya Cathcart, lying in the hallway outside the nursery.

"Do you know what color the eyes were drawn in on the killer's palms?" Jo said.

"No. The room was lit only by moonlight. The children said the eyes were 'dark.' Black, maybe gray, but it's impossible to know."

"Black and gray can both indicate strength and stability," Jo said. "Of course, Western culture associates black with darkness, evil, and death. It's the color of shadow."

Caitlin had thought they were getting maybe a little *too* deep, but the repeated mention of shadow stirred something in her. Not a thought so much as a cold feeling.

"Everything about this offender is shadow," she said.

Jo paused and regarded Caitlin carefully through the video link.

Caitlin leaned back. "He's a negative. Slippery. I'm not too cut-and-dried to say it spooks me. And I pay attention to that feeling."

"Paying attention to that kind of intuition can keep you alive."

Jo's expression suggested that she knew this from firsthand experience.

The psychiatrist mirrored Caitlin and leaned back. She picked up a coffee mug. A diamond ring gleamed on her left hand. Caitlin's eyes were again drawn to the framed photo of the man in the pararescue uniform.

"Congratulations," Caitlin said.

Jo's smile was instant and genuine. "You feds are quick on the uptake."

Caitlin smiled warmly in return.

"One final point on the symbolism of the drawings," Jo said. "In English, there's the homophone. *Eye* equals *I*."

"He's the one who's watching."

"Part of him is." Jo set down the mug. "Eyes obsess and frighten one group psychologically—paranoids."

Caitlin sat up straight.

"What terrifies a paranoid isn't that another person sees him. It's that for one moment, contact with another human eye forces him to see *himself*."

Caitlin gripped the pen.

"Paranoid people project their self-hatred and aggression onto others. When you hold the gaze of a paranoid, that hatred and aggression are reflected back at their true source. There's a moment of self-realization," Jo said. "You want to know why the killer gouged out Maya Cathcart's eyes? It was his way of grabbing the mirror away from the victim."

"Jesus."

They were quiet for a moment. Caitlin ran a hand through her hair. She felt uneasy. Excited.

"Paranoids may fix their eyes relentlessly on you," Jo said. "In every social interaction, these people are watching for criticism. Expecting it. Observing every aspect of the environment for threats. It's known as the 'paranoid stare.'"

"Do you think he has paranoid personality disorder?"

"I don't have enough evidence to determine that," Jo said. "Staring, vigilance, even hypervigilance don't on their own indicate paranoia. Watchfulness isn't necessarily pathological. It can be an adaptive survival response. In police officers, for example."

"I knew you were going to get to that."

"And corrections officers, prosecuting attorneys, and mental health care providers."

"Really."

Jo tipped her screen down so Caitlin could see her outfit. Besides a black crew-neck sweater, she wore khaki combats and Doc Martens.

"On rounds in the secure ward, I see schizophrenic gang members. They may think I'm the queen of the lizard people, and they're resourceful at fashioning drinking straws into shivs. I dress to run."

Caitlin was starting to like this shrink.

"How would paranoia manifest in social situations?" she said.

"In a pervasive mistrust of others and a profoundly cynical view of the world. These people tend to be cold, aloof, and distant. Argumentative. Few if any close friends. Guarded and secretive. Sarcastic. Hostile."

"And they stare."

"Sometimes." Jo held up a hand as if to slow Caitlin down. "You know the phrase 'shifty eyes.' It's a characteristic pattern of eye movement in people with paranoid personality organization."

"That's useful. Very." Caitlin thought. "Shifty eyes. Is that neurological? Brain chemistry?"

Jo shook her head. "Often it indicates a combination of fear and shame."

"I doubt this killer experiences much of either."

"Not all serial killers are stone-cold psychopaths. Everybody is unique. And this guy sounds singular."

"Exceptionally."

"There can be significant crossover between paranoia and psychopathy." Jo was silent for a few seconds. "Both paranoid people and psychopaths are concerned with issues of power, and they tend to act out. But paranoid individuals can love. Maybe ambivalently—but they're capable of deep attachment," Jo said. "Though if this killer is psychopathic, he may attach only to children and animals."

Caitlin propped her elbows on the table. "Paranoids deal with their negative qualities by disavowing and projecting them. Correct? The rejected qualities then feel like external threats."

"Yes. A number of serial killers have murdered their victims out of the conviction that the victims were trying to murder *them*. It's destructive projection run wild," Jo said. "And because they see the sources of their suffering as coming from outside, disturbed paranoids are often more dangerous to others than to themselves. They're much less suicidal than equally disturbed depressives." She paused a beat. "But they sometimes kill themselves to preempt someone else from destroying them. Even when the looming 'destruction' is purely imaginary."

"Good Christ."

A dozen thoughts ran through Caitlin's mind. How would paranoia affect an attempt to arrest the Midnight Man? If he was on the run or, worse, cornered, would paranoia influence his endgame? Did it mean that, unlike other serial killers, he would *have* an endgame, even if it wasn't consciously planned out?

"Paranoid people often have angry, threatening qualities, but they also suffer from fear and shame," Jo said. "Bringing me back to 'shifty eyes.' It's a downward-left eye movement. And it's a compromise. A horizontal-left glance indicates pure fear. A straight-down look signifies undiluted shame."

"All paranoids?" Caitlin said.

"Even the most grandiose paranoid lives with the terror that others are out to harm him." Jo sobered. "It explains the Midnight Man's behavior at the Cathcart home." She paused again, choosing her words. "The fear paranoid people feel is annihilation anxiety. The terror of being destroyed. It's horrendous dread."

Caitlin listened, processing.

"As for shame, paranoid people can deny and project their feelings so powerfully that any sense of shame becomes unreachable to them. Instead, they spend all their energy on thwarting people they believe want to shame and humiliate them."

"But when the mirror forces them to see the truth …"

"Finding himself at the end of a gun barrel forced the UNSUB to experience the ultimate shame—being powerless and humiliated and in total fear of annihilation. Confronting that fear and shame was unbearable."

"So he acted out by shooting Maya Cathcart. Taking her eyes. Destroying the mirror."

"Yes," Jo said.

Caitlin thought for a dark minute. "Is he preemptively annihilating all his victims?"

"As children, paranoids often feel overpowered and humiliated by a domineering parent. They come to expect mistreatment. As adults, instead of enduring that anxiety, they'll lash out."

"I'll hit you before you hit me," Caitlin said.

"Absolutely." Jo took a thoughtful moment. "I should make special mention of malignant paranoia. These people are sadistic. Intimidating, callous, and vengeful."

"Sounds like our guy."

"Paranoids try to enhance their self-esteem by exerting power against authorities and people they think are important. Feeling triumphant gives them a sense of both safety and righteousness," Jo said.

"Safety. I'm convinced that's an issue for the Midnight Man. He wants people to feel *unsafe*."

"That's part of malignant paranoia. These people are capriciously tyrannical," Jo said. "They need to challenge and defeat the persecutory parent."

Caitlin leaned back. "You're working up to something."

"The entire script of these murders." Jo had become increasingly grave. "Every move the killer makes, and every person he interacts with when he invades a home and commits these crimes, plays a symbolic role. There's the mother. She represents child-rearing, nurturance, homemaking. The father—he signifies law and order, and authority."

"And the children …"

"The children and *himself*," Jo said. "The son. That's a psychological role too. Young, irresponsible. He's committing some of society's most taboo acts. Matricide and patricide. But he's not killing his own parents. He's repeatedly carrying out the psychodrama with surrogates."

In safe neighborhoods.

"And I think there's symbolism in the theater with the children," Jo said. "They represent his undifferentiated self."

Caitlin tried to get her head around it. "Does this mean that because he's paranoid, he's unlikely to harm the kids? Because he's less likely to commit suicide?"

"No," Jo said. "It means that when he finally sees himself reflected in the eyes of a child, he may preemptively annihilate them too."

The tinsel on the flat-screen television shivered as people walked around the war room. It set Caitlin's nerves crawling.

"One other thing." Jo scrolled through the information Caitlin had sent. "There's a detail in the Cathcart crime scene report. The killer sliced out and removed a square of hallway carpet." She paused. "The victim confronted him with the shotgun. It likely terrified him."

Fear. Caitlin saw it now. "He wet himself."

"He literally had the piss scared out of him. He took the evidence to hide his humiliation."

"So he has a weakness."

Jo's voice lowered, and her face grew somber. "That's not a weakness. It's a trigger. If anybody fights back, his fear enrages him. He'll escalate his violence."

18

As the clock headed toward midnight, the Sheriff's cruiser pulled into the McDonald's in East San Gabriel. The roads had quieted—temporarily. The witching hour was approaching. The deputy figured he had a brief window of time to caffeinate and get wide-eyed and ready for late-night lunacy.

The four-lane avenue was unexceptional, lined with car dealerships, chain restaurants, and strip malls where Christmas lights hung inside store windows. The McDonald's offered him a warm, clown-colored embrace. He cruised a circuit in the parking lot, checking the rear of the building. A couple of cars were parked by the back fence, unoccupied, probably belonging to employees. Dumpster, telephone poles, darkness beyond the fence, a residential street, hedges, trees. Everything placid. He coasted to the front of the lot and parked facing the street.

He rocked himself out of the car. He was in his midthirties, solidly built, wearing a jacket against the December chill. Inside, he bantered with the skinny teen behind the counter, a kid who had more pimples than he had whiskers in his *I Can't Believe It's Not a Mustache*.

The kid acted jumpy, avoiding the deputy's eyes. Flicking a gaze at him, then glancing quickly away, as if touching a stove with his bare hand.

The deputy maintained a friendly posture, relaxed and alert. Your Neighborhood Protector. No way to know if the kid simply got anxious around cops or whether he came from a neighborhood where you didn't act friendly toward the police. Or whether he had some other reason for feeling nervous. The kid's anxiety was patent. But if you didn't know any cops, didn't have them in your life as family, friends, or neighbors, a lot of people got twitchy—even just serving an officer a cup of coffee.

Then the boy brought the big to-go cup, carrying it like it was nitroglycerin, and the deputy decided the kid was just new at the job.

The boy set it on the counter and flexed his hands and actually blew on his fingers. Hot. "Would you like anything with that? We got apple pies."

The kid gestured toward the kitchen, like a French chef was back there sculpting treasures out of sugar and lard.

The deputy handed over two bucks for the coffee. "Nah. You eat the pies. You can use the calories more than I can. Keep the change."

He lifted the coffee cup in a *cheers* motion and pushed through the doors from the shiny plastic interior to the chilly darkness outside.

He sipped, eyes sweeping the parking lot, the street, listening for revving engines or drunken voices raised in anger. But it was peaceful, lights flowing across the shiny asphalt, adding a watery festivity to the emptying night.

The coffee was good. One thing about McDonald's—it was reliable. Everywhere you went, day or evening or midnight, the product could be counted on to give you exactly what you expected. He walked to the cruiser, realizing the coffee was indeed freaking hot. *Jeez.*

He was reaching for the driver's door handle when the window fissured with a hard *crack.*

He dropped the coffee and ducked as he drew his weapon. Then he was in motion around the hood of the car, seeking cover behind the engine block, listening for further fire before he knelt by the front passenger tire, heart pistoning. He bent to his shoulder-mounted radio.

"Shot fired. Officer requires assistance."

Crouched by the wheel, he heard the dispatcher calling for backup. The night had turned brighter by several orders of magnitude and he was breathing like he'd run an all-out sprint. He tried to see where the shot had come from.

No car speeding away. Nobody running. No movement in the shadows.

He had a clear view into the garishly lit interior of the McDonald's. A single customer sat at a table, burger in one hand, phone in the other, chewing and reading. The pimply teen was wiping the counter. The kid had put earbuds in and was singing along with the tune that was bouncing through his head.

The deputy was sixty feet away. Between him and the door was an open expanse of asphalt. No cover. But the people inside were targets, and oblivious to the danger.

The kid behind the counter looked outside and saw him.

The boy stopped wiping the counter, hand on the rag, as if in suspended animation. The deputy's radio spat at him. Multiple units in route.

The kid leaned forward, mouth opening, as though trying to believe he was really seeing what was in front of him. The deputy waved at him violently. *Get back.*

But the kid was yelling toward the kitchen, and jumping over the counter, running through tables and booths, his red shirttail hanging out, flapping. He skidded out the front door. And before the deputy could shout, the kid came running at him.

The deputy yelled, "Get inside."

The kid stopped. "Dude, you okay?"

In the distance, the deputy heard sirens. He bolted from his crouch, charged across the parking lot, and grabbed the kid's elbow. He pulled him inside, yelled at the customer to get down below the windows, shepherded him and the kid and the cooks to shelter in the kitchen. Flashing lights rose and reflected from the windows and counters and aluminum kitchen equipment.

He glared at the kid, and pointed a finger, wanting to reprimand him for his naivete and foolishness. What came out of his mouth was, "Thank you. Thank you, son. But if you follow me outside again, I'm going to have a heart attack. Then kick your ass for giving it to me."

It was only when the parking lot filled with cruisers and uniforms and the block was locked down that the deputy walked back to his car.

The window had what looked like a bullet hole. It looked like nothing else.

But when he opened the driver's door and examined the interior, he couldn't find the spent round. There was no hole in the dash, the seats, the floor, the passenger door.

He replayed in his mind the moment when the window shattered. He heard the hard, flat crack of the glass breaking.

But now he couldn't recall hearing gunfire. He bent to the window. Leaned inside the cruiser.

On the driver's seat he found chunked safety glass and a chip of white debris the size of a molar.

Something had come out of the dark and cratered the window.

The deputy could have protested. He could have insisted that he'd truly been shot at. But he couldn't. Because he knew.

This had happened before.

19

At a food truck around the corner from LAPD headquarters, Caitlin paid for her breakfast tacos. The morning was clear and brisk. The air felt velvety. Nearby, Rainey waited, steam rising from her coffee.

Their phones buzzed as the cook handed Caitlin a rustling paper bag.

"Thanks," she told him.

Rainey read the text. "Emmerich. We need to deliver the profile to the task force today."

"Then we'd better take a fresh run at the problem."

The problem being that, despite the BAU team's combined decades of investigatory experience, the Midnight Man's mind and motivation remained elusive. They felt like they were tugging on clouds.

They walked up a broad sidewalk toward HQ. City Hall poked above the roofs of office buildings, chalk white.

"How should we categorize the UNSUB?" Caitlin said.

Rainey's sunglasses burned with the rising sun. "He could be a visionary killer."

"Don't toy with me before breakfast."

"Gotta start the ball rolling. He does scrawl eyes and claw marks, and declares, 'I am the Legion of the Night.'"

Visionary killers were driven by apparitions or voices commanding them to murder. They believed they were compelled to act by Satan, microwaves, or as the Son of Sam long claimed, the neighbor's dog. And, like the California man who thought that killing strangers would prevent earthquakes, visionary killers generally acted in the grip of a psychotic delusion. That eliminated the Midnight Man.

"Hedonistic?" Caitlin said.

Hedonistic killers murdered for lust, thrill, or material gain. Rainey considered it.

"A psychopath whose greed escalated to murder?" she said. "He is an experienced burglar. But it would imply he kills the adults in the house because they're expendable obstacles to robbery."

They paused at a crosswalk for a red light. Traffic guttered past. Simultaneously, they shook their heads. The light changed, and they crossed the street.

"And his desire to torment kids doesn't fit," Caitlin said.

"That suggests he's a power-control killer."

Caitlin thought about it. Power-control killers sought to dominate their victims.

"Given that many power-control killers are maltreated as children," she said, "and made to feel weak and inadequate as adults, it could fit with the Midnight Man's apparent paranoia. But ..."

She trailed off, searching for a precise way to frame a slippery thought. Rainey glanced over.

"... but it doesn't square with his treatment of kids at the crime scene," Caitlin said. "The McKinley twins—it fits like a glove in that case. Kicking in the bedroom door, looming over them as they hid in the closet, intoning his ... *creed* at them—he absolutely intended to dominate and reduce them to abject fear. But in Monterey Park, he walked across a toddler's bed. In Arcadia, he drew an eye on the forehead of an infant. Those scenes were full of terror, but for adults."

Rainey nodded. "They're a message to the rest of us."

"When a killer expends energy sending a message to people who aren't directly in front of him, it indicates that his motive isn't simply power and control." She turned her head to Rainey. "Is he mission-oriented?"

Palm trees went past along the curb. Skyscrapers toothpicked the blue sky.

"Mission-oriented killers act to rectify some perceived societal ill," Rainey said. "To cleanse the world of people they loathe. Prostitutes. Gays."

Sinners, Caitlin thought, recalling the Prophet and the Ghost. The Prophet had clothed his deadly crusade in a parody of poetic justice and called his lethal misanthropy righteous.

"If so, who's the Midnight Man trying to eliminate?" Rainey said.

"I don't know."

"He's killed across ethnic groups. It's possible he's racially motivated but absent substantive evidence, I think we need to keep that idea to one side."

"I don't want to ignore the possibility."

"Gut feeling?" Rainey said. "He's no more conscious of a racial component in choosing victims than he would be choosing a checkout lane at the grocery store by eyeballing the checker. It could be there, but it's not what drives him hardest."

"Families with kids," Caitlin said. "Nuclear unit. The primal human group. But he says he's above it. Outside it. Proclaiming himself 'beyond good and evil' suggests that he sees himself playing a cosmic role."

Rainey drank her coffee. "It's certainly grandiose. Declaring himself God. Or anointed by a deity."

"Isn't God the very definition of good?" Caitlin said. "Doesn't God oppose evil? What could be beyond them both?"

"An asteroid."

Caitlin shook her head. "I'm talking about people."

"God isn't human. God is *holy*," Rainey said. "God is absolutely *other*. Awesome and terrifying."

They weaved through foot traffic and rounded a corner to the LAPD complex, shining in the morning sun.

"Absolutely other?" Caitlin said. "Aren't we supposed to be made in God's image?"

"According to Abrahamic tradition. I grew up with altar calls in a Baptist church. When I say *God*, that's what I mean," Rainey said.

"Not so other faiths. Have you heard of Kali? Hindu goddess of time, doomsday, and death. And a powerful symbol of motherly love."

"You've been drinking coffee for hours, haven't you?"

"May I tell you about our lord and savior, Dark Roast?"

Caitlin half laughed.

"Don't fall prey to the idea that God is engaged in an eternal battle against a supernatural force called 'evil.' That's heretical." Rainey became thoughtful. "I know you're talking about free will. Responsibility. Guilt. The Midnight Man says he's past all that."

"He's lying. Claiming that he has a hall pass. That he's exalted or exempt. No way."

They crossed the plaza and headed in. Upstairs, crime scene photos were spread across the war room's conference table. They set down their things. They hadn't resolved any of the questions they'd been debating.

"We'll discuss the neurobiology of psychopathy another time," Rainey said. "Maybe the Midnight Man was born without a conscience. But even if his brain's wired in a way that prevents him from feeling compassion, he's legally and morally answerable for his actions. He'll pay."

She turned to the photos. Caitlin dropped her peacoat over a chair.

Rainey stilled, examining a photo, as something caught her eye. She opened her computer and pulled up the evidence inventory.

"Something interesting?" Caitlin said.

"Arcadia crime scene. Take a look at that photo."

Caitlin picked it up. The photo showed the broken window in the Cathcarts' living room.

"The UNSUB smashed the window, then reached inside to unlock it and gain access," Rainey said. "Terrence Cathcart was in the kitchen making a sandwich. He'd only turned on a single under-cabinet light. He'd closed the swinging door between the kitchen and the living room, presumably to keep from waking Maya or the baby. From outside the window, the living room would have been dark. I don't think the UNSUB saw the light. He didn't know Cathcart was up. He didn't expect anybody in the house to be awake. Didn't think they'd hear the glass break."

She scrolled through the evidence inventory. "Check what's on the floor inside the window."

Caitlin examined the photo. Morning light glinted off the jagged remains of the windowpane. Glass littered the sill and floor. Some shards were an inch long, some the size of a pizza slice.

It wasn't immediately obvious to her what had caught Rainey's attention. Hardwood floor. A Navajo rug. Baby shoes.

"Debris?" she finally said.

Rainey stopped scrolling. She read from the inventory. "'Found on the floor of the house, inside the window that was broken to gain entry.' Shards of glass and a 'ceramic chip, one point two centimeter diameter.'" She pointed at the photo. "There."

Caitlin could see it—a small irregularly shaped white object. It was about the size of a pinto bean.

"No other ceramics in the photo. In any of the photos. No broken plates or porcelain vases. Just that distinctive bit on the floor." Rainey sat down, typed, and pulled up the forensic report. Her head tilted to one side. "The chip's made of a heat-resistant aluminum oxide ceramic."

Caitlin's cop radar warmed up.

Rainey read on. "It's from a spark plug."

Caitlin leaned over her shoulder to scan the forensic report. "It's a ninja rock."

Rainey glanced up. "That a street term?"

Caitlin nodded. "Spark plug ceramic is harder than tempered glass. Broken chips—tiny, light, concealable—shatter car windows more easily than a hammer or crowbar."

"He used it to break the Cathcarts' living room window," Rainey said.

"In a thief's hands, ninja rocks are part of a burglary toolkit. Possession with intent is illegal in California." Caitlin straightened. "Using one on the living room window would have been quick and easy. Ninja rocks hit more quietly than a hammer or a brick. Like tossing a pebble at a window to wake somebody up. Except the glass disintegrates."

She examined the photo. "He's so careful to collect all evidence from the scene. Was this a mistake?"

Rainey drummed her fingers on the table. "Yes. Because the homeowners confronted him and fought back."

She turned. "He shatters the window with the ninja rock. Little white chip, the size of a tooth my kid puts under his pillow for the Tooth Fairy, fits in his pocket, right? And he plans to scoop it back up once he climbs inside. But despite the house being dark, somebody's awake, and on his feet, and ready to protect his family."

Rainey mimed the living room space. "The UNSUB is standing, maybe crouching, inside the window, on top of the broken glass and the ceramic chip. And Terrence Cathcart charges out of the kitchen. Young, fit, pumped up, and armed with a carving knife."

"The killer's instantly in the thick of a fight," Caitlin said. "A fight he's always avoided—until this moment."

"He picks dark houses precisely to give himself an advantage over the homeowners. Entering an occupied dwelling where you don't know the layout is a high risk for a home invader. But a late night, a dark house—he presumes he'll have an unimpeded first shot."

Keyes came through the door, windblown, his cheeks red.

Rainey positioned herself in front of the table, as if she was the intruder. Caitlin advanced toward her, hand out, playing Terrence Cathcart wielding the knife.

"The killer sees him." Rainey raised her arm, making a finger gun. "Cathcart gets near. He's shot in the middle of the living room at close range. He was charging."

"And the gunshot rouses Maya Cathcart." Caitlin paused. "This is like his other attacks, because shooting the man wakes up the woman. But this time, the killer isn't standing at the foot of the bed to enjoy her confusion and terror. He's on the far side of the house."

"He's in the living room, checking that Terrence Cathcart's dead," Rainey said.

"It gives Maya extra seconds."

Keyes watched, absorbed by their discussion.

"Then here comes Maya down the hall, carrying her grandpop's Winchester," Rainey said.

Caitlin mimicked aiming a long gun. "Before the UNSUB can collect the ninja rock, he's on the back foot, defending himself against her."

Rainey nodded, energized, then drooped. "And that goddamn gun was too old."

Caitlin lowered her arms. The awfulness of the scene could only be subsumed for a few seconds at a time.

"His script went awry," she said. "It distracted him."

"Maya faced him down and pulled the trigger. That overwhelmed his neural network, his memory, his planning, his cleanup scheme," Rainey said. "I think she fried him so hard that he forgot to collect the ninja rock."

"It's our luck. And it's a data point. But it means that if anybody fights back, it focuses him entirely on violence to the exclusion of all else. And the danger to potential victims increases."

She and Rainey dropped their posed positions. Across the room, a television rattled. Conversation burbled at desks. On the flat-screen the tinsel danced in the air currents.

"Leaving the rock was an anomaly," Caitlin said. "It wasn't deliberate."

Rainey seemed to shake off the darkness that had briefly wreathed her. "Maybe it can be more than that. Keyes?"

He stepped up. Espresso-eagerness on his face.

"We've been looking at behavioral similarities at the crime scenes."

"Signature," Keyes said.

Rainey nodded. "But let's look at MO too. I doubt the Midnight Man's career in burglary began with home invasion murder. Let's go back."

"And sideways," Caitlin said.

Keyes tilted his head. "You think he's out there committing other burglaries now?"

"Good chance."

"If he's got a drug habit, he might be supporting himself through theft," Rainey said. "Search for burglaries and break-ins committed with ninja rocks in Southern California."

Keyes opened his laptop. "Parameters?"

"Start with the last twenty-four months. Los Angeles County."

"Home invasions? Burglaries of both residential and commercial property?"

"Everything," Caitlin said. "Auto burglaries too."

He nodded, accessing a database. Rainey gave the crime scene photo a final once-over.

"That was sharp," Caitlin said to her.

"Turn, turn, turn. Keep exploring new angles." She pushed the photo away. "And it was Maya Cathcart who was sharp. She took point, though it killed her."

It took Keyes barely half an hour. He leaned back, his eyes wide.

"Ooh, doggy," he said.

Caitlin nearly laughed. He would have sounded like a rube, if not for his knowing expression. The sunshine reflected off his laptop. She and Rainey rounded the table to peer over his shoulder.

His screen displayed long list of incidents, summarized in dry dispatch codes and acronyms. He hit a key. Instantly the list narrowed.

"What in ..." Rainey said, leaning closer. "That is ..."

"Minor league freaky on its own," Keyes said. "In light of the Arcadia attack, perhaps important."

"Not perhaps," Caitlin said. "Definitely."

Keyes had discovered a serial vandal who used ninja rocks to attack police cars.

Since the spring, seven police or sheriff's vehicles had been hit and had their windows shattered by ceramic chips. Every vehicle had been struck from a distance. Two while stopped at traffic lights. One while answering a late-night silent alarm at a warehouse. Two at fast food restaurants. One while the officer had responded to reports of a person unconscious at the wheel of a car that, it turned out, had been abandoned. The perpetrator had never been seen. Never identified.

"Attacks always occur after dark," Caitlin said. "In two of those cases, I suspect the vandal is the one who brought the cops to the scene."

"He set off the alarm at the warehouse and called in an anonymous 911 request for a welfare check on the abandoned car. Then he laid in wait," Rainey said. "The other attacks—the fast food restaurants ..."

Keyes said, "Map. Hang on." He sent a map to the big-screen TV and highlighted the locations of every incident of vandalism.

Caitlin walked to the screen. "Want to bet the McDonald's and that Starbucks are frequent stops for cops on duty?"

"Stand-alone buildings, meaning an attacker nearby could gain a vantage, and concealment, and pick his target," Rainey said.

Keyes read, tapping his thumb against his bottom lip. "In every case, the officers involved initially thought they were under fire." He drilled down into the incident reports. "In all but one attack, the officer reported shots fired. It was only when no spent rounds could be found—and the ninja rocks were discovered—that they figured out that the sharp report they heard was the ceramic hitting the window."

Caitlin slowly shook her head. Something didn't add up. "Ninja rocks are generally thrown at car windows from three to five feet away. They're incredibly effective, especially when flung with a good fastball motion," she said. "It doesn't take brute strength, either—I could shatter windows with a fingernail-size bit of spark plug."

"But you can do the FBI Academy obstacle course at Quantico. You've got plenty of brute strength," Keyes said.

"Skinny teenagers and strung-out heroin addicts do it every day, is my point," she said. "From close up. An irregularly shaped ceramic fragment, so light weight, quickly loses its force. How is this guy hitting the cars from such a distance that the officers not only can't see him, but he has a solid head start on getting away?"

Rainey crossed her arms. "Take it from the mother of two boys. This guy's firing a slingshot."

Keyes nodded. "Yeah."

"That's … so immature," Caitlin said.

"These attacks are taunts. They're meant to terrify," Rainey said. "This guy is scouting locations where cops hang out, or finding ways to lure them to a scene, and he's scaring them. With simulated gunfire. They respond as if they're in imminent danger. Picture Mr. Ninja Rock watching them duck and cover, watching them *cringe*, feeling his power over the police."

"It's minor league sadism," Caitlin said. "He enjoys the spectacle and slinks away basking in a feeling of power."

"Getting his rocks off …" Rainey returned to the forensic report on the ceramic chip found at the Cathcart crime scene. "There was a partial brand ID on the chip. Hardcastle Spark Plug. Batch number, so they can trace the date it was manufactured."

Keyes held out his hand. "May I?"

Rainey gave him the report. Five minutes later when he lifted his hands from the keyboard, he wasn't wry, or jokey. He was intense and grave.

"The ninja rocks fired at patrol cars match the one found at the murder scene," he said.

"They're connected," Caitlin said.

Keyes leaned over his computer again. "Give me some more time. These incidents expand the number of data points for the geographic profile."

Caitlin picked up the crime scene photo. The ninja rock was small but revealing.

"Rainey. We still need to categorize the killer. I'll stick a pin in the board. Domination. Humiliation. Preemptive annihilation. He's a power-control killer who's stewing in malignant paranoia."

20

At Bay Rise Elementary School, dismissal was cacophony.

That was Hannah Guillory's vocabulary word of the day. *Cacophony.* She walked from her classroom under the bottle brush trees, eating her after-school apple, red Chuck Taylors catching the sun. The day was cool but with the sunshine everybody was talking louder than usual. She finished up, dropped the apple core in the trash, and ran to join her friends as they headed home, backpacks weighing them down. For a minute, Hannah felt normal. Then she heard them talking.

"They bought a badass home security system," Caleb said. "Alarms on all the doors and windows, strobe lights if anybody comes on the property. Cameras they can watch even when they're away. They get a text alert, like a police siren, if they're somewhere else and the doorbell rings. It's like an X-Men base."

Lots of people were getting home security systems. They'd all seen the service trucks driving around town. They'd all seen new window stickers or yard placards stating, PROTECTED BY HOMESECUR.

But not everybody could afford home security systems.

"I heard my parents," Olivia said. "Whispering. They were nervous. Dad said installing a system would cost two thousand dollars."

Sam whistled, or tried to. Olivia's eyes looked weirdly uncertain. And shiny.

"I watched the news," Hannah said. "Even if you want to buy a security system, there's a waiting list. It's like two months."

That thought seemed to sober even the enthusiastic talkers.

"Some people are bolting up fake video cameras," Sam said.

"Cool," Caleb said.

"But where do you *get* fake video cameras?" Hannah said. "If you can't get a real system, where are you going to find a fake one? At a swap meet? On eBay? You'd still have to buy it."

"My aunt and uncle tried to buy an alarm system but they're on the waiting list," Madison said. "So they tied bells and chimes to their doorknobs and backyard gates."

"That's a supersmart idea."

Madison licked her lips before speaking. "We got a guard dog."

"Where?" everybody said.

"The animal shelter."

"A trained guard dog? Like from the army, or a junk yard?"

Madison shrugged. "He's big. He has scars."

Hannah went quiet again. They weren't talking about what she'd heard on the news. That people weren't just buying dogs. The shelters were nearly empty, even of little dogs. Things that could make noise.

Softly, she said, "People are buying guns."

Nobody reacted. Out front of school, the buses were full. The pickup zone was jammed, a long line of cars and trucks trailing back to the street. Like never before.

Hoisting her backpack higher on her shoulders, Hannah headed for the crosswalk. The crossing guard was waiting.

"You coming, Madison?" she said.

Her friend shook her head. "I have to wait for my brother to pick me up." Her brother was a senior in high school. "He's skipping soccer practice and coming straight here after his final period."

Hannah paused, really noticing the heavy car traffic and empty sidewalks. Across the street from the school were neat houses, packed close together. Scraggly palms and overhead wires. Small cars and pickups parked along the street, the occasional boat. Only a few kids were walking home today.

A very few, like her. Because it was sunny, and her dad was at work at the Port of Los Angeles, and her mom was home with Charlie, and the killer wasn't called the Daylight Man. She gripped the straps of her backpack.

For a moment her group of friends held together, a pack unwilling to break apart. Sam spoke hesitantly.

"My parents take turns on watch every night."

All eyes turned to him.

"They make sure somebody's always awake. Always up. Always has their phone in their hand." He glanced back and forth between them. "You think a gun's going to stop the Midnight Man? He never even steps into the light. Never even makes a sound. You have to be *right there* and ready to go. Otherwise you're dead meat."

It was early afternoon when Emmerich edited his notes a final time and stood up from the conference table. "Let's go."

He gave a heads up to Detective Solis across the room. Solis clapped his hands and gathered the task force detectives around his desk. Weisbach appeared worn and anxious. Several plainclothes officers and two detectives from the Arcadia Police Department opened notepads. The Sheriff's Department detective, Alvarez, looked neat and pressed and exhausted. A wad of gum distended his cheek.

Solis straightened his tie. It was a frantic red against his white shirt. "Special Agent Emmerich and his team have put together the behavioral profile of the UNSUB. Agents?"

Emmerich stepped forward. As always, he had the emotional energy of a thrown hatchet, propulsive and sharp. "We've analyzed some new information, enough to deliver a preliminary criminal profile. I must emphasize the word *preliminary*."

Caitlin felt a strange, unsettled energy in the room. Solis stood with his arms crossed, rocking side to side like a metronome. Around the fringe, officers she didn't recognize listened raptly. They'd either been passing through the Homicide Special Section or had been drawn by the massive interest in the case—uniformed officers in blue, and a plainclothes officer in a mom-appropriate coral twin-set. Given the subject matter, her outfit seemed jarringly out of place.

Or not. These people had families and wanted to keep them safe. And the LA area was freaking out.

The case had devoured the local news—especially the channel playing silently on a television in the corner. People felt desperate to protect themselves. This killer was a lightning bolt who could strike anywhere. And everybody had to sleep sometime.

Even the task force detectives were thinking: Is he going to hit my home?

"The killer is probably Caucasian, aged twenty-four to thirty," Emmerich said. "He's an expert burglar but his motive isn't theft— it's domination. He kills from a desire to wield absolute control over authority figures and seize emotional power for himself. So he may fence some of his victims' stolen valuables, but almost certainly keeps their wedding rings as trophies. He's intelligent, and meticulous in his forensic countermeasures. For example, when he drives to and from the scenes he takes extreme care not to violate traffic laws. But his success at burglary doesn't carry over to the rest of his life."

Emmerich nodded at Caitlin. She passed around printed summaries of the profile.

"At most, the UNSUB has completed high school. He may have started college, but soon dropped out. If he's currently employed it's in an entry level or minimum wage job. He hasn't lasted long at any job he's had—except perhaps a family business—because he's repeatedly fired for stealing."

Officers bent their heads to read the printout, or scribbled notes. Weisbach started pacing at the back of the group.

"The killer has a deep suspicion and loathing of authority. So he won't have a history of playing team sports. If he belongs to any clubs or organizations, they'll be groups he creates or can take over. He may haunt conspiracy websites but insists that his opinions alone are true."

Emmerich peered around the room. "He was raised in a Christian household—'Legion' is a New Testament reference—but rejects the church and organized religion. He may have joined the military because he loved the idea of becoming a trained killer. If he did, he chafed at the command structure, and was discharged soon after enlisting, possibly for unauthorized absences."

Alvarez scowled. "He doesn't play well with others."

"Hardly. But because he lacks marketable skills, has a poor job history, and struggles to get along with others—including potential roommates—he probably lives with family," Emmerich said. "And he's had repeated contact with the justice system, which his long-suffering relatives know all too well."

He scanned the assembled officers, carefully, assuring himself that they were taking everything in.

"The root of the UNSUB's behavior is paranoia," he said.

Solis nodded. Alvarez stuck a fresh toothpick between his teeth, eyes narrow.

"He's suspicious of others, mistrustful, and vengeful," Emmerich said. "He'll be known as secretive. But assertive, intolerant—and cruel. He acts out, verbally and physically, against family, coworkers, and the few friends he has." He paused. "And anybody who's crossed paths with him is likely to remark that he has a penetrating stare."

Weisbach stopped pacing. "Penetrating."

"It seems like a small detail but sticks with people who interact with malignant paranoids. The intensity of the gaze."

Emmerich rubbed the wristband of his watch. Caitlin knew, from the gesture, he was uncomfortable with how imprecise the profile sounded. The entire team felt the same. But the cops needed something—even an ambiguous sketch—to help focus their investigation.

He turned to Weisbach. "You brought us a glimpse of that gaze."

"You're right," she said.

Weisbach headed for the big screen and put up a still image. The Midnight Man, sauntering down the middle of the road in Benedict Canyon.

Even with the distorted, photo-negative image, one thing stood out on the killer's blurry, flat visage. His furious eyes.

"I'd call that stare the definition of penetrating," Weisbach said.

Emmerich nodded. "Nobody who's met him is going to forget that look."

The image stayed up as the briefing ended. Repelled but magnetized, Caitlin found herself standing in front of the screen. A cold finger seemed to scrape down her back.

"He's not even staring at another person," she told Weisbach. "He's staring into the night. He's staring through that lens at all of us."

"Thousands of people are wiring up their homes with security systems. He's going to get caught on camera again." Weisbach stared at the image for another moment. "Let's hope we don't get that look in person, on full burn. It's something I never want to see."

The first video came in less than an hour later.

The junior task force detective was rumpled, as if he'd gone through a few rinse cycles in a laundromat washing machine—tie limp, khakis creased. His eyes were glassy with sleep deprivation. But despite his fatigue, he was stoked. He slid a memory stick into his computer.

"CCTV from a convenience store two blocks from the attack at the McKinley residence."

Caitlin pictured the young twins, Noah and Natalie. Their stunned stares and near-catatonic grief. *I am beyond good and evil.*

The detective hit PLAY. The camera monitored the convenience store parking lot and avenue beyond. The night was late, the video as cheap as it came. The better cameras, Caitlin knew, were inside the store, covering the door and the cash register. The street was empty, traffic nonexistent. She held her breath.

After ten seconds, here he came.

The video provided the same eerie white-on-black glimpse of the Midnight Man as before, rambling down the street after committing double murder. Hoodie, ball cap, head down, walking on his toes, twirling a phone in his hand.

He was on screen for six seconds, then gone. Caitlin exhaled.

"Which direction did he head?"

"North."

Caitlin pictured it. "Coming downhill, toward the Valley."

The young detective nodded and pulled up another video clip. "This we got from a camera on the street behind the McDonald's where the sheriff's cruiser was hit with the ninja rock."

Residential street. Trees, ranch homes. No traffic.

"Time stamp shows it's three minutes after the deputy called for assistance."

A figure walked along a suburban sidewalk. His distinctive strut was instantly recognizable. Once again, he appeared to be in no hurry. Same basic clothes, same head-down pose. Hands in his pockets.

"Hoodie's bulky. He could be hiding a slingshot in the waistband of his jeans," Caitlin said. "Along with a handgun."

"Easily," Weisbach said.

He seemed utterly calm, as if at home in the neighborhood. He had a definite pep in his stride.

Ten seconds into the video, the reflection of flashing lights illuminated the trees.

"That's backup inbound to the McDonald's," Caitlin said.

The figure on the screen slowed and stopped. The lights swept past toward the restaurant. The figure slowly turned on the sidewalk to watch them go.

"Jesus," Caitlin said.

There was absolutely no question in her mind that this was their UNSUB. She felt excitement welling. She felt unnerved.

The figure continued to turn, doing a lazy pirouette, watching the flashing lights of the sheriffs' cruisers sweep past a block from where he stood. He was in a peaceful residential neighborhood, among dozens of homes where families slept. Within arm's reach of them.

But he seemed uninterested in the hundreds of people he walked among. Not that night. He finished his pirouette and continued down the sidewalk out of sight. Thirty seconds later, off screen, a car's headlights came on, glowing up the road. They swept in a circle as the unseen car made a U-turn and faded away.

"It's him," Caitlin said. "This is great work."

"That U-turn put him heading west," the detective said.

"Send me everything, would you?" she tapped a fist against his shoulder. "Thanks."

She turned to go but had another thought. "You said the time stamp on this video starts three minutes after the deputy radioed for assistance. How far from the McDonald's was the camera located?"

"Half a block. Maybe sixty yards."

She calculated. "It would take him roughly thirty seconds to walk that distance. That means after he shot the ninja rock at the cruiser, he stayed put for two and a half minutes. He could have maintained concealment to avoid discovery, but I think he stayed to watch the chaos he unleashed."

"Enjoying it."

"Lording it over the deputy who thought he was under fire." She looked at Weisbach with something approaching disgust. And a chill.

She thanked the detective again. As she headed for the stairs, she called Keyes.

"Got something for you. Saddle up."

Keyes was tossing a baseball back and forth between his hands, eyeing his laptop as if urging it to steal home, when Caitlin found Emmerich in the hallway, speaking to Weisbach and Alvarez. She waved them toward the war room.

"Keyes is almost ready," she said.

When they approached, Keyes knuckled the baseball. "I'm compiling the environmental data. Weather, temp, moonrise. Also pulling the historical Google Maps imagery from the dates of the killings and integrating it with the FBI's latest satellite data. I'll have the geographic profile in a minute."

His eyes were shining. His hair was a poodle mass falling over his forehead. He nudged his frames with a knuckle and put a map of the LA basin on the big screen. He clicked. Four red dots appeared. And seven yellow ones.

"Yellow dots are the police car vandalism." He gestured. "North Hollywood. Southgate. Van Nuys. Miracle Mile. Buena Park—that's Orange County. East San Gabriel." He turned. "Each in a different LAPD or LA Sheriff's patrol area, or in a city with its own police department. Seemingly a small-bore problem, unlikely to become widely known across divisions or between departments. It's a form of camouflage and counterforensics."

Alvarez nodded. "He's a knowledgeable fucker."

"Psychology influences what 'least effort' means to a criminal choosing between various possibilities." Keyes circled the table and picked up the baseball again. "So 'closest' can be a difficult thing to determine. Isotropic surfaces—spaces that exhibit equal physical properties in all directions—are hard to find in real life. Maps can look flat, but on the street, travel will be easier in some directions or along certain routes, and harder along others. The navigation apps on your phone will give you exact travel times down to the minute, day or night. But they don't tell us the psychological comfort a particular person gets—or doesn't—from taking a certain route."

Keyes' laptop caught his attention. He leaned over it and started typing. "That's what I mean by 'mental maps.' What the offender's atti-tude is toward a place. It's his subjective feeling about a neighborhood." Keyes stared at his computer screen. "Here we go."

His voice sounded both excited and uncertain. Hitting a key, he sent the results of his calculations to the TV. The geographic profile appeared.

He straightened. "Huh."

On the flat-screen was a 3-D rendering of the Los Angeles basin.

Overlaid on it were rings like the slope of a volcano—ramping up to the lip of a crater and falling away to a central hole, like a caldera.

Caitlin knew what the map represented. The high peaks around the lip of the crater were comfort zones, which included the sites of the Midnight Man's attacks—and locations where he was likely to commit further attacks. Their gradual outward slope indicated distance decay. The hole in the middle of the caldera showed his home ground.

Weisbach whistled. It wasn't in admiration. It was in confusion.

The result of Keyes' algorithmic computation didn't show an area where the killer lived. It showed two.

One zone was in the San Fernando Valley, centering on the Van Nuys / North Hollywood area.

The second zone was right downtown, practically on top of the LAPD HQ building where they were standing.

"That's unexpected," Keyes said.

Caitlin's hopes receded. Each of the two buffer zones was roughly two miles in diameter.

Keyes' voice grew distant. "The Midnight Man's hunting style is dispersed, which aligns with a power-control killer, but I didn't expect this."

If this were some patch of desert where the population was six people per square mile, they'd be on their way out the door to surveil and arrest somebody. But in the second largest city in the United States?

Keyes frowned hard at the screen, his gaze jumping. "No—I've seen something like this before. An English case, serial rapist, the geographic profile indicated two buffer zones. Manchester Police were able to focus their searches. The offender was a truck driver who lived in one zone and visited his mother's house in the other. So don't despair."

Alvarez glowered at him from under heavy brows. "Despair isn't my first reaction, cupcake."

Keyes' eyes flickered, registering the remark, but he continued scanning the screen. He didn't crack back at the detective.

"This is accurate," he said. "Based on all the information the task force has gathered. You can concentrate your offender searches, your patrols, on these two zones."

"And what about his next attack?" Alvarez said. "Where can we concentrate our resources to prevent it?"

Keyes voice went flat. "You can't."

Gnawing on his wad of gum, Alvarez cut a glance at Emmerich. "Thought this was your big gun, gonna give us not just a target but a bull's-eye."

Caitlin's hackles rose. "Come on, Alvarez. You know that Keyes couldn't, wouldn't, and didn't promise that. Blow off your steam outside, not at Nick."

Weisbach set her shoulders back sharply. A dragonfly sweep.

"We can use this. Thank you, Mr. Keyes." She nodded at Emmerich and jabbed a pointed glance at Alvarez. "And we have information to put out to the public. Let's prep a press conference."

The podium had an emblem on the front, the Los Angeles Police Department's insignia with the motto TO PROTECT AND TO SERVE. It was set up between the US and California flags in front of a beige wall in a nondescript conference room on the first floor of LAPD headquarters.

Behind the podium stood members of the task force, including the BAU team. The media provided the other half of the show. Television lights, handheld microphones, boom mikes, photographers with big lenses, TV correspondents, print reporters with smart phones recording the proceedings, all massed symbiotically around the front of the room, with a no-man's-land blank space between them.

A buffer zone, Caitlin thought.

The commanding officer of Robbery-Homicide, a man with yardstick posture and a neat white mustache, introduced himself, along with the commanding officer of the Los Angeles Sheriff's Department's Detective Division. They'd stepped into these glaring lights on a Friday in the run-up to the holidays in a show of force and seriousness, to try to reassure the thirteen million people in the region that law enforcement was doing everything humanly possible to keep them from ending up dead on the floor in front of the Christmas stockings.

By force of trained habit, Caitlin scrutinized everyone in the room. But this press conference wasn't open to the public, only cops and press. She saw the same grim-faced officers who had been upstairs when Emmerich presented the profile. They were even grimmer-faced now.

The Robbery-Homicide commanding officer held forth, stating that they had assembled to request the community's assistance and put out information regarding the series of murders that was ongoing in Los Angeles County. He was dry and thorough, and the press was antsy.

After running through the basics, he turned the stage over to Detective Dave Solis.

Solis grabbed the podium by both sides and read from a printout. "We have information to release about a person of interest in these murders." His gentle voice, gravelly with fatigue, sounded gruff. He waited until a video was cued up on a nearby screen. "We've obtained images of a man we'd like to talk to."

The new CCTV videos of the Midnight Man played. The atmosphere in the room instantly turned electric.

When the video that had been taken near the McDonald's ninja rock attack reached its end, it paused: a shot of the white-negative figure across the street from the camera, caught midspin as he sauntered away from the scene. Wild and eerie. A white flame.

"We're requesting the public's assistance in identifying this individual," Solis said.

The video should have provided a clear identification of the murderer, but instead showed a faceless golem, draped in baggy clothes, hooded, loose in the world, unconnected to the streets he floated through with his malign designs and gamma-ray eyes.

Solis took questions for several minutes. He thanked everyone for coming and ended the conference. His microphone shut off. The group behind the podium dispersed. The lights of the television cameras shut down.

Rainey watched the reporters and assorted officers scatter. "We'll see."

The Robbery-Homicide commanding officer strode past with a nod. Emmerich shook his hand. Solis came over. His attitude was both bleak and dogged.

"Somebody knows him," he said. "Somebody knows exactly who he is."

"The city's hooked into this," Emmerich said. "There's an army of amateurs out there right now, trying to figure out how to identify him."

Keyes started to mutter something, then stopped himself. Caitlin thought he'd been about to say, *Good luck.* Enhancing videos the way TV cop shows and movies did it was a fantasy.

"Let's hope it goes viral," he said. "And this guy's boss or girlfriend gets a funny feeling that it's him."

"We'll be ready," Solis said. "Thank you."

He shook everyone's hand and left. The BAU team followed, into the lobby of the building. It was vast and echoing, and the afternoon light had passed overhead to leave them in shadow.

It was Friday. The task force was going back upstairs to continue winnowing information and reading interviews and staring at crime scene photos and adding tips to their lead board. To stay up through another night, skipping school plays and soccer games and holiday parties and dinner with the family.

For a minute the BAU team hung in the lobby.

Emmerich said, "Thank you all. That's it for now. I'll see you Monday morning at Quantico."

From here, it was up to local law enforcement.

They'd given the task force all they could. But the UNSUB remained at large. It felt like a lit fuse.

21

The day was chillier. The sun hung at a sharper angle at the crest of the coastal mountains. Pink light above it, soft in the winter sky. Birdsong and the smell of wood smoke. Caitlin's face stung from the cold.

The feeling in the air was *welcome*. It reminded her of college, of finishing finals and rolling into the driveway in her beat-up old Subaru after the drive down I-5. Of her mom waiting up with the lights on in the kitchen. The tactile memory of long starry nights, happy times with candlelight and a warm house full of laughter.

She jammed her hands deep in the pockets of her peacoat and walked up the path to the town house. The sycamores let the last of the dappled light hit the grass. Behind the complex, the sunset reflected red from windows high in the Berkeley Hills. It had been a short flight after a long week. Bringing her home to a city where she no longer lived.

The town houses were wood-sided, cozy, nestled far enough from Telegraph Avenue to provide a feeling of calm amid the Berkeley frenzy. Caitlin paused at the door for a gut check and knocked.

She counted slowly, figuring it would take a while. Peered at the fish-eye of the peephole. After hitting twenty, she raised a fist toward the door.

Before she could knock again, it opened. "If you're selling Avon, I'm not buying. Your makeup looks like shit."

"Look who's talking."

Michele Ferreira stood in the doorway, lips pursed.

The sun hit her face full on as she gazed up at Caitlin. She was half a foot shorter and, leaning on a cane, seemed small and crooked. Her pixie fauxhawk was messy. She wore raspberry scrubs and a threadbare expression.

For an interminable pause they stared at each other. Then threw their arms around each other, fighting back tears.

Michele backed up, relying heavily on the cane. "Come in, goddammit."

The stiffness in her body drove a sharp ache through Caitlin. This was Michele, the mighty mite of their running club, who in years past frequently dared Caitlin to race her down crazy inclines in the hills, swearing viciously as she pounded for the finish before spitting and laughing and tossing Caitlin a beer. Today she could barely hobble the five yards to her living room sofa. She had been seventy feet away when the bomb exploded in the ER.

The town house was tidy, modern, with a patio and small play area overhung with birch trees. The décor was preschool artwork and a passel of dinosaurs on the coffee table.

Michele eased herself onto the couch. "You look like a goddamn FBI agent. What are those—*slacks?*"

She was smiling. Her shoulders were tight. As she settled herself, the strain seemed to ease. Caitlin hated seeing her like this.

"Chips and salsa?" Caitlin was already walking to the open kitchen, and Michele waved her on. She grabbed a bag of blue corn chips and a tub of pico de gallo from the fridge. She nearly plopped on the sofa next to Michele but caught herself at the last second and sat without jarring the cushions.

An ID badge from Temescal Hospital sat on the coffee table amid the velociraptors. Michele caught Caitlin eyeing it.

"New security features on all staff and visitor badges," she said. "Biometrics. They're changing the entire security protocol for the hospital, all hospitals in Alameda County, working with local fire and police departments and Homeland Security."

She made jazz hands. "We've hit the big time."

But the attack on the hospital hadn't come via a breach in staff security. The bomb was brought into the emergency room strapped to the back of a woman who had been found incoherent on the street near the University of California campus.

The woman had worn layers of dirty clothing and a heavy coat. Her wrists were wrapped with barbed wire that ran up her arms under her sleeves. She wouldn't let the firefighter-paramedics remove it. She bit at the EMT who tried to unbutton her coat. The paramedics rolled her into the Temescal ER on a Saturday night, unsure whether she had overdosed, sustained a brain injury, or gone off her meds.

As they departed, an RN managed to cut away the patient's blouse. The sleep-deprived trauma resident got a pair of surgical wire cutters to remove the barbed wire digging into the woman's wrists. The RN saw that the patient's torso was extravagantly wrapped in duct tape, and delicately lifted the woman so she could see what was so bulky against her back—

Caitlin had seen the video feed from the ER.

She'd watched it hundreds of times. It showed the raw, final milliseconds in the lives of everyone in the exam room.

The patient thrashed on the exam table. She was in her early forties, carried no ID, and nine months later, still had not been identified. She fought the doctor and nurses, who tried to understand what she was saying. *Garbled utterings*, the paramedics had written.

Now, Caitlin thought the woman must have had an inkling. She knew what was coming and was trying to stop it. The explosion left little of her to autopsy. Toxicology had struggled for results. Metabolites of what could be hallucinogens.

In the final instant, the RN saw wires protruding from a package that lay flush against the patient's spine. The wires ran up her back to her arms, where they intertwined with the barbed wire.

The scene was etched into Caitlin's retinas. The resident, tall and tired and bent entirely to the task in front of him. The nurse at his side, holding the patient's arm still as the woman tried to jerk it away from the wire cutters. The RN who saw the danger, frantically throwing herself across the exam table at the resident, mouth wide. Yelling, Caitlin was sure, "Don't!"

And in the corner of the video, a tiny sliver of the view beyond the ER bay, a woman moving into frame. Small and coiled and competent, raspberry scrubs, a stethoscope draped around her neck. Michele, turning the corner, walking straight at unfolding disaster.

The time stamp on the video, 19:49:50.6, was frozen in Caitlin's mind. The wish. The hopeless dread, the *if only*. One second sooner. If the RN had been taller, her arm longer, the resident less focused on the few square inches of flesh and barbed wire before him. Maybe, then.

19:49:50.7.

The flash. Static. Black screen.

The people in the ER bay died instantly. The patient, two nurses, the resident. Another patient and a hospital orderly died within the same second, when the blast wave and fire blew over them at 3,400 feet per second. High explosives gave no quarter.

You couldn't outrun them, not like in the movies. The explosion propagated faster than the speed of sound. You couldn't dive away from blooming red flames, balletically spinning in slow motion. Before that thought could spread from one synapse to the next, you had been swallowed by the detonation.

It was a miracle that Michele had survived. Everybody said so.

Caitlin didn't believe in miracles. She believed in luck and preparation and Tier 1 emergency response. But this, she thought—Michele sitting on the sofa beside her—might qualify. Might need to be submitted to the Vatican, credited to some saint-in-waiting.

Caitlin's throat tightened. She scavenged her emotions and shoved them into a back pocket, crumpled and messy.

New security measures at Temescal were good. Because something more than frustration, more than injustice or the lack of "closure," ate at her and had to gnaw Michele to the bone. It was lingering fear.

Who was the bomber? Where was he now? When would he strike again?

Michele grabbed a handful of chips and slumped back. The house was quiet. Sadie was with Sean. She'd been with Sean most of the time since the bombing.

"I'm getting there," Michele said, though Caitlin hadn't asked a question. "It's coming back into focus an inch at a time. Not a day at a time. An hour. A minute. I'm holding on."

"How's work?"

Michele was doing a desk job. Limited hours. Temescal had been good about that.

"Calm. Placid. It's paperwork. Data entry. HIPAA compliance. Nothing requiring me to move fast or make fateful decisions," she said. "I hate it."

"You never were the soothing-music type."

"I miss the ER," she said and stopped. "I mean, we all miss it."

It was gone. Temescal was open, because it was a major hospital for the Oakland-Berkeley metro, but the new ER was months from completion. Right now it was a construction site.

Michele's eyes welled. "I thought walking into Temescal would get easier after the first day. But it only gets harder." She clenched her fists. "Nine dead, forty-eight injured, no arrests, no claims of responsibility. The bomber's kicking back somewhere, laughing at us."

Michele had dropped the pseudo-relaxed attitude. Her eyes were shiny. Caitlin noticed that the town house wasn't merely tidy. Michele was keeping surfaces clean, sight lines clear, destroying reminders of everything she couldn't currently do. Neither of them said *PTSD*, but they didn't need to. Michele was hypervigilant and being eaten away.

Caitlin took her hand. "The cops and ATF are going balls-out to catch this guy."

"Sean is practically obsessed." Michele hung on. "Do you think it's the Ghost?"

Caitlin felt a sick chill. *It's my greatest fear.*

She put an arm around Michele and pulled her close. "There's no evidence for that."

Her friend felt like a wounded cat under her embrace, shivering and ready to pounce.

Caitlin left Michele with a plate of food she'd heated, the television on, and her evening meds parceled out. She embraced her tightly and kissed her cheek and Michele said, "Hug my girl for me tonight."

Caitlin got in her cheap rental car and headed across Berkeley toward the bay. She glimpsed the firefly sunset on the water, and the glorious sparkle of San Francisco beyond it. To the east the sky was bluing to black.

As she pulled around the corner into Sean's neighborhood, she still felt unsettled and downbeat. The narrow street was lined with parked pickups and hybrids, crowded with houses, illuminated by warm lights behind living room windows. Sean's front yard was just large enough for a single orange tree. His F-150 took up the entire driveway. The gingerbread eaves of the Victorian house glowed red, blue, and green with Christmas lights. It didn't soothe her, not after seeing Michele's state, not enough.

Not until she parked and climbed out, carrying Thai takeout in brown paper bags, and spotted the curtains in the front window dropping back into place did she begin to calm. She strolled up the walk to the front steps as the door blew open and Sadie blasted out.

"Cat!"

The little girl leaped on her like a monkey. Caitlin tried to hold onto her while keeping a grasp on the takeout. She didn't need to worry. Sadie's grip was wiry and relentless. Her hair smelled like watermelon shampoo. Her arms squeezed Caitlin's neck tight, hard enough to choke, but Caitlin didn't care.

Sean appeared in the doorway, backlit by amber light.

"What did you bring to eat?" Sadie said. "Is it pot stickers? Pad Thai? I'm *starving*."

"All that and green curry too," Caitlin said.

Sean ambled out and pried Sadie loose. He propped her on one hip, smiling. With his free arm he grabbed Caitlin and twirled her. Caitlin laughed.

He slowed, his face close to hers. "'Bout time you got here."

She kissed him. The world folded around her shoulders, stars and night and life and his smile and heat enclosing them, surrounding her with everything she needed right then.

Later, after she tucked Sadie into bed and told her a story, after she kissed the little girl good night and jogged down the narrow stairs, she and Sean shrugged into their coats and headed to the backyard. Sean lit a firepit. Bathed by its orange heat, they sat under the stars and let the cold night settle around them. Sean poured tequila shots.

"Michele's hanging in there," Caitlin said. "But it kills me to see her struggling so hard."

"There's trauma counseling for the survivors. Took her a while to agree to it, and I had to drag her into the first group session like pulling a stubborn bulldog by the leash." He warmed the shot glass in his hands. "She's nails, that one."

The fire heated Caitlin's face. She didn't react to Sean's remarks. She felt that wisp of unease, deep inside, about his feelings for Michele.

But she was the one who had brought it up, and knew Sean needed to talk about the case. They both wanted to. It was like sharing a needle. Their fix.

"How'd your week play out?" she said.

"Couple of leads we got from the wholesaler who sold the wiring for the Temescal bomb might be solid," he said. "We're digging, even if the bomber's still a phantom."

The bombing campaign went back fifteen months and led from New York City to Monterey, San Francisco, and Oakland. On the map, it seemed to coil in a spiral—like the barbed wire that had been wrapped around the Temescal Hospital victim.

"Could be anybody," he said.

The first two bombs, planted at New York Presbyterian Hospital and outside the Defense Language Institute in Monterey, had been pressure-cooker-type devices that used hydrogen peroxide. The lethal devices that exploded at a biotech firm in San Francisco and at Temescal had not only been packed with screws and razor blades but used PETN and boosted TNT.

High explosives weren't easy to come by. You couldn't grab the ingredients off the shelf at Home Depot. And wiring bombs wasn't like plugging in your toaster. Sure, some amateurs got away with it, but others ended up in bits, plastered against their basement walls.

Sean downed his tequila shot. "Anybody. But the Ghost knows explosives."

The Ghost had lured Sean to an abandoned warehouse on a false tip about stolen blasting material. After sabotaging the explosives in the BART tunnel, he left Sean near death on a train platform.

The problem: Sean had no memory of the man who set him up. All he had was a spooky sense of déjà vu that overcame him when he saw grainy security videos of the bomber. A figure in a black full-length duster, hoodie, and sunglasses. Five nine, possibly Caucasian. Sex indeterminate.

Caitlin had seen the Ghost once, in person, without knowing who he was. A skinny young guy walking past her in a dusty bar, heels of his boots scraping on the wood floor, giving her a stony side-eye. She'd been in his presence for a few creepy seconds. White, skeevy, cold.

The skeevy and cold parts could have been camouflage.

"The Ghost is a parasite," Caitlin said. "He found the Prophet and piggybacked onto his crimes, then betrayed him. I don't know whether he'd instigate a new series of murders on his own."

"He said he'd bring you down. The bombings could be part of that plan," Sean said. "After all, here you are."

Caitlin felt a surge of guilt. "If I'd caught him on the BART platform that night …"

"You didn't even know he existed that night."

"But I was there. And he escaped," she said. "And now he's loose."

Sean's voice quieted. "I was there too."

He gazed into the fire, maybe beyond, and back. The light flickered on his face, orange, hot. Caitlin realized the weight he was bearing.

She set down her shot glass, got up, and straddled his lap. She brushed his cheek with her fingers and took his hand.

"Anything I can do to help. Anything you need," she said.

"I need you." He pulled her close and wrapped his arms around her waist. "And I need you to remember that you're not alone."

She rested her forehead against his. She shut her eyes.

"You took your badge off," he said, "but it doesn't matter. I can tell that the Midnight Man's spinning through your head. You're running scenarios backward and forward, ten dozen ways. Working every angle." He tightened his arms around her. "You can talk."

With her eyes closed, she could hear him breathe. She could scent the wood smoke from the firepit. Could shiver from the heat of the flames. She could feel the sureness of Sean's embrace. She could let go, just a little, knowing that he would hold on.

She could taste the tequila on his lips when she kissed him.

Sean poured them each another shot. "I mean it. Your mind's full of this. Your veins. I can feel your pulse beneath your skin. Tell me what's going on with the case."

She held back only another second. "This guy is like nothing I've ever dealt with. Any of us. Including Emmerich and some senior LAPD Robbery-Homicide detectives."

She told him everything—the killer's fascination with eyes, his paranoia, the eerie videos, the vandalism of police cars. It poured out, electric. Talking to Sean was cathartic. But it was more than that. It was an opportunity to slide under his skin, to pump his veins full of everything too. It was a wish for insight.

"The eyes," Sean said. "Are they his 'legion?' Who are they watching? Who's supposed to see?"

"I don't know. He kills sleeping mothers and fathers with absolute brutality. The police car attacks are petty in comparison," she said. "He's striking out at authority. But it's bizarre."

"Daddy. Mommy. The Man," Sean said. "This guy wants them all dead. But he's scared of facing the cops. So he hides and torments them with this childish game."

Parents and cops. Caitlin's stomach lurched. The smoke that had clouded her thoughts about the killer abruptly seemed to clear.

"You're right. Jesus." She stood up. "Sean. What if he's a cop's son?"

22

At her family's home in Bay Rise, Hannah Guillory lay in bed, staring at the ceiling. Her parents and four-year-old brother were asleep. So was their cat, Silky, burrowed against her shoulder. But Hannah was extremely awake.

She could hear traffic on the 110 freeway. And somebody's dog barking down the street. The shadows of the trees brushed back and forth across the walls. She pressed her Fitbit. 12:52 A.M. She wanted to stay awake, but it was boring. And spooky. Her stomach was twisty. Also, she was hungry.

She got up. Without turning on the lights, she tiptoed past her parents' room to the kitchen for a glass of milk. The house smelled like their Christmas tree. Wind rustled the bushes. It was unusually dark outside. The streetlight was out.

She opened the refrigerator and got out the milk, blinking against the glare of the fridge light. It cast its shine on the sliding glass doors and patio beyond.

And she saw it. Out there. A shadow. Man shaped.

She slammed the fridge door. Her heart pounded. Had she imagined the shadow?

Her eyes adjusted. The shadow stood there, facing her. Tall, skinny, motionless.

Her legs went stringy, like puppet legs.

Hoodie. Brim of a ball cap. The same as the killer on the video the police had shown on TV.

Real, it was real, of course it was, just like she knew it would be. He wasn't her imagination. She didn't move. If she moved, her puppet legs would noodle and she'd fall tangled to the floor. She locked her knees.

He had to have seen the light from the fridge. He knew she was there. He knew the family was home.

If he was the Midnight Man, that would make him want to break in. Because the Midnight Man crept neighborhoods sniffing for houses where families lived, so he could slither through cracks in the windows and walls to murder moms and dads.

He stepped toward the sliding glass doors. Hannah stifled a cry and ducked behind the kitchen island. He shook the door handle. It was locked.

Hannah peered around for a way to escape the kitchen without him seeing her. She couldn't. The sliding glass doors were clean and shiny. That was her chore—to wipe the doors down. Clean off dust and smears and little handprints. The doors were spotless and gave a perfect view of the room.

Crouched behind the island, she whispered, "Go away, go away."

Outside, footsteps moved across the patio toward the corner of the house. Fingernails scraped the stucco wall. He was rounding the corner to try the window over the kitchen sink.

Hannah tucked herself into a ball. *Go away* …

Behind her, a small sleepy voice said, "Hannah, you spilled your milk."

Her head popped up. Her little brother Charlie stood nearby, his blanket trailing on the floor.

The starry night glittered in Charlie's eyes. Outside, the scraping fingernails stopped. The shadow appeared outside the kitchen window.

Hannah swept Charlie into her arms and pulled him against the counter out of sight.

He inhaled in surprise. She pressed a hand over his mouth. Shook her head frantically.

Was the window locked? Her dad had checked the doors earlier, tugging on every lock to make sure it was secure. But the windows?

Their house didn't have a burglar alarm. Didn't have flood lights or cameras or a guard dog. They had Dad, and Mom, and Silky, who had claws but didn't respond to commands, wasn't an *attack cat*, and Hannah squeezed Charlie with tears stinging her eyes and *please please let the window be locked.*

The man popped the screen and shoved the sash. The window didn't budge.

Hannah clutched Charlie. Felt his confusion, felt him catching her fear.

Her legs were paper. Her throat was a straw. But the Midnight Man was *right there.* Charlie was in danger and hiding here wouldn't save him. They had to get out of the kitchen.

"Follow me," she whispered. Charlie whimpered.

They inched along the counter. Risking exposure, she pulled him across the floor and under the kitchen table.

She caught her breath. The noise at the window had stopped. Was he gone? Or was he standing there, waiting, hoping to fool her into crawling into the open?

Tiny voice. "We're going to run to Mom and Dad's room. On three." She held up her fingers. "One."

She heard a sound in the laundry room. Horrified, she peeked.

An arm snaked through the cat door and reached for the doorknob.

She grabbed Charlie and bolted. The house was so dark and the Christmas tree was a looming tower and she ran past, and she couldn't breathe, and Charlie was running beside her, his little hand in hers, and she *ran*, the hallway like a telescope collapsing in front of her. She burst into her parents' bedroom.

"Call 911!"

Startled from sleep, her parents rolled slowly under the covers.

Charlie broke into tears. Hannah hit the light switch. The ceiling light came on harsh white.

"Call 911 now now he's here the Midnight Man call 911 hurry he's getting in *now!*"

Her mom was squinting and sleepy but all at once rose like a cobra and grabbed the phone. Hannah hugged Charlie tight as his cries turned long and loud. Her dad flew out of the bed in his boxers, hair crazy straight up. He reached down and grabbed a baseball bat from under the bed.

Her mom pressed the phone to her ear. "Police. I need the police immediately. A prowler's breaking into our house."

Her dad ran to the doorway with the bat cocked. Pointed back at them. "Shut the door and lock it. Hannah!"

He charged down the hallway.

Lip quivering, Hannah slammed the door and turned the flimsy lock. Charlie's cries grew piercing.

The porch light came on. Outside, footsteps pounded.

Hannah ran to the window.

Her mom turned, phone to her ear. "No—Hannah, *stop.*"

But Hannah was already at the window. Dad was out there somewhere. Was he chasing the Midnight Man? Was he okay? She pushed aside the curtains.

She saw the shadow jump into an SUV.

He started the engine and pulled away, staring back at the house. Straight at her.

Then he was gone.

Four minutes later, the police cars came screaming in.

23

The sun was breaking the eastern horizon, sharp and gold, when Caitlin arrived back in LA on the first flight from Oakland Saturday morning. The streets, the sidewalks, the park across from LAPD headquarters were all quiet, as if slowly stretching in the cool blue of the morning, before the bright day poured over them.

The quiet contrasted with the news channels, talk radio, the papers, social media, the red chyrons that screamed from every television. FAMILY ESCAPES MIDNIGHT MAN IN NEW ATTACK. And the sense of calm lasted until Caitlin stepped into the war room.

She walked off the elevator into a room striated with sharp light and fizzing with energy. The detectives she'd said goodbye to less than twenty-four hours earlier, who had been worn and bedraggled, were all there, and all of them were jacked.

Solis was at his desk, phone to his ear, talking in rapid bursts, writing notes. Alvarez was in conference with the detectives from Arcadia. Weisbach, looking scrappy in jeans and a UCLA sweatshirt, her curls erupting from a ponytail, saw Caitlin from across the room and waved her over.

"You're quick," Weisbach said.

"I was close. Bay Area. The rest of the team is on their way."

She was glad she could make it here so quickly. And she felt lousy that once again her time with Sean—and Sadie and Michele, not to mention her own mother—had been cut short.

Weisbach rocked up and down on her toes. "This is a break. Huge."

She tucked her arms under her armpits, like a coach on the sideline with time running out. "But just a break. Not the dam bursting."

Weisbach, like everyone else, was not just stoked but frustrated. Despite the 911 call, the killer had managed to elude them.

"Patrol units tried to track his escape route from the Bay Rise neighborhood. But he crossed city limit boundaries and then 911 dispatch sectors. It screwed with communication and coordination. And he struck during a change of watch again," Weisbach said. "Bad luck for us."

"Bad something," Caitlin said.

She was jacked, too—and angry. She had brooded all night, and during the flight down the coast. What Weisbach had just told her only amplified her anger.

The UNSUB had outmaneuvered the police, seemingly by using their own procedures against them. 911 dispatch sectors. Who knew that, except obsessives and insiders?

It cemented her suspicion that the killer was a cop's son. To a cop's daughter, it felt like the breach of a sacred trust.

Every officer in the war room was running on adrenaline and fear and hope and pure devotion. Give them a glimpse of the UNSUB and they would dig until they dropped. The thought that the Midnight Man was the son of somebody who devoted himself to protecting the endangered public filled Caitlin's throat with acid.

She'd had tough times with her dad. The awful cases he brought home had broken him down. They'd drilled holes in the family. But even in her darkest moments, she had never thought of lashing out at the police or the public. Only at herself.

Turning a cop's knowledge against innocents, using police procedure to terrorize and kill? The acid taste burned her tongue.

But she didn't bring it up—not yet. Because, despite losing the killer on the back streets of LA, the task force was excited.

They had a witness. A witness who saw the vehicle the killer was driving. Saw which way he went. Saw his face.

She was sitting at a desk by the windows.

"Her name's Hannah Guillory," Weisbach said.

Hannah sat alone, feet dangling. She wore a *Moana* T-shirt and pink leggings and scarlet Chuck Taylor high-tops. Her brown hair was messily tucked behind her ears. She was sitting on her hands. She appeared not so much disoriented as drowsy.

"Take it she didn't get much sleep last night," Caitlin said.

Weisbach shrugged. "Patrol initially questioned her, and detectives from Harbor Division. When it became clear they were dealing with a new Midnight Man attack, they called me and Solis. We brought her in."

"She's been here all night?"

"A trooper, too." Weisbach didn't sound uncaring, but she wasn't a softy either. "She's been telling her story. And we've had her working with a sketch artist. And going through mug books and photos of vehicles. She described an SUV but can't pinpoint the make or model."

Against the broad wall of windows, Hannah looked small.

"She by herself?" Caitlin said. "Are her parents here?"

"Her dad left twenty minutes ago—he's a crane operator at the port and his shift starts at seven A.M. Her mom stepped out a few minutes ago with Hannah's younger brother. The little boy's done. Fried. A family friend's coming to get him. Mrs. Guillory will be back shortly."

They walked to the desk. Hannah watched them approach.

Weisbach said, "This is Agent Hendrix. She's from the FBI."

Hannah gave Caitlin a considered look. She seemed to find her appearance unexpected, though Caitlin couldn't tell for certain through the girl's fatigue. Hannah appeared to be taking in the Saturday morning race-to-the-airport version of an FBI agent—the peacoat, jeans, and Doc Martens—against a pop culture image. She did glance at Caitlin's hip, undoubtedly checking for the holstered gun. Everybody was in down-and-dirty mode this morning.

"Call me Caitlin." She pulled over a chair and sat. "Hannah. That's a great name."

The girl had wide brown eyes. "It's a palindrome."

"Cool. The same backwards as forwards."

From across the room, Solis beckoned Weisbach.

"I'll be back." The ice-pick glance Weisbach gave Caitlin as she walked away said: Do some stuff here. Dig out information the rest of us haven't.

Caitlin took a second. She didn't want to pounce, not on this kid.

"You've been telling everybody the same story all night long, I hear."

"It's important."

"It is. So I'm sorry if I'm going to ask you to go through everything again, if it's boring or scary."

Hannah shifted. "It's okay."

"Because when you tell it to me, I might hear some things the other detectives haven't. I'm trained to listen for certain things they might not be. They're the best, but I investigate cases from a different angle sometimes."

Hannah nodded.

"You'd heard about the Midnight Man before last night, right?" Caitlin said.

Hannah's nod became vigorous. "We talk about him all the time at school."

"What about?"

"How to defend our houses from him."

Hannah's gaze dropped to the floor. Caitlin recalled what the forensic psychiatrist, Jo Beckett, had said about eyes—a straight-down gaze indicated unalloyed shame.

"Did you think you could protect your house from him?" Caitlin said.

Hannah's shoulders rose as she took a breath. A half-shrug.

"I could have written a list," she said. "A checklist. All the doors and windows. Made sure they were locked."

She had stopped swinging her feet. Her red Chucks hung abjectly. "Because I didn't think of the cat door. I was in bed when Silky came into my room and jumped up and nuzzled me, and he was cold, his nose and his fur were chilly, so I should have known he'd been outside." Her bottom lip trembled. "If I'd made a checklist, the cat door would have been on it. Would have been locked."

Damn, this kid felt responsible for a lot.

"The checklist sounds like a smart idea," Caitlin said. "You and your family can work on it." She offered a smile that felt melancholy.

Hannah blinked, but kept looking down.

"Hey." Caitlin leaned both elbows on the desk. "I'm not throwing shade at you. Not making fun of your idea. It's smart. Do it. But Hannah."

The girl looked to the side. Fearful.

"It's not your job to be the one who sees every problem before it happens," Caitlin said. "That's for grown-ups."

Caitlin sensed that Hannah was a quiet kid who didn't know how courageous she was. And something else. That Hannah saw fine details others missed. Her recollection about the cat's chilly fur, for instance.

"Hannah, if I tell you something, will you promise to be cool?"

Shrug.

"You were freakin' brave last night."

Hannah blinked again, seemingly surprised.

"Freakin' isn't really the word I want to use, but you're twelve, and I'm a federal agent," Caitlin said.

Hannah looked up.

"You didn't freeze. You took action. You helped your little brother. You warned your mom and dad." *In the nick of goddamn time,* she held back. "Because of that, because of *you,* your family's okay, and these detectives have some really important clues."

Hannah took a deep breath. She looked at Caitlin and didn't turn away.

"Can I ask you about what happened before you got up last night?" Caitlin said.

"Okay." Barely audible, but there was a flicker of interest, and openness.

"Which way does your bedroom window face?"

"The backyard."

"Did you have the curtains open?"

Hannah hesitated. "I closed them when I got my pj's on but after Mom told me good night and turned out the light, I got up and opened them."

"Why?"

"So I could see what was outside."

She seemed to want to say something else. Caitlin nodded. *Go on.*

"Sam Hernandez, from school, his parents take turns keeping watch all night. I thought I could maybe too."

A pang went through Caitlin. "What did you see?"

"Not him."

"That's valuable information," Caitlin said.

"It is?"

"It confirms what the police think—that he came into the backyard through the gate on the other side of the house. He didn't jump the fence and come across the lawn."

"Okay. Wow."

"When it's nighttime, what can you usually see in the backyard?"

Hannah thought for a moment. "The concrete of the patio. It's pale. The swing set, because it's metal. The trees are just shadows."

"Why can you see the concrete and metal?"

"Because … the streetlight out front is tall enough that it shines over the roof into the yard." She sounded surprised that she'd analyzed it.

"Could you see the patio and swing set when you got up last night to go to the kitchen?" Caitlin said.

Hannah's gaze extended. "No." Emotion filled her face, a mix of excitement and fear. She looked at Caitlin directly now. "It was super dark outside, but I didn't notice until I got to the kitchen."

"Did you hear any sounds before you got up? Outside sounds."

"A dog barking. Up the street somewhere. The Gonzalezes have a cocker spaniel. I think it was him. He always barks at weird sounds in the distance."

"Good. Anything else?"

"The freeway. At night, sometimes, after everybody's asleep, I can hear traffic on the 110."

Caitlin nodded, encouraging her. She wanted Hannah to open herself to every sensation she'd felt in the early hours of the morning. It was a technique called cognitive interviewing. It helped a witness do more than simply recall events. It got them to relive the experience.

Eyewitness testimony was notoriously unreliable, prone to gaps, confirmation bias, prejudice, and blind spots caused by terror. Cognitive interviewers talked to eyewitnesses in a way that could enhance their ability to retrieve memories of an event—without creating inaccurate accounts or confabulations. The technique focused on getting witnesses and victims to be aware of everything that took place, the entire context and environment of the crime. Sights, sounds, emotions, the weather—everything that could bring the scene fully and deeply alive in the witness' memory.

"What else did you hear?"

"Wind. Silky purring, for a while, until he went to sleep."

Caitlin nodded. "What did you smell?"

"The Christmas tree." Hannah's response was instant. "As soon as I walked into the living room. It made me feel ... better. For a minute." Her expression softened, and her gaze extended. "When I went in the kitchen I smelled coffee. Dad had put it in the coffeemaker for the morning." She tilted her head. "The leftover étouffée when I opened the fridge door." She closed her eyes. "Charlie's breath."

Her jaw tightened, and her lip quivered again. She was *there*, back in the kitchen, holding her little brother for what was literally dear life.

"Now move on, to your parents' bedroom." Caitlin's voice was smooth and low. "What did you hear?"

Hannah's breathing rate increased. "Mom on the phone to 911. Charlie crying. Long, long cries. Scared cries. Dad running down the hall. Footsteps—" She paused, lips open. "Footsteps running, outside, on the grass and driveway."

"What did you see?"

"Mom told me to keep away from the window, but I was so scared for Dad. The porch light came on, so I knew he was at the front door. And I heard footsteps, but they weren't barefoot." Her eyes widened. "They were shoes. If you're barefoot, nobody can hear you running on the grass. So it had to be *him*. I knew it but didn't know it. But I looked out the window …"

She blinked. Stopped.

In cognitive interviews, one technique to improve recall was to ask the interviewee to take a fresh vantage point on the scene—to mentally place themselves across a room, or a street, and describe what somebody standing there would have seen. To describe, sometimes, what the perpetrator would have seen from his vantage point.

When Hannah stopped, Caitlin considered asking her to place herself in the point of view of the man she saw running across the lawn. Then Hannah seemed to submerge herself once again into the scene.

"He was running. In a straight line, diagonally across the lawn. Fast. Not crazy out of control or scared, just sprinting," Hannah said. "He was running fast enough that his sweatshirt was flat against his front and flapping behind him."

Caitlin nodded softly.

"He crossed the lawn and kept going in that straight line across the street. That was when he faded out. The porch light doesn't shine all the way across the street."

"His vehicle was parked on the opposite side of the street?"

Hannah nodded. "Up where the streetlight is. The one that was out. So he wasn't parked in front of our house."

"Can you estimate how far away? How many houses?"

"Four houses to the streetlight. So, there," Hannah said, and her brow crinkled. "Police always say 'vehicle.' Why?"

"Because there are lots of categories of motor vehicles." This kid was sharp. And she loved words. *Categories* seemed appropriate. Don't talk down to her. "Autos. Pickup trucks. Big rigs. Motorcycles. Station wagons. Until we can narrow down the description, we use the word that covers all of them. What did you see?"

"The Midnight Man drove an SUV."

"Can you tell me what size it was?"

"Not the biggest." Her eyes widened, seemingly with a thought. "Not as big as the ones the FBI drives. On TV, I mean."

"Not as big as a Chevy Suburban."

Hannah shook her head. "It was a dark color. Blue or black."

"It went past the front of your house?"

"Yes." Something popped into her expression. "With the lights off."

"When it drove past your house, did the porch light reflect off the grille?"

Hannah nearly jumped in her seat. "Jeep."

Caitlin's breathing paused.

The girl abruptly thrummed with energy. "It said Jeep. On the front. Above the grille." She paused. "The name almost looks like a palindrome."

"Good." Caitlin kept calm. She wanted to high-five the girl. "What else?"

Hannah seemed temporarily caught by excitement, too present.

"You were standing at the window in your mom and dad's room, looking across the front lawn," Caitlin said. "And the Jeep drove into the glow of the porch light."

"Heading from right to left. West," Hannah said. "But in the middle of the road. Right up the center of the street."

"Think about the Jeep. Did you see anything else about it? Hubcaps? Dents? Scratches?"

"It had a sticker on the windshield."

"Okay."

Fine details. Caitlin had been right. Presuming that Hannah wasn't imagining or confabulating.

"Where on the windshield? Can you see it?" Caitlin said.

"On the side closest to where I'm standing. The driver's side."

"What color's the sticker?"

Hannah's gaze stretched. Her lips pressed together. She regarded Caitlin fretfully. "I don't know."

Caitlin eased off. She couldn't force it.

Then Hannah's face cleared. "It had letters. A picture and letters."

"Keep seeing it."

"So did his sweatshirt."

That made Caitlin inhale. "The Midnight Man's sweatshirt."

"I saw it when he ran across the lawn. I told you it was pressed flat against his chest from running fast, and in the wind. The sweatshirt was dark but had a logo. The logo was red. That's why I didn't think of it until now. The red blended with the black."

"It's fine. Remembering now is great."

"The logo was—like an animal." She paused, thoughtful. "Like a mascot."

"Excellent." Caitlin tried not to let her excitement bowl the girl over. "Keep going."

Hannah squeezed her eyes shut. "Some of the letters were S-H."

"That's what was on the sticker?"

Hannah nodded. Then shook her head. "I don't know."

Caitlin took a risk. "Picture yourself behind the wheel of the car. Staring out the windshield. The sticker is where?"

"Bottom left." No hesitation.

Hannah's face went distant again, but with intensity, not dreaminess. Caitlin worried that the girl was putting herself thoroughly into the point of view of the driver. Worried, because if Hannah followed that thread to its end point, she would spot the corollary to the fact that she had seen the Midnight Man. He had seen her.

But she was concentrating. "The sticker. Some of the letters were S-H. I know it." She nearly gasped. "That was what I saw when he was driving away. And it's what he saw when he looked at the sticker, too. Because that's how the letters looked on *inside* of the sticker. The *back* side." She thought for a sharp moment. "From the front side it would be H-S."

HS. Caitlin froze.

"What I saw from the back side looked like S-H-something-something. From the front, the sticker would say something-something-H-S."

A jolt ran through Caitlin. HS. A logo like a mascot, on a sweatshirt.

Everything they had struggled to understand about the Midnight Man—everything that didn't seem to fit—sharpened into focus.

"High School?" she said.

Hannah brightened. "Exactly. Like a school parking sticker. With its mascot on it."

Their profile of the killer was off. He wasn't in his twenties.

He was a teenager.

24

Caitlin's mind fizzed like a road flare.

As she sat across the desk from little Hannah Guillory, with the morning sun spangling the windows, everything Caitlin knew about the Midnight Man spit and blazed in phosphor-white images behind her eyes.

High school.

It seemed off the charts. A ruthless serial killer who was crazed with hormones, a teen's oppositional defiance, and a belief in his own immortality. An annihilator who sat in math class.

But everything about the Midnight Man was off the charts.

Hannah observed her with sharp interest, then rubbed her eyes as if they were gritty.

"You hanging in?" Caitlin said.

Hannah nodded.

"Hold on a minute. I'll be back."

She crossed the room to Weisbach's desk. "Jeep. With a parking sticker that features a high school mascot."

Weisbach spun on her chair. "Jesus."

"Be right back. I have to make a phone call."

Weisbach jumped to her feet and headed toward Hannah. Caitlin stepped into the hallway and called Emmerich.

He picked up with the noise of a cavernous building echoing behind his voice. "Hendrix."

"I think our profile is off."

She ran through her suspicions—that the Midnight Man was much younger than they had imagined. The noise on Emmerich's end caromed in her ear. He was at Washington Dulles Airport, waiting to board a flight to Los Angeles. He'd been home less than an hour before turning around and heading back to the terminal.

"A teenager," he said.

Caitlin paced, waiting for his reaction, hoping he wouldn't dismiss her reasoning.

"Hold tight till I get there. We need a united front to present this theory."

She inhaled. "Safe travels."

She returned to the war room, her fingertips tingling.

At the desk by the windows, Weisbach and Solis were leaning over Hannah. Detective Alvarez paced behind them. Hannah frowned at the desktop computer, hunched forward, concentrating. When Caitlin neared, she saw that the screen was covered with high school mascot logos.

"Keep scrolling," Solis said to her. "Tell us if anything looks familiar." Hannah's shoulders drooped.

Caitlin approached with a confident smile. "How about breakfast first?"

Hannah popped up like a puppy that had just heard the word *walk*. Solis and Weisbach acted less enthusiastic.

"On me," Caitlin said.

The LAPD detectives hesitated. Caitlin maintained the sunny smile. Hannah scooted to the edge of the desk chair, eager, awaiting permission. Caitlin winked at her. The girl got up.

Alvarez conceded. "On you sounds good."

Downstairs in the bustling cafeteria, the aroma of food perked Hannah up. She took a tray from a stack and turned hopefully to Caitlin.

"Anything you want. Go for it," Caitlin said.

"Cool."

Hannah slid her tray along the line, eyes as round as quarters, investigating the food under the orange heat lamps, darting up and down the line to thoroughly examine the entire menu. She was wiry, and sparrow-quick. Caitlin suspected that she kept a million deep thoughts to herself as they swooped through her head. A canteen server smiled at Hannah and she nodded enthusiastically at pancakes, eggs, bacon, and sausage.

As the girl filled her tray, Caitlin turned to Solis and Weisbach.

"Thanks. I didn't mean to bigfoot your interview with her. But she was starting to remind me of Oliver Twist peering into a bowl of gruel."

"Sure," Solis said.

"I know you're running on less than empty," Caitlin said. "And that you don't want to waste a minute."

Weisbach grabbed a tray. "We don't have a minute to waste. But we're here now."

Caitlin tried an ingratiating smile. "I was pushing the kid too, until I stepped out for a moment and realized what I was doing."

Alvarez reached for a plate. "Jeep SUV. Dark blue or black. How many of those are licensed in California?" He raised a hand. "I know— it's a start. It's great. And Hendrix is right. We need a break before we turn on each other."

Solis, the bags under his eyes grayer than usual, grunted. "Tens of thousands of Jeeps are undoubtedly registered with the DMV. We'll have the kid look at makes and models. And if the vehicle was stolen, the killer may have gotten sloppy wiping it down when he dumped it after fleeing the scene. Maybe we'll get lucky."

Weisbach asked the server for a helping of scrambled eggs. "We need to define our search parameters for high school mascots. Public, private, parochial schools …"

Alvarez said, "You think the girl's reliable? That's a pretty specific bit of information to remember. She may have been trying to be 'helpful.'"

Caitlin moved along the line with them, piling her tray with fruit and yogurt. Then eggs, sausage, and a waffle. And French toast. In answer to Alvarez's question she tipped her hand back and forth. *Maybe, maybe not.*

"It's possible," she said. "But Hannah's reaction was genuine surprise—a moment of illumination. Not the kind of fakey enthusiasm some witnesses give you, and not a reluctant, 'I guess so ...' You know what I'm talking about."

"I do. And she's a little trooper, I'll give you that. But she's twelve."

"And she'll last a while longer once she gets some calories into her. But not too long."

She turned to see if Hannah was still scooting back and forth, or whether she'd heaped her plate so heavily that she would struggle to carry it. The girl was no longer in line.

"Where'd she go?"

The others turned. The tables in the room were full. With adults. Detectives, support staff, officers in uniform. No Hannah.

Caitlin left her tray on the rack and crossed the room, searching. Soon the detectives fanned out. Hannah's tray sat on the rack in front of the juice bar.

But she wasn't in the canteen. She was gone.

Weisbach stepped into the hall. Caitlin was right behind. No sign of the girl.

"Could her mom have come back while we were talking?" Caitlin said. "Left with her?"

"No. The desk downstairs would have called to let me know if Mrs. Guillory came in. She needs an escort to the war room." Weisbach craned her head up and down the hall. "You check whether Hannah went back upstairs. I'll see if she's in the women's room."

Caitlin ran up the stairs and ducked into the war room. Hannah wasn't there. Nobody had seen the girl.

Weisbach texted.

???

Nothing

Didn't leave by the main exit—front
desk didn't let her out.

That should have eased Caitlin's swelling sense of concern. But it
didn't. *She has to be here someplace. Where would a kid go?*
What the hell had happened to her?
She didn't think she was overreacting. Unless Hannah had
freaked out and run, something untoward had happened. She texted
Solis.

Floor-by-floor search?

Alvarez is starting at the top. I've
notified people to hold her if they
spot her attempting to leave.

Going back to canteen to
retrace her steps.

She ran down the stairs and met Weisbach coming up the hall.
Weisbach shook her head and led Caitlin back into the cafeteria.
Hannah's abandoned tray remained by the juice bar.
The detective's face, often anxious, now looked apprehensive. "How
did we lose her?"
"We didn't consider the possibility that she might go anyplace
while we were talking." *Stupidly.* "How long has it been?"
Weisbach checked her watch. "Ten minutes."
"Dammit."

Caitlin could run a mile and a half in ten minutes. She could drive twenty miles, with lights and sirens. She'd never realized how long, and gaping, ten minutes felt when a kid was abruptly gone.

"I should have …" She ran her fingers through her hair. "Why would she just leave? She wouldn't. Would she?"

A young voice said, "Wouldn't what?"

Caitlin and Weisbach turned. Hannah was standing right behind them.

"Where were you?" Weisbach said.

Hannah's face, open and baffled, turned wary. She stepped back and knotted her fingers together. "What's the matter?"

"You left without telling us," Weisbach said. "You shouldn't have done that."

Weisbach moved toward her, which only caused the girl to retreat another step.

"I'm sorry." Hannah's face flushed pink. "The other detective said I should go with him."

"What other detective?"

She pointed at the door. "The one who came in while we were in the line. He took me downstairs to talk."

"Who?"

"I didn't mean to do anything wrong."

The girl's voice broke. Weisbach brought herself up short.

"Of course you didn't."

Hannah's chin was quavering. Weisbach put a gentle hand against her back, led her to a table, and sat down beside her. Caitlin took a seat across from them.

"It's okay," Weisbach said. "We were just concerned."

Hannah wiped her eyes, trying to be surreptitious about it.

"Who was the detective who asked to speak to you?"

Weisbach spoke in a calming tone but shot Caitlin a glance. Something seemed amiss—to both of them.

"I don't know who it was," Hannah said. "He didn't tell me his name."

At the canteen door, Solis appeared, followed quickly by Alvarez. Their worry evaporated to relief, then confusion and annoyance—until they saw Hannah's face. They walked over.

Caitlin said, "Do you see the detective in here?"

Hannah shook her head.

"You didn't recognize him from earlier, when you were upstairs?"

Another shake.

Weisbach said, "What did he look like?"

"Dad age," Hannah said. "Dressed up. In a nice jacket and jeans."

"White? Black? Asian?"

"White and pale. His coat was blue. I didn't see him before," she said. "He had a lanyard and a name badge hanging from his neck. He was all official."

"But you didn't get his name?" Weisbach said.

"The badge was flipped around. All I could see was the back."

Hannah scrutinized the assembled detectives. From her face, it was clear she knew something wasn't right.

"What else?" Caitlin said.

"He had a cellphone. He said to record our conversation. That it would make it my certified statement."

Solis inhaled and shifted. Shook his head. Pulled Weisbach and Caitlin away.

"It wasn't anybody on the task force."

Weisbach's worry lines were deepening by the minute. "What if it wasn't a cop at all?"

"Cellphone to record their conversation? Jeans? Badge on a lanyard?" Solis said. "This 'detective' sounds like a tabloid journalist."

"Best case," Weisbach said.

"You thinking—"

"Could be a conspiracy nut."

Caitlin frowned. "Or a serial killer groupie. Or a stalker."

Alvarez, from behind Weisbach's shoulder, spoke quietly. "Or it could be him. The Midnight Man."

Solis' shoulders lowered, as if sandbags had been draped across them. Weisbach's mouth pursed like she'd bitten into a lemon. "Unlikely."

"But possible," Solis said. "Hannah only glimpsed the perp's face for a half a second, as he drove away. Dammit."

Caitlin held her tongue. For a second. "I have to disagree. It—"

"Doesn't fit the profile, yeah," Alvarez said. "Screw the profile."

She *really* bit her tongue. "'Dad age' sounds a lot different from what both Hannah and the McKinley twins describe."

Solis glanced past her shoulder. "Hannah? What do you think?"

The girl had squirreled around in her seat to listen in on their conversation. At Solis' question, she blushed, caught out and flustered. "I don't know."

"Did the detective look like the Midnight Man?"

Her shoulders ratcheted up. "Kind of did. But not. Older and tireder. Maybe."

She glanced between them, seeking approval, or hoping to keep from being scolded again.

The detectives turned toward each other. Sotto voce, Solis said, "Pull video from every camera in the building."

25

Hannah's mother took her home soon afterward. The girl first browsed through high school mascot logos, fruitlessly, and watched video from the building's front desk, but couldn't identify the man who claimed to be a detective. Her eyes turned glassy. Her mom, petite and fierce with a black ponytail swinging halfway down her back, clasped Hannah's hand and marched her from the war room. Weisbach escorted them out, her flat-ironed cool masking her frustration.

Watching them go, Caitlin scribbled her name and phone number on a Post-it and jogged after them. She caught them at the elevator and put the note in Hannah's hand.

"Just in case," she said.

Hannah held her gaze until the doors slid shut.

Caitlin grabbed her gear, checked into the hotel, and headed to Bay Rise. The FBI team was inbound and would meet her there, to see firsthand the scene of the Midnight Man's foiled attack.

The South Bay neighborhood was bounded by freeways. Small houses bumped flanks and whitewashed garden walls bordered yards the size of a king bed. The boulevards were smattered with tire shops and noodle houses. The Guillorys' home sat on a tidy street among dozens of tidy streets laid out in a grid like a silicon chip.

Caitlin stopped eighty yards from their house, near the spot Hannah had said the Midnight Man parked his Jeep. She wanted the same view he'd had. She killed the Suburban's ignition. The ticking engine cooled.

The modest neighborhood would have been a smorgasbord laid out in front of him.

The wide street was lined with parked cars, pickups, and boats on trailers. The Guillorys' house sat squarely in the middle of the block, a hundred yards from the cross streets at either end. Up the way, a couple of boys shot hoops against a driveway backboard.

Caitlin could hear the rush of the freeway, a quiet thrum beneath the day—the neighborhood's background noise. To the south, the terrain ran flat to San Pedro, Long Beach, the ports, the ocean. The Palos Verdes Peninsula hovered toward the west, a blue-green vision. To the north, a hill protruded above the homes, brown with long grass. It was undeveloped except for billboards advertising liposuction and personal injury lawyers. Telephone and power lines crisscrossed the road. Streetlights were spaced every seventy yards or so.

Soon, in the rearview mirror, Caitlin saw Emmerich and Rainey pull up in another Suburban. She climbed out and was walking toward them when Keyes rounded the corner and hopped out of a Lyft.

They all wore their game faces. Focused, purposeful, ready to work. Caitlin knew what they'd given up to be here today. Rainey had planned to take her boys to an ice hockey training camp. Emmerich's daughter Lily was supposed to arrive home from UVA for winter break. Keyes had gone to San Diego to spend the weekend with a friend—or maybe lover—and had caught the Amtrak back to LA.

Behind his Ray-Bans, Emmerich's face was flat. He stood beside the Suburban, hands on his hips, seeming to download information about the scene in silent gulps.

"Blue-collar, aspirational community," he said.

"Another safe neighborhood," Caitlin said.

Rainey gazed around. "It was."

Keyes had on a slouchy gray ski cap, his hair squirreling in curls from beneath it. His black frames provided a sharp counterpoint to his pale skin.

"Safe is the operative word," he said. "For everybody."

He stuffed his hands in his pockets and turned in a slow circle. "Working-class neighborhood, ethnically mixed but majority Anglo, low crime rate. Nothing exciting about Bay Rise, but it does have good schools and parks and Vietnamese restaurants where you can get decent pho." He peered up the street. "Families live here, and they mean to put down roots. It's not transient."

"You're saying it's not just residents who feel safe here?" Rainey said.

"Precisely that. This attack site is the farthest the UNSUB has traveled from the center point of his nearest buffer zone. It's a definite stretch, in terms of pure mileage. *But.*"

He paused to make sure he had their attention—which was unnecessary, given that he was virtually jittering.

"But remember? When defining an offender's comfort zone, raw distance from his home base isn't the only consideration."

Emmerich nodded. "Terrain, access to transport, road conditions, all matter."

"So does security. An UNSUB is much less likely to attack in areas where he *personally* feels at risk." Keyes pointed toward downtown. "Between the Midnight Man's buffer zone and this little suburban street, the metro is solidly built up. There are no swamps or firepits. But there are parts of town where a white offender—especially a very young one—might be concerned that he'd be noticed and identified."

"Compton," Rainey said. "Watts."

"I'm guessing his mental map told him to stick to the 110 freeway and drive straight past cities where he would feel uncertain about being seen on the street alone late at night. Where he might be regarded as suspicious. Maybe he was concerned about his personal safety in communities of color. Maybe he just didn't want to stand out."

Caitlin said, "*Huh.* White boy been told all his life to stay out of South Central."

"Basically."

Keyes was practically bouncing on his toes. Caitlin felt his nervous energy leaching into her. Rainey's lips were pursed. Emmerich was breathing slowly, the way he did at the firing range when sighting on targets. They all felt a sense of urgency.

"So he's territorial, but his comfort zone extends farther than we'd thought," Caitlin said. "And he's gaining confidence, expanding his range."

"Definitely."

Emmerich turned toward the Guillorys' house. "When Hannah scared off the Midnight Man, she likely saved her parents' lives." He stopped for a beat, seemingly considering the luck, and bravery, that had taken. "But that's not all she did. She frustrated the UNSUB. His urge to kill must be intense."

"He's pent up and pissed off," Caitlin said. "When he lashes out again, it'll be furious."

"It'll be soon," Rainey said. "An adolescent won't control his urges for long."

"Days, possibly," Emmerich said.

Keyes rocked on his toes. "The two buffer zones in the geographic profile could represent the killer's home and school. Or, if he's from a divorced family, mom's house and dad's."

Relief and validation coursed through Caitlin. The entire team supported her conclusion about the UNSUB's age.

At the Guillory house, the curtains on the front window swept open. A woman stood inside, half hidden by the noontime glare, black ponytail, arms hanging at her sides.

"Hannah's mom," Caitlin said. "Let's say hello. I don't want her to think we're surveilling her. And I know what it's like to be on the other end of an FBI stare."

She glanced at Emmerich. She had first seen him standing beside a Bureau SUV at a crime scene, abrading her with his gaze. She'd felt dissected. And at the time, she'd been a cop.

Keyes said, "I'll meet you back here in a minute." He walked up the road toward the T-junction at one end.

Caitlin crossed the street with Emmerich and Rainey. A cold wind gusted. The woman in the window backed away from the glass. By the time they came up the walk, she stood at the open front door.

"Just got my little boy down for a nap, so let's keep our voices low. You are?"

She wore Uggs and jeans and ten silver rings in her left ear, along with one in her nose. Her face said she was done dealing with this havoc for the foreseeable future.

Caitlin extended her hand. "Special Agent Hendrix."

After a second's hesitation, the woman shook. "Mina Guillory. You were at the police station."

Caitlin introduced Emmerich and Rainey, and said, "We don't want to intrude further on your day. We do want to assure you of our concern. We're working to help the police apprehend the suspect."

Mina Guillory stepped onto the porch and softly pulled the door shut. "Then why are you here?"

Emmerich removed his sunglasses. "The more we see firsthand, the more we can infer about the perpetrator. The better the police can target their investigation. The sooner it'll be over."

"You figure why he targeted us, let me know." She nodded at the door. "Hannah'll be telling all her friends. They have a kids' squad gonna keep us all safe." She lowered her voice even further. "She's probably in the hall, listening. What I want is for you to figure how to keep him from coming back."

"We want this to end ASAP. We're doing everything we can."

Mina raked her gaze up and down him. Maybe she'd noticed he made no promises.

"Please see everything there is to see. Inspect it with a microscope or a psychic or a Geiger counter. Then do me a favor and drive downtown to discuss it. Because the longer you're here, the likelier that one of the neighbors will post photos online. Of you. And the house. And us." She propped a fist on a hip. "And before you know it, we've got news choppers overhead and conspiracy theorists shouting that we're crisis actors making this up, while my four-year-old reverts to sucking his thumb and Hannah hides in her room building serial killer traps out of darts and fishing wire."

Emmerich nodded sharply.

Mina opened the door and stepped back inside. "And thanks for getting Hannah breakfast. She said the cop waffles were good."

She shut the door.

26

The team walked across the street toward their vehicles. Keyes said, "I need to see more of Bay Rise. We should find the nearest Denny's."

Rainey gave him some side-eye. "That's an oddly specific piece of information to feed into the algorithm. Even for you."

"No. I'm ravenous."

They ended up getting deli takeout and carrying it back to their hotel, where the staff opened a conference room for them. Caitlin grabbed coffee and silverware from the restaurant. Gathered around a conference table, they dug into salads and fat sandwiches.

Emmerich set a pocket notebook on the table, its edges lined up with his knife. "We need to reexamine the profile of the Midnight Man, and we need specialist analysis. Juvenile multiple-murderers are beyond my depth of expertise."

He adjusted the notebook, though Caitlin thought it was already perfectly aligned to North on the compass and perhaps to the center of the galaxy.

She removed her tablet from her bag. "Let's get the professional in on the conversation."

Dr. Jo Beckett answered the video call within a few seconds. "Happy Saturday, Agent Hendrix."

"Got ten minutes to put on the government tab?"

Jo was in line at a busy San Francisco coffeehouse, surrounded by animated conversation and the clatter of mugs. Behind her a wide window gave a view toward the piers. A cable car rolled past, bell ringing.

She took in Caitlin's tone and expression. She put an earbud in. "Shoot."

"We suspect that the UNSUB is a juvenile, and perhaps the son of a law enforcement officer."

The forensic psychiatrist's face registered both alarm and rabid curiosity, before she varnished it back to neutral. "Hang on."

Taking her coffee, she pushed through the door onto a narrow street. The sky was puffy with white clouds. People passed her, bundled up and ruddy-cheeked. It was the day Caitlin should have been enjoying in the Bay Area herself.

Jo checked the street for traffic, jogged across, and headed to a pocket-size park. "Fill me in."

Caitlin introduced the others, summarized the evidence, and explained how she had come to suspect that the Midnight Man was in his teens. Jo sat down on a park bench in the sunshine, brow furrowed, drinking her coffee.

"We're not one hundred percent certain the Midnight Man's a teenager, but …"

"Intuition, experience, and circumstantial evidence leads you that way," Jo said. "What do you need from me?"

"Tell me if I've run off track through a guardrail," Caitlin said. "And if I haven't, tell us how being so young would affect the UNSUB's behavior—and the risk he presents to the public and law enforcement."

Jo stared into the distance, thoughtful. Then turned to Caitlin.

"You're not off track. Vandalizing police cars with the slingshot and ninja rocks is a classic bit of juvenilia. The fact that the behavior is repeated and enthusiastic suggests that it's literally childish," she said. "I work with prisoners. The guys who are down for murder are overwhelmingly young, but they're men—by the time they reach San Quentin they've abandoned those kinds of pranks."

"Even murderers in their early twenties don't behave like this, you're saying."

"Rarely. I think there's a high probability you're correct about his age."

Emmerich leaned in. "Doctor Beckett, your analysis of the UNSUB's malignant paranoia guided our development of the profile."

"This new information doesn't change my assessment. That was based on his crime scene behavior. It holds," Jo said. "And if he's a juvenile, it doesn't make him less dangerous. Quite the opposite."

"Lack of a lengthy time horizon, immature impulse control, the feeling that all the world is a playground," Emmerich said.

"That, mixed with the painstaking care he takes to eliminate forensic evidence and evade detection. He's not just highly knowledgeable. He's cagey. Sly. Smart. That makes him a deadly adversary," she said. "And I need to emphasize a particular aspect of malignant paranoia."

"Sadism," Emmerich said.

"These people derive pleasure from inflicting pain on others. When they strike out, they're not merely preempting imagined attacks on themselves."

"They enjoy causing suffering and humiliation," Emmerich said.

She nodded. "Sadism, of course, isn't unique to malignant paranoia. And I suspect your next question is about antisocial personality organization."

Rainey pulled her chair closer to the screen. "Psychopathy?"

"That's the jackpot question, and I can't officially answer it. Because people under eighteen cannot medically be given that diagnosis."

"Semantics," Rainey said.

"Sometimes. I'll get to that. First let's talk about some differences between antisocial and paranoid personalities." Jo's hair whipped in the wind. "They're both highly concerned with issues of power. But for distinct reasons."

Caitlin said, "Exercising power against authority figures bolsters a paranoid's ego and reduces their feelings of fear. Have I got that right?"

"Yes. Whereas a sociopath's entire psychological defense system can be built around exerting command as a way to deny and avoid shame—in the sense that they don't want ever to reveal what they regard as weaknesses."

Rainey said, "I thought psychopaths didn't feel shame. Have no conscience, so don't even recognize it."

"Lack of conscience manifests in their absence of attachments to other people," Jo said. "What they want is to *influence* people—to get over on them. Their greatest desire is to parade their power. Sociopaths will outright brag about their crimes. Scams, con jobs, robberies. You all know that—they can readily confess to homicide if they think it will impress you."

"To a shocking degree," Rainey said.

"But these same people will lie and conceal comparatively trivial offenses—compulsive masturbation or stealing a couple of bucks from a murder victim's pocket."

"Because they think it makes them look pathetic."

Jo nodded. "A sociopath's primary psychological defense is omnipotent control. Exerting sway, projecting dominance. Above every other aim, wielding power takes precedence. Because it defends their psyche against shame."

Emmerich crossed his arms. "And it can present as malignant grandiosity."

"In cruel ways. They share sadism with malignant paranoids."

"And when somebody's personality mixes paranoia and sociopathy?" Caitlin said.

"It's vital to know whether an offender is primarily paranoid or primarily sociopathic. Communicating with them will be tough in any case, but impossible with someone who's deeply paranoid," Jo said. "A sociopath might assume that outreach from you is an attempt to get something from him. He'll think you're working an angle—because *he* is. If you act with absolute honesty, you can sometimes break through and get him to begin a dialogue."

She brushed her hair from her eyes. "But paranoids assume from the get-go that you're planning to betray and attack them. They analyze every word and gesture for hidden motives. They presume you're lying and sabotaging them. So the more you know about how the Midnight Man's personality's organized, the better you'll be able to predict his behavior. And choose your tactics if you engage him in pursuit. Or, God forbid, if he ends up with hostages."

Emmerich's eyes were sharp. "Juvenile psychopathy."

Jo drank her coffee and peered across the park before answering. "That's a diagnosis no doctor wants to give. It's a label that's simply too horrifying to apply to kids. So pediatricians and child psychiatrists don't. The APA doesn't recognize it in the *DSM-5*. Because it's worse than telling parents their kid has inoperable cancer. It's a hopeless diagnosis that carries not just a stigma but actual moral horror."

"And yet," Emmerich said.

"By the time certain young people reach legal adulthood, they've been diagnosed in ways that tell the story. Conduct Disorder with Callous Traits, for one. They've often been analyzed, drugged, arrested, incarcerated, institutionalized, and fended off with actual sticks by their terrorized families. Sometimes they've planned elaborate mass casualty attacks. Think of Eric Harris."

Columbine. Keyes rubbed his eyes.

"Juvenile psychopathy is both tragic and extremely dangerous. It arises from a mix of nature and nurture—brain architecture and the child's home environment. It's not insanity. It's a poverty of compassion that manifests in cold calculation," Jo said. "It's incurable. And from everything you've told me, it fits the Midnight Man."

Caitlin scraped her knuckles across her forehead. She wasn't surprised, but felt a strange sense of sorrow mixing with her anger.

Emmerich spoke pensively. "A juvenile psychopath with paranoid traits. That means there's almost no way of building trust with the UNSUB. If we try to contact him, he won't listen to us."

"No," Jo said.

The wind gusted over her and clouds covered the sun. A storm was blowing into San Francisco.

"His sadistic tendencies and malignant paranoia have elements of fanaticism," Jo said. "The way he draws eyes, wanting people to see—he has a message for the world, and he's not going to back off from it. He's grandiose and intensely angry."

"He's a piece of work," Caitlin said.

"I wouldn't use that terminology in an official report. But yes."

Emmerich spread his hands at the team. None of them had any other questions.

"You've been extremely helpful, doctor. I appreciate your time," Emmerich said.

"If you need me, you know how to reach me."

"Thanks, Jo," Caitlin said.

Jo gave Caitlin a lingering look. "Good luck." She ended the call.

The room abruptly felt flat and strangely empty—maybe of hope.

"Suspicious, violent, sneaky, and smart," Rainey said.

Emmerich spoke distantly. "Familiar with counterforensics, and so well-informed about local police procedure that he apparently takes advantage of shift changes and the boundaries between dispatch sectors."

"Not just hypervigilant and knowledgeable," Caitlin said. "Young, strong, quick, and willing to take physical risks like so many teenage boys."

Keyes spread his hands on the table. "Say it. He's a terrifying opponent."

Rainey's expression was veiled. She seemed uncertain and unnerved. "It's like he's a freshly made vampire. A creature of the night. He's wild with bloodlust and has eyes that see in the dark."

The table fell silent. Keyes pushed his plate away.

WFS, Caitlin thought. Weirder Fucking Shit, every day.

Outside the conference room, on a sunny hotel patio, a family walked past. Cheerful grandparents, their son pushing a stroller, a young woman with a toddler on her hip.

A shadow fell across the patio behind them, trailed by engine noise. Caitlin leaned toward the window and glanced up. An LAPD helicopter.

She thought, *Vampires never surrender*.

Emmerich stood and absently cleaned up the remains of his lunch. "Let's check into the hotel. Then regroup. Meet in the lobby in half an hour to head downtown."

Caitlin walked from the conference room snarled in thought. *Game it out*, she told herself. Think through every scenario in which they might confront the Midnight Man. Envision the UNSUB's behavior and design strategies to capture him. She visualized possibilities. Traffic stop. Gunfight in a victim's home. Tip called in by the killer's own family.

Confrontation at a high school locker. Knife fight at the winter formal.

As she headed for the elevator, her phone pinged. Sean.

Miss ya.

She exhaled. Telling the others she'd catch up with them, she headed outside and placed a video call. She crossed the hotel driveway toward the busy street, where she wouldn't be overheard.

When Sean appeared on her screen, she said, "Ya, too."

He was walking down the road outside his house, hair windblown under lowering gray clouds, his jean jacket pulled over a Cal sweatshirt. He turned the phone so Caitlin could see Sadie ahead, wobbling along the sidewalk on a tiny bike with training wheels. When he turned the screen back around, he was frowning.

"You don't look happy about what you've learned today," he said.

"It's beyond disturbing."

"Tell me," he said.

The wind raked Caitlin's face and hissed through the palm trees above her head. "Calling him 'The Midnight Man' is a misnomer. He's the Midnight Boy."

She told him as she paced back and forth on the sidewalk. Then she continued gaming scenarios out.

"What'll the killer do if he's identified? If his face is flashed across every television screen in the city? If the authorities confront him?"

"Nothing peaceful," Sean said.

"He'll have to be taken by surprise," she said. "He'll need to be surrounded and subdued before he has a chance to react. Otherwise, he'll never go quietly."

"You're picturing yourself face to face with him, aren't you?"

She slowed. "Yes. A troubled, potentially abused, maybe neuro-logically compromised teenager. Sneaky, smart, capable, but not an adult."

"Deadly."

"And a cop's son."

"That's really eating at you," Sean said.

She stopped. Traffic grumbled past. "I guess it is."

"Even more than it was last night. Now that you think he's a teenager, you look ready to punch a garbage truck."

She pinched her nose. "Flip a garbage truck, maybe." She started pacing again. "I don't know why."

"Yeah, you do. You've been a cop's teenage kid. You're thinking about what that did to you in high school."

Sean knew her history of self-harm. Knew that, lonely, distressed, and isolated, she had believed her life was out of control and spiraling down, down, endlessly down.

Most of the time when she reflected, she remembered what it was like to be Mack Hendrix's kid. The daughter of the detective who went off the deep end. But all cops' kids dealt with the pressures of their parents' jobs.

"You're not the high school hero when you're the son of the Man," Sean said.

"No, you are not."

Like her, the Midnight Man had probably felt the pride and fear that came from seeing a parent pin on a badge. Felt the pressure to grow up as straight as an arrow. Known the distrust of schoolmates. Like her, he may have had the word *narc* spat in his face.

A kid who felt all eyes on him, all the time.

"Part of you wants to tell this kid that high school's survivable. That everything will be okay," Sean said.

She recalled herself at fifteen—thinking that a police officer's life was a nightmare for everybody in his orbit. She'd sought desperate, false refuge in cutting herself. For months, until she accidentally cut too deep and ended up in the ER.

"You want to grab this kid and tell him there's a way out," Sean said. "But Caitlin, you're too late."

Annihilation. The black nowhere. As a teenager, she'd heard it call to her—only to claw her way back from the idea in terror.

The Midnight Man, drowning in paranoia, had a consuming dread of being obliterated. A vision of annihilation poured down on him ceaselessly. His dread, apparently, was so unbearable that to end it he might rush into annihilation's embrace.

Maybe their visions had the same bitter roots.

She tried to see his face. Somebody who could never fit in. A smiling kid.

Holding a gun, and a knife, and buzzing with shame, and terror, and rage.

"Cat," Sean said. "You're thinking about what happens if this UNSUB forces you into a position where you have to use deadly force."

The air seemed to flicker. "He's lethal."

"And you're not cold enough to sight on him like he's a paper target at the range—thank God."

"You wouldn't either."

"Maybe. Neither of us wants to find out," he said. "You know you'd never be the same if you pulled the trigger on a kid. That's what's eating at you. Even though he's a killer."

She let her gaze lengthen, to the gleam of traffic and the shadows on the mountains.

"I've got to go. He's out there." She put her fingers to her lips, then to the screen. "Thanks, Sean."

His gaze pierced her. "Eyes wide, Hendrix. He knows as much as you did at that age, and he has no limits."

She ended the call and walked back toward the hotel. The ground felt insubstantial beneath her feet.

27

By the time the BAU team walked into the war room, Caitlin's nerves had turned acid. The room was hot. The writhing silver tinsel seemed feral.

Detective Solis glanced up when Emmerich approached his desk.

"We need to update the Midnight Man's behavioral profile," Emmerich said.

Solis removed a pair of reading glasses and studied him. Emmerich's expression was metallic.

"Right." Solis beckoned Weisbach and Alvarez.

Alvarez had rolled up his sleeves. His forearms bulged with veins. His USMC tattoo practically throbbed.

He was back to gnawing on a toothpick. "What's up?"

"The Midnight Man may be a teenager," Emmerich said.

For a fraction of a second, nobody reacted. Then Solis rocked back. Weisbach's eyes narrowed.

Emmerich outlined the team's reasoning. Alvarez shook his head.

"Where's this coming from? The sticker that Hannah Guillory thought she saw on the guy's windshield?"

"That's one factor," Emmerich said.

"Could have been a stolen car."

"True," Caitlin said. "But the logo and letters on the UNSUB's hoodie match those on the car. That, I think, significantly increases the chances the car belongs to him."

"Could be a teacher. Janitor. Could be borrowing his kid sister's car."

"Absolutely," Emmerich said. "But he could be a student himself. Investigating that possibility will allow us to narrow the suspect pool. It will *give* us a suspect pool."

Alvarez threw away the toothpick. "Juveniles commit felonies every day. They join street gangs. Work as runners for drug dealers. But it's almost unheard of for a teenager to become a serial killer."

"It's rare," Caitlin said. "Rarer than it is for a teen to commit spree killings or mass murder in a continuous rampage." She held Alvarez's eye. "But very young killers aren't unicorns. Unfortunately."

Alvarez crossed his arms. Outside, the wind whistled past the windows. The storm that had already reached San Francisco was rolling down the coast.

Weisbach broke her silence. "Alvarez is right. It's too broad, too vague. I think it's more likely that the killer is an immature young man in his twenties."

Emmerich's voice was calm but pointed. "This isn't a wild guess."

Keyes had his laptop open. "One more data point. The UNSUB has repeatedly invoked the idea of 'Legion.' That term doesn't just have biblical and occult connotations. It's a storyline in a top-selling video game. *Demonocalypse.*" He spun the laptop. The game's website was up. "The demographic is male gamers ages fourteen to eighteen."

Solis, the dark circles under his eyes increasingly sooty, said, "I can see it. It's worth investigating."

Emmerich didn't react, but Caitlin knew he was relieved.

The BAU wasn't in charge of this investigation. They were working the case solely at the request of the LAPD. The murders were state crimes and the FBI couldn't have taken over the investigation even if they'd wanted to.

This was the task force's ball game. But the BAU had thrown them a curve. *Worth investigating* wasn't a random phrase. Devoting resources to this avenue—time, money, patrol officers, detectives—meant that other avenues would get short shrift. It was a choice. It would inevitably come at a cost.

Solis said, "Let's look at this suspect pool. Give it the weekend."

Alvarez said, "Where we supposed to start?"

Emmerich straightened his already straight posture. "Juveniles who've had contact with the criminal justice system. The Midnight Man isn't a neophyte. He knows the system from the inside out. White males, home addresses within the buffer zones in the geographic profile."

"You know how many that is? Hundreds of thousands."

The vibe among them was confused and grumbling. Caitlin knew her next remark might intensify that. But it was important.

"It's not hundreds of thousands. We can narrow it down tremendously," she said. "Because there's something else we need to add to the profile. I think the killer is the son of a cop."

Alvarez blew out a hard breath. "No way."

Weisbach took off her glasses. "I've been wondering something similar."

"The persistent vandalism of police vehicles. His familiarity with 911 dispatch sectors. The way his attacks have all occurred within thirty minutes of a shift change at the station nearest to his target."

Alvarez shook his head. "Because this asshole hates law enforcement, you think he's striking back at Daddy? Give me a break."

Weisbach was small, and stern, and stood her ground. "He's too knowledgeable. Somebody's either guiding him, educating him, or he's picked up an intense amount of understanding as to how local law enforcement operates."

Alvarez's neck was growing red. "So he's smart. I don't think we need to add these off-the-wall ideas to our workload."

Solis, who was the senior Robbery-Homicide detective, ran a hand over his stubble. "It's a possibility. An unpleasant one."

Alvarez's carotid artery throbbed. He had to be exhausted and frustrated, but his resistance seemed deeper rooted than that.

"Teenager. Cop's kid. Fine." He pointed at Keyes. "You've got the software. Get yourself access to every database in Southern California and knock yourself out. But I've got real leads to follow." He turned to walk away, got five feet, and spun back around. "FBI flies all the way out here and you're taking potshots in the dark."

Exhaling harshly, he did stalk off, head lowered. Keyes pulled off his slouch cap.

"I'm on it," he said. "LAPD, LASD, Arcadia, CHP, every police department in Los Angeles county. Sworn officers, civilian staff, active and retired. Federal agencies too. Give me logins and I'll rock and roll."

Weisbach raised her hands. Maybe in conciliation, maybe surrender. "You got it."

She gave Solis an indecipherable look. They walked away.

The FBI team stood alone, the golden afternoon light angling sharply across the walls.

"That went well," Rainey said.

Caitlin said, "Like a fastball to the head."

Four forty-six P.M., the sun spat its final burning rays and plunged beneath the horizon, bleeding red along the surface of the ocean. A cavernous blue fell through the void it left, and a deepening cold, as night soaked the city. He could taste it, the night. It was him now—what he told them to call him, the Midnight Man. *His.*

He climbed the last few flights of stairs and shoved open the broken fire door to the roof. The scarlet crevice along the horizon was a scar being sewn shut. The hustle and noise of downtown lay far below. Blazing lights, billboards, Staples Center glaring to the south, millions of people staring at televisions or driving cars. Holiday time. Hell time—a long, dying animal howl. Nobody seeing. *Him.*

Up here, he was invisible by design. The building was abandoned. He could keep watch, three hundred sixty degrees, seeing, unseen. The giant towers that crowded the heart of downtown technically overlooked his aerie. But the building's roof was tar paper, black, like his clothing, and gloves, and hat, and movements. Here, he could eye them all, and practically hear their scheming.

The wind blew from the north, cold with menace. Turning, turning.

Spin the wheel, let's see which way to go tonight.

He put his earbuds in and turned up the music beneath his hood. It filled his world. Made him here, and not.

He was hungry.

And more. He was brimming with indignation.

Bay Rise was down there, along the snaking white line that was the 110 freeway. Unaware, ignorant—so oblivious that even with its eyes open, it was asleep. So many neat little homes crammed ass by jowl but each so sharply defined, each thinking it was insulated, protected. *Asking* for it.

But he'd been shut out. Run off. That house, the solemn little bougie home on the tidy little bougie street, he'd shot out the street light with a ninja rock this time and nobody had even stirred. One dog had barked, but after that, nothing. The gate at the side of the house was well oiled, no rusty hinges, no creaking. Mommydaddy asleep, everything perfectly dark, the wind such a welcome cover, hissing as he strolled to the backyard and enjoyed standing on the patio, eyeing the choice of windows, catching sight of his star-flecked reflection in the sliding glass patio door. Standing there, an absence, giving away nothing, nobody able to see him, the only eyes his, on the lock, the ease of opening it, and the lesson that would be unleashed within.

Then the light boomed from the fridge in the kitchen. Poured out across his feet and legs and the girl in the kitchen ...

He turned up the music in his ears. It shredded, a pirate recording of an Every Time I Die concert. Here, he could let it throb through him. Drawing power and inspiration and cocooning himself in it.

The girl. *Littlesister bloodblister.* She'd shut the door, slammed off the light, the white heart of vision, and he'd seen her duck. Tiny coward, hiding. But he'd slid along the side of the house and found the cat door, easy-peasy.

And then the girl, and her family, turned it all to shit.

Thwarting him, after he'd done his research. Checked the map, located the substation. After he spent an hour, more, driving, feeling, needing, working up to it. Leaving him empty-handed.

It was an outrage. How dare those people try to stop him?

The city lights shimmered. The wind rose. A storm was rolling in.

He climbed down from the roof and slipped through back streets to the car.

Time to feed.

28

In El Segundo, night had settled over the streets. The neighborhood was hushed. Kiki Bingham had been deeply asleep, but knew she'd only been out for ten or fifteen minutes. Then, *pop*, awake. She wasn't surprised. This zero-to-alert reaction had become ingrained since she'd had the kids.

She lay with her eyes closed, hearing no sounds from the boys' bedroom. Rob was snoring softly behind her, his knee nudging her in the back. Maybe that's what had woken her up. She fluffed the pillow and hoped she could drift back to sleep.

But her mind fizzed. Christmas presents to wrap. Cookies to bake. Liquor to buy for the office party.

She smelled the strong whiff of petroleum from the city's oil storage tanks. The pong was heavy tonight, permeating the back of her throat. An onshore breeze must be blowing in from the beach. El Segundo had one of Southern California's prettiest stretches of coastline, if you didn't mind the cyclone fencing and power station and the vast oil refineries that lined Vista del Mar. She pulled the covers up around her ears. A jet roared, taking off from LAX.

A jet—that must have been what woke her. Though after living in this friendly, crowded neighborhood for three years, she should have been able to tune out the noise of yet another departing airliner. The airport's south runway was three hundred yards away. On this street, you learned to pace the rhythm of your speech when the evening KLM flight to Amsterdam commenced its takeoff roll. Search for their

177

house on street view, you saw an A380 lifting off in the background, photobombing them.

She was wide awake now, her mind pinballing in random directions.

The jet howled away, over the ocean. The engine noise was thunderous. The smell of oil was too sharp. She opened her eyes.

The bedroom sheers, ghostly in the thin starlight, were ballooning under a breeze. The window was open.

She jerked up—too late. At the foot of the bed, a shadowed figure raised a gun.

He held his arm straight out and fired.

The shot hit Rob. Then Kiki was scrambling, a shriek sliding from her throat, kicking off the covers, clawing the wall behind her, and she knew who it was, knew it was real, and then he turned the pistol on her.

He worked speedily. He had it down now.

Despite his pounding heart, his dry mouth, the excitement, the purity, the *righteous vengeance* of it, the incredible, liberating *rage* of it, he worked efficiently in the dark, kneeling on the bed, knife digging. His gloved fingers found the rounds. Clock on the nightstand said 12:37 A.M. He mined the bullet from the man's body, and the woman's, and he slipped them into his pocket. 12:41 A.M. He opened the bedroom door and walked down the hall, wondering why he hadn't heard a single sound from the children. Maybe they'd barricaded themselves in their room.

In the living room, he stopped. The blinds were up and gave him a clear view of the neighborhood outside. All around, lights blazed. At the house next door. Across the street, every house—porchlights, front windows shining. Dogs barked.

He glanced over his shoulder at the parents' room. Their window was open. That was on him. He'd found it unlocked, climbed in silently, and left it wide. He had wanted the cold breeze to provide a hint, a tickle, wanted it to wake the mommydaddy for a last sensory moment of confusion before he clarified things. Mistake. The open window meant the neighborhood had heard the gunfire.

He stalked back down the hall, gun hanging from his hand. In his pocket, the bullets that had canceled the parents clacked against each other. Such power, so hot, all his. Stopping at the door to what had to be the children's room, he grabbed the knob.

Locked. He stepped back to kick it down.

Outside, flashlights. Running across the street in this direction. The glowing blue rectangles of phone screens. Voices.

He ducked into the living room again to peer out the front window. Far side of the hill, the flash of blue lights. Cops. And the mob. They were coming.

The kids' door remained closed. Right there, like a taste, a lure, an unblemished meal just ripe for his teeth. More lights outside. He grabbed a Christmas stocking, ducked back down the hall, and climbed out the parents' window. He ran across the backyard, scaled the fence, and sprinted for the car. More blue lights, red too, hitting the fence, the lights arriving as the same time as the storm, cops and rain both pouring down.

Evie Stevens heard the ocean. Thought she did. That sound was what woke her, maybe. She was still half in her dream, and could be it was the ocean, because her house was a quarter mile from the beach and in Torrance, in the middle of the night when the wind was blowing the right way, you could hear it sometimes, the surf purring onto the sand. She hated waking up in the middle of the night. Especially on a Saturday, her first night of winter break, no eighth-grade math or history for two weeks, no first-period gym class when it was freakin' fifty degrees outside, practically Antarctica. Just her warm bed and sleeping in till whenever and *vacation*.

She rolled over. Fumbled for her phone on the floor by the bed and squinched one eye open. 1:26 A.M. Ugh.

She dropped the phone and nestled deeper into the covers. She couldn't hear the ocean now that she was awake. But she heard the rain. Splashing on the roof and patio outside the french doors.

She heard the rain, and she smelled it. Wet fabric. Or fur.

Double ugh—had Churro been out, then nudged his way into her room, soppy and reeking of wet dog? She felt something move at the foot of the bed. *Ughhhh …*

Evie tossed off the duvet and propped herself up on her elbows. "Churro …"

She blinked twice. Her eyes popped wide. And she froze, like a clear stake of ice.

It wasn't the dog. She was staring at something bigger.

At the foot of her bed, etched around the edges by dim light coming through the french doors, was a figure in a hoodie. Face nothing but an empty space in the darkness. The wet fabric smell was coming from him. Sweatshirt, jeans.

He was crouched on the balls of his feet, like a gargoyle, breathing on her.

Evie screamed.

She screamed, no dream, real, the sound filling her head, and she scrambled. Backward, crablike, but the headboard was there, and the screaming and the rain were all she could hear. The sheets tangled around her legs and she tried to spin and get out of the bed.

He launched.

She spun and her hands hit the floor, her feet still tangled in the sheets, kicking, pumping, her fingers clawing the carpet to *move, get away …*

The figure, the shape—*Midnight Man, oh my God*—landed on top of her, and then he was on his feet, hauling her off the bed by her waist, and she kept screaming, and Dad was upstairs, the house a split level, but he had to hear her—somebody had to hear her. She couldn't get her feet on the ground, was clawing at the air, and the man, wet man, strong, light, holding her. But he couldn't stop her screaming.

Then he could. He whipped the lamp off the nightstand and wrapped the cord around her neck. The plug ripped from the wall in a spray of sparks. All at once the rubber cord was a garrote, choking her, and no sounds came out. She grabbed at it, but he was dragging her out the french doors, the cold rain hitting her in the eyes as she thrashed, her feet slipping on the concrete of the patio, past the mini soccer net to the gate, she could see the side gate was open.

The cord was impossibly tight, strangling her. She couldn't get her fingers under it, it was wet now, slippery, and he was dragging her by it, along the walk into the front yard. She couldn't, *omigod*, couldn't breathe. They passed beneath the spreading branches of the Monterey pine and the rain briefly eased and she saw a dark vehicle parked at the curb.

Evie couldn't let him get her in the car.

But she had to breathe—*had to, had to*—and she clawed and pulled and couldn't get the cord loose.

Stop trying to. Go for him instead.

She flung her arms over her head and grabbed at *his* neck, *his* face. Scratching and clawing.

He flinched. Growled, "Stupid *pig.*"

She dug her nails into flesh. Her vision was spiked with stars. *Dig, hurt, don't stop, damage him, make him let go.* But she couldn't breathe. It was agony. It was going away, all of it, if he got her in that car. And the only sound she could hear was the pounding of her heart in her ears, all she could see was flying yellow stars, all she could smell was the wet, the man's breath, the grass beneath her feet.

Until she heard something else. Immeasurably distant, dim, like hearing a cannon boom from beneath the entire weight of the ocean.

Barking.

Dim, everything dim, even the stars turning red and being swallowed by the black. But the barking. Then the Midnight Man pulling harder, running, and then, abruptly, no more. He dropped her.

Evie hit the grass in the rain, almost gone. Fumbled at the lamp cord. Pulled, crazily, and unwrapped it. She gasped. A huge, gulping breath. Another.

She rolled. Got up, and grabbed the lamp, backing up, ready to swing it. She tried to scream but all she could do was keep gasping. Till the stars receded and the night, the yard, reality, reappeared.

The Midnight Man was on his knees on the sidewalk. He'd been knocked down.

Churro was on him. The family dog had burst through the french doors in Evie's bedroom and chased him down. Sweet Churro, their Doberman. Evie staggered back, the rain plastering her face.

The Midnight Man kicked free, clambered to his feet, and ran. With Churro chasing him, he careened toward the dark SUV parked on the street. Behind Evie, the lights in the house came on. The Midnight Man fled.

29

Caitlin's phone sang on the nightstand, beetling in a circle. The thrum woke her from twilight sleep. She rolled, stabbing for the phone, eyes sliding open to see her hotel room, skyscraper lights spangling the night outside. She was on top of the covers in her clothes.

CJ EMMERICH, the screen read. The bedside clock, a stinging red, registered 1:34 A.M. Caitlin jammed the phone to her ear and tried not to sound anything less than completely alert.

"Boss."

"He struck. Sheriff's deputies are in pursuit. We're joining."

She was on her feet before he could end the call.

She ran down the stairs, forcing herself to complete wakefulness, needing to be fully engaged, and slammed through the fire door into the hotel parking garage to see Rainey emerge from the elevator. Brianne's face was iron. Warrior focus. Mother wolf intensity. Hunt an UNSUB who destroyed families? Rainey would end him, without mercy.

Caitlin held up the keys. They ran to the Suburban. As they climbed in, tires squealed and Emmerich rounded the corner.

He braked in front of them. "Sheriff's dispatcher will vector us. I'll lead."

He pulled away sharply. Caitlin fired up the engine and followed him out of the garage, buckling her seat belt as she steered one-handed. Emmerich lit the Suburban's flashing light strip on the windshield. Caitlin followed suit. The rain hit them, loud and hard.

"You have the Sheriff's Department radio frequency?" Caitlin said.

Rainey nodded and dialed it in. "Thought it never rained in LA. You like wet roads?"

"Born to them."

Water sheeted across the windshield. Caitlin flipped on the wipers and accelerated, even as Emmerich pulled away.

"All I got is that the Midnight Man struck again," she said.

"Two dead in El Segundo, man and woman. Children unharmed. Gunfire drew the neighbors' attention, and the UNSUB ran before he could terrorize the kids." Rainey dialed the radio. "He struck again forty-five minutes later in Torrance, seven miles south."

"He hit twice tonight. In under an hour."

"Attacked a fourteen-year-old girl."

"*Fourteen*." Caitlin turned to gape at Rainey. "The girl. Dead?"

"Alive. Family dog tore after the UNSUB. He ran."

"Hell yeah, dog." The windshield wipers slapped back and forth. "The UNSUB didn't recon thoroughly." She shook her head. "He ignored the parents and physically attacked the daughter. And absolutely smashed his previous age barrier."

"There may have been no overt signs that the home had a dog. But this was a slipup. I think he was still in a pressurized mental state after his initial attack tonight."

"Because he wasn't able to complete his ritual at the first crime scene."

"The neighbors interrupted him," Rainey said. "Spoiled his script halfway through the fantasy."

Ahead, partially obscured by the deluge and tire spray, Emmerich tapped the brakes and took a sharp corner. Caitlin followed. On the radio, chatter ramped up. The flat tone of the dispatcher's voice belied the urgency of the information she was relaying. The interjections from deputies in pursuit were terse and strained.

Caitlin's voice turned brusque. "Assaulting an eighth grader. Forty-five minutes between attacks. The escalation is *insane*."

Rainey turned up the radio. Caitlin heard cross talk and the words *black Jeep*.

"Jeep. Hannah Guillory pegged it," Caitlin said.

Rainey phoned Emmerich and put the call on speaker. "CJ—details on the pursuit and the UNSUB's vehicle?"

Caitlin raced up a freeway onramp behind him, bottoming out. Emmerich's voice came through tinny but cool.

"Torrance attack, the girl was dragged onto the family's front lawn. She described him getting into a dark, late model SUV," he said. "Her father jumped into his car and gave chase."

"Oh, man," Caitlin said.

On the southbound freeway, traffic was sparse, five lanes wide open in front of them. Sodium lights picketed past, furry in the rain.

"The father couldn't get close enough to the suspect's vehicle to read a plate number or specify the model but kept it in sight as the UNSUB made it to Pacific Coast Highway and headed east. The father was a couple blocks back but the road's straight, and he was on the phone with 911. He got Torrance PD and LA Sheriff's deputies to join the pursuit."

Rainey held onto the dash as they took a bend. "Still no positive ID on the make, or the plate? Air support?"

"Negative on all three. Sheriff's air division is grounded. Weather."

The two Suburbans ate up the roadway, center lane, flying past traffic. Under the *whap* of the wipers and the spray ahead, Emmerich's tail lights were blurry.

"How long as the pursuit been in progress?" Caitlin said.

"Eleven minutes."

In some places that would be a long time. In Southern California, where pursuits could last an hour and span counties, eleven minutes was nothing.

Rainey had a tablet, and brought up a navigation app. It took her a minute to mark some waypoints and pull up a diagram of the pursuit so far.

"Eight, nine minutes in residential neighborhoods and on surface streets," she said. "But he jumped on the 405 sixty seconds ago."

The 405 freeway—that was good news and bad news. Good because pursuing officers could more easily keep a target vehicle in sight on a freeway, and because their vehicles frequently had more horsepower than the suspect's. Their top speed was likely higher than his. Bad because freeway speeds meant that any crash could be catastrophic.

"How far to the junction?" Caitlin said.

"Four miles."

Caitlin kept her grip firm, her foot heavy on the gas, sticking to Emmerich's tail. She was trained in advanced pursuit and emergency driving. She had years on wet Bay Area streets as a patrol officer. And the last time she'd engaged in a high-speed pursuit was when she chased a convenience store robber in Alameda. She knew the risks.

Not just the risk that a fleeing suspect might turn on pursuers with deadly force. Across the nation, on average, somebody died because of a police pursuit every day. Sometimes it was the suspect. Sometimes it was a crime victim or bystander. Sometimes a cop.

Over the radio, fresh reports came in from deputies and the dispatcher: A crazed driver was running motorists off the road. Black SUV, white guy at the wheel.

The dispatcher. *"Be advised, suspect vehicle has exited the 405. Heading east on Norcross Avenue."*

Rain obscured Caitlin's view. Ahead of her, Emmerich barreled along.

"Suspect sighted heading northeast on Willowbrook Boulevard, one mile north of the 91 freeway."

Rainey zoomed in on her navigation app. "Emmerich, do you see the interception route?"

Flashing blue lights surrounded Emmerich's Suburban like a strobing aura. Caitlin was pushing eighty-five. Emmerich came back, curt.

"We can cut him off."

"I'll call it in." Rainey radioed their location to the dispatcher and other cars in pursuit. "Repeat, two FBI vehicles are inbound, heading south on the 110. We will vector east to get ahead of the suspect and cut him off."

They roared past a fuel tanker and swept off the freeway onto slick surface streets.

A suburban area, strip malls, golf courses, tall banks of trees and sound walls that butted up against the freeway. Stoplights. Streets that, while nearly empty, were pocked by dumpsters and parked vehicles and overhanging trees that blocked the view. Cross traffic.

The road curved. The dispatcher reported a traffic accident south of them—two cars had collided when they swerved to avoid a black SUV running a red light.

"That's only a quarter mile away," Rainey said. "We're gaining. We're ahead of the interception point."

They passed a city park. When the trees gave way to telephone poles and auto dealerships, they saw, through the rain, several blocks southwest, a tsunami of flashing lights. It was moving, paralleling their track.

"Go, go," Emmerich said.

Caitlin jammed the pedal to the floor.

The dispatcher. "*Suspect reported one block east of Rio Verde Avenue, heading northeast. He has entered a residential neighborhood and cut around several corners at high speed.*"

Rainey zoomed on the map. "He's pulled away from the units in pursuit. Those flashing lights are way behind him. Quarter mile. But we're not. We're still on course to make the interception point."

"He got off the freeway ASAP. He's trying to break visual contact with the pursuing vehicles. He knows that's how to lose the cops." She cut a glance at Rainey. "Officer's son. Hundred percent."

Caitlin gripped the wheel. Emmerich was sixty yards ahead, swallowed by the spray from his tires. To the south the bubble of flashing lights grew brighter.

Emmerich's voice came over Rainey's phone. "Three more blocks, cut right."

There was a traffic light ahead of him, green.

"Roger," Caitlin said.

Rainey stared at the nav app. "We'll cut through a park, come out in a residential neighborhood, if we're lucky we'll get to an intersection in time to block it. I Iem him in with the Sheriff's closing from behind."

"Got it," Caitlin said. "You have the conn. Tell me where to park it."

Emmerich arrowed through the green light, Caitlin right behind.

"Hundred yards," Rainey said.

They were going ninety. Caitlin eased off the gas. Emmerich pulled away, then his brake lights came on. The rain turned to sheets.

Barely visible under the curtain of water, headlights appeared from a side street. A car pulled out in front of Emmerich.

Caitlin didn't have time to gasp. Emmerich had no time at all. He swerved.

Caitlin hit the brakes. The car from the side street was directly ahead, a goblin-black compact that might as well have been invisible, on a roadway slick with oil and pounding rain.

"God," she said.

Emmerich's tires lost grip. Going at least fifty, he hydroplaned across the roadway.

Caitlin gasped. "No—"

Emmerich's Suburban spun one-eighty, scrubbing speed. Almost made it. Squealing backward, it vaulted the curb and hit a telephone pole.

The Suburban slammed to a stop. The telephone pole swayed. The SUV's headlights glared into the street.

Caitlin braked, hard. Rainey was calling Emmerich's name into the phone, calm but urgent.

He shouted back. "Keep going."

Caitlin glimpsed him holding the wheel, checking the dash. He turned his head and pointed at her.

"*Now*," he yelled. "I'll rejoin. Go."

Caitlin gave Emmerich a last brief look and gazed up the road. Nothing but red lights and open lanes. To the west, the bubble-wave of flashing blue was stringing out.

Rainey said, "Now, or he'll get past us."

Caitlin floored it.

The back end of the Suburban fishtailed. She straightened it out and raced up the street, running the red lights, checking peripherally for cross traffic, hoping the Suburban's flashing light strip would alert other drivers.

The radio chatter had paused, nothing but dead air. That was an ominous sign.

"Right at the next light," Rainey said.

Caitlin swung wide for the turn and cut close to the curb, veering onto a curving avenue.

"What's ahead?" she said.

"Neighborhoods. A greenbelt. A park and playing fields."

The streets tightened into a maze of crossroads and dead ends. On the radio, everything they heard suggested bad outcomes.

"*He turned off the boulevard,*" one pursuing deputy radioed.

"*He's on Reinhold. No—dead end …*"

Through the radio they heard sirens. Cross talk. The pursuit was growing disorganized. The killer was dodging the cops.

Rainey peered at her navigation app, then the darkened street.

"Best guess," Caitlin said. "Choose."

"Right. Then left. No, that left." Rainey pointed.

They were now navigating by a combination of phone app, last-known-location reports, 911 calls from drivers reporting crashes, and the wet, ever-nearer flash of blue and red lights in the night. Caitlin pushed the Suburban around a corner down a residential street. It was absolutely quiet, the houses lit by her flashing lights.

"What's at the end of this road?" she said.

"Cut-through to the road where the main pursuit is. Go right."

Caitlin hit the brakes and nearly slid around the corner. The road ran straight toward the mass of the flashing light storm.

A new voice broke into the radio cross talk—an agitated deputy.

"*The suspect has abandoned his car. He's fleeing on foot.*"

Rainey cut into the radio chatter. "This is FBI Special Agent

Brianne Rainey, in pursuit. What's the location, and direction he's running?"

The deputy yelled back the name of a nearby street. "He ran toward the park."

"Do you have him in sight?"

"Negative." His voice was young. He sounded like he'd been sprinting, though they knew he was at the wheel of his cruiser. They could hear the engine and siren.

Rainey aimed her hand at the windshield. "Forget hitting the main street. Left at the corner, that's the street where he has to run to get into the park from this side."

Caitlin gunned it around the corner and down the street. The road ended at darkened woods.

She screeched to a stop. No sign of a Jeep. No sign of the Midnight Man.

The agitated deputy's voice came through. *"It's Ohlmeyer. I'm at the playing fields on the far side of the park. Rain's so heavy, I need my headlights and side spot. I'm ... hold on."*

They waited for a second, doors open, listening for the deputy to continue, but the radio went to static. Briefly locking eyes, Caitlin and Rainey jumped out of the Suburban.

The rain immediately soaked Caitlin, cold, blowing in her face in the gusting wind. They ran down a path under overhanging trees, weapons in their hands, flashlights aimed ahead. The mud was slick beneath Caitlin's Doc Martens.

Rain pounded the overhead leaves. Branches bent to the wind. Caitlin's breath feathered in front of her under the beam of her flashlight.

A hundred yards along the path, the trees opened. Ahead, white light poured across the ground—headlights. More diffusely, red and blue police lights popped in the rain. Slowing, they checked every direction. Rainey eyed their six. Caitlin listened for footsteps and rustling brush and hunted for shadows moving in an unnatural direction. Nothing.

All the intensity, the violence, the dark pursuit of this specter, gathered and permeated the air. He seemed a relentless scythe. Yet a vision of a young face floated behind Caitlin's eyes—lost, striking out. Too young to buy a beer. Reloading, maybe. Her head buzzed.

Where are you?

Who are you?

They stepped from the tree-lined path.

They emerged onto a flooded football field. A sheriff's car sat on the fifty-yard line, driver's door open. A Crown Vic, high beams and side spot aimed downfield at the goal line. Raising their guns, Caitlin and Rainey advanced across the field.

Their shoes splashed, water soaking Caitlin's legs. The cruiser's engine was running, idling high.

The car was empty.

They were both breathing hard. They'd lost radio contact with the pursuit once they left the Suburban. Now they heard it from the deputy's car. Rainey cast the beam of her flashlight at the grass by the open driver's door. The field was submerged in two inches of water, but directly outside the door they saw clearly defined shoeprints, heavy tread, filled with mud. The shoeprints led away from the car.

"He jumped out." Rainey turned her flashlight in the direction Deputy Ohlmeyer had apparently run.

Carefully, heads swiveling, they followed the footprints. Chewed up grass, glare of pooling water. The rain hammered them. They kept out of the direct beam of the cruiser's headlights, trying to stay shadowed, knowing they were backlit to anybody lurking in the trees. Rainey's shoulders rose and fell with every breath, but her Glock held steady.

Where the headlights faded, they found Ohlmeyer.

Face down, jacket starting to float. The water around him swirled red with blood. One gunshot wound to his back. Another to his head.

"Oh, God," Rainey said.

They rolled Ohlmeyer over. Caitlin knelt at his side and pressed cold fingers to his neck. Felt no pulse. Above her, Rainey scanned the field. Caitlin grabbed the deputy's shoulder-mounted radio.

"Officer down."

Tearing her gaze from the young man's lifeless face, she got to her feet. She and Rainey backed against each other, gaining 360-degree visibility, and swept their flashlights across the field, searching for the shooter. Nothing. Nobody moving.

Then, as Caitlin turned, her flashlight caught the gray reflection of stone. She inhaled.

Headstones. They were outside the entrance to a cemetery.

The buzzing returned to Caitlin's head, overwhelming her thoughts, ringing in her ears. The killer was gone.

From the empty patrol car, the radio blared. *"All units."*

She and Rainey returned to the car. Rainey leaned in and picked up the radio transmitter. The dispatcher's cool voice was ragged along the edges.

"Suspect vehicle last sighted on Alamagne Drive."

A new voice broke in to the cross talk. Emmerich.

"Am at the Alamagne Drive location," he said. *"The suspect's vehicle is no longer there. Repeat, no longer there."*

Rainey hesitated before pushing the radio transmit button. She looked at the deputy's body. Caitlin slumped against the cruiser. The Midnight Man had escaped.

30

The overhead lights in the war room were silver-white, mind-numbing, relentless. Caitlin stared at the whiteboard. She had a cup of coffee in her hand. When she took a swallow, she was surprised to find the coffee cold. How long had she been standing there?

She found the clock on the wall. It was three thirty A.M.

The room was bright and beyond dismal. The silver tinsel had fallen off one corner of the large-screen television and hung like a strangled snake. Across the floor, Solis was speaking to a group of LAPD brass. Caitlin didn't recognize any of them except the commanding officer of Robbery-Homicide, who had come downtown in the deep of the night shortly before Christmas because events had turned desperate. The atmosphere was so jagged that Caitlin could practically hear it humming beneath the lights. Grief, and anger, and dread.

She stared into her paper coffee cup. The milk had curdled. She drank it anyway.

Her eyes burned from exhaustion. Her boots and jeans were wet, her shirt too, where the rain had sneaked down the back of her coat. Her hair stuck damply to her head.

The whiteboard, at which she was staring blankly, hadn't been updated. None of tonight's attacks had been added to the timeline. Stiffly, she walked to the board, uncapped a marker, and started to write her thoughts. The pen squeaked across the board.

The Midnight Man was escalating on multiple fronts.

His attacks were coming closer together.

He had crossed new boundary lines—he broke an age barrier, attacking an eighth grader. He attempted to kidnap the girl.

He killed a cop.

The marker hovered in her hand. She capped it and tossed it on the table. She didn't need to write down the final twist.

The killer returned unseen to his vehicle. And he got away.

She felt a tap on the shoulder and turned abruptly.

Keyes handed her a long-sleeved T-shirt. "It'll be too big, but it's dry."

An unexpected tightness squeezed her throat. "Thanks."

Keyes' Jack Russell energy was subdued. He was normally both enthusiastic and patient, confident that if he fed data into his program and let the software digest its meal, the answer to the problem he was working would appear, crisp and clear and statistically significant. But tonight he looked at sea.

He read her scribbled list on the whiteboard. "It doesn't lead us closer to him, does it?"

She shook her head.

"I have to do something," she said. "If I write it down, maybe an answer will pour out through my fingertips when I can't consciously see the solution." She stared at the words on the board, and her eyes unfocused. "I ..."

She cleared her throat. Across the room, the LAPD brass headed toward the door, heads together, talking in low tones. Solis dropped into his desk chair and ran a hand over his face.

Caitlin turned to Keyes. "I should have known what he was capable of. But I didn't."

A wave swept through her, cold and terrible. They were up against somebody darker than she had ever encountered.

"The UNSUB is ramping up at an exponential rate," she said. "His inhibitions are dropping. His bloodlust is increasing. Cops are now his targets." Her voice cracked. She breathed again. "And he won't hold off harming young children forever."

Keyes' fierce eyes revealed a pain she hadn't seen before. It was fear. She should have been able to reassure him, to present a confident attitude. Team spirit. But Keyes' expression shook her even further.

In her peripheral vision she saw Rainey come through the door with Emmerich. Rainey's shirt and pants were as wet as Caitlin's. Emmerich looked worn and frustrated.

She straightened, though she felt unmoored. "Glad you're all right."

Emmerich waved away her concern. "No injuries, no damage to the other car. The Suburban's still drivable. But ..."

He pressed his lips white and rubbed his watchband. He didn't say more. *But I wasn't there soon enough.*

Keyes reached into his computer bag and handed Rainey a T-shirt. "Get warm."

Her face softened with gratitude.

Emmerich eyed the whiteboard. "The deputy apparently knew the park well. So well that he almost succeeded in cutting the UNSUB off when he abandoned his vehicle and ran into the trees." He shook his head. "But for whatever reason, Ohlmeyer stopped his cruiser in the middle of the field. He got out without being aware that the killer had circled around behind him in the dark. The rain, the engine noise, the adrenaline ..."

"The killer wasn't cornered," Rainey said. "He didn't shoot the deputy as self-preservation." She turned to her colleagues. "Ohlmeyer pursued the Midnight Man to the field, but the killer had a clear path of escape. *More* than a clear path. Ohlmeyer had lost sight of him. All the UNSUB had to do was run through the cemetery. But he didn't. He circled around behind the deputy and shot him in the back." She shook her head. "This wasn't desperation. It was escalation."

Behind Emmerich, a figure stormed through the door. Dark hair, darker eyes, wet LASD windbreaker. Detective Alvarez. He aimed straight for the BAU team.

As the expression on Caitlin's face changed, Emmerich, Rainey, and Keyes all turned.

Alvarez pointed at them. "All your fancy profiling, and you didn't see this coming."

The other task force detectives in the room stopped what they were doing. Alvarez came at the FBI group like a freight train.

"Shoveling bullshit about the guy being an officer's kid," he said. "You thought the police car vandalism was harmless."

He practically vibrated, like a machine that was revving out of control, with all the subsurface elements about to shake loose. But it had been a Sheriff's deputy floating facedown on the football field. Caitlin knew he was seeking a target for his anguish.

Didn't make it feel any better. Or fair. It felt like shrapnel hitting her in the heart.

"Harmless. You thought him using a slingshot meant it was a joke. That he'd never go after an officer. That he wouldn't dare. *Wrong*," Alvarez said.

Emmerich stepped toward him. "I don't know if the vandalism was a prelude or a harbinger. But I'm sorry."

"Fuck sorry."

Everybody was watching. Nobody moved.

"A deputy's *dead*." Red-faced, Alvarez jabbed an accusing finger at Emmerich, then swept it at the rest of the team.

"Useless," he yelled. "Worse."

Emmerich held the detective's gaze, unshakable, waiting for a moment to speak. Detective Solis approached and put a hand on Alvarez's back. Alvarez shook it off, raised both hands, and stalked out the door.

The air seemed to shimmer with leftover vitriol. Solis merely raised a hand and shook his head.

"I know," Emmerich said.

Keyes' hands hung uselessly at his sides. Rainey said, "Back at it." She took the T-shirt Keyes had given to her and headed to the women's room to change.

Caitlin felt a strange weight pressing on her shoulders. It was emotional, she knew, but it felt like a lead apron, and standing up under its weight seemed staggering.

She grabbed her empty coffee cup and, unable to speak, raised it with a question on her face. Keyes and Emmerich shook their heads. She headed out the door in the general direction of the vending machine.

In the hall, with the cold lights reflecting against the empty darkness outside, she threw the cup in the trash and shoved through the fire door to the stairwell. The invisible lead apron was heated. She needed to get it off of her, get rid of the strangling heat and deathly weight. On the ground floor she banged through the doors into the night.

The cold enveloped her, a shock. The rain was still coming down. She walked away from the vibrantly lit building, down the sidewalk, past dark palm trees. The streets glistened black and green and red with reflected traffic lights. She needed to calm down. She was going to be here all night, all day if it took that, and she needed to regroup and *get her shit together.*

She reached a small outdoor parking lot, slowed, and turned her face to the rain. After a minute, the lead apron no longer felt hot. Her hair and shirt were soaked through. The weight remained.

Parked nearby in the lot was Emmerich's dented Suburban. The back end was a shiny mess of crumples and scraped paint, a half-torn bumper. She peered back at the building. Lights ablaze, catching her. She walked around to the far side of the Suburban and leaned against it.

Cool. The hell. Off.

The building's lights reflected from the SUV's side mirror. The glass had a crack in it. She saw herself: hot-eyed, ashamed, enraged.

She was more than ever convinced the killer was a cop's kid.

Like her. Raised in Blue World, from day one. Bathed in it, baptized, submerged in it.

He was like a dark, fissured reflection of her.

Cop World. Dad in the morning, putting on his aftershave and his Smith & Wesson .38. Watching him and loving it, feeling the pride, always hearing the needle of worry beneath her mom's send-off: *Be safe.*

Good times, Dad walking her through the sheriff's station, holding her hand, introducing her to his colleagues. Bad times. Dad drunk and raging. Mack Hendrix, senior homicide detective, losing it, in public, at Sizzler, because the case from hell was scooping out his insides. Because the case had taken a physical toll on him that nobody would realize for decades. Caitlin with her fork in her hand, food in her mouth that she all at once thought would choke her. Mack backhanding his drink from the table. Hearing it shatter on the floor. Her mom moving to clean it up, and Mack saying, sharp as a rifle crack, "Leave it, Sandy."

The glass wasn't what Sandy Hendrix left. Eventually, Mack was.

And across the Sizzler that night, two of her classmates had been watching.

Later, at school, those schoolmates snarked to their clique, within her earshot, about *Captain Crazy.*

Now, the rain hit Caitlin's shoulders, a fall of icy needles. She felt alone, as alone as at that moment in school.

The odds of solving this case were far worse than she had imagined. And it wasn't just the killer who was ahead of them. With tension eating through the task force, capturing the UNSUB would be harder than ever.

The sense of loss and helplessness broke through her last defenses. She seemed transparent to the rain. As if it were ice-picking through her skin, her heart, hitting the ground as if she were nothing. It turned her blindingly hot.

"*Fuck.*"

She smashed her elbow into the Suburban's side mirror.

The glass broke. The sound, the *crack*, felt cleansing. Her energy returned, sharp and bright. She inhaled. Felt present again, felt cleansed. The rain retreated to purifying coldness, running off her face and shoulders.

Half the glass in the mirror had fallen out. She felt a twinge of regret.

"Oops."

She would have to tell Emmerich about that. Apologize. Write it up for the after-action report. Send it into the maw of the Bureau's filing system. Have it go on her permanent record.

Worth it, she thought. For the cathartic release.

Her vision felt honed, the shapes of surrounding buildings razor-edged. Her pulse echoed in her ears when she exhaled. She bent and cleaned up the slice of glass that had fallen from the mirror. Her arm was stinging.

Under the reflection of a streetlight, she saw the silver shine—a sliver of the mirror embedded in her arm. She wiped her hand on her jeans and went to pick the flake from her skin. She stopped. The chip of glass looked alive with light.

The wave gathered itself again. The night swelled, and loomed, and bore down once more. She stared at the sliver of glass. It didn't sting enough.

Don't.

You've been here before, she thought. Long ago. The scars on her arms reminded her. Her tattoos reminded her.

Back away. Swim to shore. Don't.

She pressed the sliver of mirror in and drew it through her flesh.

She sliced a cut on her forearm. Blood rose and beaded. Pain flooded her system.

The chill of the rain disappeared. The rain itself seemed to evaporate. The fatigue vanished. The night. Everything distilled to the brilliant pulsing bead of glass pain she herself had given rise to.

She felt exhilaration and relief. She felt soothed and punished. She felt *control*.

She knew, deep down, that it was an illusion. That shame would soon follow. In the moment, she didn't care.

She stood in the dark and tugged the silvered mirror from her flesh. She put it in her pocket.

31

In the morning, the storm blew out. Under the rising sun, the streets glistened in shades of gold and oil-slick. Caitlin emerged from the hotel elevator and finished a text to Sean.

> Hope so. Haven't booked
> flight to OAK yet. Depends
> on today.

Whether she made it back to Berkeley for Christmas, or New Year's, or at all, depended on how the violence of the last twelve hours played out. The two murders in El Segundo, the fourteen-year-old's attempted abduction, the killing of the deputy. The increasingly urgent and rancorous investigation.

She jammed her phone in her back pocket beneath her peacoat. She had her Glock holstered, her handcuffs on the back of her belt, a huge cup of room-brewed coffee, her computer case slung over her shoulder, and lace-up boots for whatever the day turned into. Her black turtleneck covered her arms down to her fingertips.

The lobby clattered with the click-clack of roller suitcases and smelled faintly of pancake syrup. The corporate wallpaper and These-Are-Shapes prints were pinkish in the morning sun, giving her the sense that she was standing inside an enormous mouth. When the doors slid open, a cold breeze rushed in. Rainey stood outside under the portico, one earbud in, speaking on the phone.

"Bo, that's the best I can do. Won't know more until we sync up with the task force. I'm sorry."

Caitlin hung back. Rainey, it seemed, was having the same hate-to-disappoint-you conversation with her husband that Caitlin was holding with Sean.

Above the check-in desk, a television played a network morning show. The hosts should have been talking about cookie decorations and last-minute holiday gifts. Instead, they sat rigidly, peering hard into the camera.

"Southern California is on pins and needles," one said.

The newscast showed scenes of citywide panic. Police roadblocks. People yanking down their Christmas lights and putting up halogen spotlights instead. People packing up and getting out of town.

Caitlin felt a presence at her shoulder. Keyes looked strangely haunted and uncertain, like a deer caught unaware in a meadow. Together they watched the report.

A mother clutched her children and leaned toward a microphone, seemingly angry enough to bite it. "I want to know when the cops are going to catch this killer."

A map of the LA Basin appeared. Crime scenes were marked in red—a vast, indiscriminate, blood-spattered shooting gallery for the Midnight Man.

The elevator chimed and Emmerich walked out. He nodded good morning and they fell in with him. The ride downtown was nearly silent.

This early on a Sunday morning, LAPD headquarters was one of the few busy spots in downtown Los Angeles, along with Skid Row storefront missions and Our Lady of the Angels Cathedral. The streets were empty. But the war room was up and running on acid-based energy, determination, and fear.

As they came through the door, Emmerich said, "We'll get the morning briefing. Then I want Hendrix and Keyes to visit the El Segundo crime scene. Rainey, you go speak to the girl in Torrance, Evie Stevens, who escaped from the UNSUB."

"Will do," Rainey said.

"You've got it," Caitlin said.

She wanted to retrace every step along the path of the previous night's rampage. She wanted to tear into it, expose the UNSUB's deepest roiling needs and wants, and use them to rip off his hood and identify him.

Across the room, Detective Solis seemed dog-eared. His white shirt had wilted. His red tie lay tangled on his desktop. He finished a phone call and walked over.

A Sheriff's Department detective trailed him—Alvarez's partner, Will Durand. The young detective wore jeans and a cool expression. His mouth was a tight line. Everybody was wired.

Solis said, "ME is completing the autopsy on Deputy Ohlmeyer as we speak. I expect preliminary results any minute."

"Good," Emmerich said. "Crime Scene have anything yet?"

"Imminent."

Durand crossed his arms. "I hear you think the killer is the son of a cop."

"Strong possibility," Emmerich said.

"What is that? Trying to dropkick the blame into law enforcement's lap?"

Caitlin, low on sleep but stoked on caffeine and endorphins, shook her head. "Cop's daughter here, detective. Years on patrol myself. I'm the one who realized the Midnight Man might be a cop's kid. And we're including federal agents in the search pool. So back it up."

At Caitlin's side Rainey stood like a strong safety ready to charge downfield and tackle anybody who crossed her line of sight. Keyes seemed to stand several extra inches taller than normal. Durand's neck retracted, maybe in surprise.

Emmerich spoke mildly, but his gaze could have sanded the man's skin off. "It's our considered, unanimous opinion. Make use of it. It will narrow the search field for the killer."

Solis held up a hand. "We are making use of it, even though some of us disagree with that opinion. But no matter what we think of the possibility, it stays in this room. We keep this suspicion confidential."

He paused to eye each of them. "The UNSUB is at large. Press is baying for an arrest. If the idea that the Midnight Man is connected to the police gets out there, things go nuts."

Caitlin understood the instinct, but resisted it. She opened her mouth to speak, and Solis shook his head at her.

"Nobody mentions this unless we get convincing evidence to support it," Solis said. "It would be a disaster. There'd be media hysteria. We'd lose public confidence. Stop getting tips, witnesses wouldn't know whether to trust us when we interview them. No." His gaze sizzled. "And before you say anything, I have the backing of the brass on this. It comes from the top."

Emmerich's composure was uncrackable, but Caitlin recognized a pewter chill in his eye. "Understood."

"Not off the record, not on deep background, nothing."

"We're here to assist." The metallic tinge spread to Emmerich's voice. "Glad we agree."

At his desk, Solis' phone rang. He fixed them with a final stare, then strode across the room to answer it. Durand lingered a moment, more abashed than when he'd arrived, and followed.

Keyes took off his glasses and cleaned them on the hem of his shirt. A self-soothing gesture, Caitlin thought.

"That was fun," he said.

Rainey's voice dropped to a murmur. "Pulling up the drawbridge."

Emmerich picked up a file from the table. "Comes with the territory."

Caitlin watched Solis walk away. He wasn't wrong about what would happen if their suspicions about the UNSUB leaked. But keeping the information within this room could throttle the investigation. It eliminated the chance that the people she thought most likely to know and identify the suspect—members of law enforcement—would learn what they needed to know.

"I know the pressure's intensifying," Emmerich said evenly. "That's for me to deal with. Don't let it affect you. I'm the heat shield. You're doing your jobs. That's what matters—keep it up." He checked that they'd all heard him clearly. "Back to work."

Caitlin felt a wash of loyalty, and despair, and gratitude. "El Segundo. On it."

Emmerich's gaze momentarily warmed. She grabbed her coat, said, "Let's hit it," and walked with Keyes toward the door.

Halfway across the floor, she caught a shift in the air. At his desk, Solis absently dropped the phone onto its cradle, face agape as he peered at his computer screen.

"Keyes," she said.

They slowed.

Solis turned his head and met her gaze. He looked gutted.

She veered through a maze of desks toward his. The morning sunshine cut a vicious stripe across Solis' face. His eyes were shot through with pain.

"Detective?" she said.

He said nothing for a moment. "Autopsy—ME recovered two rounds from Deputy Ohlmeyer's body."

The news didn't surprise her. She and Rainey had reached the football field almost immediately after the shooting. They'd probably driven the killer to flee before he was able to dig the spent bullets from the deputy's body.

"Fast-tracked those rounds to forensics," Solis said. "Ballistics just came back."

He turned his computer screen so she and Keyes could see.

On screen was the ballistics report on the deputy's shooting. The round that killed him had been identified: 230-grain jacketed hollow-point Winchester Ranger T-series ammunition.

She went very still. Looked at Solis.

"It's an LAPD-issued round," he said.

32

The shock Caitlin felt came not as a sonic boom, but as a hush. LAPD ammunition had killed Deputy Ohlmeyer. Detective Solis stared numbly at his computer screen. Across the room, Emmerich sensed the change in the air. He looked up, saw her face, and crossed the floor.

He read the report on the computer screen and stilled.

The room's cold light seemed purifying. Caitlin's nerve endings thrummed beneath her skin. Confirmation. It felt great. It felt clarifying. And horrifying. And portentous.

Solis picked up his phone and punched a number. "Alvarez. Get down here."

He slumped and put both hands over his face.

The news hit the task force like a log barreling downhill. Twenty minutes later, gathered at Solis' desk, the detectives slumped, flattened. Solis spoke in a monotone.

"We need to look at current and former officers who might have a disturbed son."

Weisbach let out a rough breath. "How broad a look? How are we going to define 'disturbed?'"

"We don't have to start from scratch," Emmerich said. "Like we've been saying, we're sure this young man has been in contact with the justice system."

His tone was measured. Caitlin was certain he was restraining his relief and excitement over the ballistics evidence.

"The Midnight Man's more than a defiant kid. He's been in trouble from an early age. He'll have an arrest record—juvenile, adult, or both. He'll be known for persistent aggression. Fire setting or animal cruelty. Vandalism. Gratuitous lying and indifference to the pain of others." He turned. "And Dr. Keyes has been cross-referencing employee and court records."

Keyes nodded. "Between the LAPD, LASD, CHP, federal law enforcement agencies, and police departments in Los Angeles County, it adds up to more than forty thousand active sworn officers and staff. Not all records are available. Some juvenile proceedings are sealed. What I have is partial, but it's a starting point. Especially if we focus first on LAPD connections." He paused for emphasis. "Thirty-seven initial possibilities."

Weisbach nodded crisply. "Send them. We'll split up the names and begin contacting people."

Solis said, "Start digging, people."

Keyes sent the list, and the detectives scattered. Emmerich motioned to the team.

"Get to last night's crime scenes while the sun's still up."

Caitlin grabbed her coat. "I'm there."

Emmerich turned to Solis. The circles under the LAPD detective's eyes were the color of fireplace ash.

"Whatever you need, detective," Emmerich said.

"He's devolving," Solis said. "Figure out what his next play will be."

The train slid along, smooth, humming, the city a slur outside the windows, sunlight hissing in his eyes as they passed a string of buildings. *Light dark light dark light.* He shoved the brim of his cap lower on his forehead, tugged the hoodie around his ears, and turned up the music. "Winter in My Heart," by Vast. The claw marks on his back, the bite, throbbed.

A dog. Why did it have to be a dog?

The Red Line train swept underground. Soon it decelerated into the swooping futurescape of the Hollywood/Highland station. When the doors opened, he eyed the people flowing out, flowing in, walking past him, not seeing him. He was a still point in the arterial pulse.

A Doberman. No sign of it when he scoped the house. It had simply appeared, loosed on him. Trained, undoubtedly—aimed, sniffing, waiting for *him*. Ready to attack.

His opponents' legion was fighting back.

Fuck them.

The doors kissed shut, silent behind the music. A woman walked toward him, about to take a seat. He spread his legs. She moved away. He tugged again at the hoodie. The scratches on his neck had scabbed over, the swipe that Arcadia woman had given him. They didn't hurt anymore, but they were identifying marks, and nobody else needed to see them. The train accelerated. It tongued north through the tunnel toward the Universal City / Studio City stop.

That dog. A beautiful Dobie, and it had been deliberately *turned* against him. The scratches burned like a bastard. He'd seen its eyes, smooth marbles in the dark, lost and distorted as it lunged at him.

Everybody lied.

The train slid through the tunnel. The one time he skipped doing mommydaddy first, and they'd sent a dog after him. Too cowardly to save their shrieking spawn themselves. Dog didn't know what was happening. The dog obeyed. The dog was loyal. Threw itself into danger on mommydaddy's orders. Didn't know he might have had to kill it. *Merry Christmas.*

Using the dog infuriated him. Thwarting his work infuriated him.

Last night—Torrance—wouldn't happen again. Sheriffs, multiple pursuit vehicles, even the FBI. The actual Eff-Bee-fuckin'-Eye out to get him. From the cemetery he'd seen them, two agents on the football field. Reapers, guns gleaming as they scythed silently across the flooded grass in the storm.

One of them had looked right at him. Red hair, pale face, scorching eyes. Or maybe she'd looked right past him, but he hadn't chanced it.

He'd ducked. She *saw* things. Agent Darkstar. A black hole. Get too close, you couldn't escape. She was an event horizon. See him, and she would have him. For good. He'd be gone.

From now on, the mommydaddies would experience the full show. Spawn first. Dog if they forced him. They would *see*, and know their error. Trying to get him was a mistake. A bad one.

The train slid through the night of the tunnel. A new song came on. "The Space in Between" by How to Destroy Angels. He turned it up.

33

The afternoon had deepened to cobalt by the time Caitlin and Keyes got to El Segundo. The low white sun was pitching toward the Pacific. The last moments of crystalline daylight, just after four thirty.

A gasoline tang from the Chevron refinery hung sharp in the air. The roar of turbofan engines reverberated every ninety seconds from LAX.

At the small home that belonged to the Bingham family, Day-Glo police tape crisscrossed the front door. An El Segundo patrol car was parked at the curb outside. Caitlin greeted the officer at the wheel, then joined Keyes on the flagstone walk in front of the house.

"What drew the killer here?" she said.

Keyes turned in a three-sixty. Houses crowded the sidewalk, shoulder to shoulder. Parked cars lined the street. A lone lemon tree stood in the Binghams' front yard.

"Whim," he said.

"This is from Dr. Data Analysis? Try again."

Keyes stepped back with something approaching alarm. "I'm not being flip. Sorry."

"And I don't mean to grind your gears. But I do need you to elaborate." She raised a hand. *Proceed.*

He turned in another, slower, circle. "The Midnight Man's target selection depends on several factors. Use the freeways. Stick to the comfort zone. Avoid homes on dead-end streets, find dark spots, steer clear of police stations. But some of it—I still picture him rolling hard, music pounding, seeing only as far as the headlights. His ultimate decision about where to strike will be impulse."

She caught a fresh sting of petroleum on a gust of wind. The sky sank to indigo. Christmas lights were coming on. It was deep in December, but the holidays had blurred past her. Now Christmas decorations struck her as garish and out of place.

She nodded at the Bingham home. "This house. Evaluate its location along with the home in Torrance and the route he took to escape. Can that tell you which of the two buffer zones he's using as his home base right now? Where he is tonight?"

"His hunting zones separate sharply into north and south sectors. Roughly the San Fernando Valley versus the LA Basin. I think the Santa Monica Mountains form a mental barrier for him. When he leaves his home base to hunt, he sticks to whichever side of the hills he's on."

"So he's nesting downtown right now."

"Probably."

At LAX, a heavy jet went to takeoff thrust and poured down the runway. The roar reverberated through Caitlin's chest. The jet lifted off into the dusk. As it rose into the scintillating sunset, its thunder faded. Caitlin felt her phone buzzing in her pocket before she heard it.

Keyes pulled his phone out at the same moment she did. They both had a text from Rainey.

Call just came in to the task force from
Hannah Guillory's father. Vandalism in
their neighborhood.

Keyes looked up. "Vandalism? Another police car?"

Caitlin's phone rang. She didn't recognize the number. "Hendrix."

"Caitlin?"

The voice was young. It was scared.

"Hannah?" Caitlin said.

"You told me I could call you," the girl said. "Are you coming? Here to my house? Because I think the Midnight Man is watching us."

34

At the curb outside LAPD headquarters, Keyes jumped out of the idling Suburban. The complex's icy walls were starkly lit. Cold air soaked through the vehicle.

Rainey jumped in. "Thanks."

With a wave, Keyes shut the door. Caitlin pulled out.

"Patrol unit is on scene at the Guillorys', detectives en route," Rainey said.

"Good. Hannah sounded freaked. And I want to see firsthand what's going on."

It was around five P.M. and full dark had settled over the city. Downtown was a yin-yang of night-black sky and dazzlingly lit streets. The evening was bustling. Shoppers were out, restaurants full, holiday concerts in swing. A Lakers game was scheduled to tip off at Staples Center. Caitlin rolled by City Hall and past a church with a banner strung above the doors. *Welcome the Prince of Peace.*

Her stomach tightened. "*Gloria in excelsis. I am beyond good and evil.*"

"Legion of the night. The newborn king."

Caitlin shook her head. "Impossible. I don't care if this killer was born without a conscience, or whether he was made into a monster. He's intelligent. Vicious. And sane."

"Somebody topped off your iced tea with vinegar," Rainey said.

"He's not beyond anything. He knows the terms 'right' and 'wrong.'"

"But doesn't *feel* them," Rainey said. "So he doesn't feel bound by them."

"Sucks for him that feelings don't count under the law."

Caitlin accelerated onto the freeway. Traffic was swift. Headlights formed a shining river.

"He knows that laws exist," she said. "There's right and wrong. And, for us, *righting* a wrong. That's never beyond good and evil."

"No? Thinking everything you do is righteous makes it easy to fall into the shadows. And being God is above your pay grade."

Caitlin ground her hands on the wheel. "I don't want to be God. Or even an avenging angel. I just want to protect others."

And she wanted to keep control over her life. The sleeves of her sweater covered her arms down to her thumbs. Nobody could see the fresh cuts on her arms. There were more of them now.

She felt both powerful and clearheaded. And confused, and drowning. Each cut staved off submersion for a few pure moments.

"The Midnight Man's just trying to drill a hole into children's heads with those words," she said. "Hitting them with an emotional hollow-point."

"So he can leave them alive, but blown apart." Rainey exhaled. "We do whatever it takes to keep him away from any more kids."

"A-goddamn-men."

She said it with conviction, but a voice deep in her head whispered, *Whatever it takes? Really? You ready to own what that could mean?*

"Using deadly force against a teen …"

Rainey gave Caitlin a hard look. "If he was endangering my life or the lives of others? Without hesitation." She turned and stared through the windshield. "And it would be like shooting myself in the heart. We don't want it to come to that."

When they reached Bay Rise and pulled off the freeway onto the Guillorys' street, Caitlin said, "Damn." The road was crowded with cop cars—and news vans.

"Exactly what Mina Guillory didn't want," she said.

But the news crews weren't aiming their cameras and microphones at the Guillory home. TV lights blasted the hill behind houses further down the street, where billboards overlooked the neighborhood. Caitlin parked the Suburban near the corner, well away from the cameras' glare. There was a nerve-racking buzz in the air. She and Rainey walked down the street.

"Jesus on a poodle," Rainey said.

One of the billboards had been painted wall to wall with red eyes.

Dave Guillory opened the door six inches wide. Body-blocking the entrance, he sized up Caitlin and Rainey with mistrust. He was a wiry man with ropy arms inked with tattoos. Caitlin and Rainey held up their FBI credentials.

From inside, Mina called, "Get them in and shut the door, Dave. Now."

When Caitlin stepped into the front hall, she could almost smell the sense of siege. In the living room, two LAPD patrol officers were speaking to a detective. Mina Guillory held little Charlie on one hip.

Dave gestured toward the cops. "Join the party."

From the back of the house, Hannah emerged, running. She slowed, sliding on the parquet floor in her socks.

"You came." Her eyes were too wide, her face flushed.

"Told you we would," Caitlin said.

Her parents turned sharply toward the girl. Mina said, "You phoned the FBI?"

Abruptly Hannah blushed a deeper red. "I …"

"I told her to call if she needed anything," Caitlin said.

Mina hoisted Charlie higher on her hip. "Then do your thing. Whatever it takes to make this nightmare go away."

Caitlin put a hand on Hannah's shoulder. "Let me and Special Agent Rainey talk to the police officers for a minute. Okay?"

"Okay." Hannah's reply was almost a sigh of relief.

In the living room, Caitlin and Rainey introduced themselves. The LAPD detective told them that thus far they'd found no witnesses to the billboard vandalism. And no other evidence that the Midnight Man had returned to the neighborhood, much less the Guillorys' property.

Rainey drew Caitlin to the front window, out of the family's earshot. She put her hands on her hips.

"Something's off." She hung a long, slow gaze on the spotlighted billboard. "This would mark a brazen change in his MO. And the drawings strike me as … wrong."

With her phone, Rainey snapped photos of the billboard.

Caitlin glanced at the cops near the Christmas tree. "The fact that the killer paints crime scenes with bloody eyes has been *closely* held." She crossed her arms. "And we haven't heard a peep to suggest that it's leaked."

"He painted eyes on the nursery walls in Arcadia. Plenty of people saw that. Patrol officers, crime scene technicians, EMTs, the ME's staff … It's possible."

"Why would anybody besides the UNSUB paint the billboard? Publicity? Chaos?"

Rainey's lips pursed. After a second she shook her head. "No. There's no evidence that somebody else is the culprit. The Midnight Man had to have come back here and done it."

From the living room came a flurry of activity. The LAPD detective spoke to Mina and Dave Guillory. The parents conferred, nodded, and ushered Hannah down the hall. As the girl headed toward her room, she darted to Caitlin's side.

"We're leaving. Will you come with?"

The detective ambled over. "Think it would be a good idea for the Guillorys to get away for an hour or two. Until we can process the scene out there. And until the media leaves."

Mina said, "I called a friend. We're going to hang at their place until the spotlights shut off." Charlie fussed on her hip. "Hannah, grab some books and snacks, and Charlie's toys."

Caitlin patted Hannah on the back. "Go on. I'm not leaving."

Hannah skipped down the hall to her room. Caitlin lowered her voice.

"Loading the family in the minivan and driving off with a police escort will only draw the attention of those television cameras," she said.

"What do you suggest?" the detective said.

"Misdirection."

Hannah knelt and kissed the cat on the head. "You'll be okay, Silky."

She stood and schlepped her backpack onto her shoulders. Silky, a blue Burmese, almost silvery in his sleekness, rubbed against her legs. Hannah held out her hand to Charlie.

"Ready for our big escape?"

"Ready." He nodded extravagantly and put his index finger to his lips, as Hannah had shown him. "Shh."

It was dramatic, but Caitlin didn't mind. Letting the kids feel that they were having an adventure was better than having them feel cornered and helpless. She and the LAPD detective walked the family to the kitchen.

Rainey had driven the Guillorys' pickup past the news vans. The uniformed officers were out on the street, canvassing neighbors about the graffiti on the billboard. In the kitchen, Dave Guillory opened the sliding glass door and led his wife and kids out the back.

The family who lived directly behind the Guillorys had agreed to let them use their yard for a quiet trek.

Caitlin and the LAPD detective helped the kids and parents over the fence. When they reached the street, Rainey was waiting with their truck.

Caitlin retrieved the Suburban. Then she and Rainey escorted them out of the neighborhood and away from the cameras.

At a quiet apartment building in Long Beach, they accompanied the Guillorys up the steps to their friends' door. The cold air had the honeyed brush of the ocean. Christmas lights were strung inside the apartment's front window.

Mina Guillory hugged the woman who let them in. "Thanks, hon. Couple hours, that's all we need."

On the walkway, Rainey scanned the complex, though Caitlin had taken countermeasures to avoid being followed. Neither of them had seen any signs of a tail.

Dave Guillory nudged Hannah through the door, but the little girl turned to Caitlin.

"Are you coming in?"

"No. We need to get back to work."

"Don't go." Hannah squeezed her hands into fists.

Caitlin crouched in front of her. "You've got your books, right?"

Hannah nodded tightly. "*The Golden Compass*."

"You've got Dr. Seuss for Charlie—I saw you stick *Horton Hears a Who* in your backpack."

"It's his favorite." Hannah's voice was small.

Inside, Charlie raced around the living room, laughing at high pitch.

"I think you'd better read to him."

"Maybe I'd better," Hannah said. "Or he'll get overstimulated and have a meltdown."

"Big sisters always have that responsibility, don't they?" In her pocket, Caitlin's phone pinged with an arriving email. "And there's the office, telling me to hop to it."

She smiled. After a few seconds, Hannah made a half-hearted attempt to smile back.

"And you've got my phone number."

Hannah exhaled.

Caitlin stood. She held up her hand and Hannah gave her a high five. Caitlin nodded crisply.

As she and Rainey descended the stairs, she took out her phone. She opened the email while she walked to the Suburban.

RE: NEW MM VIDEO.

"Whoa. It's a new clip of the killer."

Caitlin slowed. As with the other videos, this one was high-gain white, a photo negative of the UNSUB. As with the others, he was sauntering down a nighttime street. Hoodie, ball cap, baggy jeans.

Rainey said, "CCTV?"

"Looks like a home surveillance camera. Don't know where it was captured—hold on."

The UNSUB's step had the familiar looseness, but something about this video seemed to have a different intensity. He appeared less … what, postcoital? More focused. Hungry.

He passed a street sign. Caitlin paused the playback.

"Whitehorse Drive," she said.

"I've seen that." Rainey's brows knit. "Tonight." She pulled out her own phone. Checked the map. "Whitehorse is eight blocks away from the Guillorys' street."

Caitlin's pulsed ticked up. In the corner of the screen was a time stamp. "Video's dated." She looked up. "Tonight."

Rainey's eyes widened. "The UNSUB was definitely there."

"So he must have painted the eyes on the billboard."

Even as she said it, her voice drifted. Something seemed wrong. She zoomed on the time stamp.

Caitlin gasped so loudly that Rainey grabbed her hand and turned the phone to see the screen.

Rainey read. "Time stamp says 6:11 P.M."

"Twenty minutes ago."

"Oh, hell no."

"*Tonight*. The killer's there *now*."

Rainey broke for the Suburban, placing a call as she ran. "I need police dispatched to Whitehorse Drive," she nearly shouted to the 911 operator, giving her FBI badge number.

Caitlin raced at Rainey's heels. Her hands shook. On the screen of her phone, the UNSUB stalked down the darkened street toward homes full of unsuspecting families.

35

When Caitlin squealed around the corner onto Whitehorse Drive, every shred of hope drained from her.

Police cars and ambulances filled the street.

This time, Rainey was the one who gasped. "No. Oh, Jesus."

The flashing blue light strip in the windshield of the Suburban took on the fevered vibration of a migraine aura. Caitlin yanked the vehicle to the curb and had the door open before she remembered to put the SUV in Park and kill the engine.

She rushed with Rainey to a house in the middle of the block. She tried to walk and to avoid shoving aside EMTs and uniformed cops but couldn't keep herself from running up the front walk. The door of the ranch house gaped wide. She stopped at the threshold.

Emmerich stood inside, his face bleak. He wore latex gloves, and paper booties over his hiking shoes.

"The family?" Caitlin said.

He turned his head to spot her. He took a beat. Seemed off balance. "The father's dead. Mother critically injured. Gunshot wound to the chest. She's on her way to Harbor-UCLA Medical Center."

"Kids?"

The blue flashing lights were joined by red. They lashed the walls, and Emmerich's face, and Rainey's shoulder as she pulled on gloves and booties and spoke in a low voice to the officer logging people into the scene. Caitlin didn't move.

"The kids?" she said again.

"Alive."

Caitlin found that she too had put on gloves and booties. She handed back the pen and saw her signature on the log-in sheet. She was in the house, following Emmerich down an entry hall that felt like a throat.

"But?" she said.

His voice went flat. "But the kids were tied up. Drawings of eyes were cut into their palms with a knife."

Caitlin breathed through gritted teeth. Emmerich led her around a corner, past forensic techs fingerprinting the door to the master bedroom. Inside, half visible, a man sprawled by the foot of the bed. He'd been cut down as he charged at the attacker.

A boy's bedroom was across the hall. Caitlin stepped in.

On the wall, in the child's blood, was written TRUE NIGHT BREED.

Caitlin stood before it. How much blood did the killer claw from the hand of an agonized kid to write that message?

Voices tumbled around the hallway and the front of the house. Outside the curtained window, the migraine lights shrieked and spun. On the boy's bedroom floor, below the windowsill, Lego blocks were scattered.

The killer was long gone.

Caitlin felt short of breath. Her chest seemed to have a steel band cinched around it. She turned and walked past Emmerich and Rainey, out the front door, past the ambulance and uniformed officers and black-and-whites with squawking radios. The spinning lights felt like the blades of a sickle, slicing her across the eyes. She headed blindly down the street.

She pressed her fists to her forehead. Dug her nails into her palms.

The kids in that house had tried to protect their family against intrusion—with *toys*. The UNSUB had walked right over them.

The FBI did nothing to stop him.

They'd been literally around the corner earlier, at the Guillorys' house. They'd left. Left the neighborhood, left the family in the house on Whitehorse Drive bare and exposed. They had failed them.

She found herself in the middle of the street beside the Suburban. The night felt icily hot, slippery, atomized.

The Midnight Man seeped through cracks like black oil, and she couldn't get a grip on him. She felt utterly defeated.

She put a hand on the Suburban and staggered around to the far side. In the dark, she pressed her back to the side the SUV and slid to the ground.

The wave was gathering itself again. It was a darker dark than water, colder, heavier, malevolent. It was a rising wall of rage and fear, inexorable, inescapable. She scraped at the scabs on her forearms. A row of cuts now ran between her wrists and her elbows. She wrestled off her peacoat and shoved up the sleeves of her sweater and scratched everywhere the cuts could be torn open.

The pain was insufficient.

She wanted a razor blade. Needed it. The blade was clean. The blade executed her intent. The blade drew straight and shockingly true. The desire was overpowering.

She took out her drop-point knife.

Just one cut, she thought. One cleansing, flashbulb burst of pain. Then she'd be in control.

Under the glow of a nearby streetlight, she saw her reflection in the gleaming surface of the knife. She looked indistinct. Distorted. Beaten.

The knife trembled in her hand. *Just once.*

She turned her left wrist up, toward the night sky. Her skin was winter pale, except where it was scored with half a dozen stripes. The knife hovered over her arm.

She hesitated. *Just once* was a lie. There was no *once*. Just as there was no such thing as being in complete control.

But there was something else. She knew there was. Trying to reach her.

Creating the pain would be so easy. All it would require was gravity. Let the knife fall toward her arm, let it punish, bring forth blood, flood her system with adrenaline. Resisting was harder. Why defy the urge, when she wanted, lusted for, the pain? Why hold back, when the night, the earth, the seething angels that bit at her conscience, said, *Do it?* Why fight the monstrous beautiful pull of the wave?

The knife gleamed, light licking it. Yet she didn't cut.

Sean's words came back to her. *I need you to remember that you're not alone.*

The blade waited.

Her voice came as a harsh exhalation. "What am I doing?"

Sean hadn't just been mouthing platitudes. He'd been serious. As serious as blood. And here she was, curled on a curb, leaning against the wheel well of an SUV, thinking of calming herself with a knife.

She needed to get her ass off the ground and get inside the crime scene.

Forcing herself to breathe, she sheathed the knife. For a second she stared into the night.

The cold centered her. She closed her eyes and breathed in, breathed out. More of Sean's words came back to her. *The eyes. Who are they watching? Who's supposed to see?*

She thought. The eyes painted on the billboard near the Guillorys' house—they seemed to be peering down. Not, as at the other crime scenes, directly ahead.

Why?

As she thought, she opened her eyes and refocused. Her gaze lengthened to take in the spread of Whitehorse Drive. And the street sign at the corner, where the emailed video had shown the killer walking less than an hour earlier.

She stood. Shoving down her sleeves and grabbing her coat, she headed for the street sign. Her pulse pounded.

Whitehorse Drive ended in a T-junction at the corner. Beyond it, across from the street sign, there was nothing but a vacant lot. No homes, no buildings.

No surveillance cameras.

"The hell," she said.

She ran across the street to the vacant lot, pulling out her phone. When she rewatched the video, her blood turned colder than the air.

The camera in the video hovered, not always steadily, several feet above eye level—approximately at the height of the street sign. *Hell no.* She looked at the night sky. The stars sparkled, breaking through the haze of light pollution. She heard muffled conversation and police radios up the street, and the distant rush of traffic on the 110 freeway a few blocks away. Directly overhead, there was no sound. No planes, no helicopters, no birds.

It was quiet, but how many times recently had she heard a buzzing noise?

She ran across the intersection and up Whitehorse Drive, back to the crime scene. At the front door she stopped.

"Emmerich," she shouted. "Somebody's been watching everything with a drone."

36

Inside the ranch house, Emmerich turned, alarmed. He left the detective he was speaking to and came out to the porch.

"Drone," Caitlin said.

She explained in a brusque burst, playing the video as she walked with him along the sidewalk toward the street sign.

"Who sent the video to you?" Emmerich said.

"It came to the LAPD. I'm on the distribution list." She forwarded it to him.

He continued walking as he phoned Keyes. "Need you to trace the incoming path of an email."

At the dark corner of Whitehorse Drive, Emmerich played the video of the Midnight Man. His breath wreathed his face in the cold air.

"It's almost steady, but at the start of the video, the camera seems to be in motion," he said.

"The drone getting into position?"

"It had to have been following him for at least a few seconds before this. The video's been edited to appear that it was a stationary camera and he simply walked into frame."

His phone rang. He answered, "Keyes. Talk." He listened, said, "Thanks," and hung up. "The email address has been spoofed."

"So who sent the video to the LAPD?"

"And why camouflage the original address?"

"Today's version of an anonymous tip to the cops?" Caitlin said. "Was it a journalist? A random voyeur? A vigilante?"

Emmerich glanced skyward and peered around the street. "Possibly it was a lucky break. Somebody could have surreptitiously launched their drone earlier when the LAPD was called to investigate the billboard vandalism."

"Undoubtedly illegal."

"FAA rules would preclude flying at night, or near a police operation. Not to mention invasion of privacy if the drone filmed someone's family or personal activity without permission."

It made sense. But from the way Emmerich was examining the night—like an owl, eyes alert—he had the same doubts Caitlin did. Luck seemed too fortuitous. And as a detective, she'd become cynical enough to think coincidence rarely existed.

"This isn't the first time somebody has intruded in the investigation," she said.

His head swiveled.

"When Hannah came downtown to the war room. Somebody lured her out of the canteen at LAPD headquarters. He claimed to be a detective."

Emmerich spun and walked briskly back toward the crime scene, with Caitlin hurrying alongside.

"Get downtown," he said. "Check it out."

The war room still felt brightly dismal, but the tinsel had been restored to the top of the big-screen TV. When Caitlin swept in, the room was busy. Detective Weisbach was at her desk. Eyes gritty but energized—possibly with equal doses of apprehension and purpose. As Caitlin approached, she stood and shook her head.

"I checked—the man who claimed to be a detective when Hannah was here hasn't been identified."

"Even with video covering the main entrance to the building? Have you narrowed it down?" Caitlin said.

Weisbach spread her arms, gesturing around. "Multiple buildings in the complex, multiple points of entry. He could be one of many people who signed in before the incident."

"How many is many?"

"Over a hundred."

"Let me see the videos."

"It's hours' worth."

"All I have right now is time."

Weisbach sent Caitlin a link and she opened her laptop.

"We presume he isn't actually an LAPD detective, patrol officer, or employee," Weisbach said. "And that he may have presented a fake ID when he signed in at the desk."

Caitlin cued up the surveillance videos. She found herself holding her breath.

The videos unspooled, silent, jerky, minute after minute running by in accelerated time. She felt a queasy itch beneath her skin. After a few minutes, she realized why.

She feared that she might recognize the fake detective as the Ghost.

But she could identify no one. Not a single person who entered the lobby on the videos looked familiar. She felt no spooky sense of déjà vu. She was simultaneously relieved, baffled, and disappointed.

She sat down at the conference table and scraped her fingers through her hair.

Did the man who spoke to Hannah also send the drone video? If so, why the subterfuge?

She realized how twisted she had become about the Ghost. He had wormed his way deep into her head. There was zero—less than zero—evidence that he was in Los Angeles, or somehow involved in the Midnight Man case.

She wondered if she and Sean had spun an equally baseless conspiracy theory that he was involved with the bombings. That they'd tangled themselves in emotional barbed wire.

She texted Emmerich.

> No luck identifying the man
> who tricked Hannah into

talking. No link I can find
to the drone video. Will
continue digging.

A cold finger seemed to run up her spine. Damn. She had spirited
the Guillory family away from the news cameras. But if a drone had
been hovering, it could have followed her. She would never have heard
it above the Suburban's engine.

She phoned Mina Guillory.

"Agent Hendrix. Is something going on?"

"Just checking in to make sure everything's okay."

"Yeah. We're fine. Wanted to get the kids home and put them to
bed, and our friends didn't need so much commotion at their place. We
only got home a minute ago. All the cops and news vans are gone from
our street, but ..."

Caitlin pinched the bridge of her nose. She didn't want to have to
break it to the Guillorys.

"... but we caught sight of police cars in the neighborhood. I heard
what happened."

"Yes."

"He was back in Bay Rise. I'm sorry I got snippy with you earlier
at the house. You were watching out for us. And I'm extremely grateful
you got us far away while"—Mina's voice dropped to a near whisper—
"what happened on Whitehorse Drive was going on."

"It's my job."

Caitlin heard the relief in Mina's voice, and appreciated it, but felt
unsettled as well. "Are there any patrol units on your street?"

"Yeah—absolutely. We let the detectives know we were coming
home. Police officers met us here and searched the house to make sure
it was safe before we came back in. There's a squad car stationed at the
curb outside for our protection."

"Good." That, at least, reassured her. Caitlin said, "Tell Hannah
good night," and ended the call.

She set her phone on the conference table. She should get coffee and calories. Outside, headlights and taillights rivered through the streets, a solid glow. As full night descended, the city had grown ever busier. She stood up.

The Guillorys were all right. The cops were there. But a feeling nagged at her—that she was overlooking something.

"Weisbach," she said. "Where are we with the thirty-seven cops' kids with behavioral issues?"

The detective pressed her fists into the small of her back. "Working through the list. Eight have alibis, most still need to be contacted."

Caitlin nodded. The nagging feeling endured. Did it relate to the Midnight Man? To the bombing case?

She didn't know.

As the evening lengthened, the Guillorys' house fell quiet. The Christmas tree lights sparkled in the living room. Tucked in bed, little Charlie plunged into depthless sleep. Mina and Dave stretched out on the sofa, exhausted, watching television.

The police car sat at the curb with its windows rolled up against the wintry cold. The cop behind the wheel blew on his hands and periodically fired up the engine to run the heater.

Bundled under her covers, Hannah lay dressed in her clothes, holding a hammer, trying to stay awake and keep watch.

In the attic, the Midnight Man hunkered, listening.

37

Mina Guillory squinted an eye open. Her shoulders felt stiff, her fingers chilly. She had dozed off with the TV droning. At her side, Dave was snoring.

The room seemed cold. She fumbled for the remote but before she turned the television off, she felt a draft. She stilled. Cold night air was unquestionably seeping through the house.

The draft was wafting down the hallway. She flipped on a lamp. Beside her on the sofa, her husband stirred.

"What?" he mumbled. Then he was instantly alert. "Mina?"

She stood, her stomach queasy, and walked to the top of the hallway. The draft felt stronger. She flicked the switch for the hall light.

The hatch in the ceiling that led to the attic was open, a yawning black square. Directly beneath it on the carpet were dusty footprints.

"Get the cop."

The baseball bat was leaning against the living room wall. She grabbed it and ran for Charlie's room. Dave tore out the front door toward the police car, yelling like a banshee. Mina raised the bat, threw open Charlie's door, and charged in.

The door smacked the wall. Mina cocked the bat, like Big Papi winding up to swing, teeth gritted.

In his bed, sheets rumpled around his feet, Charlie lay with his butt in the air, sound asleep.

Relief poured through her, then more fear, like a rain of needles. She threw open the closet. Nothing. Outside she heard voices and a slamming car door and feet pounding across the lawn. Charlie stirred. She spun and ducked back into the hall.

The draft wasn't coming from the attic. It was coming from Hannah's room.

She ran toward it, heart racing, fears flailing, as Dave came charging around the hallway corner with the officer.

He pointed. "There."

The door to Hannah's room was open a few inches. The officer said, "Step back, ma'am," but Mina poked the end of the bat against the door and shoved it all the way open. She flipped on the light.

"Jesus lord."

Hannah's bed was empty.

The curtains shivered. The window gaped wide. The screen had been kicked out. Mina and Dave ran to the windowsill. Footprints marked the grass outside. Two sets.

Hannah was gone.

38

Caitlin muscled the Suburban around a corner onto the Guillorys' street. Ahead, Solis and Weisbach braked in front of the house. Everyone jumped out into a night soaked with cold. The home, the road, and nearby intersections were swarming with patrol cars and uniformed officers. LAPD cruisers were parked crossways at corners. Flashlights swung through the bushes in nearby yards. Searching. Overhead, above the dazzle and darkness of the city, the stars raged down.

They were in overdrive, juiced on sick adrenaline. Caitlin caught up with the LAPD detectives as they hurried toward the house. The strain on Weisbach's thin face spoke for them all. If they couldn't locate Hannah in the next few hours, the girl was dead.

Every window at the house blazed with light. The Guillorys were chasing away the night the only way they could and lighting the home like a beacon. *We're here, Hannah.*

Uniformed officers were already inside. In the living room Dave Guillory was digging through papers at a desk near the Christmas tree. Charlie slumped on the sofa in his pajamas, feet dangling, thumb in his mouth. Mina sat beside him, stroking the little boy's hair. When Caitlin and the detectives walked in, she jumped up. Her eyes were as hot as a blowtorch.

"How'd he get in? The police searched the house. We locked up. How?"

"We're going to figure that out," Weisbach said. "But first we need to find your daughter."

Dave pulled out the drawer and dumped it on the desktop. "This has got to be where I put the login password for Hannah's phone. I'm sure."

He continued digging through papers. In the kitchen, several other drawers had been pulled out and rummaged through.

Caitlin spoke evenly, hoping to cool Mina down a few degrees. "I'm playing catch-up. I take it you've searched the house for the phone."

"Every inch. Called it. Not here."

She glanced at Solis. "Cell tower triangulation?"

"The phone company's on it," Solis said.

Dave rifled papers. "But if I can access the account, I'll activate 'find my phone.' Locating it with GPS will be quicker and more accurate. Right?"

"Right," Solis said.

"I should have set that up already. Should have posted the login someplace obvious. But Hannah's so responsible, I didn't think she'd lose the phone. Or that we'd lose ..."

His voice cracked. He clenched his jaw, pressed his fists against the desktop, and breathed.

"Keep looking," Solis said. He turned to Mina. "And you can help us best by telling us everything that happened tonight, down to the last detail. And everything about Hannah."

Mina forcibly calmed herself. "We gave a description of what she's wearing to the patrol officers. We gave them photos of her. We'll give you anything."

Behind them on the sofa, Charlie softly began to cry.

Mina turned sharply, as though to hush him, then went to the couch, sat, and pulled him against her side. Her eyes remained fiery.

A uniform approached. He was young and pale, and from the way he avoided looking at Mina, Caitlin guessed he was the officer who'd been stationed outside the house when Hannah was taken.

"She was apparently wearing street clothes," the officer said. "Her pj's were folded on her desk chair and her Chuck Taylors aren't in the closet."

Caitlin said, "She told me she's been wearing her clothes to bed and trying to stay awake like a sentry."

"That may explain the hammer we found on the floor in her room."

Oh, girl.

"Good chance the phone could be in her pocket," the cop said. His gaze flicked to the backyard. "Or at least that it was when he took her out the window."

The officer's face was drawn. Caitlin knew why. Nobody had searched the attic. Nobody had considered the possibility that the Midnight Man could have been hiding up there.

"Got it," Dave shouted.

Hands shaking, he pulled out his own phone, bent over the desk, and peered back and forth between a Post-it and his screen, typing.

After a couple of shaky wrong entries, his breath left him in a rush. "Here."

He handed Solis his cell. In the center of the screen, overlaid on a map, was a throbbing red dot.

Solis nearly swelled with urgency. He lifted a portable police radio to his lips.

"All units." He rattled off the location of the cell phone.

Mina jumped up from the sofa and clamped her hands around Dave's arm. Pain, hope, and fear poured from Dave in waves. Caitlin felt a sick ache for them. Less than forty-eight hours earlier, she'd become alarmed when Hannah disappeared for ten minutes—at the headquarters of the LAPD. Tonight, Hannah had been swept into a vast and voracious darkness. With the most indiscriminately violent killer Caitlin had ever confronted. How the Guillorys were holding it together, or simply standing, she couldn't conceive.

Charlie slid off the couch and padded over, blanket trailing. He leaned against his father and wrapped his arms around Dave's leg.

Dave stared at the throbbing red dot. "They on their way?"

"Multiple units are on their way," Solis said.

Dave nodded. Caitlin, however, pressed her lips tight. On the map, the red dot pulsed, but didn't move.

Dave scraped his knuckles across his forehead. "I'm going to the location."

"Let our officers handle this," Solis said. "Please."

"I can't sit here. I'm going."

Solis put a hand on Dave's shoulder. "It's safer for everybody to let us do this. For you, our officers, and Hannah."

Dave clenched his fists, took a breath, and stalked to the window. The radio squawked.

"We found it," a staticky voice said.

Dave spun back around. Mina grabbed his hand. Solis turned and walked out the front door.

The Guillorys looked stricken.

Caitlin knew that Solis wanted to hear the news, no matter what it was, out of their earshot. Dave and Mina started after him. Caitlin put a hand on Mina's arm to stop her.

"Give Solis a minute."

Mina tried to shake her off. "That's my daughter out there. Not his."

"But it's a police operation, and he needs to focus. Let him do his job, which is to reduce the danger to Hannah. One minute."

Thinking, the cop on the radio said *it*. Not *her*. And the pulsing red dot hadn't moved an inch.

Though tormented, Mina relented. On the front porch, Solis stood heavily, staring into the distance, listening to the report from the responding officers. Raising a finger, Caitlin asked Mina to stay inside. She stepped out, pulled the door shut, and drew near enough to Solis to hear the voice of a cop at the scene.

"*Laying in the dirt a few feet off the roadway. Face is smashed up pretty bad.*"

Caitlin's legs went stringy.

"*We'll bring it in. Maybe the tech guys can recover data from this thing.*"

Caitlin put a hand against the wall of the house, hoping it wouldn't be obvious that she was steadying herself. Silently praying into the deep. *Thank you. But, please …*

She saw Emmerich, Keyes, and Rainey jump out of a Suburban and jog across the lawn toward them.

Caitlin stepped toward Solis. "If your techs want backup, Keyes is the man. He can get anything broken to sing like an opera star."

Solis nodded. "Bring the phone in. Immediately."

Caitlin waved to Keyes. "You're up."

Solis eyed her. "Phone was thrown onto the roadside three miles from here, at an on-ramp to the Artesia freeway. You read that like I do?"

She nodded. "It took the UNSUB that long to figure out Hannah had the phone on her. He was focused on other things until then. And pitching it out the car window instead of destroying it sends us a message."

"He doesn't plan to use it to communicate."

"He *is* communicating. The Midnight Man's telling us he has her, and more. He's saying, 'I could be taking her anywhere. You'll never find me.'"

Solis' exhaustion was evident from the gray scale of his skin. Caitlin took a calming breath.

"You get to tell the Guillorys we think Hannah's alive," she said. "That's everything they need to know right now."

39

The screen of Hannah's phone was cracked, the glass riven and spidery. The charging port had been choked with mud. But in the Electronics Unit of the LAPD's Technical Investigation Division, Keyes and one of the LAPD's techs had laid the phone on a workbench under high-wattage strip lights. When Caitlin walked in, they were bent over it like neurosurgeons massaging a tiny brain back to life.

The electronics lab reminded Caitlin of the garages of Silicon Valley coders and hardware wizards she knew, packed with laptops, snaking cables, HD screens, soldering irons, and the confident air of swashbuckling nerdmanship. Hannah's phone was connected to power, and as Caitlin hovered, Keyes played with the keyboard. The LAPD tech, a young Latino man in a maroon dress shirt, said, "Now."

Keyes hit a command. The phone's screen lit with a logo.

"Okay."

The tech was calm, but his voice was breathless. Keyes nearly shouted.

He caught the question in Caitlin's eyes. "Don't even breathe. This thing's on life support."

"I'm not even thinking loud thoughts."

It took five more minutes of delicate resuscitation. As they worked, Caitlin dimly heard a helicopter lift off from the heliport on the roof of the building. Then the tech abandoned the forced calm.

"Holy shit," he said.

The phone was failing, but they'd goosed it enough to download its contents to another drive. Keyes mirrored it to a desktop screen and displayed the phone's most recent activity.

"Double holy shit," Caitlin said.

"*High* holy shit," Keyes said.

Hannah had snapped a photo. It showed a dashboard—from the front passenger seat.

"She was in that vehicle." Caitlin saw the time stamp. "Had to be just a minute or two after the UNSUB took her."

She wanted to yell. Wanted to grab the phone and kiss it, to keep herself from slumping over the table and shaking.

The Midnight Man had unquestionably taken Hannah with him alive.

The photo was blurry, poorly exposed. Caitlin could barely grasp the audacity it took to attempt the shot. The killer must have quickly seen what Hannah had done, or tried to do, and thrown the phone out the window.

But did he know she had actually snapped the photo? Wouldn't he have deleted it if he had?

"I think he saw her holding the phone and figured she was trying to call 911, or her parents. Grabbed it from her and chucked it out of the vehicle."

On the desktop, Keyes was manipulating the photo to improve the exposure and resolution.

He brought up the gain. "Vehicle's manufacturer logo is on the steering wheel. It's a Jeep."

The LAPD tech swung a laptop around and searched for images of Jeep dashboards. It took him less than a minute. "Renegade."

Caitlin was on her own phone, texting the task force.

"There's a parking sticker on the windshield," Keyes said. "Hard to isolate because the steering wheel's in the way, and there's exterior glare on the glass. But …"

The tech leaned over Keyes' shoulder. "Sharpen it. There."

The image on the screen turned etched, and distorted. But legible. Distinct, and indisputable.

RVHS.

Above the letters was the logo of a high school mascot—a hawk.

"It's the UNSUB's SUV," Caitlin said.

The tech craned his neck. "Alter the focus."

Keyes zoomed out. In the windshield was a reflection of the driver. Male. Dirty blond, hoodie, ball cap. Caitlin's skin prickled.

"And that," she said, "is the Midnight Man."

Buzzed on an electric thread of hope, Caitlin and Keyes drove back to LAPD headquarters as every law enforcement agency in Los Angeles County got the word: be on the lookout for a late model Jeep Renegade. Inside, Caitlin grabbed a cup of coffee. As she was returning to the war room, her phone rang. She pulled it from her pocket.

SEAN RAWLINS.

"Hey." She heard the rush of energy in her own voice—and the note of surprise at hearing from him.

"Want you to have a heads up," he said.

Engine noise nearly obscured his voice. Turboprop engines. His tone sent her veering to the windows, where she'd have a bit of privacy.

"Sounds like you're on the move," she said.

"On a taxiway lining up for takeoff. Not going to get airmiles for this one."

She stood at the window. The street below was streaming with vehicles, headlights a white flow. Sean was telling her he was on a government flight. His obliqueness told her to hold the news close to the vest.

"The case?" she said.

"Team-building trip to Garlock. SRT will meet us there."

She knew Garlock. She'd driven through. It was a Mojave Desert ghost town—a collection of played-out miners' shacks fifty miles north of Edwards Air Force Base. Garlock was tumbleweeds and hills and brown, brown, brown to the desiccated horizon. And it was sunbaked desert rats who built crazy scrap-lumber cabins and God knows what kind of home-brewed fortresses back in the canyons and gullies.

SRT was the ATF's Special Response Team. Their tactical unit.

The urge to know was like an irresistible salt taste on her tongue. "Whatcha got?"

"The lab completed their chemical analysis of the last two bombs," Sean said. "Managed to identify a detection taggant. EDGN."

Caitlin tried to recall—in the United States, EDGN was added to Semtex, among other high explosives. "US manufacture. Obtained in the country."

"They also identified sourcing for components of the Temescal bomb, including its detonator and barbed wire."

She put a hand against the window. The glass was cold. "What are you searching for out there, Sean?"

"We have a name."

The noise on his end flared. The plane sounded like it was beginning its takeoff roll.

"Going to lose the call in a second," he said. "But want you to know. We have a suspect. We're on our way to a remote cabin he owns."

Caitlin's mouth felt dry. She inhaled slowly, feeling a powerful sense of excitement. And concern.

And she realized what had been nagging at her earlier in the evening. "The barbed wire," she said. "It's not just his signature. It has to symbolize a manifesto. He'll use it again." She kept her voice level. "Watch for booby traps. Stay safe."

"Plan to." He paused. "Talk to you afterward."

Her heart felt wrapped in thorns. Sean had been working toward this, toward something like this, for what seemed an endless age. It had half eaten his gut. He didn't need her to send him off with only a caution.

"Get him, Sean."

"You too, Cat."

It was as close to declarations of love as they would get when surrounded by cops and federal agents in the deep of a deadly night. She ended the call.

As she lowered the phone, voices rose across the room. She turned from the soothing cool of the windows. Detective Weisbach beckoned. Caitlin jogged to her desk.

Weisbach jabbed a finger at her computer. "I found the mascot logo. Rio Vista High."

The Rio Vista Hawks. The school logo was the swooping profile of the bird, red against a black field—the school colors Hannah had identified on the UNSUB's sweatshirt.

Weisbach pulled up a map. Keyes crowded in. Rio Vista High was in the east end of the San Fernando Valley, less than ten miles from where they stood.

Keyes said, "It's in the northern buffer zone of the geographic profile."

At another desk, Detective Alvarez shouted. "Got it. ID'd the Jeep Renegade. And its owner."

The energy in the room rose so abruptly that the overhead lights seemed to flare. Alvarez put up a photo on the big-screen TV.

"Hayden Maddox."

The photo was of a driver's license, but Alvarez read from a rap sheet.

"Maddox has a petty criminal record. Shoplifting. Theft from a vehicle. Breaking and entering. Vandalism." He shot a glance at Keyes. "We cross-referenced him against the thirty-seven names on your preliminary suspect list."

Caitlin walked toward the screen. The photo showed a Caucasian face. Bright blue eyes transfixed by the blare of the DMV flash camera. Blanked of personality. Blond.

Keyes' voice floated behind her. "Cross-referenced against … oh."

Caitlin heard Keyes pause, but didn't turn. She kept walking toward the screen, trying to see into the photo, those eyes, that glowing, unknowable face.

"He's the son of an LAPD officer," Keyes said. "Plainclothes with the Burglary/Pawn Unit. Gretchen Maddox."

Caitlin stopped in front of the screen. Alvarez approached.

"He's a sophomore at the high school," he said.

Caitlin read his date of birth on the driver's license. Hayden Maddox was sixteen.

40

The convoy pulled out: the LAPD Robbery-Homicide detectives, Alvarez and his Sheriff's Department partner, the BAU agents. SWAT was coordinating. They would lead the entry at the residence of Hayden Maddox—a modest ranch home in the Valley owned by his parents, Gretchen and Robert.

Emmerich drove, grave and focused, rolling hard behind Solis up the 101 through Cahuenga Pass. He, Rainey, and Caitlin wore ballistic vests. Glocks holstered, Remington 870 loaded. No lights, no sirens. Radio silence. No bulletins or alerts, not yet. Nothing to tip the public, the media—and especially the suspect—that an operation was in progress to arrest the Midnight Man.

Riding shotgun, Caitlin scrolled through Hayden Maddox's records. Pages and pages of information, glowing with unearthly intensity from her screen in the Suburban's dim interior. The SUV ate up the road as they crested the pass and descended into the electric shimmer of the Valley.

Hayden's record went back to grade school.

Truancy. Chronic truancy.

Arrests. For setting fire to a middle school trashcan. For shoplifting candy bars and condoms from a 7-Eleven.

"How old when he stole the condoms?" Rainey said from the backseat.

"Thirteen," Caitlin said. "Don't know if he actually had a girlfriend or just thought he might eventually have sex. Either way, it says something about him. Possibly that he was paranoid about getting an STD. Or that a girl who got pregnant would have power over him."

She continued reading. Dropped charges. Juvenile court diversion programs.

Apology letters. *Dear Principal Nguyen, I am very sorry for my immature and destructive behavior after the eighth grade dance last week. I have learned my lesson.*

Counseling. Anger management.

Probation. Restitution. Community service.

Caitlin read aloud, and between the lines: Hayden Maddox was a kid out of control, playing the system, getting breaks every time he turned around.

Rainey said it for all of them. "Because he's a cop's son."

The Maddox neighborhood could have been lifted from a '70s sitcom about a white-bread suburban family. Edged lawns. Rose trellises. Illuminated Nativity scenes and rooftops atwinkle with flying plastic reindeer.

LAPD vehicles blocked both ends of the street and SWAT silently, invisibly, deployed. Caitlin climbed from the Suburban into bracingly cold air.

The Maddox house was dark. There was no sign of the Jeep Renegade.

Nobody answered the bell. But inside, they heard a cry that sounded like a dog whimpering.

A SWAT officer in a black helmet and khaki fatigues stepped up. The door was heavy but when he swung the small battering ram, the wood splintered.

The cops flowed inside. From the rear of the house came a smash, SWAT breaching the back door.

Caitlin followed Emmerich in close formation, with Rainey on her shoulder. Down the front hall, through the living room. Noise, voices calling, "Clear." Her heart thundered. Her vision seemed ultraviolet. She held her hopes and fears tight in the back of her chest, calling, "Left clear. Right clear."

The house was small—kitchen, three bedrooms, family room.

Searching, flowing, step by step, room by room, pistols and rifle barrels swinging, until there was no question.

"All clear," the SWAT commander called.

Hannah wasn't there. The thunder in Caitlin's heart became a roar.

From the back of the house, Weisbach called, "In here."

On the floor in the master bedroom, they found Hayden Maddox's father.

Robert Maddox was in his mid-forties, stocky, and blood-drenched. He sprawled beside the bed, his hands stretched overhead, tied to the bedpost.

He had a gunshot wound in his upper chest. Blood glistened on his shirt. He'd been kicked heavily in the face.

As they stood in the doorway absorbing the gory scene, a sound returned: the whimpering moan they'd heard before, the dog-like cry for help. It was coming from Maddox.

His lips were cracked. His voice was a rasp. He opened a single gleaming eye.

"Help me."

41

With her knife, Caitlin sliced the zip ties that bound Robert Maddox's wrists to the bedpost. His hands dropped to his lap. He groaned and slumped against the bed. Rainey knelt at his side and took his pulse, then ripped open his shirt. The entry wound was neat and small and seeping blood. She grabbed a throw blanket from a bedside chair, folded it, and pressed it to Maddox's chest. Weisbach radioed for an ambulance.

A crowd had pushed into the room—uniforms, detectives, and SWAT officers. Weisbach waved people away. "Give him air. Literally. Everybody back."

Emmerich ushered them out. Together, Caitlin and Weisbach eased Maddox away from the bed and lay him flat on the floor. Rainey propped pillows beneath his feet to elevate his legs and prevent shock, then crouched at his side, keeping pressure on the gunshot wound. Maddox's eyelids swam up and down.

If Maddox had been shot with the same ammunition that had killed Sheriff's Deputy Ohlmeyer, the neat entry wound meant nothing. A hollow-point wreaked its damage below the skin.

"Mr. Maddox," Caitlin said. "Who did this?"

The whimper returned, a long moan.

She gentled a hand on his shoulder. "Sir."

Maddox squeezed his eyes shut. "Hayden." A sad cry fell from his lips. "My son attacked me."

Solis ducked into the room. "Gretchen Maddox didn't turn up for her shift at Burglary this afternoon. Phone in the kitchen has six new voicemails from her shift commander."

Weisbach leaned toward Maddox. "Robert. Is your wife here? Where's Gretchen?"

His eyes opened. "I don't know. But ..." A rough breath. "I'm afraid. Something's wrong. Please find her."

"Working on it," Solis said, and headed out of the room.

Maddox told them Gretchen drove an Acura and gave a sketchy idea of what she had been wearing.

Rainey eyed Weisbach. "How long till the paramedics get here?"

"They're coming."

Rainey turned back to Maddox. "Stay with us, Robert. We need you to do that." She pressed the blanket against the wound. "Tell us about Hayden."

Robert Maddox peered up at them. His lips retracted, a rictus. And he began to talk.

Two paths can lead to psychopathy: one dominated by nature, the other by nurture. For some children, their environment—living with abusive parents, fending for themselves in dangerous neighborhoods—can turn them coldhearted and violent. If those kids are given a reprieve from their situation, they can be pulled back from psychopathy's edge.

Other children, Caitlin had learned, had a combination of neural wiring and ingrained personality organization that only constant intervention could keep in check. As Robert Maddox spoke, in choked and broken sentences, a picture formed of a son who seemed born to be violently antisocial.

"He just ... *shot* me," Maddox said. "I don't know why. I knew he'd been upset—he's hardly been home the past couple of months, but ... I looked up and he was standing in the doorway. He said, 'Dad.' Then raised the gun. Said, 'Time's up.' And pulled the trigger."

His voice sounded painfully dry. Caitlin ducked outside and grabbed a bottle of water from the Suburban. When she returned,

Weisbach was running Maddox through a series of questions. When was the last time he'd seen his son? Was he driving the Jeep Renegade? Was the girl Hannah Guillory with him? Who were his friends? Where might he have gone?

Maddox had no answers.

Caitlin raised his head and gave him a sip of water. She took his hand. "How young was Hayden when you understood that he was struggling?"

For a second he held back. Then, as if deciding that years of shame and secrecy were no longer worth it, he continued. His voice sounded clearer. But his eyes were clouded.

"Three," he said.

"Three years old?"

"I heard Hayden counting. 'One, two, three, four ...' I was proud of him, being so little but knowing his numbers. I came around the corner to praise him. He was crouched by the fireplace, counting the times he stuck the guinea pig with a sharp pencil."

Nobody reacted. Caitlin considered that a feat.

Straight from the womb, Maddox's description made clear, Hayden was a pitiless child. He was bright, imaginative, and charming. But he was a compulsive liar. And a thief. Aggressive. Self-centered.

"He's always been suspicious of others—so suspicious. I don't know why. Somebody must have hurt him, a bully. For him to be so vindictive," Maddox said. "He had to learn it from somebody who hurt him."

Caitlin didn't think Hayden must have been bullied. His own bullying could have been entirely self-generated.

"Was he physically violent with people at an early age?" she said.

Maddox was pale, but the tap had opened. "I thought it was boys being boys. At first. But my wife's a cop—she sees so much, and she knew Hayden was different. Nothing we said had any effect on him. 'Don't hit your friend—it hurts him.' 'Don't slam his hand in the door.' It didn't penetrate. Hayden didn't care. He *liked* hurting people. He was ... cruel." He squeezed his eyes shut. "It scared us."

Caitlin held his hand. Maddox described a boy who from the time he entered grade school was capriciously, gratuitously violent. He explained how he and Gretchen tried everything to control Hayden. Stern discipline. Corporal punishment. Tough love. Bribery. Prayer.

"Things would go great for a few weeks. Hayden would say he was sorry. That he was trying harder. That he loved Jesus and was changed. But a month, six weeks, and he was back to his old tricks. And lying about it, or *angry* if we pointed out he was backsliding. Making out that it was our fault. Somebody's. Never his. Then …"

Maddox paused, as if deciding whether to open a vault he kept tightly locked. He breathed. Pain, either visceral or emotional, seemed to swell, and the tumblers clicked.

"When Hayden was twelve, we reached out for help. We asked Gretchen's brother to take him under his wing."

Rainey and Caitlin exchanged a glance.

"What's his name, Mr. Maddox?" Rainey said.

"Trey. Trey Laforte," Maddox said. "It's good for kids to have an adult they can trust and confide in."

"Of course."

"Trey, he's Gretchen's younger brother. Ex-military. Army Ranger, fought in Iraq," Maddox said. "He was the real deal, somebody we thought could channel all Hayden's … *unruly* energies. We hoped Trey could put Hayden on the right road. Get out his frustrations. Hayden's always been very physical, but also very much inside his own head. Trey, he could give Hayden a cut-down version of army discipline. We thought learning survival skills might straighten him out."

Fresh pain swam through his eyes.

"And?" Rainey said.

"It seemed to work. Hayden loved tracking, trapping, learning military tactics and guerrilla warfare. Ninja shit, he said, was cool." Passion flecked his voice. "He finally had *something*."

His lips quivered. Caitlin squeezed his hand. He seemed to be coming up on a *but*.

He inhaled. "Then came the hunting trip."

Teach the boy to shoot, Uncle Trey said. Hayden was fourteen, plenty old enough. Have him bring down a buck, smear his kill's hot blood across his cheeks, and he'd feel like a warrior.

"It was supposed to be a bonding weekend," Maddox said. Him, Hayden, and Uncle Trey. "The Sierras, early in Christmas season. Take the dog, too. Give Hayden positive focus. Man time."

Early in Christmas season, Caitlin thought—past deer-hunting season, probably. Poaching season. She continued to hold Maddox's hand.

"But when the moment came and Hayden took his shot," Maddox said, "it wasn't a clean kill. The boy's first time hitting a moving target with a big rifle, not at the range, real life, couldn't blame him. And he did hit the deer. But it stumbled away, wounded. Then …"

He winced. Caitlin pressed his hand, encouraging him.

"Hayden was furious he'd missed," Maddox said. "And—Trey and I told him not to stomp off, not to kick rocks, he had to complete the kill. We were … very emphatic."

Caitlin grimaced, picturing a boy facing withering shouts to finish the job.

"It happened so fast. Trey yelling, the dog barking. Coho, our black Lab, he was loud as hell. And the deer crashing through the underbrush, trying to escape," Maddox said. "Hayden tore into the forest, firing. Just firing. He ran, I saw him pulling the bolt on the rifle, again and again." Another breath. "When he reached the deer, it was dead."

He looked down. "Coho was wounded."

Anguish knifed through Caitlin. She could only imagine her dog, Shadow, being shot, picture her crying in pain and confusion.

"We were miles deep in the high Sierra," Maddox said. "Hours from a vet's office. There was no way"—he shook his head vehemently—"no way at all to save Coho."

He gazed between her and Rainey. "Even though Hayden begged. Even though he tried to hoist the dog across his shoulders. That dog was the only creature Hayden ever cared about. But there was no way."

Rainey's expression had gone distant and hard. Maddox's hand, in Caitlin's, was cold.

"And it was Hayden's dog," he said.

Hayden's fault the Lab was doomed. Hayden's responsibility to rectify the situation.

"Man up," Maddox said.

His voice trembled. "God help me. I made Hayden shoot that dog."

On the window and walls of the bedroom, icy lights spun blue and red. A siren whined and died. The ambulance pulled up outside.

A voice in the doorway spoke grimly. "Keep talking."

It was Emmerich. Telling Maddox to finish the story.

"After the hunting trip, Hayden acted the same at home. Charmer. Liar," Maddox said. "But he became a full-time schemer. And hater. And thief."

Quietly, Hayden became consumed with punishing anybody who tried to exercise control over him. Anybody in authority.

"And he never looked me in the eye. Not from the moment he stood over that dog and pulled the trigger," Maddox said. "He'd stare, but if you looked back? Catch his gaze, you were in for trouble."

He gasped, seemingly closer to tears than physical pain.

"Hayden's out of control," Maddox said. "And the boy doesn't care. Nothing stops him." His hand trembled in Caitlin's. "His mother said, 'Keep this up and you'll be nothing but a small-time thug.' Hayden sneered. Said he'd never be a small-time anything. Gretchen told him to be careful or he'd eat those words. Hayden smiled. Just *grinned*."

Maddox's eyes widened as desperation, recognition, something honest broke through his defenses. "Hayden thinks that no matter what he does, he'll be protected. By his age, by his ability to con people—and by the fact that his mom's a cop."

Outside, vehicle doors slammed. The paramedics were unloading.

Emmerich approached. "Has your son ever been diagnosed by a psychiatrist?"

Maddox averted his gaze like a dog caught eating the trash.

"Hayden's been given multiple psychiatric diagnoses. Emotional detachment disorder. Oppositional defiant disorder. Conduct disorder with—" His voice caught and dropped. "With callous and unemotional traits."

He went silent, as if the tape had run out. He didn't say the rest. Maybe he couldn't bring himself to.

Hayden was a psychopath.

Quietly, Emmerich asked, "The hunting trip. Did Hayden's mother have any involvement?"

It took Maddox a moment, deciding. "Before Hayden put the dog down, he called her. Begged her to get him out of it. It was pathetic. Almost made me change my mind. Almost. Then ..." His voice rose, a spiral, toward something uncontrollable. "She said, 'You made your bed. You have to lie in it.'"

Maddox's last words slid toward incoherence. He sounded utterly broken. Two paramedics entered the bedroom, wearing blue latex gloves and carrying a medical kit.

Detective Weisbach stepped into the hall and spoke into her police radio. Putting out a BOLO for Hayden. "The suspect is armed and extremely dangerous."

Maddox broke into sobs. "Don't hurt him."

The paramedics took control of the space. "Let us get to work. You can talk to him again later."

Caitlin and Rainey moved back, and the paramedics knelt at Maddox's side. The bedroom suddenly felt hot and crowded, rife with the smell of blood and desperation. The paramedics took Maddox's vitals, but he didn't seem to notice. He stared straight at Emmerich. His voice spiked.

"It's not Hayden's fault that something's wrong with him," he choked. "Don't hurt him. I know he did this to me, but I love my son."

42

Don't hurt him.

The words seemed to shove Caitlin backward.

She retreated from the bedroom. The paramedics took Robert Maddox's pulse, put ECG leads on his chest, palpated the gunshot wound, checked his pupils for signs of head trauma from the kicking he'd taken. Maddox breathed shallowly, pleading for his ruthless son, his hand grasping toward Caitlin as she backed away.

Rainey joined her in the hallway. Her face was stark with shock, her mind working behind her eyes. Emmerich was beyond somber.

"Hayden's moved past surrogates to attacking the sources of his rage," he said. "He's building toward a finale."

On the floor in the bedroom, Robert Maddox moaned incoherently.

A warning blared in Caitlin's head. "Confronting a malignant paranoid can trigger homicidal violence. Preemptive annihilation."

"The BOLO specifies armed and dangerous," Emmerich said.

"If he's cornered, nobody's likely to talk him down. He'll strike out. If Hannah's with him, it'll be exceptionally dangerous for her. If she *isn't* with him when he's confronted, using deadly force could seal her fate anyway. We'd never find her," she said. "Taking him alive has to be a priority."

"Nobody wants to turn their gun on a high school sophomore."

The look she gave him said, *On what planet?* "I don't."

I love my son.

Hayden existed without the ability to love, so emotionally

250

impoverished that he didn't even know he was lost and starving. He was a boy. If she pulled the trigger, what would she become?

Officers edged past them in the hall. The house was about to be excavated. Armed with a warrant, the LAPD would search the home from top to bottom for handguns, ammunition, spent rounds, ninja rocks, shoes matching the prints in the hallway at the Guillorys' home, a black hoodie and ball cap, wedding rings, and more.

In Hayden's room, Weisbach and another detective were examining every millimeter of space—the dresser, desk, bed, bookshelf, and closet. Weisbach had Hayden's laptop open. Caitlin heard her say that the computer was password protected, but that task force officers had begun searching his social media and tracing his activity. His social footprint seemed skimpy.

Caitlin wasn't surprised. A paranoid like Hayden was unlikely to share information on easily accessible forums.

The paramedics brought Robert Maddox out, strapped to a stretcher, an oxygen mask on his battered face. Solis trailed them. Caitlin followed them out the front door as they hurried Maddox through the cold air to the ambulance.

Its flashing lights popcorned against the darkness. The paramedics lifted the stretcher inside, and Solis clambered in with them.

Up and down the street, clusters of people stood on porches and lawns, backlit and shadowed. Neighbors—alarmed, curious, confused.

Rainey approached. She took the neighbors in. "Word'll spread. We've lost the chance to take him by surprise. We need to get out ahead on this with public announcements. Now."

"The BOLO, public bulletins, saturate every channel with Hannah's photo."

Thinking of Hannah caused Caitlin's chest to hurt. She pressed a fist to her sternum and forced a breath.

Solis hopped down from the ambulance and slammed the door. The engine fired up, lights and siren, and pulled away.

He hiked over, bearish. "Got more from the father. The kid doesn't just have wheels. He's got money—he took his dad's wallet. Credit cards if he's sloppy enough to use them. Couple hundred in cash otherwise."

Enough to stay out of electronic sight for a while. Hours at a minimum. And when a child's life was at stake, every hour was a lifetime.

Rainey said, "We have to figure out where Hayden might go to ground."

Solis nodded. "I pressed him. Maddox thinks the most likely place the kid would seek refuge is with his uncle. Trey, the ex-Ranger." His eyes, under the porch light, crackled.

"But?" Caitlin said. "What's the hitch?"

"Trey Laforte has fallen off the grid," Solis said. "Seems Trey has a few issues of his own. Substances, anger, inability to keep a job. He got evicted from a fleabag apartment a few months back. Asked to move in here, but Maddox objected. Had enough trouble with Hayden, didn't need more turmoil under his roof. Maddox doesn't know where the guy is."

"Some mentor," Caitlin said. "Drunk and stoned, teaching Hayden survival skills, urban guerrilla tactics, how to be a silent, invisible 'ninja' …"

"Trying to scare him straight with stories of his time in combat. Not likely to be pretty, especially if the uncle was trying to knock the kid's head one-eighty in some kind of tough-love boot camp."

"The guy who screamed, 'Shoot the dog' at an eighth grader might not be the role model to turn the kid away from sociopathy."

"We're contacting military records. See if we can get a current address. At least information on where Laforte's VA benefits land."

Weisbach leaned out the front door and beckoned to Solis with a two-fingered wave.

Solis stepped inside. He and Weisbach held a brief, intense debate. Scowling, Weisbach made a phone call. She shook her head, hung up, and Solis came back out.

"We're going to release Hayden Maddox's name to the public. Make an announcement."

"Good," Rainey said. "And?"

"On the guidance of the top brass and LAPD's lawyers, we're going to withhold his photo."

"Fuck that. Pardon my Russian."

Caitlin felt punched. But she said, "This was inevitable."

"Hayden Maddox is a juvenile," Solis said. "By a significant margin. He's not coming up on eighteen. Nowhere near it."

"He's suspected of committing multiple murders," Rainey said.

"And despite the gravity of the case, the law firmly requires us to guard his privacy." The bags under his eyes were the color of charcoal. "I love it just as much as you."

He stalked toward his car.

Rainey looked ready to spit tacks, but Caitlin just shook her head.

"The kid's protected. And you can bet he counted on this," she said.

At the end of the street, where two LAPD cruisers blocked access, a tall figure showed ID and squeezed past. Keyes jogged up, eager and grave.

He gazed at the unexceptional ranch home, eating up every detail. "This is it. Ground Zero in the UNSUB's buffer zone."

Emmerich's voice came from the front hall of the house. He stood backlit in the doorway. "No longer an UNSUB." He waved them inside. "Let's talk."

Emmerich gathered the team in the living room, near the cold fireplace.

He crossed his arms and spoke pensively. "The hunting trip."

"December," Rainey said. "Start of Christmas season. That's a nasty trigger."

She regarded the living room. A scraggly Christmas tree had been tipped sideways into the wall. Possibly by cops searching the room, more likely by an angry Hayden.

"Goddamn mind job," Caitlin said. "Maybe Hayden's poor dog couldn't have been saved. But what a cruel thing to do to a kid. Even to a budding psychopath. Damn."

"'Man time,'" Rainey said. "But the kid blew it. How'd that affect him? Mortification. Shame. Which he turned into rage."

Emmerich nodded. He paused for a moment. "Do you know the concept of liminal space?"

Caitlin shook her head. Keyes nodded, slowly, as if making a connection.

"Liminality relates to times, or places, or experiences located at a sensory threshold," Emmerich said. "It relates to the transitional. The in-between. It's the moment of falling into sleep. Dusk is a liminal time. So are dawn and midnight. Highways are liminal spaces. Airports. Hotels. Borders. Crossroads."

"The Twilight Zone," Keyes said.

"Precisely."

Caitlin felt a pull, something drawing her into thoughts both opaque and icily clear.

"Liminality is unstable," Emmerich said. "It's alluring and disorienting. Every ritual has a liminal moment—when participants are no longer their old selves but haven't yet attained their new status." He paused. "Screw up the transformation, and you're stuck. In some traditional societies, people who fail a ritual passage are branded as dangerous."

"Hayden Maddox failed his rite of passage to manhood," Caitlin said.

Emmerich nodded. "The hunting trip trapped an exceptionally dangerous boy in an unstable psychological space and lit a smoldering fuse."

"He's been ritually tormenting children," Caitlin said.

Keyes shook his head. "He's nowhere. Always in a seam. No wonder it's been a nightmare to build the geographic profile."

Emmerich took a second to catch each of their eyes. "We have to get into that space ourselves—mentally and physically—to figure out how to predict his next moves."

They were silent for a moment. Caitlin said, "Hiding places. He's paranoid. He'll have secret places—some between the walls …"

Rainey spun toward the hallway. "His room."

She hurried down the hall and leaned through the doorway to speak to the detectives searching Hayden's bedroom. Then she leaned back out, alert and alarmed, and waved.

Caitlin joined her. The LAPD detectives stood at the open closet.

One had shoved clothing aside and was examining its back wall on his tiptoes with a flashlight. The other was tapping on it.

"A false wall," Rainey said.

"We have a hidden compartment," the detective said. "And it's booby trapped."

He froze, then stepped back, grim.

"There's a trip wire. If you open the compartment without deactivating the rigging, you'll stick your hand straight into a nest of firecrackers. M-80s. They'd blow your fingers off."

He appeared disagreeably surprised but determined. "Don't worry, we'll disarm the trip wire and find whatever's in his hidey-hole."

At the top of the hall Detective Solis appeared. "LAPD Command is putting together an emergency bulletin, and we're going to hold a press conference. I'm heading downtown."

Emmerich said, "You need one of us to join you in a show of unity for the cameras?"

"Please," Solis said. "Our commander thinks that releasing Hayden's name may spur him to flee Los Angeles. Consensus is, he'll dump his car first."

"Can't say they're wrong."

"LAPD's posting patrols at Metrolink and Amtrak stations, and at bus terminals."

"Good."

He led them to the front door.

"We're also searching for Gretchen Maddox." Solis' voice took on a deeper tone of disquiet. Blue-on-blue concern for a fellow officer. "And we've issued an Amber Alert for Hannah Guillory."

"Great," Caitlin said.

With the team, she walked toward their Suburban. The arching sky seemed to blast her. Huge, infinite. And all of them so small beneath it, Hannah most of all.

After a second, she found the North Star. She hung her gaze on it. Sean had taken to the night sky not that long ago. He and the

ATF team were somewhere under that star, beyond the horizon. They might already be conducting their raid on the bombing suspect's cabin. Starlight, needle-white, nicked at her.

They reached the Suburban and Emmerich unlocked the doors.

"One last thing," he said. "Tonight is a liminal moment."

Keyes said, "How's that?"

"December twenty-first." He paused, hand on the door handle. "The winter solstice. It's the longest night of the year."

43

The Metro bus pulled up outside Union Station in downtown LA at 9:42 P.M. Though it had been dark for hours, the city was busy. Traffic all the way in. People on the streets and heading into the station. When the pneumatic door of the bus hissed open, he strolled down the steps. Playing it relaxed. A lanky teenager, heading home from a movie or a game. His hood was pulled over his baseball cap.

Hayden Maddox didn't need to act jumpy. So he didn't. He was on foot, and alone. He had gotten rid of the Jeep Renegade for the night—not dumped it, but left it miles distant, in an out-of-the-way spot. Nothing conspicuous. Nothing to see here, folks—move along. Pocketed the keys and strolled off, then rode the bus back downtown to cover his trail. No need to act squirrelly.

But he did need to shake anybody who was following him. And people were. The red eyes painted on the billboard overlooking the Guillorys' house proved that. Big, all-seeing eyes, crazy-wide, staring down at the street. Somebody had spray-painted them to send a message. To *him*.

Who? CNN? LAPD? Hannah, who had *snitched* on him to the LAPD?

He had to stay on top of it.

The station was coldly lit, its white walls screaming *cathedral*. Art Deco combined with Spanish Colonial. His fourth-grade teacher had made his class memorize it on their field trip. Palm trees and a scent of old glamour, or a stench of urine from the 1930s. He sauntered inside through the side doors. The main hall echoed crazily with jabber and suitcase wheels and tinkling Christmas music. The noise bounced between the high wood ceiling and the red tile floor. The corridors were a torrent of people focused on getting someplace else. Never on who was *there*.

Screens showed the tracks for departing trains. The ticket windows were open. The only thing that unsettled him was how busy the place was, this time of night. The holidays. Families were rushing to get wherever they thought they should be to nag or scream at their relatives. People were carrying shopping bags. Drunks, pretending to be jolly, were singing along with the tinny carols. Televisions played in the waiting area, showing a news bulletin.

POLICE SEEK MURDER SUSPECT.

Good fucking luck with that. He

kept walking. Hands in his pockets, relaxed. Total calm. Total alertness. Eyes sweeping the scene. The TVs showed a crappy police sketch of the Midnight Man—less than nothing to worry about. A blank, cartoon face, nothing but formless eyes under a hat and hood. It could have been the Unabomber. He smiled.

A name flashed onscreen. HAYDEN MADDOX.

He stopped smiling. Shit.

He walked, eyeing the screens. Six of them, all announcing HAYDEN MADDOX.

Under his skin a thousand electric eels began to writhe. He kept his face slack, appearing as half-interested as the rest of the people rushing for their rides out of downtown.

He thought. Who the *hell* gave his identity to the police? Hannah the snitchwitch, who'd lain in wait in for him with her Chuck Taylors and her daddy's hammer? (Lotta good that did.) The FBI? Agent Darkstar?

Cops were stationed inside the doors.

Hayden could guess why. He figured they had to have his photo.

The TVs, the police, none of them were flashing his face. Just his name. But ANNOUNCING HAYDEN MADDOX meant they would have pulled his driver's license pic from the DMV. Yet the TV news wasn't broadcasting it. The cops weren't flashing a photo at passing travelers and asking, *Have you seen this person?*

Because he was a minor.

That was good. That was his backstop. It wouldn't matter if he tore the head off the Queen of England and drop-kicked it down the steps at City Hall. He had rights. They had to protect his privacy.

But the cops themselves had the photo. They were all gaping at it. Memorizing it. Out to get him. Every single one.

But they were facing precisely the wrong way.

They stood ten yards inside the doors, facing the glass. They were watching people coming into the main station entrance—looking for somebody they figured was desperate to get a train out of Los Angeles.

Not somebody heading into the heart of downtown.

Cop 101: Look behind you. Fa la la la LOL, idiots. Ambling, he glanced again at the TV screens. AMBER ALERT.

Don't slow down. Don't. The fuck? It was Hannah. Last seen in his Renegade.

The writhing eels seemed to crackle and bite. Every eye in the station, the televisions, the departure screens, the phones in people's hands, all felt like they were pouring their hot sight onto him. But the cops continued eyeing people coming in through the main doors.

Hayden hunched into his sweatshirt and strolled straight past them into the longest night.

44

Under the war room's cold lights, they spread out evidence seized from Hayden Maddox's home. Every task force detective, every uniform, every tech they could round up, had arrived at LAPD HQ. The atmosphere was spiky, the tempo intense.

The rat's nest behind the false wall in Hayden's closet had been wired to terrify and maim. If tripped, the string of M-80 firecrackers would have set the wall on fire and destroyed the trove inside. But demolition would have given Hayden concrete proof that his foes were spying on him.

"I'll get you before you get me," Caitlin muttered.

And from the evidence stuffed behind the false wall, raging against imagined foes was one of Hayden Maddox's obsessions.

"This is going to keep forensic psychiatrists busy for years," Rainey said.

There were journals. After they'd been photographed, scanned, and logged, the task force put on fresh gloves and started speed-reading. They needed to mine the journals for information that could lead them to Hayden—and Hannah.

As she read, Caitlin felt herself being dragged into a rain-swollen gully, as if she'd been swept off her feet by a flash flood. The waters were cold, riddled with rocks as sharp as teeth.

HAYDEN MADDOX.

They watch. They plot. "How can we humiliate Hayden today?"
They think I don't see it. Idiots.

They think they can trick me yet again into swallowing their mindrape arglebargle. They talk about right and wrong and good and evil but the Theory of Relativity says it's all just your point of view. Turn around, see the people conniving against you, you'll discover the truth. Good means SUBMIT. Right means CRAWL.

Wrong means FREEDOM. It means I decide.

So turn the tables. Make them see. Make them know.

Make them pay.

Right now, I can take them unaware. Slack, snoring, weak. Before they even know what hits them. Except when they do, and then it's even more beautiful.

But soon I will take them at length. And drill it into their heads, all their heads, like a wild WOLF tearing through them with its claws, fighting back, rising up in LEGIONS to crush them like bone meal.

Caitlin flipped through the journal, page upon page of power fantasies, fears, elaborate plans for REVENGE.

A photo was taped inside the journal's back cover. She felt a wash of grief. It was a picture of a black Lab. Written in Hayden's crabbed scrawl was COHO.

She spun the journal around and shoved it to the middle of the table. Rainey took it in solemnly. Her phone beeped. She read a text.

"Detectives at his house found a fireproof cash box. Stuffed with prescription meds and a roll of bills."

"What meds?" Caitlin said.

"Adderall and Zoloft. Hayden's prescriptions. Seems he hasn't been taking them, just selling them."

Keyes came in with his laptop. "His wall stash included a manila envelope containing camera memory cards. This kid is old school. Doesn't upload his business to the cloud. He kept it within literal arm's reach." He sat down. "He wants control."

He cued up a video. Caitlin and Rainey came around. Keyes hit PLAY.

The video had been filmed with a camera set up on Hayden's desk.

Caitlin recognized the posters on the wall. The clip was short, twenty seconds.

Under the glare of the overhead bulb, Hayden walked into view. Every inch of skin on Caitlin's arms prickled.

"*You.*"

It was the figure from every CCTV surveillance video the cops had found. The lanky male frame, the sidling walk. But this video wasn't high-gain negative. It was the Midnight Man with the lights turned on. The blindingly white figure brought frothing into full color.

He pointed a finger at the camera. "*You lying pile of dogshit.*"

He was blond. Bright-eyed. A cold scoop of vanilla ice cream. A high school boy that sophomore girls would gape at and giggle over and call *cute*.

He rushed at the camera, his face getting inches from the lens. "*Claiming it's me—that I'm the problem. Blaming me for everything. All you little sneaks, you pussies crying in your beds, laughing at me. All you wannabe SS guards, you're nothing. Nothing like the real thing.*" He widened his eyes, hamming it up, pouring on the cheese. "*But guess who is. You'll see. You'll pay.*"

The clip ended.

"Jesus," Caitlin said.

Weisbach was standing at her shoulder. She sounded as dry as sandpaper. "These pissant demagogues always drool over the SS. They just can't stop jacking off to the dream of the Third Reich."

Keyes gestured at the screen. "I've gone through a dozen of these. Same theme in all. You'll suffer. You're weak. Everybody who's persecuting me, from the school principal to the girl behind the counter at Taco Bell, is going to hurt. He has an enemies list ten miles long."

"And now Hannah's at the top of it," Caitlin said.

She rubbed her eyes. Then told herself: *Shut away these aching thoughts about the danger Hannah's in. Eat your fears. Focus.*

"He started breaking fresh barriers a couple of days ago," she said. "But what's gone down tonight is escalation on a whole different scale. Incredibly bold. Attacking in the early evening instead of waiting until families are asleep. He's unspooling his revenge on us all. Hannah's some kind of icing on the cake. What he has in mind, I can't even …"

Keyes nodded. "So far I've found nothing to help identify where he might take her. I'll keep looking."

Emmerich walked in with a stack of eight-by-ten photo blowups. He stuck them on the whiteboard. They were childhood photos of Hayden.

Caitlin felt a fresh disconnect.

Family snapshots showed an apparently happy-go-lucky kid. The boy had a sunny, shy smile. Picnic photos had a relaxed air, his dad engaged, his mom, Gretchen, quiet but observant. She was sturdy, with her blond hair swept up in a big hair clip, her jeans tight, her bare arms tanned and lithe. Something familiar in her expression, maybe a cop's watchfulness. Hayden ate hot dogs. Hayden played tag. Hayden made goofy faces.

Caitlin was well-used to criminals who appeared polite, neat, and amiable. Even murderers didn't stomp around screaming like figures from a Hieronymus Bosch hellscape 24/7. They watched television and grilled hamburgers and updated their LinkedIn profiles hoping for that promotion. Only a few unlucky people saw the mask slip, the rage uncoil, the knife emerge. Everyone else got the bland platitudes from the guy in the corporate polo shirt with the assistant manager's name tag pinned to his chest.

Caitlin expected that. But this was different. In these photos, the acid rage that had eaten Hayden Maddox from the inside was nowhere even a shadow. The screaming, strutting ham actor on the home videos, the casually euphoric killer dancing away from death—none of that showed.

She approached the whiteboard. In one shot Hayden was about seven years old, angelic, arms around his black Lab.

In another, he stood with his mom in a third-grade classroom. Bring Your Parents to School Day. One father had on a dentist's white coat. Another wore a hard hat. Gretchen wore her LAPD uniform. Her hand squeezed Hayden's shoulder. He was gazing up at her. His smile seemed strangely desperate and poignant. In that smile Caitlin saw fear, and a longing for approval and security.

She had a photo like it in an album somewhere at home.

Stop it. That kid had curdled and hardened into someone relentlessly dangerous. But as she examined his expression—the anxious longing he poured out—she couldn't help feeling a twisted compassion for the boy in the photo.

Could I take his life? What would be left of me afterward?

She stepped back mentally. If Hayden saw compassion on her face, or heard it in her voice, he would use it against her. Because Hayden thought compassion was a weakness.

He tormented children because, in part, he had observed that children's pain upset most people. He would try to turn that distress against anybody who came for him. He would use Hannah to manipulate people's compassion to his advantage. To stage his ultimate victory.

She had to keep him from winning that.

And if he forced her into a corner?

Don't let it come to that.

But time was short. How, in the sprawling darkness of Los Angeles, could they possibly locate him?

Solis approached, a printout in his hand. "Hayden's uncle, Trey Laforte."

"The Ranger who's gone off the grid," Caitlin said.

"You're not going to believe this." Solis held up the printout. "Laforte was here the day the fake detective interrogated Hannah."

Caitlin grabbed it. "Hell no."

The printout showed a photo of a man signing a visitors' logbook. The camera was overhead, the image poor quality, but the man wore black jeans, a polo shirt, and a blazer. Sunglasses tucked in the V of his collar. He was smiling, appeared to be chit-chatting with the desk clerk. The time stamp was a few minutes before Hannah had disappeared from the cafeteria.

"Hannah watched videos that were recorded at the front desk. She didn't recognize this man," Caitlin said.

"This isn't from the front desk," Solis said. "He came into the complex through an entrance that's used almost exclusively by officers and staff."

Caitlin handed Emmerich the printout.

He examined the image. "Laforte acts like he knows the clerk."

"He's been here before, visiting his sister. I've put a call in to the clerk, but I'm guessing if she remembers Laforte coming that day, he claimed it was to see Officer Maddox."

Caitlin shook her head. "Hannah told us. When Alvarez asked her if the detective looked like the Midnight Man, she said he kind of did. But 'older and tireder.'" She flicked a finger at the photo. "Of course he does. He's the Midnight Man's uncle."

She studied the photo. Trey Laforte had the same strong build and striking features as Hayden and Gretchen.

"Hell," she said.

"What?" Emmerich said.

She turned to the whiteboard. The Maddox family picnic photo. Judging by Hayden's age, the snapshot had been taken almost a decade ago. Caitlin now knew why something in Gretchen's eyes seemed familiar.

"Officer Maddox." She tapped the photo, her jaw slackening. "She's cut her hair short. It's brunette now. And she's lost a bunch of weight."

"You've met her?" Solis said.

"No, but I've seen her."

"Where?"

"Here in this room." She spread her arms. "When Emmerich delivered the UNSUB's profile to the task force. The room was packed—uniforms, staffers, officers and detectives from other units." An image of Gretchen bloomed in vivid shades. "She wore a coral twin set. I thought—that's a mom."

Rainey approached. "Got her current ID photo?"

Solis, ruffled, found a terminal and pulled it up.

Gretchen Maddox had lost the sparkle and with it, her youthfulness. She couldn't be much older than Rainey but looked like she'd lived several additional lifetimes.

"She was here," Caitlin said. "She's not assigned to the task force, but she attended the briefing. She heard us describe who we were after."

Solis said, "That's not out of the ordinary ..."

Rainey said, "The next day—she attended the press conference, too."

"Lots of officers were there," Solis said. "Strength in numbers."

But his keenness to find a non-suspicious reason for Gretchen Maddox's repeated appearances was ebbing. Especially with the photo of her brother, Trey Laforte, clenched in Emmerich's hand.

"Christ," Solis said. "I know."

Emmerich said, "I can think of only one reason why Trey Laforte would impersonate a detective and question Hannah."

"Gretchen Maddox suspected Hayden's involvement in the killings. Told Trey and got him down here to gather information on the sly," Solis said dully.

Rainey said, "Maya Cathcart clawed her attacker. I wonder if Gretchen asked Hayden where the bloody scratches on his face came from."

Solis ran a hand over his stubble. "So she got Trey to play detective and ask Hannah if the Midnight Man had any gouges on him? Yeah. At least." He shook his head. "Goddammit. We still can't locate either Laforte or Officer Maddox."

Emmerich said, "Given how Hayden attacked his father, I'm less concerned they're aiding Hayden than I am they're in danger."

Solis almost laughed. "What have we come to, hoping one of our own is 'just' in danger, and not aiding a serial killer?" His face was dark. "I'll issue BOLOs on both Gretchen and Trey."

As he walked off, Rainey took the photo from Emmerich. "They may not be aiding and abetting Hayden. But if Gretchen and Trey have suspected things for days, and Trey inserted himself into the investigation to surreptitiously interrogate a little girl ... what else have they done?"

45

For a moment longer, Caitlin stared at the photo of Trey Laforte. She needed to think. She had to find some means to locate Hannah, because time was sliding away. But her wheels were spinning. She wanted to go for a hard run, to hit the streets and pound some clarity into her thoughts, step by step, breath by breath.

A sketchy idea whispered across the back of her mind.

She gestured to Rainey. "Walk with me. Coffee."

They left the jagged energy of the war room and headed down the corridor for the vending machine.

"You've got to be right about Trey and Gretchen," she said. "They jammed themselves sideways into the investigation because they became afraid that Hayden was responsible. And they didn't stop at interrogating Hannah. You know what else they—or at least Trey— probably did."

Rainey gave her a narrow stare. "It's what kicked things off tonight. That billboard in the Guillorys' neighborhood."

"Exactly. As soon as you saw it, you had doubts that the Midnight Man had painted those eyes on it."

"Because the eyes looked wrong. And because it's such a radical change in MO."

"*Too* radical. Hayden's changed his game up plenty in the last forty-eight hours. But one thing he's not going to do is stand on a literal advertising platform and display himself to the world. He's too paranoid." She jerked a thumb over her shoulder. "All those journals prove that."

267

"Somebody outside the task force did know about the bloody eyes."

"A cop, who heard it in the war room. Or found her son drawing mock-ups at home."

"Sweet freaking Jesus."

"So maybe Hayden didn't paint the eyes on the billboard after all. Maybe Trey did—to lure Hayden back to that neighborhood."

"Why would they try to draw him back to the Guillorys' neighborhood?" Rainey said.

"Because he'd taken off from home, and they didn't know how else to pull him out of the weeds. Because Gretchen and Trey knew Hayden couldn't resist the sight of the eyes—and neither could the media. The billboard hits the news, they figure Hayden'll see it and head straight for Bay Rise. I bet they were there, hoping to grab him."

"Desperate but plausible."

"Unfortunately, I think it worked, but in the worst way. It did draw him to the neighborhood. Where he attacked again."

They stuck coins in the vending machine. Rainey got a protein bar. Caitlin decided coffee was the wrong choice. She added more coins. Got two Red Bulls.

As she popped the top on one, the idea that had been whispering at the back of her mind escaped and nearly knocked her sideways.

"What's that look?" Rainey said.

"Come on." She headed back along the corridor, nearly running, with Rainey at her side. "Where's Emmerich? We need to get a jump on Hayden."

They found Emmerich coming up the stairs, head bent to his phone, with Keyes beside him.

"Boss," she said. "We need to draw Hayden Maddox out. Bait a trap and pull him in."

His face remained impassive, but his eyes lit. "What do you have in mind?"

"The Jeep Renegade," Caitlin said. "Hayden's been extremely careful to keep it from being identified. He ripped down a surveillance camera so the Jeep's plate wouldn't be recorded. And until tonight, he knew the cops hadn't ID'd it. But the Amber Alert changes all that," she said. "Now a description of the Jeep is blasting from every TV and cell phone in Southern California. Make, model, plate number. And Hayden's too careful to let himself get caught driving it. The Amber Alert will push him to dump it."

"I agree he's not going to drive that vehicle—*if* he learns of the Amber Alert."

"He's paranoid. He might try to go to ground, but he's convinced everybody's constantly spying on him. He's not going to pull a blanket over his head and hide. His mind won't let him. He's going to obsess over keeping watch on the watchers. *He knows.*"

Rainey nodded. "He's hypervigilant. His paranoia won't permit him to turn off the news."

"I'll accept that supposition," Emmerich said. "What do you propose?"

"Let's put out word that the Jeep's been sighted."

He didn't react.

"If he dumped the Jeep in a hurry, he may not have thoroughly sterilized it. It may contain evidence that points to his whereabouts. Hearing that the police have found the vehicle will make him nervous."

"Presume he thinks he sterilized the vehicle." Emmerich raised a hand. "Devil's advocate."

"But he can't be sure. He's a cop's kid. A Burglary cop's kid. He knows that the smallest, seemingly invisible detail can be missed by a suspect who's in a rush to purge incriminating evidence or escape a scene. Like he forgot to pick up the ninja rock when he fled the Cathcarts' house."

"Presume he *burned* the vehicle."

Caitlin pressed her lips tight, then nodded to Keyes. "Can you pull up callouts for car fires tonight? Jeeps. In the time since Hannah was abducted."

Keyes ducked into the war room. Almost immediately he came back shaking his head. "Nothing that matches within the last three hours."

Emmerich adjusted his watchband, wary. "You think putting out the location of a fake sighting would lure him to the scene?"

"It might." She explained why she and Rainey thought Trey or Gretchen had painted the eyes on the billboard. "That was meant as a flashing red light, to draw Hayden out. We think it worked—because he's obsessed and mistrustful. Always watching, scoping scenes out, trying to surveil and outmaneuver his enemies. Why wouldn't he think he can show up again and get away—after all, he always does."

"One major hitch." Emmerich waited, wanting her to say it.

"Sure. He knows where he dumped the Jeep. We don't."

"If he left it in Anaheim and we put out a bulletin that a Renegade's been found in Malibu …"

"I know. But it doesn't matter whether he returns to the location where he dumped it."

"Explain."

"The report that the Jeep's been found just has to seem plausible enough that Hayden will be compelled to check it out." She turned to Keyes again. "Fire up your geographic profile, slap that algorithm awake, and dig into every insight you've gained about the Midnight Man's hunting patterns." She set a hand on his shoulder. "You've dived deeper into how he moves than anybody. Figure out where we should place a decoy vehicle."

He nodded, as if revving a mental engine, and shoved his hair out of his eyes. Took a step and stopped, checking with Emmerich.

Emmerich nodded, and followed him toward the war room, beckoning Caitlin and Rainey to come along.

"You still haven't convinced me," he said.

The war room's blue-white lights added a jolt that boosted Caitlin's Red Bull buzz. "If the task force releases information that seems credible, it will set Hayden off. So …"

Rainey pointed with her protein bar. "If we announce a sighting via the media …"

"He's going to have his doubts," Caitlin said. "Because he's not simply suspicious—he's a cynic. He expects the authorities to put out misleading information."

At the conference table, Keyes brought up the 3-D representation of the Midnight Man's hunting grounds, like twin calderas around the buffer zones.

He typed. "It's like that Ukrainian politician who was 'assassinated'—then appeared at a press conference. He and the cops had faked his death as a sting. With every announcement like that, confidence in what you're hearing decays." He flung them a glance. "At least, for a paranoid."

Emmerich said, "So if Hayden would mistrust an announcement from the media ..."

Caitlin said, "He'll want to verify that this news is also on police radio."

Emmerich's expression altered. The neutrality retreated. "Because he would expect the LAPD to lie to the public, with the cooperation or unwitting compliance of the media. But he would presume that internally, the police act on the *real* information."

"Absolutely."

She was squeezing her Red Bull in her fist. The one she was drinking. The spare was squeezed in her other fist. Peripherally, she saw Detective Alvarez following their conversation.

Emmerich grew animated. "Hayden would seek a source of information he trusts. You think he has access to a police scanner?"

"He may even have his mother's radio." Worry for Gretchen Maddox brushed the back of her neck.

"He's cautious about *everything*. I would bet my paycheck that, at minimum, he has a police scanner app," she said. "In all the videos of the Midnight Man leaving crime scenes, he's playing with his phone. Why? He's not posting to Instagram. I think he's monitoring the scanner."

Emmerich mulled it. "If he's dumped the Jeep, he's probably also turned off his phone to prevent us from tracking him. Maybe tossed it, got a burner. He has his dad's cash and credit cards."

Keyes raised his head. "Detective Solis got a warrant for cell site data on Hayden's phone number. The last ping was seventy-four minutes ago. Appears he turned it off at that point." His words tumbled out, a spray. "But if we put this story out, that the Jeep has been sighted ..."

"Burner?" Emmerich said.

"No. Why do people get burner phones? Text and voice calls."

Caitlin nodded. "And Hayden's not calling or texting anybody. He has no confederates and no friends. He's not going to contact the cops or the media."

"And the kind of burner a teenager like Hayden Maddox could get—let's say tonight—with the cash from his father's wallet?" Keyes said. "It won't be a smart phone. Won't have the capability to load apps. And his laptop was left at his parents' house."

"Meaning?" Emmerich said.

Caitlin said, "Confirming the news via the police scanner app will be irresistible. Even though he knows his phone can be tracked, Hayden will turn it on. Maybe just long enough to check the app. And when he does, we can find him."

She held her breath. If this had any chance of drawing Hayden into the open—digitally at a minimum, physically if they were lucky—it would take teamwork.

Detective Alvarez walked over. His face was its usual storm. Caitlin stiffened. Of all the detectives on the task force, Alvarez was the one who most doubted the FBI's value to the investigation. He was the one who'd nearly punched Emmerich over the death of Sheriff's Deputy Ohlmeyer.

His hands hung at his sides. "Did I hear you say you need a black Jeep Renegade?"

Caitlin eyed him crossways. "Maybe."

He jerked a thumb at the windows. "Because mine's outside."

46

By 11:15 P.M., Detective Alvarez's Jeep was in place, angled carelessly along a curb outside a suburban park. The residential neighborhood south of downtown was quiet. The park featured soccer fields, playground equipment, and picnic grounds in a grove of oaks. The Renegade looked black, dusty, and alluring.

"Baitsy," Alvarez called it.

Behind a hedge that ran alongside the Methodist church at the corner, Caitlin and Emmerich waited. On a cross street, Rainey and Keyes were parked on a driveway at a house whose owners were gone for the holidays, their Suburban squeezed between a bass-fishing boat and an RV.

The street was wide, with good sight lines. The block—entry, exit, access through the park—had a defensible perimeter. Emmerich had binoculars, Caitlin a nightscope.

Keyes had gamed it out, with enthusiasm and high anxiety. Before they'd left the war room, he plumbed his geographic profile to judge the r oads the Midnight Man most frequently traveled and where, statistically, he had most likely driven tonight. From that, he extrapolated locations where Hayden might want to dump his Jeep.

"Somewhere he thinks it'll be safe," Keyes said. "Because I can't believe he wants to give it up. He'll want it as a backup. So he's not going to drive it into the LA River, or some vacant lot where he's afraid it would be stolen and sent to a chop shop."

Alvarez said, "It's a misconception that cars left in low-rent neighborhoods are instantly jacked or stripped. Most people who live in low-rent neighborhoods drive cars, and nobody gives them a second glance."

"I know. I know," Keyes said, almost tripping over his own words. "But Hayden may not. And he doesn't want his Jeep to get jacked."

"No," Rainey said. "He's paranoid. He doesn't want to relinquish control. Doesn't want anybody to get into his business. If he can't destroy the Jeep instantly and completely, he'll park it someplace he thinks is safe."

"Right," Keyes said. "And under pressure, 'safe' is going to register as 'familiar.' So I judge that he'd park the Renegade within his hunting grounds, along a path he knows well. And"—he held out his hands—"someplace where he can access further transportation. Metro Rail, bus stops, anonymous, easy ways for him to split from the neighborhood."

"We found a receipt in his bedroom wastebasket for a monthly Metro travel pass," Alvarez said.

Keyes' shoulders dropped with relief. "That confirms all my suspicions."

Rainey asked Alvarez, "Can you track his movements with the pass?"

"We can get a solid map of where he traveled in the last month."

Keyes put the geographic profile up on the big screen. "Hayden attacked his father midafternoon. Then he headed south. He crossed the mountains and kept going. He attacked in Bay Rise. He grabbed Hannah from Bay Rise. All south." He took a breath.

Caitlin stared at the screen. "When he shot his dad at their home, he destroyed that buffer zone. He's not going back."

"Right. Psychologically as well as geographically, I think, he's still on this side of the mountains. Centering in the south buffer zone. That's where he dumped the Jeep."

He walked to the screen and indicated. "Near one of these freeways. Because they intersect with major bus and train lines that run downtown."

Everybody agreed. Alvarez said, "So where do we plant the bait Jeep?"

"That's the beauty of it," Keyes said. "We park it where *we* want, not where *he* left his."

Now here they were. A middle-class area patrolled out of the Sheriff's Carson station. A quiet street. Equidistant to the 110 and 405 freeways.

And easy walking distance to a Metro Rail station.

Alvarez had modified the license plate on his Jeep to appear—from a distance, in poor light—like the plate number registered to Hayden Maddox. Baitsy wore camouflage. Parked at the curb, it was now bracketed by two Sheriff's cruisers.

Road crew spotlights had been set up, glaring down on the Renegade. Deputies walked around the scene, supervised by Alvarez and his partner, Detective Durand. Two other officers were searching the vehicle, dressed in white Tyvek suits, as if they were from the forensic unit.

Once the stage was set, the play had been put in motion. The Carson sheriff's station put out a bulletin: the Jeep being sought in the Amber Alert had been stopped.

Community reporters had picked it up, and the social media feeds of local newspapers and television channels. No further information had been made available.

Over police-band radio, however, it was different.

Through Sheriff's Department patrol units, dispatchers, and task force detectives, they spread word that when the suspect vehicle had been pulled over, the person driving it was not Hayden Maddox. It was a man who had hot-wired it.

"Wait—you're saying the Amber Alert vehicle got stolen from the kidnapper?"

"Unbelievable but apparently true. Driver was not the owner of the SUV. No question."

"Deputies stop a vehicle sought by every cop on the street, and the guy at the wheel is a car thief?"

"Yeah. 'It's not mine, I'm not the Midnight Man ... I just stole it. Honest.'"

Laughter.

"Guy's been arrested for GTA."

"That interrogation will be fun."

A stern voice broke into the banter. "Enough. Keep it off the air."

"It's a good setup," Emmerich murmured, binoculars to his eyes.

"It's a roll of the dice. But I'm glad everyone anted up."

Caitlin was cold and amped. And fearful that this was a mistake. Rushed. Overkill. That they would go home empty-handed.

That Hannah would never be found.

She put the nightscope to her eye and scanned the view. The air was dry, which meant her breath didn't wreathe when she exhaled. That was good. The sleeves of her sweater pulled against the scabbed cuts on her forearms. The sensation, she realized, was annoying. Her skin felt sore and tender. And the tugging was only physical. At least for now, every craving to cut had evaporated.

In her earpiece she heard Keyes, speaking on an encrypted radio frequency that police scanners couldn't monitor.

"I'm on with the phone company," he said quietly. "They're monitoring Hayden's phone in real time. Let's hope it pings a cell tower."

Concealed behind the hedge, Caitlin had a clear view of Alvarez's Jeep. She thought: *Walk into view, Hayden. Then come quietly. Please.*

If he didn't, if nobody showed up, they were burning minutes that Hannah didn't have.

Emmerich checked his diver's watch. The illuminated dial showed they'd been in place half an hour. It felt like a century.

Then the wind dropped. A dog barked, distantly.

And another, closer. Caitlin raised her scope.

At the park, beyond the soccer fields, a figure lurked in the band of trees. Magnified in night-vision green, his eyes swept the view and settled on the Jeep. Caitlin's pulse picked up. The view through the scope pulsated, emerald.

Emmerich murmured into his radio. "Subject at ten o'clock."

At the Jeep, the detectives continued searching it, without a twitch. They knew that if Hayden was watching, it wouldn't take him long to realize the vehicle wasn't his.

That didn't matter. Getting him securely within the perimeter did.

Caitlin watched the distant figure in the trees. He crept forward like a cat, smooth and slow and focused, keeping himself tucked among the oaks.

Caitlin's words fell as a whispered breath. "Come on."

The moments before, those uncertain seconds, the holding back, were agony to her. Impatience and anxiety bubbled along her nerves. *Let's go,* she wanted to shout. She held still, her head throbbing.

The figure in the trees slunk forward. Almost into the open.

They couldn't move before confirming it was Hayden. If they leaped on the first person who wandered inside the perimeter, they would lose the element of surprise. And if Hayden, paranoid watcher, was hiding and observing from another vantage, he would melt away before they ever spotted him.

In her earpiece, Caitlin heard Alvarez. "Is it him?"

"High probability," Emmerich said. "Same build, hoodie, ball cap. But the trees provide too much concealment. We don't have a positive ID yet."

"I'd grab this sneaky bastard in the trees, but Hayden has cash," Alvarez said. "I wouldn't put it past him to pay somebody from the bus stop to jog to the park, spy on the scene, and report back. All the while peeping to see what happens."

Keyes broke in, a top note of insistence in his voice. "Phone company got a ping on Hayden's phone."

Caitlin felt a white flash of elation—and validation. "Where? When?"

"Downtown. Forty-seven minutes ago," Keyes said. "That's after the Amber Alert went out."

Emmerich said, "Just one ping?"

"I'll get back to you," Keyes said.

In the trees, the figure slid to the left.

"He's moving," Emmerich said. "Still within the trees."

Rainey's voice came through the earpiece. "He's changing vantage points to get a better angle on the Jeep. Think he's trying to get a look at the tag."

Keyes came back on. More excited. "Second ping, twenty minutes ago. Five miles south of downtown. He's moving this way."

Alvarez said, "Is it pinging *now?*"

Caitlin stopped breathing, eye to the nightscope. The greenish figure, a shimmering revenant, darted along inside the tree line. Light on his feet, an ease in his stride even as he employed what resembled military stealth.

"Subject walks like him," she said. "I'd stake everything on it."

Rainey said, "I've lost sight of him from this angle."

Emmerich had the binoculars to his eyes. After a second, he said, "We're not going to get a one-hundred percent confirmed ID as long as he's in the trees. Your call, Alvarez."

Alvarez stood beside his Renegade, facing Emmerich and Caitlin. Behind him, across the park, the figure in the trees stepped sideways.

"He's moving," Caitlin said. "Few more steps, he'll be in position to read the Jeep's plate."

Alvarez unzipped his jacket for quick access to his weapon. "Right. We move." He drew a visible breath. "On my count of three."

At the edge of the oak grove, a pickup truck rounded a corner.

"Dammit," Caitlin said.

They hadn't locked down the neighborhood—no roadblocks, no stop-and-searches. They couldn't have, not without scaring off the Midnight Man. The roads were open.

The figure across the park was standing just within the tree line. When the pickup arced through its turn, its headlights striped him.

The driver braked and hit the high beams.

The headlights overwhelmed the nightscope. Like a phosphorous grenade exploding, everything went greenish-white. Caitlin turned her head and pulled the scope from her face, hissing.

Her vision was skewed, one eye painfully night-blind, the other clear.

And she saw: Hayden Maddox stood frozen the glare of the headlights. He stared.

And bolted.

"He's running," Emmerich yelled into his radio. "Go, go, go."

They broke cover, hard in pursuit.

47

Caitlin tore from behind the church hedge and ran across the street, past the Jeep Renegade, onto the playing fields. Ahead of her Alvarez sprinted for the tree line, gun in his hand. Hayden had disappeared into the dark cover of the oaks.

Alvarez shouted into his shoulder-mounted radio, calling the unmarked Sheriff's cars positioned around the perimeter. "Suspect is fleeing on foot, east toward Devine. White male. Black hoodie. Presumed armed and extremely dangerous."

Caitlin accelerated. "Take him alive. We have to know where Hannah is."

Alvarez repeated that into the radio. Pointed to Caitlin. "You go left. I'll go right."

From all around them, headlights and engines fired up. Flashing red and blue lights. Back at the church, Emmerich squealed out of the parking lot in the Suburban.

His voice in her earpiece. "I'm heading east to intercept him."

The other FBI Suburban roared down the south side of the block, Rainey's voice terse over the radio. "Same."

Caitlin sent a quick glance Alvarez's way. He nodded, and they entered the trees.

Already breathing hard, Caitlin let her eyes adjust to the darkness of the grove. Listening. She held her Glock barrel down. Raising the nightscope again, she did a fast sweep of the grove, a hundred eighty degrees. Caught a green glow from Alvarez to her right, gun and flashlight raised, advancing steadily. Swept left. The headlights and light strips beyond the trees threatened to overwhelm her vision again. She blinked, gun held alongside her right leg, as she scanned.

On the street, a Suburban swept past. Emmerich.

Behind it, a swift figure raced from the trees and darted across the road.

"He just crossed the street heading north. Toward houses," she said into her radio.

Jamming the nightscope in her pocket, she ran. Alvarez's footsteps joined hers. Ahead, Emmerich braked hard and reversed.

She and Alvarez left the trees and crossed the road. Ahead, dogs barked. The gate along the side of a house was swinging.

"There," she called.

Alvarez followed her through the gate, radioing Sheriff's units to cover the next street over.

On the back patio a dog burst toward them, barking frantically. Caitlin saw bearish fur and teeth. She slid past just as the dog reached the end of its chain and jerked up short. Alvarez hurried to the back fence and pulled himself up to peer over.

"Bushes crushed. He jumped. This way."

He scaled the fence. Caitlin took a running leap and hauled herself over after him.

Alvarez ran across the lawn, radioing his location. Caitlin touched her earpiece and did the same. House lights were coming on. Porch lights. Voices. More dogs.

The loudest dogs were barking in the yard next door.

"Alvarez." She ran to the side fence and hauled herself up to peer over. Her skin goose-bumped. She wondered, abruptly, whether Hayden lurked on the other side, aiming a gun her way loaded with LAPD ammo.

Instead she saw dogs at the far end of that yard, barking at the fence as if berating a fleeing raccoon. In the yard beyond that, motion lights flipped on.

"This way," she shouted.

Alvarez ran out a gate toward the street. "I'll take the sidewalk."

She scaled the fence, scrabbling for purchase in her boots, and dropped into the next yard. Ran across, past dogs barking so crazily that they didn't notice her. Took the next fence and dropped into the yard wildly lit by the surveillance lights. A man threw open his patio door and raised a samurai sword.

"FBI. Get inside, sir." She shouted it, hoping he wouldn't charge her, that he'd spot the jacket with the letters F-B-I ten inches tall.

The man blinked and retreated, the sword catching on his swirling curtains. At the far side of the house came the noise of trash cans falling over.

Voice in her earpiece. Alvarez. "Suspect just ran across a front lawn and up an alley."

She rounded the side of the house, nearly collided with the spilled trash cans, and jumped them as she ran out the gate. On surrounding roads, lights and sirens were headed north. Across the street Alvarez raced into the alley.

"Emmerich," she said into her radio.

The Suburban powered around the corner, high beams blaring. She jumped in, pointing at the alley. Emmerich spun the wheel and floored it. She slammed against the door as he turned. She put her seat belt on, lowered her window, and heard more dogs barking. A cacophony was rising, the chase spiraling rather than focusing. Hayden had again created havoc and slipped into a seam of shadow.

At the far end of the alley, Alvarez stopped, his head swiveling back and forth. Emmerich pulled up beside him.

"Which way?" Emmerich said.

The street was empty. No barking, no security lights.

Alvarez pointed behind the Suburban. "I think he doubled back."

"What happened to our perimeter?" Caitlin said.

"Sneaky fucking teenager," Alvarez said.

Radio static interrupted. "All units in the vicinity of Obsidian Drive, report of a stolen vehicle."

Emmerich turned it up. White Corolla stolen from outside a home—a pizza delivery driver's car.

Alvarez grabbed the window frame. "Obsidian, that's three blocks south."

Detective Durand slewed around the corner at the wheel of Alvarez's Jeep. Alvarez motioned him out of the driver's seat, jumped behind the wheel, and they raced off. Emmerich followed. By the time they reached Obsidian Drive, another 911 call had come in. Dangerous driver heading west.

In her earpiece, Caitlin heard Alvarez. "I think he's trying to make it to the freeway. But he's in a delivery car with an illuminated plastic pizza on the roof. He won't outrun us for long in that thing."

"What other resources you got?" Caitlin said. "Who's coming?"

"Air support's inbound." Alvarez was shouting to be heard over the sound of his Jeep's racing engine. "Sheriff's Department helicopter. LAPD too. Both have FLIR."

Forward Looking Infrared. Thermal imaging cameras that could spot heat signatures.

"Good," Caitlin said.

Emmerich was silent at the wheel, pouring along the road, streetlights striping his face. Caitlin glanced up through the windshield. The skies were clear. Flying would be no problem.

Emmerich opened a channel to the rest of the BAU team. "Rainey."

"Here," she replied. "We're near the park—in case he doubles back."

"Cancel that. He's in a vehicle heading for a freeway at high speed. Contact the Tactical Aviation Unit."

He wanted an FBI helo in the sky, and Rainey with it.

The road swept past, strip malls brightly lit, busy with late-evening diners, Christmas parties, bars and clubs full.

"He's in the open," Emmerich said. "We have to get him before he slides back into the seam. We're not letting him slip through our fingers again."

But Hayden had escaped from one police pursuit once already by using deadly force. There was no reason he wouldn't expect to elude this one. And no reason he couldn't succeed.

But not forever.

"He can't keep it up," she said.

"With anyone else I'd say this is the end, but not the Midnight Man." Emmerich's voice had a strange, attenuated tone to it. His mouth clamped shut, a white line.

"What are you thinking?" A feeling like cold water poured down her back. "GSK?"

He drove, silent. Confirming her suspicion—he was thinking of the Golden State Killer, who eluded an FBI agent and disappeared into a dark Santa Barbara neighborhood one autumn night. At the time, the escape of a neighborhood prowler had seemed merely unfortunate. But the GSK went on to murder at least ten people, beyond several he'd already killed in Northern California. Forty years later, when his statewide reign of terror was laid bare, the prowler's escape came to be seen as a disastrous turning point. After that night, he left no victims alive.

Radio static again. The Sheriff's dispatcher. "Hit and run at the intersection of Garnett and Criner. Suspect vehicle is a white pizza delivery car, heading west."

Emmerich jammed the pedal down. The flashing blue of their light strip reflected off roadside buildings. Caitlin brought up Criner and Garnett on GPS.

"Half a mile ahead."

They blazed along. Up the road, flashing lights became visible.

Alvarez came on. "We have the vehicle in sight and multiple units inbound. We're going to blockade the road. Cut him off."

Caitlin put a hand to the dashboard. Ahead, through traffic, she caught a glimpse of white.

"I see him."

The car was a block ahead, its pizza sign shining. It burned through a red light at the intersection. The Sheriff's cruisers followed. Alvarez. The Suburban. Gaining.

Several blocks ahead, a wall of flashing lights filled the street. The roadblock was taking shape.

The pizza car arrowed straight toward the next intersection. Red light. Three lanes of stopped cars. He braked. Smoke rose from his tires.

He veered toward the curb, but telephone poles and a bus stop prevented him from cutting onto the sidewalk.

"He's penned."

Caitlin's pulse was pumping. She gripped the dash. *Come on. Stop. Surrender.*

The pizza car slewed, tires squealing, and skidded sideways. Its passenger side bashed the back of a car waiting at the red light. The line of stopped cars accordioned.

"Jesus," Caitlin said.

The driver's door of the pizza car flew open and a swift figure climbed out, slid across the hood, and caromed between crushed vehicles whose drivers were still too shocked to react.

"He's running," she said.

Emmerich's voice was an icepick. "Do not lose sight of him."

And she thought: *Don't carjack anybody, Hayden.* Don't put a hollow-point round through another person's head. Run—and we'll catch you.

He ducked from view behind a delivery truck.

"Hell." She opened the door and leaped out.

Ran between vehicles, through a jumble of cars whose horns were blaring nonstop, hoods crumpled, radiators blowing steam. She ran past the delivery truck. Where was he?

A man shouted, "*Cocksucker.*" And a motorcycle engine revved.

A bike whizzed into view and sped past her. The bike's owner was on the pavement, climbing to his feet, pulling his helmet off. He saw her and spread his arms.

"Asshole stole my bike."

The motorcycle jumped the curb into a strip mall parking lot and cut into an alley. Caitlin ran back to the Suburban.

"He's on two wheels." She pointed. "Heading for the 110."

Lights flashing, hand on the horn, Emmerich worked his way past the crash. Sheriff's units, bright spikes of light, tore after the bike.

"He got on the freeway," Alvarez said over the radio. "In pursuit."

A few seconds behind, Emmerich hauled the big SUV up the on-ramp. Despite the hour, the freeway was busy. Emmerich followed Alvarez's Jeep. Radio chatter. The Sheriff's helicopter was two minutes out.

"He's dodging between lanes," Alvarez said. "Little shit knows how to drive that thing."

Traffic thickened. Emmerich pulled onto the left shoulder and raced along, inches from the concrete median barriers. The helicopter swept past overhead. Its spotlight painted the road.

The freeway took a bend, and in the distance Caitlin saw the cloverleaf interchange with the 105 freeway. Four levels of twisting concrete. A stack interchange. Autopia dystopia.

"He'll try to lose us there," she said.

The interchange approached. Alvarez swung to the right-hand shoulder, stopped, jumped out of the Jeep, and ran to a guardrail. Below the rail was scrub and dense brush.

Emmerich squealed up beside them. Caitlin put down her window. Alvarez pointed. "He drove the bike off the road. Down there."

The interchange took up acres of land. A set of cloverleaf bends half a mile in diameter, it was ten swirling lanes of concrete and ramps that curved a hundred feet overhead. Caitlin listened for the blatt of the motorcycle engine. She couldn't hear it against all the traffic.

Alvarez radioed their location. Called for CHP backup, LAPD, everybody. Then he said, "Screw it," climbed over the guardrail, and pelted down the shoulder and into the night-darkened brush. Caitlin looked at Emmerich.

"Go," he said.

She jumped out. The noise was overpowering, headlights whipping past, eighteen-wheelers rolling by with massive drafts of air.

This interchange wasn't just sweeping ramps. It sat amid dense residential neighborhoods. Major surface streets led in all directions. And, at the center of the interchange complex: escalators, elevators, and platforms for the Metro Rail Green Line. A level up from the 110 roadway was the Silver Line express bus station.

A few people stood on the brightly lit rail platform, their attention drawn to the flashing lights of the vehicles stopped on the freeway shoulder. Caught, perplexed, by the strangeness of people on foot, standing at the roadside. Stillness amid the constant flow. Caitlin hopped the guardrail and followed Alvarez down the slope, pebbles and dust flying from beneath her boots. The helicopter's engine droned high overhead, but the sound dimmed as she scraped through chaparral and ran past the massive concrete pylons that supported one of the cloverleaf ramps.

Following the beam from Alvarez's flashlight, she pushed through the brush, aware of the cold, the smell of exhaust, the weird no-man's land. As she caught up, they heard the revving of a motorcycle engine. They exchanged a glance. Abruptly alone, together. They raised their weapons and stepped around opposite sides of a pylon.

The motorcycle lay on its side on the dirt. Engine gunning, back wheel spinning. They swept their flashlights around the scene.

Hayden was gone.

Caitlin's skin tingled. She and Alvarez turned back to back. Everything was darkness, invisibility, speed, motion.

"We can't lose him, not now." She swiveled her head toward the Metro Rail station. Her heart dropped. "We need to get people watching the trains. The buses." She was breathing hard. "Goddammit."

In her earpiece came the voice of Nicholas Keyes.

"Hayden's phone just pinged again."

48

aitlin ran back up the slope to the Suburban. Traffic arrowed past it.
Emmerich stood on the hood, binoculars to his eyes, sweeping the
view, blue-tinged by the flashing light strip, talking over the radio to
the Sheriff's Department helicopter. At the Metro Rail station, a fresh
crowd of people eyed them.

In Caitlin's earpiece, Keyes spoke rapidly. "I got that one ping. Cell
tower multilateration put him somewhere to your northeast. Two
minutes ago."

Emmerich jumped off the hood and hurried back behind the wheel.
Caitlin hopped in the passenger seat and slammed the door.

"One ping?" she said.

"Triangulation. He's turned off GPS. And he's powered down
the phone again. We can identify the strongest signal among the three
cell towers he pinged, and narrow down his location to within fifty
meters—of where he was then. But he's been moving. Fast. All I can do
is hope he turns the phone back on."

Emmerich said, "We need a direction to head. Northeast isn't
enough."

"Keyes," Caitlin said. "Did you hear that we found the motorcycle?
Dumped. He ran."

"Figure he turned on his phone when he abandoned the bike,"
Keyes said. "Hold on. The strongest cell tower signal … it was near the
eastbound 105 on-ramp. Hold on."

Emmerich held still, waiting.

"Tracking Hayden's phone via cell tower pings is tricky in real time, but ..." Keyes' voice jumped half an octave. "He pinged again. Hold on."

Caitlin stuck her hand out the window to signal Alvarez. Keyes came back.

"Hayden's vectoring downtown. He's retreating to his buffer zone."

Emmerich said, "Then let's get ahead of him."

Racing downtown on the freeway with Emmerich, Caitlin zoomed in on the 3-D map of the Midnight Man's hunting grounds. It throbbed with false color. Overlaid on the teeming landscape of Los Angeles County, it resembled a psychedelic representation of speakers booming out spikes of sound. Yellow, orange, red, falling to drips of purple. And, in the center, the flat blue-green circle of the downtown buffer zone.

It was a bull's-eye over downtown Los Angeles, two miles in diameter.

They were diving into the bright, shadowed, thumping core of the city. The most densely populated urban metro in the country. The buffer zone included thousands of addresses. Hundreds of streets and freeways. Skyscrapers, stadiums, parks, homeless camps.

And the night was full of people. Though the clock hovered around midnight, LA was out in multitudes. Christmas shopping was at its peak. The Lakers game at Staples Center had just finished. So had a benefit concert at the Music Center.

Alvarez was ahead of them on the freeway. Keyes was driving in from West LA. Emmerich had sent Rainey to join the FBI air unit.

The LAPD was out in force, but many of their officers were detailed to traffic and event security.

Emmerich rolled past the electric purple-blue glow of Staples Center, and the shimmering Ritz-Carlton, and pulled off the freeway.

"If he's on foot, or was delayed stealing another vehicle, we're in good shape," he said.

He didn't mention the alternative. If Hayden was on an express bus, a Metro Rail train, or had lucked into finding a fast car unlocked on somebody's driveway, they were in a race.

And Hayden knew where he was going. Could take a straight shot, a ballistic voyage, directly there. His pursuers were driving semi-blind, hoping to pick up his scent. The police could stop buses, could monitor train stops, could set up more roadblocks, but not everywhere, and not soon enough.

And somewhere, maybe in the heart of the city, was Hannah Guillory. Maybe. And maybe her heart was still beating.

Caitlin's throat constricted. She forced a breath. Emmerich crossed an intersection, office buildings rising on either side, restaurants spilling the last of their diners. Outside a hotel, limos waited to shepherd partygoers home from some swanky bash.

Caitlin tracked their path on the tablet. "We just crossed into the buffer zone."

The stars were gone, overwhelmed by the artificial lightning of the electric grid. Emmerich turned off the Suburban's light strip and slowed to a crawl. Caitlin scanned the sidewalks. On a cross street, an LAPD unit cruised past. Downtown, the FBI and cops provided dozens of eyes, but they couldn't see well enough in the crowded night.

They needed more. They needed a signal from beyond visual range, deeper in the electromagnetic spectrum.

Emmerich cued his radio. "Keyes. Where are you? What do you have?"

Static came back. Nothing.

"Keyes," Emmerich repeated.

"Here," Keyes said breathlessly, distantly. "Had to stop. I'm on Wilshire, heading your way. Pulled over because I can't type on the laptop and drive at the same time."

Emmerich stopped at a light near Figueroa and Seventh Street. There was a shopping center ahead, and a Metrolink station catty-corner to them. A park nearby. People flowing. Caitlin tried to mentally set her brain to search for lanky men with a light, carefree saunter to their stride. Probably with a note of fatigue now. Maybe even jumpy, glancing around over their shoulder. For her and Emmerich, perching here and watching was as good as prowling. Unless they could get definite information to direct them.

Over the radio, she heard Keyes breathing. Typing. Then, frantic. "I found his phone."

She sat up straight.

"Vector," Emmerich said. "We're at Seventh and Figueroa."

"East," Keyes said.

Emmerich pulled around the corner. Caitlin suppressed the thought that Hayden might deliberately leave his phone on a train or bus.

"The pings are intermittent," Keyes said. "But five minutes ago, he turned the phone on long enough to capture its progress from one cell site to the next. It's east of City Hall. Hold on," he said again, like a priest intoning *amen.* "Overlaying a map of active cell sites—there's a zone where it's like a black hole."

Emmerich headed east, easing through intersections.

"There's a major construction zone southeast of City Hall. A quarter mile from LAPD headquarters. Skid Row adjacent," Keyes said. "Several cell sites in the zone have temporarily been taken out of service."

Between buildings they caught sight of City Hall, white and towering. The bustle and flow of shopping petered out. Restaurants were farther between. Bars dingier.

Emmerich swung around a corner into a warehouse district. Some buildings had been converted to loft apartments. Others were abandoned. He radioed their location.

Keyes came back on. "The center point of the buffer zone is two blocks ahead."

Emmerich braked to a stop. Dead ahead was a fenced-off four-square-block redevelopment project. Old office buildings and hotels slated for demolition were cordoned behind screened construction fencing. It comprised a city neighborhood. It was bigger than entire downtowns in some cities. It was darkened and desolate.

"I think we found it," Caitlin said.

She gave Keyes the coordinates.

"That's it," he said. "That's the core of the buffer zone. His phone pinged a cell site just outside it."

It was dark. No street lights. No lights in the empty buildings beyond the fencing.

Ground Zero.

"If the phone's there, we can assume Hayden is too," Emmerich said.

Caitlin's throat squeezed tighter. Hannah could also be there. With Hayden closing in on her.

"We have to go in," she said.

Emmerich paused, eyeing the emptiness across the street. Radioed. "Keyes. Alert the task force commanders. Now."

Emmerich's face was sere. He seemed to have boiled off any extraneous thoughtfulness, emotion, anything except cold focus.

"Right now, we have thin backup," he said. "The perimeter of this zone is massive. The LAPD can be marshaled in force but can't quickly secure it."

Caitlin brought up a detailed city map. "These blocks were cordoned off to keep out scavengers, looters, and squatters during demolition. But this construction fence clearly isn't impenetrable."

"Hardly. Hayden has obviously found access."

She thought about the zone. Scanned the fencing. There were hoardings advertising the demolition company. But also ads for the planned redevelopment. Sleek office towers, more loft apartments, gallery spaces. Dense development, much of it using the existing buildings' original brickwork.

"They're going to use the same footprint as what's there now," she said. "That means these cordoned-off blocks have access to manholes and utility tunnels."

"Underground escape routes," Emmerich said.

There were a few security lights on power poles inside the perimeter.

"I'm calling Detective Solis," Emmerich said. "He's the one who needs to liaise with the city, the demolition company, utilities, find out what's online, what's been turned off."

"If some cell sites in there are still active, it means they're connected to the electric grid. Buildings where construction's in progress will have power. Shutting everything down will take hours."

He looked at her. He didn't want to go in without a solid plan, a much more solid perimeter, and overwhelming tactical backup. She returned the look.

"We don't have hours," she said.

He pulled out his phone as he climbed from the Suburban.

Ten minutes after Emmerich made his phone call, Solis and Weisbach arrived. Alvarez and Durand. Half a dozen uniformed LAPD officers. Other units were patrolling the exterior of the cordon, and several black-and-whites were parked at the corners, spotlights on, trying to cover the fencing. The roads inside the demolition zone were blocked off by concrete barriers. Driving into the neighborhood would be impossible.

A map was spread on the hood of the Suburban. Emmerich, Caitlin, the task force detectives, and the uniformed officers planned to enter on foot and begin a grid search. Solis directed them to cover discrete sectors in pairs. They checked their earpieces.

"Silent entry," Solis said.

Emmerich nodded. "Let's go."

49

A uniformed officer snapped the padlock with bolt cutters and they slipped through the gate into the nowhere zone.

The screened construction fencing dimmed the noise and lights of the city. The air was saturated with the cold. Ahead, darkened buildings stretched for a quarter of a mile. It was an expanse not of ghosts but of nonexistence.

The search group split into teams of two and moved out silently, taking their designated search sectors. Caitlin proceeded with Emmerich, her peacoat unbuttoned, her quick-clearance holster within unimpeded reach. Within a few seconds the other teams disappeared around corners and through doorways.

They took the east side of a street two hundred yards deep in the demolition zone. The wind whistled around corners and through empty window frames of twenty-story office buildings. Beyond the fencing, skyscrapers dazzled the sky. They seemed incomprehensibly distant, separated from the dust-brushed street where Caitlin was walking as if she were viewing them through a time slip.

Drawing their weapons, she and Emmerich cleared a decrepit auto body shop, scuffing across a concrete floor that was gummed with ancient oil spots, checking the empty office, aiming the beams of their flashlights into the service pits and up to the rafters. When they exited, they drew an X on the door in white chalk. On the radio, they heard the other teams moving yard by yard, floor by floor, calling "Clear!" and talking in murmurs, signaling to each other.

Caitlin and Emmerich moved on to a corner market. The glass was missing from the front windows. They stepped through. Swept past empty shelves, open refrigerators, through the swinging doors to the stockroom and loading dock. Up a flight of stairs to an empty apartment. Caitlin's heart hammered with every corner they took, every room they entered.

And behind that hammering, she heard the steady drip of seconds running out. This nowhere zone was huge. But it wasn't endless. If Hayden spotted the search teams before they found Hannah, things would go sideways. He wouldn't simply throw down his weapon and surrender.

From the back of the apartment, Emmerich said, "Clear."

They jogged down the stairs. Caitlin radioed Keyes.

"Any more pings from Hayden's phone?"

"Negative," Keyes said. "He's gone dark. Silent running."

Caitlin climbed out the market's empty window behind Emmerich and drew an X on the wall. Up the street, hundreds of yards away, the beam of another searcher's flashlight passed between two windows of a building, four or five floors up.

"Keep listening," she said.

"Roger."

She and Emmerich jogged through a park crammed with construction equipment. And a vacant lot stacked with rusting, discarded fire escapes. They crossed an intersection. Beyond it, on the street corner, a building filled the winter sky and blocked the stars.

It was a darkened hotel. Faded brick, at least thirty stories tall—at one time it must have been a jewel. Art Deco touches, scrollwork over the grand entrance. A keening sound bent the air—wind, whining as if it was blowing through an evil harmonica. Caitlin's skin crept. Though the building ate the night, slivers of light pierced its edges. The glass in the windows was gone. Caitlin could see in one corner and out the next.

The sign above the entrance had been pried off, but rusting bolts remained. THE SWALLOWTAIL.

Emmerich tilted his head up to take the building in. "Ever hear of H. H. Holmes' Murder Castle?"

"The hotel in Chicago."

Built and operated by a serial killer. Dr. H. H. Holmes had designed the hotel himself and committed a slew of murders there during the 1893 World's Fair. The building had been fitted with windowless interior rooms, secret passageways, an asphyxiation chamber, and a basement crematorium.

"Acid vats, blowtorches in the walls," she said.

"Alarms that buzzed in Holmes' office if anybody tried to leave their room."

"Check in, never out."

"Watch your six."

Emmerich radioed in the address.

A scratchy voice acknowledged—a task force detective stationed outside the cordon to coordinate and run comms. "That's an SRO hotel. Once upon a time was high-end. Grand lobby, bar, ballroom, twenty floors of hotel rooms. Apartments on the top five floors."

Maze. Rat's nest. Final home to the down-and-out. Lair.

"We're entering."

The detective came back. "Heads up. We're cross-referencing addresses in the demolition zone with known associates of Hayden Maddox. The Swallowtail comes up as the last known address of Trey Laforte."

Hayden's uncle. Emmerich and Caitlin exchanged a glance and again drew their weapons.

The massive bronze-gilded doors creaked as they pulled them open. The lightless lobby smelled musty. Their boots squeaked on the marble floor. Their flashlights caught a vaulted ceiling, Greek columns, faded Jazz Age grandeur. A lonely pair of chairs faced each other in the lobby. A malnourished palm drooped in a pot by a fireplace. Dust choked the floor, but there were clear footprints along the main path to the bar and elevator lobby. They couldn't tell who those footprints belonged to—construction workers, or someone else.

They advanced, nerves stretched thin. Emmerich sidestepped to the front desk. It was grimy with layers of dirt. He peered around it, weapon aimed, flashlight sweeping.

"Clear," he said.

They turned and crossed toward the bar, Caitlin leading. From behind them came a *ding*.

They spun. Across the decrepit lobby, an elevator door slid open. A single dingy light bulb illuminated the elevator's interior.

On the floor inside, under its greenish glow, a man sat slumped. Legs splayed, blood-drenched, dead.

50

Caitlin and Emmerich ran across the lobby toward the elevators. The gaping doors slowly slid toward each other, the dingy light narrowing to a slice. Emmerich jammed his arm between the doors like a knife. They spread again. He leaned in and locked them open.

The man inside the elevator had been shot multiple times. Chest, face. The wall behind him was a mad spatter of blood. He sat with his hands upturned at his sides, like a penitent. Slumped, face upturned as well, pointing heavenward.

His eyes were gouged out.

A bolus of acid rolled up Caitlin's throat. She clenched her jaw, dizzy, appalled and unable to turn away.

Emmerich stepped into the elevator. Fingers to the man's neck.

"Body temp's same as mine. He just died." He put on gloves, teased the man's wallet from his back pocket, and flipped it open. "I think we just found Uncle Trey."

Caitlin didn't want to stare too long into the elevator. Her own eyes might burn with the light, and the sight. She needed to be able to see what was in the lobby, beyond the glare, in the dark. She blinked and swallowed.

Stared hard at Trey Laforte's face. There was a silver glint in the dead man's mouth.

Not the silver of alloy fillings. Not teeth. A dull gleam, mixed with a coppery color, that filled the space between his parted lips.

"What's that?"

Emmerich nudged his jaw open. The man's mouth was packed with spent bullets.

Caitlin let out a rough breath. "Jesus God."

The rounds, copper-jacketed, had peeled open when they hit their targets, blooming with a leaden shine into six-point flowers of death. From their luster, they had been washed after being dug from victims' bodies, but blood-black streaks remained. Hollow-points.

As Emmerich parted Trey Laforte's lips, the man's head tilted. The bullets poured out and down his chest. Tumbling like deadly petals, poisonous, glinting under the grimy light bulb.

Emmerich rose and backed away, staring at the body. He seemed to be struggling as hard as Caitlin was to process this. To force it to make actual sense. To believe it existed.

From the opposite end of the dark elevator lobby came another *ding.*

Caitlin turned. Down the elevator bank, another door opened. The bulb inside was winking erratically. Every nerve in Caitlin's body seemed to blaze at once.

Inside the elevator, hands bound and mouth gagged with duct tape, was Hannah Guillory.

She was standing. Breathing. Round-eyed with fear, shoulders shaking. The flickering light bulb buzzed, like a bug sending Morse Code. Like lightning.

Caitlin's heart tripped. Hannah was alive. Right there.

Behind her, his face shadowed, stood a figure in black.

It took less than a second but felt like an hour. The shadowed figure, eyes hidden beneath the brim of his ball cap, put a hand to Hannah's back to shove her out of the elevator ahead of him. Hannah stood rigid. Her eyes, like spotlights, hit Caitlin.

Caitlin and Emmerich were in motion, arrowing down the lobby. Every synapse, every muscle, every nerve in Caitlin's body was driving her toward the elevator.

The Midnight Man spotted them.

He yanked Hannah back and hit the control panel. The elevator doors slid shut.

Caitlin ran into them, almost full force. She pounded her left hand against the metal, hammering.

Emmerich flicked his radio. "All units. This is Emmerich. He's at the Swallowtail Hotel."

No reply. Again, Emmerich keyed transmit and got nothing.

"Comms are blocked." He scanned the walls. "We're in an electronic dead zone."

The fear in Hannah's eyes seemed to burn Caitlin. "Stairs."

She ran from the elevator lobby, swinging her flashlight, hunting for the stairs. She found them along the north side of the lobby.

"Here." She shoved open the fire door and glanced back.

Emmerich had his phone to his ear, still trying to contact backup. From the direction he was facing, she knew he wanted to race outside and call from the radio when he got a clear signal—or shout up the street to get another searcher's attention. It was sensible. It was procedure.

"Boss," she shouted. "Call from the stairwell. It has elevation and open windows. Please."

She was willing to go without him, though she knew that would be rash. But leaving the building, giving Hayden extra time to harm Hannah, felt intolerably more reckless. Her entire body was vibrating.

Emmerich held for half a second. Then ran toward her. Her nerves leaped.

They charged up the stairwell. Boots thudding, hitting broken bits of glass, the night dull outside, walls of other abandoned buildings looming. No echo on the concrete, because the windows were gone, the cold night wind swirling through.

On the first few floors they took turns darting out, one of them throwing open the door to the hotel hallway hoping to catch the elevator if it stopped soon—or at least get a radio signal—while the other continued to run up the stairs to the next landing. Five flights up, out of breath, Emmerich shouted into the radio, again, "All units."

A thin voice replied. "Here. It's Keyes."

Emmerich didn't slow, kept running, his voice coming in gulps. "Swallowtail Hotel." He shouted the address. "Get backup. Bring everybody. Rain down hell."

"On it," Keyes called back, his voice swimming away into static.

In the stairwell, they heard the elevator bell. They paused, listening closely, desperate to confirm the location of the sound. All Caitlin could hear was her own heavy breathing and the drumming of her heart. Emmerich pointed up. The floor above.

They climbed and emerged into a darkened hallway. It smelled close, of sweat and moldy carpet. Midway down, a dingy sliver of light narrowed, like a snake's pupil contracting. The elevator door was closing.

Beyond it, a shadow disappeared into a hotel room and swept out of sight.

Using hand signals, Emmerich directed Caitlin toward the door. Go. With an agonizing effort at silence they advanced past the elevators, past rooms with closed doors, rooms with missing doors, feeling a sharp draft that pulled threads of Caitlin's hair from her ponytail. She forcibly calmed her breathing. Needing to hear every creak and bump.

They had seen a single shadow. He'd left Hannah someplace. Put her someplace. Where?

At the door where the shadow had vanished, Emmerich paused. Close behind him, Caitlin put her hand on his shoulder and squeezed. He nodded. Signaled. Go.

He cleared the doorway. In close formation they entered the room, weapons raised, sweeping the view.

Their flashlights caught peeling paint. An empty window, a view over the demolition zone to the spangled lights of East LA. A closet. A door to the bathroom—a corner they would need to clear. No nearby noise. Caitlin's finger was on the trigger. If she sensed a sound, a dash of motion, a breath on her neck, she had to verify it wasn't Hannah before she could even conceive of squeezing it.

She smelled mildew, felt loose carpet bunched beneath her feet.

Emmerich advanced, step by step, eyes pinned on the view in his flashlight beam and the darkness beyond it.

They were five feet inside the door. Emmerich stepping silently. Caitlin was inches behind him. She heard the groaning sound beneath their feet.

She grabbed for Emmerich's shoulder. "Back—"

The floor collapsed beneath them.

51

With a nightmare snap, the floor became nothing but fabric and splinters and air. Wood squealed and split. Caitlin and Emmerich plunged through rotten beams. A nerve-sparking, breath-stealing drop. Into the empty dark.

Instinct flared. With a shout, Caitlin flung out her arms. She grabbed a rusting pipe and jerked to a stop, feet swinging. Choking on dust and wood pulp. The pipe creaked, the thick rust flaking beneath her palms, her hands slipping.

Below her came a terrible crash. She had a dreadful sense of vacant space below her dangling feet. She heard her Glock and flashlight clatter to a hard floor.

Emmerich was no longer in front of her. She knew he'd fallen, didn't believe it, couldn't bear it. The pipe creaked, whining ominously. Dark above and below. Her scalp prickled. She was exposed.

She dared to look down. Ambient light from a wall of windows played like mercury on the view below. Through swirling dust, she saw.

Emmerich had plummeted twenty feet into the decrepit ballroom. He had crashed through stacked furniture and hit hard.

Hanging from the pipe, Caitlin tried to see the room. Tables and lounge furniture. A grand bar—almost directly below her. She hung, hands grinding on the rust, and estimated the drop. Pulse drumming, she swung, held her breath, and let go. She dropped onto the bar with a thunderous clop.

She crouched and peered back up, fearing what she'd see. The sight chilled her. Overhead, the hole in the ceiling was obvious.

It was a trap.

The rug had perfectly concealed the rotting beams. As slow and careful as they'd been, they'd still moved too fast. She should have kept in mind the Midnight Man's trickery, the way he'd rigged his closet with firecrackers to injure people who walked past or reached into his realm unsuspecting. *Hell.*

Through the empty wall of windows came starlight and cold air and the distant sounds of the city. On the floor, from the midst of jumbled tables and furniture covered in sheets, the beam of her flashlight beckoned.

Aside from the sound of falling debris hitting the hardwood floor, the room itself was silent.

Crouched, she peered at the jungle of stacked furniture. "Emmerich."

No reply.

"Boss," she said, louder. "CJ."

She jumped off the bar. Cast a tingling glance at the black hole in the ballroom ceiling. Then clambered her way through the mountain of furniture to retrieve her flashlight.

She grabbed the Maglite and swept it around. Her Glock had to have fallen close by. But it could have bounced off any number of surfaces and skidded halfway across the room.

"*Emmerich.*"

A groan.

She turned. Heard the moan again, and maybe a word. *Here.*

Scrambling, pushing aside broken chairs and upended cocktail tables, she moved through the furniture castle. Still couldn't find her Glock.

Emmerich lay motionless amid splintered tables and chairs. Face down, arms splayed, right leg at a gut-turning angle. She worked her way toward him.

"Chris."

Still he didn't move. *Jesus, please …*

As she knelt at his side, his hand twitched. Fingers clawing, retracting into a fist. His head was turned away. She put a hand on his shoulder.

"Can you hear me?"

He mumbled but didn't lift his head. She didn't want to move him. She clambered over his back so she could see his face. Checked that he was breathing normally, that his pupils weren't blown, that he wasn't already gone into the dusk of death. He clawed the floor. She shined the flashlight on his face. His eyes met hers. There, not there.

No sign of his Glock either.

Overhead came a creak, scuttling noises, rat sounds. She swung the flashlight up.

A shadow slid through the hole in the ceiling. Dropped, and nimbly landed on the bar.

The city lights revealed his face. Caitlin's skin contracted.

Apple-pie features, school yearbook smile, killer's eyes. Raging confidence.

The Midnight Man, Hayden Maddox.

He crouched, the black hoodie engulfing him like a roach's carapace, breathing slowly. And drew a handgun.

Matte black, so small, seemingly so light. A familiar outline, ubiquitous, the staple of every movie and video game teenage boys played. Such a small hole in the end of the barrel. But she'd seen what came from that gun. How quickly, purely, absolutely it rendered death.

Hayden ejected the magazine, then reinserted it and slammed it home. He was between her and the door.

Ducking, Caitlin grabbed Emmerich's wrists and desperately pulled, trying to get him out of Hayden's sight. As she crabbed backward, peripherally she saw the shadow on the bar straighten to his full height. Arm extended.

Hayden's first gunshot sailed over her head and hit the wall.

She hauled, her veins hissing with adrenaline. Emmerich lay like a 170-pound sack of quicklime, his belt buckle scraping the floor and catching on slats in the hardwood.

Hayden's second shot ripped splinters from the floor six feet away. *God.*

Fear buzzed through her, an electric force. Caitlin dragged

Emmerich behind a sheet-draped sofa. Footsteps thudded as Hayden jumped from the bar onto a nearby table.

"Twinkle, twinkle, Darkstar. Come out, come out, wherever you are."

He sounded like a Cub Scout.

"*Bitch.*"

He fired again. His ejected brass landed with a *ting* near Caitlin's shoulder.

He was practically on top of her. Dropping flat, Caitlin belly crawled, sweeping her hands along the floor, searching for her gun. Hayden made a kissy sound, as if calling a cat.

Then he began to sing.

"All around the mulberry bush, the monkey chased the weasel ..."

His voice was lilting and jokey. She couldn't find her Glock.

"The monkey thought, 'I've got a gun ...'"

She had no place else to go. She turned. She was going to have to charge him.

Forcing away the image of his gun barrel, the all-devouring eye of death, she drew her knife and braced herself.

Directly above her, a table creaked. Hayden whispered. "Pop! goes the—"

"*FBI. Drop your weapon.*"

Emmerich racked the slide on his Glock.

Hayden's shoes squeaked as he spun toward the sound. He fired, the noise blaring in Caitlin's ears, and dived off the table.

She heard him hit the floor, but amid shadows and jumbled furniture, couldn't spot him. She cast a look over her shoulder. Through moonlight she caught Emmerich's eye. He'd barely moved behind the sofa. He had no angle and no strength to take a shot. He was bluffing.

Hayden's footsteps drummed, running.

Emmerich slid his gun across the floor at her. She lunged and grabbed it. Climbed to a crouch.

The racing footsteps accelerated. She swung the Glock toward the sound. It faded—Hayden was breaking for the ballroom door. Caitlin leaned around the stacked tables.

Hayden fired again. Blindly, over his shoulder. She ducked. The heavy door banged open and he sped from the ballroom.

Sheathing her knife, Caitlin scrambled back to Emmerich's side. He had pulled himself up and slumped against the sofa. His face was cornflour white and glazed with sweat. She put a hand on his arm. His skin was clammy.

Sitting up had left him panting. "Keep the Glock. Go."

She shed her coat and draped it over him. The ballroom door swung slowly shut. Hayden's footsteps thumped in the stairwell.

"He's—"

She'd been about to say, *He's fleeing the building*. But the rhythm of his footsteps was wrong. He was climbing.

In her earpiece a voice rose, distant and staticky. "There are lights on the top floor."

Caitlin leaped to her feet. "Rainey. Thank God." Hand to her ear, she rushed to the door. "Emmerich's down. Ballroom, fifth floor."

"On it." Rainey's timbre rose and became urgent. "I see Hannah."

Caitlin's blood felt radium-hot. "Where?"

"The top-floor apartment. Locked in a—bathroom, looks like. She's yanking on the door, but it won't open," Rainey said. "Glass is gone from all the windows."

Caitlin saw it clearly now. Hayden had taken Hannah to the top of the building, locked the girl in an apartment, then come back down in the elevator to lure the FBI team into his trap. She turned and peered across the ballroom at Emmerich.

"Get to her before he does," he said, his voice fading.

"You're—"

"This is his endgame."

Caitlin raised her head to look up. Top floor.

To Emmerich, she called, "Backup's on its way."

She went.

52

Stepping into the thirtieth-floor hallway, Caitlin listened to the night. She'd smashed the light bulb in the elevator so that when the doors opened, she wouldn't present a brightly lit target. But she couldn't stop the bell from ringing. She slid around the control panel into the high air above the city.

The wind whistled through missing apartment doors. Her hair swirled around her face. The Swallowtail felt like a desiccated shell. Through gaping doorways, she glimpsed city lights and heard a helicopter inbound.

From the hallway only ambient light was visible. Caitlin inched along the corridor. She had no idea whether Hayden was still running up the stairs or if he had grabbed an elevator and beaten her here.

She crept another step. The hall, the entire floor, felt empty. But it couldn't be. Rainey had seen Hannah here.

A voice broke through the radio static—Keyes. "Patrol officers have entered the building. Ascending the fire stairs. SWAT is staging. They're four minutes out."

She murmured, "I don't have four minutes."

Endgame. Hayden would kill Hannah if he reached her first.

She counted six apartments on the floor, three on each side of the hall. She reached the first doorway. Taking a long breath, she entered. The apartment was wrecked—stripped and gutted. Drywall was torn off the walls, leaving the exposed two-by-four framing. No visible electric lights on. Still, she needed to conduct a room-by-room search.

And she had to watch for fresh booby traps. Trip wires. Rugs placed over holes in the floor. Nail guns positioned to fire when she crossed an infrared beam, for all she knew. Every second ached.

Outside, a helicopter swept by, the letters FBI on its side. Its engine blatted, echoing between buildings.

Rainey's voice came through Caitlin's earpiece. She was aboard. "Have you on visual."

Caitlin crept deeper into the apartment. Boots scratching on dust and paint chips. Wind hissing through the empty window frames. No Hannah, no Hayden.

From the helicopter, Rainey's voice turned urgent. "He's above you."

Caitlin raised her flashlight and Emmerich's Glock. Saw only a water-stained ceiling. She thought, *crawl space.*

"Where? I'm on the top floor."

"No—there's another floor above you. A penthouse." Rainey's voice was calm but intense. "The apartment directly across the hall has an internal staircase that goes up."

Caitlin ran back to the hall. Outside the empty doorway of the apartment across the corridor, she pressed her back to the wall. The helicopter rounded a corner of the building, completing a sweep, its spotlight aimed above her. It slowed, dipped, and swung back around.

Rainey's voice turned glacial. "Hannah broke out of the bathroom he'd locked her in. She ran deeper into the building. He's hunting for her and closing. Hurry."

53

Her back pressed to the wall outside the doorway, Caitlin listened for noise from within the apartment. The thump of the helicopter's rotors filled her ears.

"Can't hear, won't be able to see around corners or up the stairs," she said.

"I'm your eyes," Rainey replied.

She swallowed, bolstered. "Copy."

She spun through the empty doorway into the apartment. It too was gutted, windows gaping, but the drywall hadn't been pulled down yet. Blank, impenetrable walls greeted her.

"Stairs to your left," Rainey said.

Caitlin turned the corner. The staircase ascended to a darkened hallway on the penthouse level.

Rainey radioed, "Hannah's at the opposite end of the building from you. A great room. Hands duct-taped. She's near a plate glass window that's been broken out."

Cross talk interrupted her. A SWAT commander. "Entering the building in one."

Caitlin crept up the stairs, trying to stay silent. Halfway up, she thought, *No.* Simultaneously Rainey spoke the thought out loud.

"We're past the time for stealth."

Caitlin charged to the top of the stairs and backed against a wall. Shouted, "*FBI.*"

No response.

The helicopter continued its slow crawl across the air outside the building. It turned its spotlight on the penthouse.

Rainey said, "He ducked out of sight."

The spotlight swept. Caitlin's skin skittered. Her outside eyes had just gone blind.

The penthouse took up the top floor, corner to corner, but was a warren of rooms. She couldn't wait for Rainey to find Hayden. Pulse drumming, she rounded a corner, clearing it in vertical slices, then combat-walked, gun aimed, flashlight sweeping.

She stopped.

She found herself in a bedroom. The window was covered with a dark sheet that shuddered in the wind. A second door on the far side of the room led toward the interior of the apartment. A table lamp, covered with a towel, hummed on the floor beside a sagging bed. The sheets were yellowed with sweat and grime. The wall above the headboard was pitted with bullet holes. Ghostly light seeped through them. They formed a giant eye.

Target practice. Or boredom. It was the room where Hayden had been nesting.

The smell, with the room semiprotected from the winter wind, thickened in Caitlin's nose. Urine in an unflushed toilet. Grease. A frenzy of ants crawled over a moldy blue sandwich on the nightstand. Crumpled food wrappers whisked across the hardwood floor, scuttling like crabs.

On the grungy bed lay Hayden's mother.

Officer Gretchen Maddox wore the coral pink twinset Caitlin had seen at the task force briefing. It was now torn and bloodstained. Her no-nonsense, cardboard-brown hair was tangled and matted with blood, as if she'd fought for her every breath against the person to whom she'd given life. She had been gagged with duct tape and bound to the bed frame with zip ties. Her face was puffy. Her eyes were open.

They were baby-blue, pupils fixed, as if targeting the doorway Caitlin had just come through. As if they'd been staring, unblinking, at that doorway for hours, fearing, hoping, knowing her end was inevitable and drawing close. Waiting for her only son to walk in and finish her.

To Caitlin's utter shock, she was alive.

Gretchen squinted under the beam of the flashlight. Her chest rose convulsively.

Caitlin gave a hand signal. *I'll be back.* She crossed the room toward the second door. But Gretchen bucked, frantic.

In two steps Caitlin reached the bed and ripped off the duct tape. "Which way did he go?"

Gretchen said nothing. With horror, Caitlin understood why her lower face was so puffy. Her mouth was crammed with spent bullets—and wedding rings.

She seemed close to choking, but Caitlin couldn't spare the time to help her empty her mouth. She said, "Which way?"

Still Gretchen was mute. She could have lifted her head, nodded, indicated somehow. She didn't.

But emotion flashed in her eyes. Fear, torment—and calculation.

Caitlin understood what she meant to do. Before Gretchen could gag out more than a few bullets, preparing to scream a warning to her son, Caitlin slapped the duct tape back over her mouth.

She turned and hurried to the far doorway. Shut off her flashlight and jammed it in her back pocket.

Rainey's strained voice crackled in her earpiece. "I don't have him."

On the bed behind her, Gretchen thrashed and kicked. She tried to moan, to make a sound that would break through the thump of the helicopter. The sheet over the window beat back and forth like a moth's wings.

Low, harsh, Caitlin spoke into the radio. "Hannah?"

"We're circling. Will have her in view if—*yes.* She's still in the great room. Searching for a way out. She freed her hands—she's waving at me." Rainey's voice tightened. "I signaled back but can't get to her. No visual on Hayden."

Caitlin stole to the next room, gun aimed at the floor. She presumed Hayden was waiting to ambush her. Where?

He knew she was there. Knew she was coming. But he wasn't running, wasn't blundering around. He was either sneaking or lying in wait. In the penthouse maze, how could she find him? She needed a formula, a schematic, a Magic 8-Ball. X-ray vision. She needed Keyes.

Then it came to her. She didn't need to radio him. Didn't need Keyes in the room. She already had him. She had his research on the predictability of criminal behavior.

She edged to the doorway. In the hallway hung a mirror. Antique gold frame, beveled glass, four feet high, a means for those who'd once lived here to admire themselves as they swept past in splendor. It provided a glimpse into the next room.

It was a dining room. Ornate table, high-backed chairs. A second door, maybe to the kitchen. Two tall windows.

Outside them, the helicopter's spotlight slowly panned the exterior wall of the building. It was the white of a streaking meteor. The windows turned briefly into two blind eyes.

Hayden stood between them, back against the outside wall, hiding in the helicopter's blind spot.

The gun in his right hand was raised, aimed at the door through which Caitlin had the reflected view. He hadn't spotted her in the mirror. He was waiting for her to walk down the hall past the doorway, like a target in a shooting gallery.

She needed to neutralize his advantage. To distract him, so she could get the drop on him.

And she needed to keep him from escaping to his right, through the second door, which led inexorably to Hannah. SWAT was infiltrating the hotel from the ground floor, headed up, but she couldn't wait. She had to stop him, here.

Rainey's voice came through her earpiece. "Still don't have him. Or you. Hendrix, report."

Caitlin couldn't reply without giving away her position. Outside, the helicopter tilted and flew along the side of the building, searching.

Please let me bet correctly.

The spotlight retreated, light fading. She crouched in the doorway. In her hand she held a warm, wet, jagged blossom—one of the spent bullets Gretchen had spit from her mouth. Checking her balance, she leaned from the doorway into the hall. Like skipping a pebble, she tossed the bullet around the corner, into the room where Hayden was lurking. It bounced, spun, and clattered to rest at his feet.

Hayden grabbed it. For a second, he seemed mystified. Then his head jerked up.

He peered through the doorway, into the hall. And saw Caitlin in the mirror.

54

Caitlin stared through the doorway at Hayden's reflection in the hallway mirror. From the dining room, Hayden stared back. He had a clear view of her, the indirect light providing a ghostly look at her face.

She held entirely still. *Come on*, she thought. *Do it. Do what Keyes says you should, without even thinking. Throw the bullet away to the right, and break left.*

His face, backlit by the retreating helicopter spotlight, was a shadow—the opposite of the high-gain images on all the surveillance videos Caitlin had seen. It was absence, darkness, nothingness. His hand, holding the bullet, was a fist.

He flung the bullet to his right.

Then he angled left and charged straight toward the doorway and at the mirror.

Hayden raised his gun and fired. Caitlin saw the muzzle flash an instant before the bullet hit the mirror. The glass cracked. The report boomed. The frame jumped against the wall.

Hayden, standing in the dining room, stared at the fissured glass and realized his mistake—that he hadn't fired at Caitlin, but at her reflection.

She braced, muzzle up, waiting for him to come at her. She was ready to put her gun to his head when he came through the dining room doorway into the hall.

He didn't. Standing inside the dining room, he spun to face the wall between them.

Jesus.

The wall was rotting Sheetrock. And he'd played with that plenty, shooting the giant eye into the wall of the bedroom where his mother was held prisoner.

She dropped and rolled just before his shot blew through the wall, chest high.

Chunks of drywall flew. Caitlin flipped onto her back, knees bent, Glock aimed straight back at the wall. Part of her shrieking, *Fire.* Another part hissing, *Shoot a sixteen-year-old? Unseen? Coward.* Training telling her, *Know your safe zone of fire. Know your target and what's behind it.*

Her finger hovered on the trigger. Drywall dust rained on the floor. Rounds from Emmerich's powerful Glock would penetrate the crumbling plaster as easily as they would paper plates. With Hannah downrange. She held fire.

On the far side of the wall, footsteps raced. Her adrenaline spiked and she swung the Glock at the doorway, waiting for Hayden to swivel around.

The footsteps retreated. He was running deeper into the apartment.

She scrambled to her feet. "Rainey. He's running. I think toward the great room."

Rainey's voice was staticky. "Hannah's still in there."

Caitlin charged from the bedroom into the hall. "Can you signal her to take cover?"

"Too complicated. And you're closer."

Caitlin bounced off the cracked hallway mirror and rebounded into the dining room. "Hannah," she yelled. "*Hide.*"

She sprinted past the dining room table, out the second door, into a spacious kitchen. At the far side of the room, past a hulking refrigerator, a swinging door swiveled back and forth. Caitlin rushed across, brought herself up short, and kicked the swinging door. She jumped back, yanked open the fridge door, and ducked behind it.

A shot came through the swinging door and hit the fridge, ringing against the aluminum.

Caitlin held, heart jackhammering. Keyed the radio. "Can you see Hannah? Is Hayden in the room where she is?"

The helicopter swept overhead.

"Don't have an angle right now," Rainey said. "We're making another sweep."

Gut check. *Endgame.* She couldn't wait for SWAT—she might as well walk away. There was nobody else. Just her, here, now.

Caitlin tightened her ballistic vest. She swung around the fridge and shoved open the swinging door as she dropped and rolled. No gunfire met her. She came up, sweeping the gun across the view.

The great room ran along the entire side of the building. Tall ceiling. Sconces on the wall, one with a low-wattage bulb emitting shabby yellow light. Broken coffee table and overturned wingback chairs. Smashed mirror. A velvet fainting couch. Across the room, facing the thirty-story drop, was a gaping wall of air. The frames of the windows remained, but the plate glass had been removed. A set of silk drapes billowed in the winter wind.

A second set was drifting to the floor.

The drapes had been ripped from the curtain rod with the flourish of a magician whipping aside a cape. By Hayden, who was watching them balloon and glide across the room. He stood facing Caitlin, holding Hannah tight against his chest.

The drapes. Hannah had hidden. And he'd found her.

The wind haloed Hannah's hair. Beyond her spread the immense emptiness of the night. No glass, no netting, no force field, nothing to hold her safe. Just the window frame: a two-inch-wide metal border behind her back. Not a barrier but a portal to concrete death. Three hundred feet straight down.

Hayden stood ten feet from the edge, left arm gripping Hannah's waist and pinning her arms, right elbow wrapping her neck. A vascular restraint hold—maybe he'd learned it from Uncle Trey. The semiautomatic in his right hand was aimed at the ceiling. But squeeze Hannah's neck any tighter and he would choke her to death.

Under the beam of Caitlin's flashlight, he looked ready to do it. Blood trickled from a gash in his cheek. And from cuts on Hannah's palms, and from the broken slice of mirror that gleamed on the floor nearby. God*damn*, this kid. Hannah hadn't simply hidden—she'd freed her wrists from the duct tape with the glass, then gone for him. His blue eyes crawled with rage.

As long as she had a clear shot, Caitlin could fire. It would be a good shoot. If she squeezed the trigger now, the Shooting Incident Review Group would declare it a justified use of lethal force.

That knowledge did nothing to ease the knot in her gut about firing on a high school sophomore.

And she didn't have a clear shot. Hayden was blading his body so Hannah blocked it.

"Drop the gun," Caitlin shouted.

Hayden's shoulders rose and fell. He held onto the pistol. The knot tightened in Caitlin's gut.

Outside the window, a roar swelled. The helicopter rose into view, blinding them with its spotlight.

The wash from the rotors sent dust and paint chips and paper scraps flying. Hannah cringed. Hayden turned into a backlit silhouette.

The chopper hovered and turned sideways. Rainey was braced in the open doorway, a Colt burst-fire rifle to her shoulder. Caitlin juked out of her line of fire.

"It's over," Caitlin yelled. "Drop the gun. *Now.*"

She held fire. So did Rainey, eye to the rifle scope.

Hayden looked thoughtfully at the ceiling. He seemed to consider it. His shoulder lifted—a teenager's *whatever* shrug. Then, with almost cavalier insouciance, he released his grip on Hannah's neck.

He lowered his arm, and let the pistol twirl from his index finger and clatter to the floor. He booted it away.

"Knife too," Caitlin shouted. "Kick it toward me."

He snagged a switchblade from his front pocket and flipped it onto the floor. Kicked.

She felt a trickle of relief and didn't trust it. His grip on Hannah's waist remained tight.

Caitlin inched toward him. "Let her go, Hayden. On the floor. Lock your hands behind your head."

His voice rose above the chopper, clear but strained. "You can't shoot me. I'm unarmed."

Hannah's eyes swam with light. Her shirt rippled across her shivering shoulders. Caitlin inched another step closer.

"Stop." Hayden hoisted Hannah off her feet and held her head directly in front of his.

Clever boy. Clever, paranoid, smart, deadly boy. He practically sewed the little girl onto him like a suit. A shadow. An overlay. Anything that hit him, especially a high-powered round, would kill Hannah too.

Caitlin stopped. "Let her go and we'll all walk out of here. You know that's the way it works."

He shook his head. And began turning in circles, making any shot impossible. As he spun, he reached into the front pocket of his hoodie, one-handed.

He brought out a set of handcuffs.

Fuck. He'd taken them from his mother.

He slapped one cuff around Hannah's left wrist. Then he maneuvered the other cuff around his own.

Double fuck.

He backed within eight feet of the window frame. "Go on. Pull the trigger."

He smiled. The sight of a calculating grin on his Disney-kid face chilled Caitlin to the marrow.

Even if she managed to hit him and miss Hannah, she couldn't guarantee that he wouldn't fall backward out the windows.

His gaze dropped to Hannah. The hatred on his face was so blinding that it almost reached devotion. Caitlin's nerves flashed like a sparking electrical wire.

"*No*, Hayden," she shouted. "She doesn't see you. I do."

His head jerked head up and he locked eyes with her. His spinning slowed. His gaze degenerated. Rage. Panic.

"On the floor. *Now.*"

Her heart skipped. He was so little more than a child. *One move,* she thought. *One step, one twitch, and I pull the trigger.* Even if she had to risk hitting Hannah. Dropping him would be her only chance to keep him from jumping. She could barely breathe.

His smile returned, jagged and wild.

He wanted to make her do it.

She tried to keep her voice level. "Hayden, you can't talk your way out of a nine-millimeter bullet. You won't end up in the ER, or a psych ward, or juvie. If I fire, I blow out your candle. There's no coming back."

Omnipotent control. He was desperate for it. A malignant paranoid, convinced his enemies had gathered to destroy him.

Hayden wanted to defeat her. Suicide would be his victory.

And he wanted to take Hannah with him.

His smile was whiter than the spotlight. "I uploaded a vid," he said, spinning. "Unless I yank it, it goes live at four A.M. It tells the real story. How my mom did all of this and put it on me. It's her fault. I got here to try to save Hannah but it was too late." His expression turned sly. "Shoot me and everybody will think you did it to bury the truth. I'll be a martyr."

His smile broadened. "By the time you pull the trigger we'll be halfway out the window. And you're not wearing a body cam. Nobody'll believe you. You'll be the kid killer."

Cool excitement ran across Caitlin's skin, thin hope. Over the roar of the helicopter, she shouted, "I don't need a body cam."

She nodded outside. The FBI helicopter wasn't the only copter in the air. A fleet of news choppers hovered in the distance, filming the scene.

She held the Glock steady. The moment stretched. Hayden turned in one more slow circle. Then stopped.

"Want me to let go of her?" he said. "Fine."

He spread his arms, a sweep of angel's wings. And he gave Caitlin the finger with both hands.

Hannah's cuffed hand jerked along with his, the chain clinking. Caitlin saw it in his eyes.

She dived for Hannah. "*No.*"

Hayden threw himself backward toward the window.

Lunging, Caitlin got her arms around Hannah's waist and tackled her, full bore, a cornerback bringing down the receiver. Her flying momentum jerked Hayden off balance and all three of them crashed to the dusty floor.

Hayden scrambled for the edge. Hannah screamed. Lying on top of the girl, holding on, Caitlin brought up the Glock but Hayden was at the maw. He lunged for the night and flipped over the lip of the window frame.

He dropped with shocking swiftness, jerking Hannah toward the edge. Caitlin's weight couldn't stop the slide. They skidded, fast, toward the window.

Hannah screamed in pain as the cuff dug into her wrist. The edge of the building loomed closer. *Something, anything, Jesus—*

Scrambling, Caitlin kicked sideways. The edge arrived. She jammed her shoulder into the window frame, the vertical side jamb that ran from floor to ceiling, and wedged herself against it. Hannah's handcuff caught on the bottom rail of the frame, taking part of Hayden's hanging weight.

"Hold on," Caitlin said. "Hold tight."

Hannah wrapped her free arm around Caitlin's shoulder. Her screaming was equal parts fear and anguish. The wedged handcuff squealed against the metal frame. But the chain, designed to keep crazed tweakers from ripping out jailhouse bars, didn't break.

The vertical post, lodged against Caitlin's collar bone, dug into her shoulder. She felt Hannah slide a fraction of an inch. In her earpiece, she heard the SWAT commander.

"Alpha Team is ascending in the elevator."

Rainey responded. "Enter the apartment on the west side of the building and ascend the interior staircase. Repeat, interior staircase, then south to the living room. Move, move. Agent needs backup."

Hannah slid another half an inch. Caitlin fumbled for the handcuff around the girl's wrist. She felt blood, tried to focus on anything but Hannah's unearthly cries.

Hannah moaned, "Omigod, please Caitlin don't let me fall."

SWAT wasn't going to get here fast enough.

Hayden's weight was too much. He was hanging straight down off the side of the building and seemed to be swinging and kicking. Though the cuff locked to Hannah's wrist was wedged against the bottom of the window frame, sooner rather than later it would break free of that. When it did, Caitlin wouldn't be able to hold onto the girl.

Caitlin carried her own handcuffs at the back of her belt. The key for those was in her jeans pocket. Holding tight to Hannah, she couldn't reach it.

She looked out the window at Rainey. "Do you have a shot at the chain?"

In the helicopter, Rainey didn't move her eye from the rifle scope. The chopper was hovering smoothly, but with the wind, engine torque, and the rotor downdraft washing back from the building, it was impossible for the pilot to hold it absolutely motionless.

"Rainey?"

No answer. But beneath Hannah's wails, a new voice cried, desperate and broken.

"No. No. God. Don't. I don't want to die. God. No. This was a mistake."

It was Hayden.

"Please. I'm sorry. Pull me up. Jesus Christ, help me." His pleading became a sob. "Please. Please please please."

Rainey's voice came through Caitlin's earpiece. "I have a shot at the chain."

"You sure?" Caitlin said.

"I won't miss. Not from this distance." Rainey sounded as certain as Caitlin had ever heard her. "Go or no go?"

Hayden shrieked. "Forgive me. I was wrong. I know how they all felt now. Oh, my God, forgive me."

Caitlin's chest clenched. The rotor downwash blasted the room. Rainey was waiting.

Caitlin jammed herself hard against the post of the window frame and secured her arm around Hannah.

She shouted into the night air, over the edge of the void. "Give me your hand, Hayden."

For an instant, there was no reply. Then relief and a tone of even-more-desperate fear burst from him like an explosion. "I don't think I can."

"You can do it," They had only seconds left. "Hurry, Hayden."

"Okay ... okay ..."

Securely wedged against the upright post, she removed one hand from Hannah, fumbling. Hayden's right hand swung into sight, fingers scrabbling. Caitlin stretched. And got a glimpse over the edge, at his face.

Hayden swung, nothing below him but darkness and sickening finality. He was smiling.

His pleas were a ploy.

He grabbed for her, trying to grip her wrist and pull her and Hannah over the edge with him in a victory plunge.

Caitlin moved fast. And shouted into the radio, "Shoot the chain."

Hayden howled. "I win, bitch."

Rainey fired. The bullet hit the chain of the LAPD handcuffs and broke it cleanly.

Caitlin grabbed Hannah, pulled her back from the edge, clutched the girl. Held on, shuddering, hearing Hannah cry.

Hayden's screams pierced the sky outside. Endless. Hysterical.

Frustrated. Loud, and getting louder. Hovering right near her ears.

Caitlin's own handcuff scraped against the upright post of the window frame. It was securely locked around it. The other bracelet was locked around Hayden's right hand.

She had snapped it on as he tried to grab her. He was caught, locked to the window frame, kicking and screaming in futility.

Caitlin hauled Hannah away from the edge. The girl shuddered, cradling her injured wrist. Caitlin pulled her against her shoulder.

Flashlight beams and targeting lasers erupted into the room and SWAT poured through the door. Outside the empty window, in the helicopter, Rainey lowered the rifle. Her face was unreadable in the crazed light. Caitlin lifted a hand, in gratitude and admiration. Rainey raised a fist. The helicopter turned and swooped away. Its engine faded.

Hayden's screams remained.

Winter morning twilight brightened the sky. The eastern horizon glowed blue, blazing with the morning star. On the street outside the Swallowtail Hotel, Caitlin shook hands with the departing SWAT team.

The construction company had brought in spotlights and a crane with a hydraulic lift to remove the concrete barriers that blocked entry to the demolition zone, and the street around the hotel was filled with police cars and ambulances. Detective Solis, despite his exhaustion, looked weightless. Golden. Soon the adrenaline would drain and he'd crash, good chance sleep for twenty-four hours, but for the moment, he was soaring.

He shook Caitlin's hand. "Didn't expect you to draw the short straw, but ..."

"Could have been any of us. Glad it ended the way it did," Caitlin said.

Alvarez came around the corner, loosening his ballistic vest. Caitlin smiled at him.

"Your Jeep survive last night's pursuit unscathed?" she said.

"She's damn tough."

"Baitsy deserves chrome rims and new leather interior."

He laughed and slapped her on the back as he walked toward the hotel. He was approaching the entrance when the paramedics came out with Emmerich sitting up on a stretcher. He was pale and beat up. His leg was in a temporary brace and he wore a cervical collar.

He was on the phone. "Probably this afternoon ... yes, Director."

He saw her and wrapped up the call. He asked the paramedics to wait. They shot him a look, like, *We don't work for you*, and kept walking. Caitlin fell in at their side.

Emmerich tried, briefly, to appear as if he wasn't in pain. "Fractured tib-fib," he said. "Possibly a mild concussion."

The paramedic pulling the stretcher gave Emmerich the stink eye.

"Protocol requires me to go to the ER, but I'll be back in a few hours."

"You'll be back as soon as they turn their heads, but let them take care of you, boss." Caitlin leaned toward the paramedics. "He's slippery. Don't let him get away."

She unholstered the weapon he had entrusted to her, his Glock, and held it out. He smiled and took it. He likewise unholstered the gun on his hip.

"Found yours ten feet from where you left me." He returned it to her. "Figured you'd need it back."

"Thank you."

The paramedics rolled him to the ambulance. They were shutting the doors as Keyes pulled up with Rainey in an FBI Suburban.

They were hot-eyed, worn, and almost shining with pride and relief. Caitlin waited for them with her hands on her hips.

She peered up at Keyes. "You made this possible."

"Don't know about that," he said.

"Take the credit, dude. It won't always come around."

He smiled.

Caitlin locked eyes with Rainey. She felt a welter of emotion, a dam about to burst. She held it back and squeezed Rainey's arm.

"Fine fucking shooting," she said.

Rainey nodded. Her serene exterior showed no cracks. But it seemed, briefly, transparent. The relief, the confirmation, the achievement, the daring, and above all the weight she had been able to shoulder, all shone near the surface, a heated glow.

"Let's hope we never have to call it that close again." Rainey raised her head to take in the shadowed bulk of the hotel. "I hear Hayden has fingernail scratches on his neck. Maya Cathcart did claw him. She's going to help put him away."

Caitlin nodded. It was insufficient. She pulled Rainey into a hug.

Up the street a man and woman stood at a barricade, talking to the officer controlling entry to the scene. Caitlin put two fingers to her teeth and whistled. The officer turned.

"They're good," she shouted. "Let them through."

It was Mina and Dave Guillory. The officer quickly signed them in. They rounded the barricade and ran up the street, Mina with the back of her hand to her mouth, Dave keeping his hand on her back. Caitlin pointed them toward an LAPD cruiser.

In its open front door, Hannah sat talking to Detective Weisbach while the paramedics examined her. Her wrist wasn't obviously fractured, but had sustained enough ligament and soft-tissue damage from the handcuff that she would need to have it x-rayed and splinted.

The Guillorys barely noticed Caitlin as they ran past. Their entire world had just telescoped to the girl in the car. Mina broke into a sprint. Dave broke into tears.

Hannah jumped up and didn't hit the ground before she was swallowed by her father's arms and her mother's kisses. Caitlin hung back. Weisbach met her gaze.

The Robbery-Homicide detective needed a tough hide, and a tough heart, to do this job. But the look she gave Caitlin was everything. A world. She was witness to a reunion that, as a murder cop, by definition she rarely experienced.

As Caitlin turned away, Hannah called to her. The little girl's voice, tired but giddy, had a note of anxiety. Hannah squirmed from Dave's embrace, ran up, and tearfully hugged Caitlin.

The girl buried her face in Caitlin's shoulder and gripped her like a monkey. Right then, Caitlin almost let everything go.

"Are you leaving?" Hannah said.

"Not yet. Lots of work to do here, helping the police." Caitlin lifted

Hannah's chin and took in her dirty, lucky face. "How about I give you my card? It has my work address and email at Quantico."

Hannah nodded, appearing impressed.

"We can be pen pals," Caitlin said. "Trade palindromes."

Hannah smiled. "Or do karate. I kicked my way out of that bathroom, you know."

Caitlin laughed, deeply, and gave Hannah a fist bump.

Inside the hotel lobby, Gretchen Maddox sat in a dusty wingback chair, being interviewed by her LAPD colleagues. She hadn't been seriously injured by her son. Hayden had controlled her with her own Taser before tying her up and jamming her mouth full of bullets and gold bands. But Caitlin was sure that if she hadn't shown up, Gretchen would have been Hayden's next victim. Perhaps he would have forced her to witness his suicide, leaving her to be consumed with guilt. More likely he would have killed her.

Gretchen confirmed that her brother, Trey Laforte, was the faux detective who spoke to Hannah at LAPD headquarters. And that he had painted the billboard in the Guillorys' neighborhood with red eyes.

Gretchen and Trey, terrified that Hayden might be the Midnight Man, had come up with a plan to draw the boy in from the cold. The billboard was painted as both a warning and a lure. They had hoped to catch Hayden without alerting the police. The plan backfired spectacularly.

Detectives asked Gretchen if Trey had also filmed the drone video.

"What drone video?"

That was the last thing Gretchen said to them. A zipped black body bag was wheeled through the lobby on a gurney. Gretchen shut her eyes and her words dissolved into sobs. Trey Laforte's body was taken away.

And Gretchen was left as the last lonely member of the Maddox family in the demolition zone.

Hayden was already on his way downtown, zip-cuffed in the back of an LAPD cruiser. Once he got there, he would be booked and processed and shackled in an interview room until the task force detectives arrived to interrogate him.

Surrounded by SWAT, with Caitlin's hand on his elbow, the Midnight Man had been hauled into the blue twilight narrow-eyed and hunched. But as soon as he stepped into the clear air and heard the city bubbling around him, he straightened and resumed his light-footed strut.

He glared at the tactical officers, and the uniforms, as he was marched to the patrol car. At everybody but Caitlin. He had met her eyes already, and, she thought, couldn't survive another glimpse of himself. Not while he was in custody, unable to strike out.

She had stolen his victory from him, and he knew that if he ever looked at her again he would see too much.

So he turned his head away from her and sauntered to the black-and-white, arms cuffed behind his back, his face transforming in the early morning light. Seeming to turn younger. To fill with hurt. And deliberate helplessness.

In the sky above, multiple news helicopters hovered. His video had gone live.

Caitlin knew that no matter what happened to their son, Robert and Gretchen Maddox would absorb much of the blame for his crimes. As he was put in the back of the police car, he looked up at the hovering cameras.

His face filled with a pseudo pathos. He tilted his head, like a baby bird.

He mouthed his message to the unblinking electronic eye. *"Innocent. Help."*

Caitlin watched with revulsion and something approaching wonder.

Now she headed outside into the scintillating morning air. Fresh helicopters loitered in the distance. She found coffee. It was her fourth cup in the last hour. With the bass-note drone of the rotors dulling her hearing, it took a moment to notice that her phone was humming in her pocket. She slid it free and saw a text. SEAN RAWLINS.

All her nerves instantly spun up again, and her vision throbbed, because it was always possible that one of his teammates had retrieved the phone and was trying to reach Sean's emergency contact.

She bent to the screen. After two fumbling swipes, the text opened.

We're clear.

The ATF raid was over. Sean was safe.

Caitlin took a breath and set her coffee down on a concrete construction barrier. Then, hugely relieved, sat herself down too.

She sent Sean a reply, an *A-okay* emoji, and let her hand drop, trying to get her pulse back down to triple digits.

She'd been suppressing thoughts of the raid all night. Now residual anxiety flooded her skin and evaporated in the cold.

A new text arrived from Sean.

You were right.

With a swooshing sound, he sent a photo from the cabin they'd raided in the desert. Broken windows covered with torn plastic sheeting flapping in the wind. Dun-brown landscape outside. A tight, stone-walled cabin with a collapsing roof. Single main room—fireplace, dining table, dirty kitchen.

It was filled wall to wall and floor to ceiling with coils of barbed wire.

It was an ambush. Trip wires on doors
and windows.

Caitlin gaped, stunned. She swiped the screen to phone Sean, but before she could put the call through, he sent a video.

Taken from the doorway to the house, the video alternated between gray shadow and the stark white beams of searchlights. It panned the living room of the cabin. Stuck to the coils of barbed wire that filled the room were photos. Snapshots.

"The fu …" Caitlin muttered.

The photos had been taken at bombing scenes—in the aftermath.

They were scrawled over with notes written in silver marker. One message said, EVERYTHING HAS A SPARK.

The photo showed Sean and Caitlin outside the bombed Temescal ER, jogging alongside Michele as she was taken to an ambulance.

Caitlin abruptly wanted no more coffee. "Jesus."

She tried to parse the photo, the scene, the meaning, the cold that had all at once settled behind her rib cage.

Sean's next text pinged.

Coming home soon. How about you?

I'll be there.

Want to see you. Got some news.

56

S an Francisco Bay swept past below the wings of the jet, closer, deep blue, light sparkling off whitecaps in the afternoon dusk. The hills that ringed the bay were already black in the winter twilight. The city briefly glimmered in the window as the plane banked on final approach to Oakland. The whitecaps neared, the runway slid beneath the jet, and they touched down. Caitlin leaned back against her seat as the thrust reversers roared, fighting the forward inertia. Fighting against throwing herself headlong into emotional turmoil.

But who was she kidding? Whatever was going on with Sean, something was about to change. The airliner decelerated, the engines throttled back to idle, and, as the red sunset arced through the windows, Caitlin grabbed her phone and turned it on.

No messages.

Sean had her itinerary. He should be waiting in Baggage Claim. She didn't *need* to hear anything from him in the interim. And she couldn't help worrying about why her screen was empty.

But as she schlepped up the aisle with a hundred fifty other passengers, lugging her computer case and roller bag and avoiding people hauling Christmas gifts from the overhead, she heard the cell ping. She had to wait to grab the phone until she reached the echoing terminal. The concourse was over-bright with conversation and bustle and holiday spirit. She had a text.

It was from Michele.

Did you hear?

Caitlin couldn't stand the uncertainty. She stepped away from the flow of people, to the windows, where the reedy tones of "All I Want for Christmas Is You" faded to syrupy Muzak.

Texting back would be too cowardly. And she didn't want a reply burning pixels into her screen if the news was bad. Fearing what she was going to learn, she phoned.

"Girl," Michele said.

The surprise in Michele's voice, perhaps at Caitlin's courage, or forwardness, or desperation, was blatant.

"Don't know what I've heard or haven't heard. It's been busy. Tell me," Caitlin said.

"Oh."

Michele's tone changed—as if Caitlin had rapped her knuckles with a ruler. Caitlin dropped her computer case and pinched the bridge of her nose.

"I'm moving," Michele said.

Caitlin gazed down the concourse. People flowed past her, all on the way to somewhere else.

"From your town house?" Caitlin said.

"I can't stay at Temescal. I think you know that. I think you *saw* that."

More confused than ever, Caitlin felt a needle in her heart— compassion for her friend.

"What are you going to do?" she said.

"I need a fresh start." Michele's sigh sounded both heavy and relieved. "I've been offered a job. Emergency Nursing Coordinator at Pearson-Lehman Hospital."

Caitlin hadn't heard of it. She was about to ask, but Michele kept talking. "It's in Fort Washington, Maryland."

Caitlin's lips parted. She was trying to process this. "You're moving across the country?"

"That's where Maryland is. Hey, I'm picking Sadie up from day care. Gotta jet," Michele said. "Sean can tell you the rest."

Then she was gone, and Caitlin was walking through the concourse like an automaton. The escalator down to Baggage Claim gleamed like the cheap tinsel in the war room back in Los Angeles. Arrivals was packed with people greeting holiday travelers. Which, Caitlin supposed, she was. She should have felt buoyant. She felt like a sack of thrashing snakes.

Sean was waiting at the back of the crowd. His expression was neutral. As soon as he saw her, he stepped forward. Caitlin walked directly up to him, put a hand to his chest, and stared him hard in the eye.

"Well?" she said. "The news?"

He looked so strong, so certain, so beautiful. Dark hair, raider's stare, loose and lithe and wound just tight enough. And still he gave nothing away.

"I'm transferring divisions."

Caitlin couldn't help it. Her heart grabbed. The thought filled her brain, her heart, the air: *To be with Michele.*

Sean's face was solemn. Almost regretful. "I mean, you're not planning to leave the BAU."

She shook her head.

She'd sworn to Emmerich that she was committing herself to the case, the team, the job, the mission. But this wasn't the price she'd wanted to pay. Anything but this.

Sean put his hand over hers and squeezed. She could feel his heart. Feel his breathing. He seemed to set himself more firmly on the floor.

"We're going to close this bombing case," he said. "Abso-goddamn-lutely."

"I believe it," she said, with a sense of bewilderment.

"Then I'm moving to DC." He was looking her straight in the eye. "I didn't tell you, because it's been iffy. It's been winding its way through the ATF bureaucracy for months. It's a promotion."

"Congratulations."

Now he was the one who looked bewildered. As if she wasn't as happy as he had thought she would be. She felt like she was being cast adrift on this conversation, and might get swept out the doors into the lowering darkness.

"It's close to Quantico," he said. "And Michele wants to tell you her news as well—"

"She did."

"Oh—cool." He was definitely perplexed now. "She'll be in Fort Washington, and that means the two of us can continue to coparent Sadie. We won't have to adjust the custody arrangement. We'll be within driving distance."

"What?"

He took Caitlin's face in his hands. "You and I said we'd make it work, and we will. Getting a place together would be good. As long as you don't quit the FBI."

She felt like a fool. She hoped he hadn't noticed. She could have jumped and punched a joyous hole in the ceiling.

Instead, she punched Sean on the arm. And laughed. And kissed him.

57

That night, lying in bed with Sean, Caitlin watched the Christmas lights sparkle on the Bay. A soft chill pervaded the air, and a sense of the long, welcoming night, of restfulness and unending depth, of a pause that bathed them in the ancient starlight pouring through the window. Sean brushed his fingertips through her hair. Across the neighborhood there was a palpable feeling of anticipation, people cycling up toward celebrations.

Caitlin thought about Hayden Maddox.

"He claimed he was beyond good and evil. But I'm convinced none of us ever can be," she said. "A psychopath might not *feel* remorse or compassion. But he can understand and follow the law. He can avoid deliberately damaging people."

And if he didn't want to help others live and thrive, he could leave room for them to do so. And watch, impoverished, from behind a scrim of lovelessness.

She laced her fingers with Sean's. "Have you heard of liminal time and space?"

"Like police work?" he said.

"Damn, now you're going to get deep?" She laughed. "One foot in the legal world, the other in the underworld?" She considered it. "You're right. We walk the edge."

"And have to navigate the divide," he said. "Deal with the ambiguity. Without losing the reins."

Caitlin knew these remarks were aimed directly at her. That life was complicated. That opening your heart was messy and dangerous. And worth it.

Sean tentatively turned her arm to reveal the fresh cuts she had made.

He knew her history. He had been the one to help her own up to her struggles, her choices, and to accept her scars as part of her life story. He'd suggested she tattoo her arms, claim her own skin in a new way. The literary tattoo on her right forearm, *The whole sky*, had been her response. Tonight, the whole sky felt both close and very far away.

Sean's eyes asked the question.

"Yeah," she said. "Over the weekend. But I'm done. For good."

He held on. Touch, a connection, a promise and a demand. *Will you find a way to move beyond the craving? To live in the world without needing to punish yourself for it?*

She exhaled. "Think your friend Jo Beckett could refer me to somebody?"

He pulled her closer. Nodded.

"Are you going to get these tattooed too?" he said.

She examined a healing cut. It was scar tissue, joining both sides of the wound. *Walk the edge.*

She shook her head. "These have to stand alone for now. I have to own it."

She curled against his shoulder. Their breathing came into sync. They wrapped their arms around each other and sank to sleep in the starry night.

EPILOGUE

Twenty miles west of Berkeley, on the summit of Mount Tamalpais, a figure stood at the overlook. Past the dark mass of the mountain, San Francisco Bay spread below him, shrapneled with light. He inhaled, taking it in.

The cabin in Garlock had been discovered. The name on the deed, the alias, was blown. The devices inside the cabin had been neutralized. But the photos would have been found. That was still a win. He could live with that.

It was a long game.

And he had his drone feed, which had provided valuable insights into the methods and psychology of the target he was pursuing. Patience would pay. After a minute, he spread his arms, raised his head, and let the night seethe through him.

The Ghost stood alone, and thought, *Your time is coming, Caitlin.*

ACKNOWLEDGMENTS

I owe my gratitude to a number of people whose expertise, support, enthusiasm, and hard work have helped me write the best novel I possibly could. In particular, my thanks go to everyone at Blackstone, especially Josh Stanton, Stephanie Stanton, Lauren Maturo, Josie Woodbridge, and Anne Fonteneau. For his unswerving advocacy of my writing, I'm grateful to Shane Salerno. I couldn't have a better agent in my corner. Thanks also to the team at the Story Factory, especially Ryan Coleman, and to writers who have generously encouraged readers to pick up my novels, including Don Winslow, Steve Hamilton, and Reed Farrel Coleman. A special thank you goes to Ken Price for taking an afternoon to guide me on a research tour of a major infrastructure site. It was fun, and great grist for a thriller. And above all, I'm thankful to my husband, Paul Shreve, and my children—Kate, Mark, and Nate— for their love and support.

ABOUT THE AUTHOR

MEG GARDINER is the critically acclaimed author of the UNSUB series and *China Lake*, which won the Edgar Award for Best Paperback Original and was a finalist for NPR's 100 Best Thrillers Ever. Stephen King has said of Meg Gardiner: "This woman is as good as Michael Connelly...her novels are, simply put, the finest crime-suspense series I've come across in the last twenty years." Gardiner was also recently elected president of the Mystery Writers of America for 2019.